"The Everling and the Acid King by J. Christie is a wildly inventive and emotionally charged science fantasy adventure that takes the beloved 'magical school' trope and electrifies it with sharp edges and adult stakes... I've been looking for a worthy replacement to recommend in the 'magical school' subgenre. I appreciated the balance between gritty realism and fantastical wonder that this book provides, especially in the emotional depth given to the characters... This is a rare crossover that speaks to teen and adult readers alike... The Everling and the Acid King is an unforgettable, genre-defying debut that fuses fantasy and science into something truly unique and emotionally resonant, and I'd definitely recommend it." ★★★★★
— K.C. Finn, Readers' Favorite

"Christie stirs up enjoyable comparisons to Xavier's School for Gifted Youngsters from Marvel's X-Men comics... the author sets up the fictional world perfectly... Christie is wise enough to leave plenty of room for exploring the setting and characters in future novels. The author also smartly does what few writers remember to do in series openers— resolving the main storyline while also hinting at the future..."
— Kirkus Reviews

"J. Christie's The Everling and the Acid King is one of those books that's hard to classify neatly, which is exactly why I enjoyed it so much... There's sci-fi, fantasy, horror, and humor, and it all blends in a way that works better than it has any right to. I closed the book, still buzzing from it... I don't know what's coming next in this series, but I'm in." ★★★★★
— Kyle Eaton, City Book Review

"Familiar trappings of a YA magic school may at first portend that the story will rehash Harry Potter—but that's far from what it evolves into, happily for its readers....Christie's story is satisfyingly difficult to predict; but more importantly, it's filled with surprising images, confrontations, and interpersonal connections that provide a powerful emotional draw to keep YAs and adult readers thoroughly engaged... Replete with the unexpected, delightful in its psychological connections, and atmospheric in its descriptions of a world these young adults must navigate with new insights, The Everling and the Acid King is an adventure that is hard to put down."
— D. Donovan, Senior Reviewer, Midwest Book Review

The Everling
and
the Acid King

The Everling
and
the Acid King

By
J. Christie

Wastrel Books

The Everling and the Acid King

Published by Wastrel Books.

Copyright © 2025 by J. Christie

All rights reserved.

Book Cover by Kat Valentine.

First Edition: 2025.

LCCN: 2025946670

ISBN 978-1-969056-01-7 (Paperback)

ISBN 978-1-969056-03-1 (Ebook)

For those that never got their letter...
and had to go to public school instead.

For the orphans...
my true family.

For anyone who imagined a world more magical...
and only found reality.

And mostly,
for K...

1.
The death of the Greywatch.
Portals.
Hankward.

The house shook. The trembling was frightful such that the old, floral walls threatened to buckle and fold, the faded wallpaper twisting off in places and dust raining down, turning the air thick. Voices echoed up from the stories below and into the attic above. The calls grew louder and louder as the jolts that shook the house grew more frequent by the moment. Win turned his head just as a wall split ceiling to floor, and there he glimpsed the barest bit of true sky beyond.

Somewhere in the lower floors, the death of the Greywatch unfolded. The twins, Shell and Finny Guilding, fell, overwhelmed by the molers, whose lifeless eyes and malformed faces were drooling and gripping, tearing the twins apart. Gig Godrick and his wife, Maggie, fell too, crushed, for there were so many molers that the battle became more of a clogging, clawing strain to breathe amongst the crowd. Jimmy Sedhearst still managed to run mad, though, his body afire. Some molers endeavored to grab at him, attracted by the light, but most were egressing in crazed attempts, only to find there was nowhere to flee.

But in the attic above was space amongst piles of boxes, furniture, strange electronics, the makings of crude robots and computers. All were covered with dirt and webs. And the spiders, who had taken reign, panicked across their silken nets, twisting them further in on themselves. Flies came loose and escaped. They looped around in the air, buzzing to be alive, while cockroaches below flew their secret spaces and scurried the floor over as if to dash for better cover. One ran right up on to the mendered foot of Win where he squatted.

Winnifred Baker had dark, lightly curled hair and heavy shoulders. He appeared older than he was, which was evidenced in the prematurely lined features of his still young face. He wasn't tall, but he was broad enough to be two men set alongside of each other. His eyes shimmered as if they were always slightly watery. The pair purple rimmed and nearly completely black. There was an overgrowth of beard starting around his face, and his large, loose, white teeth played contrast against the dark hairs of it.

He looked back at the crack in the wall and shook his head, gravely. He felt the bundle in his arms, held close to his body, and there was a threatening heat coming off of it. He thought to look, but a knock came from the door, drawing his eyes. It was followed by a voice that said, "Win? It's time. There's nothing else to be done. We… we can't hold them back. They're going to collapse the entire building if I don't do it. I… well, good luck," then the voice was gone along with his fiery footsteps racing away to the madness below.

Win climbed to his feet, careful with the bundle, and kicked away the stunned and lingering cockroach atop his foot. His hair, which was long, was receding in a stringy way, and it hung, limply, across his face as he rested the bundle over his ample belly. He sighed heavily, which sent him atremor, before taking uncertain steps across the shifting floor. He looked around in the discarded scrap, mumbling to himself, then he set the bundle down.

From the swaddle of old cloth peered a baby, whose mixed eyes, a blue and a green, shimmered light from the large moon shone through the cracked wall. The baby made small sounds and small movements and was altogether rather small. Winnifred Baker had held that baby in this room now for many hours, waiting. Waiting for the signal that would tell Win that he must do what he long feared he would have to. He had steeled himself for it, helpless to the cries of his friends.

Win found and grabbed hold of a small drawer, one lacking its dresser, and he toppled the contents out over the piles of junk.

Pouring forth, were remotes and strange devices, wires, cockroaches, and every sort of fuse. They scattered around in a clatter then settled. He shook the drawer and tapped it to get whatever dust he could out. Then he set it down and knelt next to the baby. "Well, here we go then," he said in a low, grumbling voice that was still soothing all the same.

The baby gave a smile to Win as Win scooped him up and set him back in the dresser drawer. Then Win tucked the blanket over the baby and picked up the whole thing. He paused a moment to listen to the soft breathing of the calm child, but the house rocked violently. So he stepped up to his feet shakily as indeterminate cries went below, mixed with the baby's muffled sounds. Win felt a pang of sorrow for the dying on both sides. And for the child. He gathered his thoughts and then spoke gently into the wooden frame. "Now, this part, well, this part will be a bit scary. But don't you worry. I've got you. I've got you right here with me."

He held the makeshift box close to his chest and stiffened his back, sniffling slightly as he did so. Green crackles of electric arcs sparked out of the skin of Win. It grew, and it touched to the floors, to the walls, to the bugs that fled around them. The man like lightning, his whole body quaking, the shockwaves of it flitting off the robots and droids, springing them to life for mere moments. They'd speak or move, a dance of functions performed. All reverberating in that green, their metal refracting the light and casting shadows around. Winnifred Baker went up in a deeper green, his body lifting into the air.

The attic door shook of a sudden. Someone at the far side twisted the knob and banged against the wood, for the door was locked. But the lightning gripped the doorknob, and a gurgled shout went up from the other side. The green sparks marked the wood, but more attempts were made to breech. The timber began to give as light broke through the crack opened near the knob. There was a face in the crack. A drooling, expressionless, and deformed face that peered in. But the eyes could not distinguish anything through the dazzling array of green.

3

Win lifted higher, just nearly to the ceiling, while the droids and robots ran around beneath him. His mouth opened, and a fresh, electric eruption shot from between his teeth. The green around him turned solid as a hole opened in the very air. Win trembled on as his body moved through the hole, vanishing. As the last of him passed, the room went dark, and the robots wound down. The door split apart and fell in pieces as shadowy, strange figures flooded in, tripping through the robots and junk. But nothing of the man and nothing of the baby remained. In the lower floors, the house had gone still. The molers in the attic looked around and then, at once, gave up before filtering back out. But the building entire erupted in flames and blew apart.

Winnifred Baker appeared before a great, stone manticore. It towered over him, and his electric spark scoured a line through its paw. He held the drawer tightly and listened to the coos from within, though a line of lightning had cut across one corner of the wood and, presumably, the baby within. "Okay, okay," Win said as he checked the boy who seemed fine. Then he looked around him, tucking the blanket back tightly. "We have many more to go. Many, many more. Can you hear me in there?"

The baby babbled back. A cockroach, or perhaps a spider, that had hitched along, fled away, and Win watched it scurry across the sand.

"Well, here goes." Win's body began to crackle again as the green electricity snaked back out of his skin. Win lifted into the air, shifting and trembling. Once again, the electric portal opened, and the man and baby moved through it.

They popped out in a neighborhood, setting off car alarms and bursting the bulbs of streetlights. Win wheezed and huffed and lifted up again. They popped out in a snowy wasteland, whose wintry ground melted around them. Win bundled himself and the drawer against the cold. He coughed at the chill wind, which raked his throat, and then he rose back into the sky and portaled through. They erupted above a city, their electric green blended with the neon glow of the adverts, which fried and sparked, but he was already up again. They came out high in the sky over a raging ocean, plummeting down and crashing in the waves, where Win held the drawer high above his head. He drifted and steeled himself, and the green came.

To jungles, to stars, to planets far away with races of other beings, to dimensions beyond Win's own grip of reality. To trainyards, to docks, to chocolate shops, to the sands about Saphill Wedd, to the hidden islands of Grammadora. They went on until Win could no longer stand, till he drooled, and his hair seemed to lose some of its color. For a while, he lay on the ground, prone, and rested. But he rose again, mumbling to himself, his breath harsh and heavy. And hair fell right out of his scalp as dead leaves from trees, but on he went. To the prison of Fieldmyre, to swamps, to bogs, to wonders, each, of the entire world, and to every possible place that Win could think of. The drawer held firm to his chest with the baby within.

When they came out at Wutherford Home, Win found himself splayed on the sidewalk before the great steps that led up to the front entrance of the old, stone building. It was two stories high and cracked in many places as it sat menacingly atop a little hill. Winnifred Baker groaned, and he carefully handled the drawer across his chest as he attempted to turn over and crawl his way up the stairs. Each stair sent pains through his bones, but, after many minutes, he had reached the halfway landing. He sprawled back out and shuddered as he let out a laugh.

"Few steps off," he murmured. He looked over at the half dozen or so remaining steps through the tears running out of his eyes and gave a big sigh. Then his body lifted again, and the lightning took the pair the remainder of the way, right to the very top. Win coughed and spat, but he did not see that there was something red in the spit. He rolled over to his belly and opened the blanket in the box carefully. The baby looked up at him from within, still smiling and wrapped in the dark cloth.

Win smiled back, and, when his voice came, it was slurred and slow. "Not so bad, eh?" Winnifred coughed. A line of spit reached from his mouth right down to the cement. "For you, at least." His smile spread wide, and his white teeth shone. "This is an alright moment, I got to say, but I'm sorry. I'm terribly sorry. I hope things will be simpler for you. I really do."

Win strained and groaned and pushed himself up to a sit. Then he steadied himself and reached into the wooden frame to lift the baby out. He wheezed as he did so, and then he hugged the baby tight and kissed him on his forehead. But the effort was too much, and he set the baby back into the drawer, still wheezing. It was another moment before he noticed the blood on the baby's forehead. He touched his own lips and saw the red that came off on his fingers. Fumbling, he went to wipe the baby clean.

Win was hurt more than he realized, and his insides were in bitter uproar. He wiped his hands absently on his menders and looked up at the clear sky above. "Looks to be a nice night. All considered." Win nodded his head, and he truly believed it in that moment. He knew then that he wouldn't remember much of anything from this night afterward. Not the death of his friends, not his escape, and not this moment. "It'll be all over soon, though. Then, that will be it. Let's hope you can stay away from us."

Win reached down a trembling hand and tickled the nose of the baby, half by accident, for his hand shook so. Then he smiled broadly at the little thing and let out a strained laugh. "So much for it all. You're the only one now. Anyway, I have a long, few days ahead of me. I don't even know how I'll make it." He gave another wry laugh then sighed. "Anyway, here I go."

Winnifred Baker laid himself back on the landing with a plop. His body erupted in the green lightning and lifted far into the sky. Below, the baby smiled up at the electric fury and watched the spark show while Win ventured on. Then, like a zap, Win was gone. The windows along the upper floors of Wutherford Home were now lighting up, one by one, while the baby watched the dark spot where Win had been, an awe about those mixed colored eyes.

The baby would not know that for two days and more, Winnifred would warp across every imaginable place again. He would warp until time lost all meaning. Till space ceased to be recognizable in any form. Till his memory had gone soft, and his words could not reach his lips with any sense to them. Till the man himself hardly seemed any man at all. Till he lay senseless and comatose and could warp no more.

The landing lights of Wutherford Home jumped into life. They illuminated the drawer, and the large door opened slowly. Blonde hair and deep, green eyes shone out as Lenna Vose peeked from within. Her eyes fell to rest on the little box, and they widened. She had seen the green light, she knew it. Twice now today. And she had heard the other children in the home talking about the light, too. This time, she was certain that she was not mad. She stepped out gingerly, in spite of her fear, edging forward. The drawer looked as if something green still glinted around it, but that couldn't be. She thought of what Ms. Bartleby would say. She had been so dismissive earlier when Lenna had told her of the light.

Lenna glanced around again, but there didn't seem to be anyone else there. Just the strange drawer. Then she leaned forward and peered inside. Instantly, her face broke into a giddy grin, and she forgot all about green lights and Ms. Bartleby. "Why, it's a baby. Just a baby." Lenna knelt down and lifted the little infant from the wooden frame. "Well, hey there. What are you doing here by yourself? Huh? It's not safe to be loitering on the stoops of random places. Don't you know that? And in a drawer, no less?"

From the foyer beyond the open door, came the craggy, sleep washed tone of Ms. Bartleby. "Lenn? What's out there, Lenna?

She turned and called back. "It's just a baby."

"A baby? Someone else leave a kid out there? That's two in one week," Ms. Bartleby mumbled, as she appeared in the light of the landing. Barb Bartleby was a heavyset woman with a pinched face and greying, bushy, brown hair that she normally kept in a loose bun on the back of her head. But, as she appeared at the doorway, she had her hair done up in rollers and pins, which crowned her head fantastically.

Lenna turned back to the infant. "Who left you here? Huh? Who did that? Who would do something like that? Tinky known it."

"They made a lot of racket dropping it here. Whoever left it. What is that? A drawer? Some weirdos." Ms. Bartleby scoffed. "They leave a note even?"

"I didn't see one."

Ms. Bartleby gave another scoff and muttered as she turned and waddled back to bed. "Woke up all the children. No note. Of course, no note. Twice in one week."

But Lenna paid her no mind. She was searching around and inside the wooden drawer but found nothing but the etched and burnt wood. It ashed across her fingers, and she examined it curiously. "That's okay. Yes, that's okay. You're going to be just fine here. Aren't you? Yeah." She wiped her hand across the blanket. "Now, what am I going to call you, little bit?" Her eyes drifted back to the drawer, and she fought to stifle a sudden laugh. "I'm going to call you Chester. That's what." She giggled, and the baby giggled with her. "And crib's taken, so we've no place to put you... so you know what that means? We'll call you Chester Nithercot."

Aris Kepler looked to the lingering electric green in the air. He beheld it with awestruck shock from behind the massive windows of Hankward Acres' office atop Acres Androids corporate headquarters. The light drifted in the distance, shimmering and fading, and he strained to keep the remnant green there, but it dissipated to nothing. Articles pinged on his versolock, updating each of the Greywatch dead as they were found in the rubble. And in moments, Hankward would come in to tell Aris that he's here. Everything was moving now, and he felt the pace of it beat in his heart. It slipped as he slipped, and the time was different.

He had a habit of finding himself in different times. Not in actuality, exactly, but his mind was built in such a way that time melded around him, and he would slip lightly from one point to another. It was both now and later for him, and Aris was, for a brief moment, stood with Chezzy Nithercot in the grassy grounds of Balefire. It hadn't happened yet, but it would. Time slipped again, and he snapped back to the office as Hankward opened the immense doors and entered.

Hankward's cheeks were flushed, and it played against the dark red of his soft, receding hair. "He's here."

Aris nodded. "And Nik?"

"He's nervous. Scared, really."

"It's understandable. You removed everything on him from the public servers?"

Hankward drew up the versolock on his wrist. "Jocasta?"

"It's done," the versolock responded, and Hankward paled against his midnight blue menders.

Aris nodded again, his hands shaking. "Keep your wits, Hankward."

"That's a bad joke, coming from you," Hankward replied, wryly.

Aris stared back, his eyes glinting with green and blue rings. "You know what I am. Now, to Nik."

11.
Bruises.
Rug.
The Fieldmores.

"Fighting again," Ms. Bartleby sighed as she drove along the country highway. "What do you think the Fieldmores will think of you? What with a busted nose and eyes all blacked. Think they'll want to adopt you then? I think not. I'll be driving back here tomorrow with some other kid for them. How would you like that?"

"I didn't start the fight," Chezzy said again. He'd been telling her as much since she had found him with Byron and his goons in the basement of Wutherford Home.

"Yes, and I had to have the doctor out for them and everything. And today of all days? You've been this close to adoption a dozen times now."

"More," Chezzy mumbled.

"Still, you carouse like you do and look what happens," Ms. Bartleby went on, not hearing him.

After a while, she fell silent, only occasionally shaking her head. Chezzy looked out the window and thought of Sarah. Right now, she and the other kids would be on kitchen duty and taking care of the little ones back at Wutherford Home. She had stayed with Chezzy in the basement, and she had tried to stand up for him to Ms. Bartleby.

"I understand you've had a hard year."

Chezzy snapped out of his daze with a wide eyed start. "What?"

She kept her eyes ahead, working against the emotion. "I know you and Ms. Vose were close. Closer than you and I ever were. And I'm sure she's the reason you did what you did to get kicked out of the Smith's house. I'm not saying it's okay, but I understand. But if you keep on the way you have, no one will ever take you. You'll spend the last four years of your childhood at Wutherford Home. And that's not healthy. Even if it's comfortable… A child needs a family. Not just overseers. You understand?"

"Yes, ma'am." He could feel himself trembling.

Finally, she looked over at the boy, but Chezzy was watching a park pass by. It was sprent with trees, swings, and springs, and children were sporting around, deep in their summer break. Chezzy and the others at Wutherford Home had studies year round, and the entire arrangement was foreign to him yet possessed a curious romanticism. Chezzy thought again of Byron, of Sarah, and of the Smiths. But most of all, he thought of Lenna Vose as he absently touched his face where he'd been kicked by the other boys. Outside, the world went from parklands to neighborhoods, and, soon, Ms. Bartleby was slowing the car.

The house situated at 1121 Morrel Drive rested at the end of a long cul de sac. Every house on the block seemed exactly the same as every other house. And every yard sported the same shrub, the same tree, and very nearly the same car in each of the same driveways. All of the houses were the same shaded brick, and, aside from their numbers, Chezzy could hardly make out how to distinguish one from the next. The whole place generated a disquieting feeling, and he found himself wondering if the people that lived in the houses were all copies of each other as well. The idea gave him a small shiver.

Ms. Bartleby pulled the car up at the end of the cul de sac, right in front of 1121 Morrel Drive. The street was empty, save a man who was entirely out of place. He was coming up the sidewalk, and he had dirty blond hair that shot up in every direction. He wore sweatpants and an unbuttoned, floral shirt, which revealed a strange looking green shirt underneath. In his dishevelry, he seemed to be watching Chezzy and Ms. Bartleby as they disembarked the car.

But Ms. Bartleby was motioning to Chezzy to retrieve the small trunk from the boot before she ushered him on. And when Chezzy looked again for the man, he was gone. He did not have long to consider this though, because Ms. Bartleby was presenting to Chezzy 1121 Morrel Drive. She smiled, and Chezzy shifted in noticeable discomfort, so he asked, "What's in the trunk?"

"A change of clothes." Her voice was nearly a whisper, and her answer came rather curtly, as if to hush him. As if speaking outside were not allowed here.

"Right." He eyed the trunk strangely, wondering if his own clothes were in it or if she had gotten him a second set like the outfit he currently donned. It was unusual for her to bring him multiple outfits for a try out trip.

"Here, let me take a look at you." She grabbed his chin and pointed his face up at her. "That's odd."

"What is?"

"You don't hardly have a mark on you at all. Did you put something on? You were all bruised up earlier. Must've been dirt from the basement. Don't know why Lenna insisted on letting you stay down there. It's a dreadful mess. Well, come along then. Let's get you inside." She moved to head up the walk, but Chezzy hesitated, prompting Ms. Bartleby to stop. "What's the matter?"

"It's just weird here."

"Oh, it's lovely," she waved him off, her voice rising somewhat. She straightened her jacket and looked around the neighborhood as if expecting a scolding as she lowered her voice back down. "Now, you're going to be nice to Mr. and Mrs. Fieldmore and to, to, uh, little Patty. That's right. You hear me?"

"Yes, Ms. Bartleby." But there was a dread mounting inside of him.

"And you're going to have a good time, too. Isn't that right?" She nodded vigorously, too vigorously, and gave him a pat, which all seemed to reassure herself a lot more than it did Chezzy. "And I'll be back along tomorrow to check on you and see how you're getting on with them."

Chezzy nodded his head, but Ms. Bartleby hardly noticed as she took him by the shoulder and led him up the front walk to the short stairs before the door. They stepped up, and Ms. Bartleby pushed the little buzzer, which was detailed with a vine like facade. They stood and waited for what seemed like many minutes, so long, in fact, that Ms. Bartleby moved to try to peek through the heavily curtained window while she reached up to push the buzzer again. But just as she did so, the door swung wide open.

Mr. and Mrs. Fieldmore stood with their daughter, Patty, posed behind the door like a catalogue cover. Chezzy sucked in a deep breath when he saw them. All three of them matched. Mr. Fieldmore's sweater vest to Mrs. Fieldmore's scarf and to Patty's bow. Mr. Fieldmore's shirt to Mrs. Fieldmore's heels and to Patty's skirt and so on. It was blinding for Chezzy to behold. Even Ms. Bartleby near gasped at the sight of them, so perfect they were, but as she recomposed, she began to find her words. "Erm, yes, this is Chester Nithercot, and, Chester, this is Mr. and Mrs. Fieldmore and their lovely daughter, Patty." Patty curtsied at the mention of her name. She appeared a little younger than Chezzy, and her bright eyes gleamed against her teeth like two incandescent orbs.

"Hello," Chezzy offered up, uncertainly.

"Now, don't be shy, there. Please, please, come on in." Mr. Fieldmore gestured broadly with a many ringed hand to his home as he smiled, challengingly. Then he led them all inside while he glanced down at Chezzy's shoes. "Now, watch your feet there. This rug was handcrafted by an isolated family of weavers in the seventeen hundreds. That's right, the seventeen hundreds."

Chezzy looked down at the colorful rug and then back up to Mr. Fieldmore's smiling, shining face. "So, you want me to…?"

"So just, yep, just walk on around it." Mr. Fieldmore outlined the safe path for Chezzy to take with his hand. Chezzy set his trunk down and took a careful step around the rug. Mr. Fieldmore, his smile unfaltering, looked quite pleased and gestured to Chezzy. "There you go. Easy, easy."

Ms. Bartleby followed around the rug likewise, her face in a forced smile, as if rising to match that of Mr. Fieldmore.

"Why would you want a rug you can't walk on?" Chezzy puzzled to Mr. Fieldmore in a grumbling whisper as they moved further into the home. Mr. Fieldmore's face turned contemplative a moment before breaking back into a shaky sort of smile.

"Chester, don't ask questions," ordered Ms. Bartleby as she jerked Chezzy tight to her. She smiled to Mr. Fieldmore. "It's a lovely rug, sir."

Mr. Fieldmore nudged at Ms. Bartleby, his teeth baring, before continuing, "Why thank you. It's decorative, you know."

"Oh, very." Ms. Bartleby's smile liked to break her whole face in two, it was stretched so wide. It seemed a sort of unspoken game had begun, and both Mr. Fieldmore and Ms. Bartleby were determined to outnice one another.

"Yes, I purchased it from the estate of Sir Pugh Fuller, himself, you know. But of course, you are familiar with him." Mr. Fieldmore led them all into a richly decored sitting room, to which he threw out his arms in a shrug of feigned modesty.

Ms. Bartleby nodded her head, her mouth agape and teeth clear, as she watched Mr. Fieldmore and then looked around at the room. "Uh, huh."

"Of course, of course. Anyway, old story, new rug. New story, old rug. You get it." Mr. Fieldmore gestured to a couch, never breaking from his pleasant expression. "Please, please. Sit, sit. Careful of the fabric, though."

Ms. Bartleby looked at the couch as if she were acid, and her mere touch would completely ruin the upholstery. Then she looked back to Mr. Fieldmore, quickly mirroring his expression. "Really, though, I should be off soon, I only meant to see that

Chester is settled, and, well, he, or all of you, will be fine, I'm sure."

Not to be outdone, Mr. Fieldmore went on, "Oh, yeah, yeah. I'm sure we will be getting on like a bundle of bees. Yes, a bundle of bees, I tell you." Then he unleashed his most startling smile yet, threatening to blind Ms. Bartleby with it. His teeth seemed like the whitest thing Chezzy had ever seen. He didn't even know that white could be that white. Or maybe it was an entirely new color that he had never seen before, because people didn't feel like white was white enough yet.

Ms. Bartleby nodded, her own eyes blinking against his brilliance, as if to concede. "Well, I'll be back in tomorrow for a little check in to see how things are going. You do recall, yes?"

Mr. Fieldmore nodded, well aware of his win. "Of course, of course."

"Oh, we will be looking forward to your visit," Mrs. Fieldmore intervened. "Won't we?" She put an arm around Patty and squeezed the girl softly.

"Yes, mother," Patty chimed in.

"See, there?" Mr. Fieldmore looked over his family, the arc of his eyes coming to rest firmly on Chezzy. "Bundle of bees. I say, I say, we'll make a lunch of it tomorrow. How's that suit?"

Mrs. Fieldmore and Patty nodded enthusiastically as they threw pleading eyes to Ms. Bartleby.

Ms. Bartleby nodded as she met the gaze of the two of them. She paused at the expectant faces before offering, "Uh, lunch? Oh, sure. We can do that."

"Then it's settled." Mr. Fieldmore clapped his hands together, the rings of each hand clanging against each other. "A tomorrow lunch." He continued to speak with Ms. Bartleby as he led her out of the house, but Chezzy couldn't make out the exchange. Instead, he looked over at Mrs. Fieldmore and Patty.

Mrs. Fieldmore smiled at him in a sort of frighteningly kind way. Chezzy shifted his feet, his eyes dropping down to the deep color of the wood beneath him. The dirt of his shoes had flaked off and crumbled as he had walked in, leaving a visible trail that snaked its way to where he stood. Chezzy looked over the trail and felt a pang of shame.

"You can have a seat, Chester." Mrs. Fieldmore gestured to the couch next to Chezzy with a long, delicate hand.

Chezzy looked up at Mrs. Fieldmore and then back down to the trail of dirt before responding, "That's alright."

"He really is rather dirty, mother," Patty seemed to agree.

Mrs. Fieldmore nudged Patty lovingly. "So were you, darling. And now look at you. Eh? Spotless. What do you think of that?"

Patty considered this a moment. "I suppose you are right, mother. Though, maybe not quite so dirty as he is. Look at his nails."

"They are rather long. As is his hair. Little dear, when did you last have a haircut?"

"Yesterday," Chezzy mumbled.

"Oh, posh. You needn't fib about it. Had to have been months, at least. Don't you worry, we'll have it trimmed posthaste."

Chezzy's hand felt up to his weird locks. He did have a haircut and a nail trim just the day before, but, as ever, both were long and frightful. A large clock tolled the time, and Chezzy looked at it, startled, before turning back to Mrs. Fieldmore and Patty. He tried to swallow his shame as both were attempting to ignore the obvious trail of mud. It wasn't so much that he was dirty. After all, he had bathed just before they left, but the grounds of Wutherford Home had been muddy from the rains. "So, why is everything so clean?"

Both of them burst into laughter. They composed quickly, though, and Mrs. Fieldmore said to Chezzy through her lingering giggles, "I suppose you aren't accustomed to being in a proper home, are you?"

Chezzy shrugged.

"Have you visited many other families?"

Chezzy bobbed his head, still looking down. "I mean, a couple." He had visited many homes, though not one of them was anywhere near as sparkling as this one was.

"A couple?"

"Yes. A couple of homes, that is."

"And what were they like? These other homes." She flipped her hand in the air in a casual way, as if at the other homes.

Chezzy brought his gaze carefully to Mrs. Fieldmore. He wondered at what she really meant by the question. "Different."

"Different how?" Her eyes had grown narrower, almost like pinpricks of light that were focused on Chezzy.

He shrugged again. "Just different, I guess. Different from yours. Different from Wutherford. In their own ways."

"And what happened with them?" Her voice had sunk to nearly a whisper with this question.

"Well," Chezzy began, but footsteps quickly interrupted him as Mr. Fieldmore strode back in, merrily.

"Well, who is hungry now? Huh? Honey? Shall we get things going?" Mr. Fieldmore asked in a rather jovial manner.

"Oh, yes, we should." Mrs. Fieldmore's entire demeanor seemed to change. She rose up and beamed at Chezzy. Then she spoke to Patty with an affectionate tone. "See to Chester, darling."

"Yes, mother." Patty gave Chezzy a warm smile, but Chezzy didn't feel warm at all. He glanced warily between Mrs. Fieldmore and Patty. But Mrs. Fieldmore was quickly disappearing after Mr. Fieldmore, leaving Chezzy and Patty alone in the parlor.

The girl stood up and nodded to Chezzy in a very formal way before she spoke, "Well, follow me," and then she led him through the parlor and into another room right off the foyer. Then they went up a flight of wooden stairs that wound around the room entire before swallowing into the second story. It took them up into a hallway where Patty turned to a door and took hold of the knob. "Don't worry," she said to him. "I know mother seemed miffed, but that wasn't it at all, you know."

"It wasn't?" Chezzy didn't really believe her.

"No. She can't stand people who pretend at being parents and toss children away."

Chezzy shifted awkwardly under the steady stare of Patty's two studious eyes. He wasn't so sure yet that Mrs. Fieldmore would hold to that. "Seemed weird."

"No. You haven't seen the weird yet."

Chezzy opened the brown paper, and the outfit he found was unlike anything he had ever worn before. He fidgeted uncomfortably after he had freshened up and changed. The new clothes sat patched across him as best he could figure them. Then he eyed himself in the mirror as everything inside of him was screaming to run. He felt this way every time, but it was worse now, for some reason. Chezzy repeatedly adjusted the garments, but they didn't really sit right on him no matter what he did. Frustrated, he balled up the brown paper in his fist and squeezed it till his hand went warm.

He dropped the paper to the floor and rubbed his hands over his forehead and up into his wild hair. He wasn't nice enough for this place. Still, he braced himself, unsure of what he should do, and opened the door. There, he was startled to find Patty waiting for him. Chezzy blushed, but Patty seemed unconcerned. "Here, let me," and she immediately set herself to deftly situating his mane, undoing and redoing buttons, retying the tie, and really adjusting the entire ensemble. Chezzy marveled at the speed and skill with which she worked. Once done, she turned him around and pushed him back into the bathroom so that he could see himself fully in the mirror. "See?"

Chezzy looked over himself. His dark xanthine tinged hair was tamed down somewhat, and, aside from that and his long nails, he looked sort of nice. "Wow. You… how'd you learn that?"

Patty gave him a soft smile. "You'll learn it too."

"Will I?"

Patty nodded to Chezzy. "Come on, we must hurry down now."

The table was a rich, dark wood and draped over with fine cloth. And upon that cloth, were assortments of foods wholly foreign to Chezzy. At two of the high backed chairs, sat Mr. and Mrs. Fieldmore, both smiling and welcoming. Patty led Chezzy to a particular chair across from Mr. Fieldmore, and then she took her own directly opposite of Mrs. Fieldmore. All of it was terribly balanced.

Chezzy pulled out the chair carefully and sat. There were subtle scratches, patched at the edge of the table under his arms. He looked up at the smiling faces of the family around him, and he felt sick down into his belly, though he couldn't say exactly why that was.

"You look just lovely, Chester. Just lovely," offered Mrs. Fieldmore promptly. "Doesn't he, darling?"

"Yes, mother," responded Patty. She gave Chezzy an encouraging nod.

"Yes, mostly, anyway," Mrs. Fieldmore amended.

"Now, Chester, how do you feel about the name Chester?" Mr. Fieldmore leveled a serious gaze at Chezzy.

"Now, Stuart, don't start on that yet."

"What? I just want to know how he likes his name, that's all." Mr. Fieldmore shrugged. "Just in case. No harm, either way. Right there, Chester?" Chezzy's name came out from Mr. Fieldmore's teeth like something stuck to them.

Mrs. Fieldmore scowled at Mr. Fieldmore while chewing a mouthful of some sort of baked and breaded chicken stuffed with what Chezzy was sure was just ham and cheese.

"Fine. Fine. We'll leave that for another time, then. Shall we, Chester?" He spooned mouthfuls of a round, green vegetable about the size of a large marble.

Chezzy nodded, not entirely sure what Mr. Fieldmore was getting at. He thought about this a moment, wondering how he would feel about another name, but either the idea or the presentation, sort of bothered Chezzy. It ate into his stomach, and he felt a new bout of anxiety hit him. "Now, don't be shy, Chester, help yourself." Mrs. Fieldmore gestured to one of the dishes before them.

"Sure." Chezzy glanced nervously over at Patty, and she nodded at him encouragingly again while she ate a modest bite of the chicken. Chezzy reached forward for a ladle, his hand seeming uncertain where to start. He settled on a single dish and scooped spoonfuls of some type of minced pie with green beans and a thick, dark gravy. He also took some sort of sweet, mashed vegetable that he did not recognize and one of the many kinds of breads. Then he ate and found that it was all very good. He chewed, and he listened as the Fieldmores made small talk amongst themselves, only occasionally addressing him in a rather awkward manner, as if attempting to include him though ultimately not knowing how he fit in.

"What sort of schooling have you done over at Wutherford?" Mrs. Fieldmore asked, struggling again to engage Chezzy.

"We do lessons, every day. From Ms. Bartleby." His words came out a bit garbled through the full mouth he was sporting.

Mrs. Fieldmore cleared her throat and blinked several times before she responded. "Every day?"

"Yes." Chezzy swallowed. "Er, yes, ma'am. And we have kitchen duty and cleaning duty and all."

Mrs. Fieldmore managed a half smile. "Isn't that something?"

Chezzy shrugged. "I guess." Mrs. Fieldmore glanced at Mr. Fieldmore and then Patty.

"Not exactly a proper education though, is it?" Mr. Fieldmore mused.

"Stuart," Mrs. Fieldmore chided.

"I'm just saying, private school is a different level. Maybe we could put him into Patty's grade. Just say he's her age. Maybe he could handle that, I mean, he's certainly small enough to pass for twelve."

"This is not the right time, Stuart."

"Right, right. Getting ahead of ourselves." He waved his hand and gave a slight roll of the eye to Chezzy, but Chezzy didn't know what the man meant to convey.

Chezzy felt hot all over, and he was sure the tie was choking him, but Mrs. Fieldmore cut in to change the subject. "They tell me you were left there as a baby. Is that right?"

"Yes. Yes, ma'am." Chezzy felt his flushed face with his hand, and he glanced at Patty before lowering his eyes to his plate and taking another bite, the scratches distracting at the sides.

Mrs. Fieldmore threw her hand to her chest and let out a dramatic, practiced gasp. "So, you've never even met your parents?"

"No, ma'am. I have not." Chezzy felt himself redden a shade. He took another bite and chewed somberly.

"Oh, you poor dear." Mrs. Fieldmore dabbed the edges of her mouth with her napkin and then did likewise to the edges of her eyes. She and the family gathered gave him a pitying look that seemed to make him lesser, somehow. It seeped with sympathy and mild disdain. It was the same look every family had given him, and, as he stayed with each, it would always turn into something else. Something far worse and far more maddening and sorrowful than anything before. Inevitably, after that, Ms. Bartleby would always return to take him back to Wutherford Home.

"Yes, poor indeed," Mr. Fieldmore agreed. "Say, Chester, do you know anything of them? Anything at all?"

Chezzy swallowed the mushed minced pie and didn't even lift his eyes to respond. "No, sir. Nothing."

Mr. Fieldmore leaned back and crossed his arms. He stroked his clean shaven face, his fork still held in his other hand. "Very curious. Right, dear?"

"Oh, yes."

"Downright strange, even."

"Mm." Mrs. Fieldmore nodded in absolute agreement.

Chezzy shrugged again. He managed to look up at the both of them. "Sometimes babies come in. I don't think they know their parents either."

Mr. Fieldmore stabbed his fork into another of the green vegetables. "And how long do those babies stay there? On average?"

Chezzy looked back and forth between Mr. and Mrs. Fieldmore before lowering his gaze, summoning softly spoken words. "Not long."

Mr. Fieldmore nodded as he wiped his forehead. Something in his demeanor was changing. "As I thought, yes. Just as I thought. That's okay. That's okay, you see. You're here for a new chance. A chance to learn and to grow and to be a part of this family. Eh? If you put in just a little more effort, you know. If you be open minded and understand that people look different. Uh, this is all different. It's a new house with new things. And that's okay, you know, because looking different isn't bad. Because we can work together to look the part. But you have to want to make it work. You have to want it. Not like before, no. Of course not. It wouldn't work. But we're a team with, uh, family and, and, presentation. You know, that's how we get through this. But you have to be open because, because you're unwanted. But that's okay to be unwanted." He took a deep breath. "We will always want you. You see? What I'm saying is, if we really just," Mr. Fieldmore held clenched fists that he shook before him, "just really try, I think we can make something here. How does that sound to you?" Mr. Fieldmore yielded his rant and wiped his face again with his cloth napkin. He looked, for a moment, completely unraveled, but he was recomposing himself.

Chezzy nodded almost imperceptibly. "Sounds good." But he wasn't sure he actually felt that way.

"Good." Mr. Fieldmore clapped his hands together, clanging his rings and refocusing, his prior confidence returning as he spoke. "Now, there are a few rules and things to sort out. Shortly, Patty will show you to your new room, which is upstairs. And, before you ask, we've already supplied it with everything you might need or want. Gladly. Yes, gladly. All we ask in return is that you keep it neat and orderly. No things lying about and all that. Patty will show you, yes. So, in the mornings, that is, every morning, you will receive word on what the dress theme will be for the day," and he smiled again, as if he were relaying a special treat to Chezzy. "On select days we will have votes for specific themes."

He gave Chezzy a little nod then went on. "Aside that, you will maintain a polite and sensibly quiet attitude during interactions and especially," he pinched both forefingers and thumbs together, "especially when guests are present. We, as a family, entertain twice a week, I'll have you know, and we're very proud of our small gatherings we hold." And he was, as was evident across his face. "Sometimes, just sometimes, we will invite nearly the whole neighborhood over for an occasion. You will be expected to maintain an air of dignity that will reflect upon all of us. I'm sure you understand, yes? And in return, you will have anything you desire, within reason. Now, isn't that right, dear?"

"Right," Mrs. Fieldmore responded approvingly. Then she positively beamed down at Chezzy where he sat.

Mr. Fieldmore nodded then turned over to Patty. "And my little Patty? Isn't that right, my dear?"

"Right," she chimed in. Patty and Chezzy exchanged a look, but Chezzy couldn't read anything on her to indicate that anything was actually wrong, even though he felt like there was something very, very wrong.

Mr. Fieldmore gestured around him. "As to the house itself, you are welcome to make yourself at home here, though, do stay out of our bedroom, the attic, and the basement. Those are off limits to children. Understand?"

Chezzy turned from Patty and nodded to Mr. Fieldmore. "Yes, sir."

"Brilliant." He smiled again, quite content with everything around him. "Then you will make yourself a nice place here, I can assure you of that."

Chezzy smiled and nodded once more. He felt like he'd just concluded a business transaction. He looked over at Patty and gave her an uncertain look. She grinned back at him and nudged his foot with her own. Chezzy wasn't sure why, but it made him feel just a little bit better. But, despite this, he couldn't bring himself to finish his plate.

Eventually, they migrated back to the parlor, where Chezzy was presented with a game called Crattleboards. The Fieldmores, each, were very excited about it as they explained the rather complicated rules. Chezzy sat, taking in the bureaucratic instructions thrown his way amongst a peppering of questions. All the while, something in the pit of his belly grew, and it gnawed at him. They were pleasant and perfectly situated, and polite, and right in every possible presentation. Yet something was wrong. Wrong beyond their staunch refusal to actually play Crattleboards after over an hour of lecturing him on how.

III.
Chezzy's room.
Mirrored.
Stuart Fieldmore Jr.

*P*atty led Chezzy upstairs and down a long hallway to his new room. Chezzy peered inside as they reached the door. The bed was tremendously tall and very wide. It had four posters that were draped around with curtains that went all the way to the ceiling. On the wall, in bold placard letters, it said *PLAY BALL*, and there was a framed jersey from some sport unknown to Chezzy. He turned to a deep wooded dresser where familial photos of the Fieldmores sat, like everything else, precisely in their intended places with not a thing askant. Chezzy stared wide eyed around the room. Then he took careful steps across the rich carpet, even though his new shoes were pristine.

"Do you like it?" Patty had followed Chezzy in. She was glowing with excitement for him, and she gripped his arm.

Chezzy turned to Patty. "Like it? It's… I've never had anything like this. It's… I guess it's nicer than the basement at Wutherford Home."

Patty's face dampened at once. "Well, we mustn't go into the basement here. You remember, don't you?"

Chezzy puzzled at her response. "Yeah. Yeah."

"Good." She relaxed a bit, but there was still a lingering hint of concern across her face.

Chezzy considered this then pressed the question. "But why?"

Patty shook her head. Her lips pulled tight for a moment before she spoke again. "That's just the rule."

Chezzy scrunched up his face. "I get that, but I'm asking why it is."

"It just is." She said this with an air of finality. "We don't break the rules here."

"But… it doesn't make sense." Every home he had stayed in had different rules, but the ones without reason always irked him.

Patty's face reddened, and she was silent until it paled again. "You'll find your night clothes on the bed. You should change. Mother and father will be in shortly to bid you goodnight. Just, just be ready before then. Can you do that?" Her tone was cold, distant.

Chezzy shrugged. "Sure…" It wasn't quite full dark out yet, and Chezzy wondered if they always went to bed this early in the evening.

"Good." Patty turned of a sudden and left. She shut the door behind her, abandoning Chezzy to his new room.

He turned and peeled back the bed curtain where he spied the new bundle of clothing, once again swathed in brown paper. He took the little package and opened the wrapping. Chezzy drew out sleep trousers with a matching, button down sleep shirt and matching house shoes. He scrambled out of his dinner clothes and hurriedly dressed in the new sleepwear. "Lot of changing," Chezzy mumbled to himself.

A knock sounded at the bedroom door followed by a voice. "Little dear? Are you dressed?" It was the voice of Mrs. Fieldmore.

"Just a moment," Chezzy replied before dashing into the bed, fighting his way through the curtains. "Okay," he added as he sunk into the thick comforter.

The bedroom door opened, and Mrs. Fieldmore entered. She was quickly followed by Mr. Fieldmore, who gave a broad and satisfied grin to the room and the bed where Chezzy lay. Mrs. Fieldmore drew the curtains aside and peeked in at him. "Settling in nicely, little Chester?"

"Yes, ma'am."

"Good. Very good."

"Good? He's sleeping with his shoes on," threw in Mr. Fieldmore with an uncomfortable guffaw. "What's that all about?"

"Sorry," said Chezzy, quickly kicking his house shoes off and on to the floor. "I didn't know what to do with them. I thought I was supposed to wear them."

Mrs. Fieldmore laughed heartily. "Oh, dear, they're just for the house. In case you need to get up. That's all."

"Okay." Chezzy felt himself flush.

Mr. Fieldmore squatted down and gathered Chezzy's house shoes. He placed them neatly together before he rose. "I'm sure you'll get it figured out. Won't you, son?"

Chezzy nodded, but he wasn't so sure he would. There seemed to be a lot of rules, and he didn't understand at least half of the ones he had learned so far. He balanced that against Mr. Fieldmore calling him son. He wasn't sure anyone had called him that before. "Am I supposed to go to sleep now? It's just, it's not very late."

Mr. and Mrs. Fieldmore exchanged a look. "Yes, but you had a big day today, and you'll be having another big one tomorrow. Best to get a little rest, don't you think, honey?"

Mrs. Fieldmore nodded. "Oh, yes, dear. You can stay up later another night, but I think it'd be best to get some sleep now. We have a lunch tomorrow." She threw her hands up to her sides, as if that settled it.

"Yes, we do. Well, you just have yourself a good night now. Come along, darling. Let him have some sleep. Big day today, big day tomorrow," repeated Mr. Fieldmore.

"Oh, you're very right." She stepped back from the bed, letting the semi sheer curtains fall shut, and they moved toward the door while giving reassuring nods back to Chezzy.

"Mr. and Mrs. Fieldmore?"

"Yes, dear?"

"Why is Patty afraid of the basement?" Chezzy knew, immediately, that it was the wrong thing to ask.

Mrs. Fieldmore stiffened and Mr. Fieldmore let out a heavy series of coughs. He slammed his hand against his chest, the rings thumping painfully. "Now, now. Now, Patty is just afraid of the dark, and that's all there is to that, you see?"

"Oh, yes. She is. She is. But, again, she is right. The basement is not a safe place for children."

"Quite."

"Yes, too many dangerous things down there for you to be going around and playing with and all."

"Yes, quite. Quite." Mr. Fieldmore agreed urgently. "Can't have you down there getting hurt or the like. Can't have that."

"No, no."

"No. Yes, they'd take you back to Wutherford."

"Yes."

"No. Without doubt. Without doubt they would."

"So, you definitely shouldn't be going down there."

"Yes. Absolutely so."

"Mhmm." Mrs. Fieldmore nodded compassionately.

"And that will be the end of it."

"Yes." And then they both nodded in unison.

"Anyway, you sleep tight." The both of them dipped out of Chezzy's room and shut the door behind them. Outside, Chezzy could hear their hushed whispers, but he couldn't quite make out any of the words. He laid there in the bed a long while, tossing thoughts around his head and waiting for dark. Something was wrong here and the Fieldmores were hiding it. Whatever it was, he was sure he'd find it in the basement.

Chezzy eased open the bedroom door. He stepped lightly out, wearing his new house shoes. But with each step, they made an odd, padding sound that seemed to boom up and down the hallway. He froze then tried walking more slowly, but no matter how he adjusted his step, they continued to thwap. Frustrated, Chezzy kicked off the house shoes and continued barefoot.

He glanced toward the stairwell heading down from the hall. The entrance to the basement was just below, and, from there, he could see that the door was ajar. Curiously, he crept down the stairs and carefully approached the door, but a shuffling, or perhaps something dropping, sounded out, stilling him. Chezzy looked around. It wasn't from the basement but from the kitchen. Someone else was still up. He glassed the double egress door for a moment and then hurried into the basement, descending the wooden stairs. But what he found when he reached the bottom shocked him.

It was a room. But not just any room. It was Chezzy's room. It mirrored his upstairs, exactly. The four poster bed, the *PLAY BALL* placards, the framed jersey, and even the dresser with the meticulously placed pictures. Chezzy felt dizzy for a moment, and he hadn't a clue what this meant. A small lamp on the far side of the bed lightly illuminated everything, and, as the air conditioning switched on, the bed curtains fluttered. Chezzy caught his breath and crept closer. Shredded. The curtains were slit all through, and it wasn't just them. The bed, the comforter, the pillows, all were cut up and spilling stuffing.

He ran back up the basement stairs, desperate for the front door. But when he reached it, he was stopped by a series of keyed locks that he had not noticed before. Chezzy wrenched open the curtain of the window next to the door and stared out at the quiet, dark street before him. He was going to break it, however, behind him came a strange, low growl. Chezzy turned and looked to the kitchen door. Whatever the sound was, it had come from there, but the kitchen held no light. The growl had changed to slurping and chomping. Bewildered, his curiosity got the better of him, and Chezzy edged forward from the foyer to the stair room. And when he reached the double egress door, he slowly pressed it open, peering beyond. A figure, the size of a large man, lurked in the corner of the kitchen, but it wasn't anyone that Chezzy knew.

The thing appeared to be chewing on something at the far countertop, and Chezzy pushed the door further in to get a better look, his eyes struggling to adjust to the blackness. Chezzy slid his body past the door and flattened against the wall to watch, while he let the door shut. As his eyes adjusted, he had absolutely no idea what he was looking at. Spikes formed around the outline of the figure, and they wobbled with the frantic chewing. Of a sudden, it grunted, and its head turned, sniffing in the air. Chezzy stiffened as he caught a glimpse of the eyes, which glowed in the dark.

The figure sniffed more, and then its entire body went strangely still before it wheeled around with surprising speed. The glowing eyes looked directly at Chezzy. Then he and the thing both let out a scream, and the spines that were all across the creature exploded outward, shooting from its body. They stabbed across the cabinets, the floor, the ceiling, and two of the spines found their way across the kitchen where they settled neatly into the chest and abdomen of Chezzy.

Chezzy looked down at the two needles puncturing his torso. Each was at least the length of a chopstick outside of his skin and about as thick as a pen. Chezzy's legs went shaky, and he sunk down to the floor. In shock, he gripped a hand around one of the embedded needles and tugged slightly. Something inside caught under the skin. The creature let out an odd groan, and Chezzy looked up to it, frozen, across the room.

Chezzy flashed with abrupt anger, his body turning hot, and he was about to climb back to his feet, but something about the sight of the thing stopped him. The creature was trembling, its head moving side to side as if in horror. The face was almost boy like, despite its animal features and glowing eyes. Its mouth opened, revealing small, pointed teeth. "Oh, no," the creature let out. "Mother and father are going to be terribly upset. Just terribly upset. Oh, no."

"What?" Chezzy managed to gasp, his stomach quivering, his body relaxing some as the anger in him melted away and was replaced with something else. He was certain he was hallucinating. Maybe there was poison on the spines.

The creature snapped out of its state and rushed forward to Chezzy. It leaned over him and spoke frantically. "Oh, no. No, no. It's okay. I can fix this, really I can." The creature gripped around one of the needles and pulled.

Chezzy let out another scream, and the creature let go of the needle.

"Oh, sorry, sorry."

The double egress door swung open, banging against Chezzy as the lights came on, and Mr. and Mrs. Fieldmore stood, aghast, as they stared down at the scene before them. Each of them wore matching pajamas to the ones that Chezzy had on. Even the creature's pants, which were torn some, matched as well. The giant bulk that was his back, however, was still half covered with spines, which would have shredded any shirt at all. His bare top revealed white fur, stomach to chin. Though, parts of his face darkened to grey that reached around the sides and across his back, even turning to blues or purples in places. Chezzy stared at him, struck.

The following hour unfolded in a baffling chaos. The lights of the house sprang on. The Fieldmores rushed around at a frantic pace. Patty came down and joined in on the fray. Mr. Fieldmore yelled at the creature as together they pulled spines from the cabinets and walls. Mrs. Fieldmore and Patty saw to Chezzy. They laid him down, and Mrs. Fieldmore worked the needles out of his skin with practiced care.

When she pulled the first one out, Chezzy saw that the ends of the needles presented with little hooks, which was why it took Mrs. Fieldmore quite some time to finagle the spines around and out. The wounds bled, and Patty held rags to them as Chezzy looked up at her worried face. He was trying to speak to her through the onslaught of distractions, but he was suddenly feeling quite drowsy. He finally managed to ask, "What was that?"

"You're okay. It was just Little Stuart," Patty replied, but the bite hadn't left her.

"Quiet, dear." Mrs. Fieldmore was prepping bandages for the wounds. Her face was stern and pale. Patty had, meanwhile, removed Chezzy's night shirt and tossed it into the trash bin. It was covered in blood.

Mr. Fieldmore had fetched a ladder and was currently pulling numerous spines out of the ceiling. "Look at the floor. Can see it from here, even. How am I to have that fixed? Can you tell me?"

"I'm sorry, father," offered up the creature.

"Sorry isn't going to fix my floors, is it? Is it?"

"No, sir." The creature shook its spiny head, and there were tear trails clearly visible in the fur of its face.

"That's right, it won't. Going to have to get a man in, again. Again. Twice this year already. Twice," Mr. Fieldmore exclaimed.

"I'm sorry, father."

"What are you doing up, anyway?"

"I was hungry again."

"Honestly, you're always hungry. You keep eating like you do, and you'll keep growing like you have. Can't have that. Where will we put you?"

The creature shrugged its massive shoulders. "I don't know. I'm sorry, father. I didn't mean to."

Chezzy was dazed. He didn't even notice as Mrs. Fieldmore was struggling to lift him up from the floor. She'd finished situating the bandages on him and was desperate to get him out of the kitchen. "Help me, now, dear."

Together, she and Patty managed to take Chezzy upstairs and to his bedroom. He could hear Mr. Fieldmore behind him going on about getting the house fixed and whether or not tomorrow's outfit scheme would even work anymore. Meanwhile, Mrs. Fieldmore fussed the entire way up. "Oh, the kitchen is just ruined, ruined I tell you. My dear Patty, how can we hope to host this Saturday with the kitchen in ruins?"

"I don't know, mother."

"And we have that luncheon, just tomorrow, you know?"

"Yes, mother."

"How will we serve? Just dreadful. And now I've been kept up in the night, so I'll have baggy eyes for the affair. What could be worse than baggy eyes for a luncheon? Baggy eyes and no way to serve properly."

"Chester has holes in him, mother."

"Oh, yes, and those. I mean, they'll be fine but even still, bandages. Bandages. What pairs well with bandages?"

"A patient's gown?"

Mrs. Fieldmore stopped at the top of the stairs and levelled a menacing look at Patty, "This is no time for jokes, Patricia."

"Yes, mother." Her tone was dry, joyless, and she shot Chezzy an unfriendly look.

They got him into his room and laid him down in his bed. Then Mrs. Fieldmore had stroked Chezzy's hair with a shaking hand as she spoke. "Now, now. You rest, you hear? We'll talk about this more in the morning, dear, alright?"

Chezzy managed a half bewildered shrug, but Mrs. Fieldmore hardly noticed. She was dabbing her face with the sleeve of her nightshirt.

"Good, good. Get some rest now." And then the both of them left, Patty giving Chezzy a head shake as the door shut. After that, Chezzy was alone in the darkness with only the muffled sounds of the Fieldmores at work downstairs to help soothe him to sleep. Not that he needed soothing. He was starved and exhausted of a sudden, and he passed right out.

Chezzy woke with a start, sitting bolt upright. His hand went instinctively to his chest, which was bare but for the bandages. There were no such things as monsters, let alone family monsters that people kept, or whatever it was he had conjured in the night. Families don't keep monsters. Especially families like the Fieldmores. They wouldn't be able to stand the mess of a monster. Not that Chezzy was familiar with the types of messes that monsters make. But the Fieldmores especially wouldn't stand for any type of mess by any type of monster and certainly not the type of mess that was made last night. Yet, here were the bandages still strapped to his body, and he looked at the small specks of blood that had soaked through them.

Chezzy wrenched the bedcurtains aside and looked out around his new room. Already drifting in, was the rich smell of bacon, and, if he strained his ears, he could hear the fat sizzling and popping downstairs over the hum of what could be conversation. His stomach let out an audible groan, and he realized just how hungry he was. He searched around his room for his house slippers, remembering that he had left them in the hall. Yet there they were, returned to his bedside. Chezzy slipped his feet into them. Then, shirtless, he braved the door and went out into the hallway.

He crept to the stairs, cautiously, and descended. A hushed, "Mother, he's coming," issued from below and gave pause to Chezzy, but then down he went. When he reached the bottom, he could still see slight swinging of the double egress door. Chezzy regarded it a moment then approached and pressed it open. Like a picture they sat, Patty, Mrs. Fieldmore, and the monster at the island counter facing Chezzy. Mr. Fieldmore was on the far side and smiling at the stovetop where breakfast meats smoked up.

All were fully dressed and in matching outfits, including the monster, though his clothes were torn through in places by the remaining spines.

"Why, good morning, sleepy head," began Mr. Fieldmore.

"Patty, you didn't set out clothes for him?" Mrs. Fieldmore asked tersely.

"Sorry, mother, I must've forgot." The edge ran sarcastic in her words.

Mrs. Fieldmore shot Patty an uncomfortable glance. "We mustn't... Patty, please, a little leeway here."

Patty gave her mother an offended look. "Leeway?" But Mr. Fieldmore cleared his throat, and the two fell silent as they looked back to Chezzy who was staring at the creature sat with them.

"I would like to introduce you to Little Stuart. Uh, Stuart Fieldmore Jr." Mr. Fieldmore gestured to the monster.

"The monster in the chair?"

"Monster is rather offensive, I daresay," pondered Mrs. Fieldmore.

The monster gave Chezzy an awkward smile. "Hello."

Chezzy's eyes widened. "He's talking to me."

"That's right, dear," Mrs. Fieldmore said. "He talks."

"That's excellent," Chezzy added as he felt for his bandages again. "How'd you get a talking monster? I mean, a Little Stuart?"

"He's our son," Mr. Fieldmore said, his voice grave. "And now he's your brother, you understand?"

"My brother? Who shot me with needles."

"Oh, yes. Sorry about that last night." The monster was talking to Chezzy again. He'd gotten up from his chair and was standing apologetically with his eyes cast down.

"No, I mean, that's so excellent. Not that you should do it again."

The monster smiled a toothy, menacing smile, then he sat back down and continued to drink his juice, slurping it with his short snout while Mr. Fieldmore beamed at Little Stuart. "You see? Not so bad, Little Stuart. Right?" Mr. Fieldmore commented. Chezzy could swear he saw the monster blush, then Mr. Fieldmore addressed him. "Now, Chester, I know this is really odd, but I'm going to need you to listen. Can you do that?"

"Yes, sir."

"Now Little Stuart has this condition, but we must not talk about his condition, or him, with other people, you understand? We must not tell anyone. I mean," he laughed, "they'd take him away, now, wouldn't they? Yes. Yes, take him right away, and I'm not having somebody take my son. No, siree. Isn't that right?"

"No, siree is right." Mrs. Fieldmore affirmed.

"Right. So, we can't be telling anyone about him, and we can't be telling anyone about your, your, your," Mr. Fieldmore waved his finger around at the area of Chezzy's bandages, "those. You understand me?"

"Yes, sir." Chezzy was grinning like a fool.

"Be straight with me, now."

"I am. Really, I mean it."

"Great. Now, are you hungry?"

It was as if Mr. Fieldmore had read Chezzy's mind, and Chezzy stared at Mr. Fieldmore with his mouth open before responding, "Yes. Yes, I am."

IV.
Ms. Bartleby.
Eyes.
Ms. Shoemaker.

The breakfast was delicious. Chezzy had been starved before, and after eating, he was sure he must have had about a half dozen eggs and eight slices of bacon alongside his hashed browns, his toast, his juice, his sliced tomatoes, and his sliced peaches. He was filled to the brim when he finished, but when Mrs. Fieldmore brought out a bread pudding for them, he somehow managed to power through and ate more than his fair share.

Afterward, he sat with his belly bulging as he talked with the Fieldmores, including Little Stuart. Little Stuart was incredible. They told Chezzy that he had been born the way he was, and that, because of this, he'd had to spend his entire life being homeschooled and hiding from other people. He was a shy, polite boy and very soft spoken, but he laughed riotously when Chezzy asked if he could touch what few of his little spikes were still poking out of him, the rest having been shot, collected, and trashed.

"Yes, you may."

Chezzy felt their needle pin ends. "Those are brilliant. How far can you shoot them out? I was all the way across the kitchen when you shot me with them."

"I don't know how far. I try not to do it, but sometimes I get startled, and it just happens. One time, Patty startled me by accident, and I sent one right through her doll's head. She like to have never forgiven me. And, of course, mother and father don't like it. I've ruined the ceiling and the floors and the walls I don't know how many times. Honestly, it's dreadful awful, I tell you. Dreadful awful."

"That's right," piped in Mr. Fieldmore. "Makes a right mess of the place near every time."

"He ruined my bedspread once," added Patty. She had steadily relaxed throughout the meal and was even slipping smiles. "And mother's painting that one time. Do you remember?"

"Oh, my painting," moaned Mrs. Fieldmore.

"Well, I thought it was the one eyed ghost," gave back Little Stuart.

"You always think it's the one eyed ghost, but there's no such thing."

"I swear it. He's always watching me."

"It's just the dark playing tricks. That's why you shouldn't night eat. You near killed Chester, here, last night."

"I know." Little Stuart's animal lips quivered, and then he lightly wiped his eyes with his too small napkin.

"I should start painting again, don't you think so, dear?" asked Mrs. Fieldmore to Mr. Fieldmore.

"No, dear. You shouldn't," replied Mr. Fieldmore.

"It's alright," Chezzy nudged Little Stuart. "I'm alright. I'm not even angry."

Little Stuart picked up a bit at this, and they went back to telling stories of all the things that he had ruined over the years. "You don't even know how many editions of Crattleboards I've ruined. They taught you about Crattleboards, didn't they?"

"Yeah…" Chezzy answered.

"Oh, it's my very favorite game. We're going to play it tons, aren't we?"

Chezzy glanced over to Mr. and Mrs. Fieldmore, the man gesturing emphatically as if painting the air. "You always stress about what to put on the canvas."

"Yes, but what if I paint the wrong thing?" Mrs. Fieldmore argued back.

"There is no wrong thing," Mr. Fieldmore exclaimed. "The wrong thing is you not sleeping. Staying up all forever, worried about a blank canvas. Whole house about falls apart."

"Aren't we, Chester?" Stuart prodded again.

Chezzy turned back to him. Patty was shooting Chezzy an encouraging look while Stuart's eyes bulged hopefully. "Tons. Right." Then Chezzy grinned. Because he really meant it, and it was sinking in that this life was his now.

"Now, now. Now, now. Now you know that when Ms. Bartleby gets here, you can't say anything to her, right?" Mr. Fieldmore cut in. He was looking at Chezzy seriously.

"Anything?" The conversation had shifted so quickly that Chezzy was startled by the sudden change in mood. He didn't even really know what it was Mr. Fieldmore was talking about.

"About," Mr. Fieldmore began but was cut off immediately by Chezzy.

"Right, right. Nothing about Little Stuart. Not a word." Then Chezzy gave Little Stuart a reassuring smile.

"Or about last night, isn't that right?"

"Or last night."

Mr. Fieldmore pointed his finger around the bandages again. "Can't say anything about that, or she'll take you back. You still want to stay, don't you?"

"Oh, yes, sir. I do. Really."

"Fantastic," he clapped his hands together, "isn't that right, dear?"

"It's wonderful, dear. Just extraordinary." Mrs. Fieldmore was alight with cheer, and it was rather infectious the way she would cast it around. Even Patty was grinning. And Chezzy seemed to fill with a warmth in his stomach and in his limbs. It was almost like he was floating. He hardly heard the doorbell ring and didn't realize that anything was wrong until he saw the panicked looks on the faces of the Fieldmores around him.

"It's much too early," Mr. Fieldmore muttered to himself. He glanced around at his family. "Positions." Little Stuart sprang up, his plate clattering to the floor beneath him and bursting into bits. His face formed apologetically, but before he could get a word out, Mr. Fieldmore was already speaking. "Doesn't matter. To the basement. Patricia, dear?"

"Yes," Mrs. Fieldmore replied. "I'll take care of it."

Little Stuart gave a huff and hurried out of the kitchen. Mr. Fieldmore saw him out then wheeled back to the others. "Good. Patty?"

A scream came from somewhere outside. For a moment, they froze, then Mr. Fieldmore turned and hurried for the foyer. As the door swung open, Chezzy glimpsed a visibly upset Ms. Bartleby through the open curtain of the window by the front door. She was shouting and banging on the glass as Little Stuart huddled, not even hidden, behind a decorative table. The double egress door swung back, blotting them from sight. Chezzy was stunned and barely heard the hissing in his ear of Patty's now shrill voice. "What?" he said back to her. His mind was racing in every direction at once.

"We have to go get you a shirt. We have to hide those right now." She was pointing at the bandages on Chezzy's body. "Do you understand?" She shook her head, her lip quivering. "This is why we follow the rules."

Chezzy was looking down at the two bandages, wavering. But Patty had already pulled him to his feet, and she was dragging him out of the dining area. They made for the stairs while trying to hide from Ms. Bartleby, who was caught in a heated exchange with Mr. Fieldmore. They paused behind the decorative table, and Chezzy spied Little Stuart, who was fumbling at the basement door before hiding himself within. Patty yanked Chezzy for the stairs but froze at the sight of Ms. Bartleby, who had just stomped right across Mr. Fieldmore's decorative rug.

"That's just the dog, the family dog, he gets startled with company, that's all. That's why we were so startled, is all, that's it," but Mr. Fieldmore's voice was quavering with fear, and even he seemed to know it was useless as he followed after her.

Ms. Bartleby came marching forward, her face livid, and her finger pointing at Mr. Fieldmore threateningly. "A dog? A dog?" she bellowed. Her face had gone a deep purple, and she was spluttering as she spoke. "What was that thing? A bear? What is going on in this house?" Her eyes swept to Patty, who had put herself in front of Chezzy in an effort to hide his bandages.

"Listen, you can't just walk in."

"Excuse you, Mr. Fieldmore, but I certainly can, and you are well aware of that. You signed the paperwork directly in front of me. Now, out of my way, dear." Without waiting, Ms. Bartleby moved Patty from between her and Chezzy. Then her eyes scanned him as her cheeks shook, her lips pulled back over her teeth. The blood drained from Ms. Bartleby's face as her free hand reached up lightly to the higher bandage. Everyone dropped silent. Even Mrs. Fieldmore, who had been in the kitchen attempting to clean, had gone still and quiet.

Quickly, Ms. Bartleby gripped Chezzy's shoulder. Mr. Fieldmore didn't dare move, and Patty acted likewise. In the kitchen, Chezzy heard the tinkling of dropped ceramic. He met his eyes to Ms. Bartleby's, and he shook his head side to side to her. "What… what have they done to you?" Ms. Bartleby's voice spilled out in a shaking, semi snarl.

"They…" he searched for the words but fell short.

"Get your trunk."

"You don't understand," Chezzy flared, his courage rising. "I don't want to leave. I want to stay here."

"Go and get your trunk," she repeated.

It was Mr. Fieldmore that interjected next with an almost timid tone. "We, uh, we actually threw that out. You see, we, uh, well, we would like to keep him."

Ms. Bartleby whirled on Mr. Fieldmore with a vibrant rage, her voice screeching with anger. "You, sir, are a fool if you think I'd leave this boy here in your hands to suffer any more harm or, or, or whatever it is that your wild animal has done to him. I can't imagine what you're doing with such a… a… And as for his trunk, well, we will fetch it from the bin or we will leave it altogether, and that will be the end of it. Furthermore, I will be submitting a report of this freakshow, and you can bet your tush you'll be getting an additional visit to review for the safety of your daughter."

Chezzy had been trying to interrupt despite the rising of her voice swelling with each word. However, upon hearing the threat about Patty, he bit his tongue in shock.

Mr. Fieldmore stood equally stunned, his mouth slack. His eyes moved over to Patty and they stared at one another. "P… Patty?" he said.

Ms. Bartleby let out a huff as she grabbed the hand of Chezzy, and he let her lead him towards the front door. No one else dared intervene. Outside, Ms. Bartleby stopped at the bin and threw it open. A pile of Stuart's needles and Chezzy's shirt stained with blood were scattered out from a ripped open trash bag. Ms. Bartleby gasped, her hand to her chest. Then she reached in to dig around, careful of the needles and the shirt.

Several moments on, she drew out the case, spilling Stuart's needles on to the concrete. Some foul liquid had spilled over the trunk, but that didn't seem to bother her either. She grabbed Chezzy once more and led him to the car, where she threw both him and the case inside. As she climbed into the driver's seat, she was muttering angrily to herself, but as soon as the car took off, she started yelling again.

"How dare they? How dare? I knew something was wrong. I just knew it. I knew it when I left, and I knew it when I woke up this morning. I could feel it. I'll have to take you to the hospital now. There's no way around it. I haven't even the slightest what they've done to you. How they've hurt you. I really haven't. Oh dear, you should have called. No, no, but of course that isn't your fault. We'll go straight to the hospital. Have the doctor tell us what it is. And when we get there, I'll call Ms. Shoemaker and let her know. Yes, that's what I'll do."

Chezzy had no idea who Ms. Shoemaker was, and he certainly didn't want to go to hospital. He wasn't even hurting. Ms. Bartleby had taken off and was weaving all over the road, and Chezzy could see that there were tears in her eyes. She was desperately trying to wipe them away, but they just kept on coming. Chezzy decided to brave a question. "Who's Ms. Shoemaker?"

Ms. Bartleby let out a wail. Chezzy had never seen her like this, and he'd certainly never heard her make any sound like that before. She sounded like a wounded cat. The wail died in simpering words. "She's Ms. Vose's replacement. She just got in this morning. First, Ms. Vose and now this mess. I'm so sorry for what you've been through."

"Honestly, Ms. Bartleby, I'm fine. The family was fine. They were really nice to me."

Ms. Bartleby looked at Chezzy. "My poor boy, what have they done to you back there? What happened?"

Chezzy looked down at his bandages, certain the injuries weren't as bad as they seemed to Ms. Bartleby. He gripped his fingertips to the top of one and peeled the tape off of him. Underneath, where a scabbed hole should be, was nothing at all. No puncture wound, no scab, nothing. Chezzy quickly grabbed the second bandage and peeled it off likewise. Again, he found nothing. Chezzy took a moment to process what he was looking at, then he thrust the two bandages forward to Ms. Bartleby and cried out, "See? See? I'm perfectly fine. They didn't do anything to me."

Ms. Bartleby glanced to the bandages and then to his body, scanning for the wounds. Her face went crimson. Suddenly, she was screaming at Chezzy, but the only words that were distinguishable were lying, wrong, and fire. He had no clue what it was she was saying, but he knew she was mad, and he knew it was somehow his fault.

She kept yelling, too, indistinguishable as it was, as Chezzy sat in stunned silence, trying to make out anything from the barrage. He couldn't even respond to any of it, so incoherent she was. One thing he knew, though, whenever he got back to Wutherford Home, he was going to be in a lot of trouble. More trouble than he had ever been in before. Then he realized that

Ms. Bartleby was looking right at him. "How could you do this, Chester? How?"

Whatever hit them seemed to catapult from nowhere, and the car they were in was abruptly flying through the air. They turned in a somersault in that big machine. It came down on its roof with a tremendous thud and the crunch of metal grinding in on itself. The last thing Chezzy remembered before blacking out, was a cloud of dust drifting around him as he hung, upside down, from his safety belt.

He awoke in an unfamiliar bed, in an unfamiliar room, sun bathing in from a large window. It appeared to be a normal hospital room, and he was draped in a hospital gown. But upon inspecting his body, he couldn't find a single burn, scratch, or injury. Chezzy puzzled at this. He was certain he remembered being in a car accident with Ms. Bartleby. Thinking of Ms. Bartleby sent a jolt through him, his body seizing. Worry went wreaking within. He could hear nurses chatting in the hall, but he couldn't manage to call out. He needed to know if she was okay.

But one shock was replaced by another as a small hole seemed to open in the air a few feet above his bed. It wasn't much more than the size of a coin, and it started as a weird discoloration before opening completely. There within, appeared a greenish blue eye. "I got you in the now, now," the eye said to Chezzy with a man's voice.

"Right…" Chezzy began, his voice relaxing, panic flowing into confusion.

"I just found another tub of that acid near the dining lab," came a second voice, that of a woman. "Wait, is that him?"

"It is," replied the man.

"Oh, let me see." The eye that Chezzy had been talking to disappeared and was replaced with a brilliantly blue and hazel flecked eye. "It's you."

"The dining lab?" interrupted the man.

"Yes," said the woman, her eye disappearing. Chezzy could almost make out their figures through the hole, but there was a lot of movement. "But him… Does this mean what I think it means?"

"It does," replied the man. "Time to fire up the ole versolock. We're going on a field trip," and then the hole disappeared completely.

Chezzy reached a hand for where the hole had been. He stared at the empty air in bewilderment. But just then, a short, pudgy woman stormed into the hospital room. She had cat rimmed glasses, a swelling face, and curly brown hair that was trimmed into a petite pile atop her head that would bob side to side as she waddled. Her thick, woolen skirt was the same dreary brown as her hair, and it matched perfectly to her blouse and bag and everything else on her. She was painful to look at in the way that you couldn't tell exactly where her hair ended and her skin began, or where her skin ended and her clothes began. All of it was exactly the very same color.

Chezzy felt downright ill looking at her. He held his breath and kept completely still, as if moving was the only way she'd notice that he was there. He didn't know why, but it seemed to work for a few moments, though her eyes did finally come to rest on Chezzy. When she saw him, she let out a bizarre snort, and she cocked her head to look at him better, her hair making a tiny wave. Every action jostled her rather ample jowls.

"Chester Nithercot?" Her high pitched voice seemed to echo back and forth through her throat.

For a moment, Chezzy considered lying, but he was sure she'd find out faster than he could escape. "Yes," he cleared his throat.

"I am Ms. Shoemaker. I am the replacement for Ms. Vose, as I'm sure Ms. Bartleby informed you. You may call me Ms. Shoemaker and that is all. Now, as Ms. Bartleby has passed on, I'll be taking control of Wutherford Home. I've already put in for a replacement for Ms. Bartleby, so you shouldn't be troubled about that." She had been holding a small satchel, and she thrust it on to the bed.

"Troubled about that?" The words were nearly involuntary as his mind was processing what she said. He felt his starved stomach near dropped right out of him as the weight of what she meant hit.

But his words meant less to Ms. Shoemaker than they did to him, and she kept talking as if Chezzy hadn't said anything at all. "I've gathered that Ms. Bartleby pulled you out of the Fieldmore home. I've also been informed that this is the seventeenth family you have failed to secure a home with. From the numerous reports and the testimonies of the parties involved, Ms. Bartleby, and even the other children, with whom I've had the pleasure of meeting, the blame of your repeated failures rests solely on you and the wealth of your abhorrent actions and behaviors. I'm here to tell you that I will not be tolerating anything of the sort. The doctor has informed me that you are in no way hurt, and, as I see it, prolonging your stay in hospital any longer would be a waste of money and resources. So." She paused, then she narrowed her eyes at Chezzy. At least he thought that she was narrowing her eyes at him, but he really couldn't even be sure what she was looking at. "So."

Chezzy realized she was waiting for a response, but he could feel the beginning of tears that he fought to control. "So?" He asked it in earnest though his voice quavered, threatening to break him.

Ms. Shoemaker pursed her lips. "So, get out of that bed and get dressed. We are going at once. I've already seen to the paperwork, and I'm not impressed by dallying." She threw some old trousers and a torn t-shirt on the foot of the bed then dropped some shoes that were easily a couple sizes too big before whipping away from him.

V.
Wutherford Home.
Daring.
The unknife.

They left the hospital in a hurry. Ms. Shoemaker didn't even stop for the doctor who chased after her, pleading to run a few more tests. She just kept walking. Chezzy glanced back to the doctor with watery eyes. She looked at Chezzy with a sorrowed and quizzical face, as if to ask him to stay, but he kept on following Ms. Shoemaker, still reeling from the news. They went out into the parking lot and to her car. If looking at her had been strange, looking in her car was even stranger.

The dashboard was completely covered with glued on figurines of penguins wearing tutus. Chezzy didn't know what to make of that. But even worse, was the back seat, which was littered with dozens of half eaten sandwiches in varying stages of rot. The stench of them was unbearable, and, upon closer inspection, Chezzy saw that every sandwich was some kind of meatball sub. Every single one. He gagged, though he did his best to hide it as he wiped the tears from his cheek.

"What exactly are you waiting for?" Ms. Shoemaker was standing half in the driver's side door and waiting for Chezzy. "Go on and get in the car."

"Right," and Chezzy hardened himself before he braved the inside. He tried to hold his breath as he sat there, while Ms. Shoemaker drove and sang along with a poppy song that sounded entirely comprised of gibberish, entirely content to pretend that Chezzy wasn't there at all. A few minutes later, however, Chezzy broke and gasped and then began to inhale the stench that had been stewing in the car for whatever indeterminate length of time. Ms. Shoemaker looked at him, snorted in an offended way, and then went back to her singing, only louder now.

She continued her practice of saying nothing to Chezzy when they arrived at Wutherford Home. But her eyes stuck to him like taffy. Judging Chezzy as he went trudging numbly up the steps to the front door and inside. All of the other children were out in the back area, and it was unnaturally quiet in the home. Chezzy habitually turned toward the door that led down into the basement.

"Where are you going?" she asked, startling Chezzy a bit from his stupor.

When he looked at her, he noted how she was blending into the wooden front door. "I'm going down to the basement."

"Whatever for?" she snarled, and flecks of spit leapt from her lips and her tongue.

"That's where... that's where I stay. In a room in the basement." He shifted uncomfortably.

Ms. Shoemaker took two steps forward and peered down at Chezzy before she spoke again. "Nonsense. All children will stay in the dorms. No one is getting special treatment or their own personal room. In fact, I'll be locking the basement to ensure that children aren't sneaking down there after I've looked it over. So, put that in your pocket." She jabbed a fat finger at Chezzy and then straightened up. Of course, Ms. Shoemaker had no way of knowing that Lenna Vose had always insisted on Chezzy staying in the basement. It never seemed like a special favor for him, but rather the other children, who were, for the most part, always slightly uneasy in his presence. But Chezzy could tell there would be no arguing with the woman.

All throughout him, he had a sickening desire to leave this place and never return again. "I really think if you contacted the Fieldmores, they would be happy to take me back."

Her eyes turned into tiny slits, and she growled, "I'll have you know that I've already tried contacting the Fieldmores several times since your departure, trying to interest them in adopting one of the more acceptable children we have at this home, and they have steadily avoided my calls. Whatever you did, your actions have lost another child here the opportunity of a nice home and family."

Chezzy was the first in the mess hall for lunch, as he was absolutely starving, and he doled himself servings of stew and rolls before taking a seat at one of the many tables. A moment later, the other children came filtering in, ushered by Ms. Shoemaker. They went quiet when they saw Chezzy, and they stared at him. The quiet was soon broken by scattered sobs and whispers that erupted from covered mouths, but Chezzy kept his eyes on his stew.

He ate with deliberate chews, and he dared not look up. He could feel his neck and forehead getting hot. From the small explosions of conversation, he could make out words like died, burned, freak, and weirdo. He guessed that they had been told about Ms. Bartleby, and it made him feel all the worse for it. He kept looking down, and, as all the other children took seats, they were careful to avoid his table. All of them, except Sarah.

She came right up to Chezzy and looked down at him. "Can I sit here, or would you rather I not?"

Chezzy nodded and fought through a knot in his throat. "You can sit here."

Sarah took the chair opposite him, and she stared at him with her dusky, dolorous eyes. They were both ringed with purple and bloodshot, and Chezzy met her gaze before quickly looking away. Even glancing at her felt like too much for him right now, so he settled for gazing back into his stew. Sarah squared her shoulders and took a quick scan of the room before leaning in to speak to Chezzy. "Are you doing alright? They're saying you didn't get hurt. You don't look hurt. But they're saying you caused the accident, too."

Chezzy shook his head and opened his mouth, searching for words, but all he managed to say in return was, "No. I didn't get hurt."

Sarah took another glass around the room before pressing the question. "But what about the rest of it?"

Chezzy stirred his spoon, looping the stew. The few pieces of meat kicked up with the potatoes in the reddened liquid. He spooned up and gulped down a sip of the broth, but he didn't answer Sarah. He didn't really know what to say to her when he wasn't sure himself what had happened. Maybe it was all his fault. It certainly felt like it was.

His thoughts drifted back to the eyes that had appeared before him in the air above his bed in the hospital. He was reminded of something Little Stuart had said, but he was quickly jerked out of his thoughts as Sarah reached her hand over and laid it on top of Chezzy's. This time, he looked right into her blackened and purpled eyes. The colors of the bruises seemed to make the hazel of her irises almost green, and he felt a pang ringing inside his stomach.

Her dark curls bobbed over her own bowl of stew, and they moved up and down slightly as she spoke. "It's okay. Really, it is. I'm, I'm sorry I asked. I didn't mean to, to upset you more. I'm sure it was horrible. Just really horrible."

And before Chezzy could respond, before he could even open his mouth, she rose and walked over to the trash can, where she dumped her stew. Chezzy watched as Sarah cleaned her bowl and cried before she left the dining hall. He finished his own bowl in solitary silence. He felt guilty for not answering Sarah, though he wasn't sure why, but the longer he thought about her, the greater an anger grew in his chest.

He glared over at the table where Byron and his friends were finishing their meals, daring them to pick any kind of a fight, even just dirty glances or whispered insults. Byron's whole group were covered in bruises worse than what they gave Sarah, and Byron himself had his arm done up in a cast. It was all Chezzy's doing, but he wanted another row. He just needed a reason, any reason, but it didn't come. They finished sullenly and left without a single eye turning Chezzy's way.

Chezzy sighed. He was feeling rather agitable, and he had taken it out on his bowl after he'd downed an entire second serving, and then a third, before roughly washing it. He saw that the other children had largely gone back outside, except a few stragglers. Sarah was out there, too, sitting alone atop the rotting trunk of a tree fell, so he opened the door and walked across the grounds to her. There, he sat on the trunk, and they were silent for several moments as they looked out at the other children, most of which were gathered in their own gloomy groups.

Chezzy spoke up first. "I don't really know what happened. I don't know why I didn't get hurt." Sarah nodded slightly and looked to Chezzy. He met her gaze. "Did Byron do all of that to you?" He pointed at her blackened eyes.

Sarah turned away and moved to cover her face. "Terry and Todd… He… It's nothing. Really, it isn't."

Chezzy looked over at Byron and the others. They were closer now than they had been before, and he could make out the scratches from his nails that were carved across their skin. Terry's face was swollen and very colorful as was the jaw of Connor. Todd's lip was busted and stitched, and Byron's arm had been put in a cast and was hanging in a sling. Chezzy leapt to his feet, and he felt all of his muscles come to life.

Sarah had let out a little squeal, startled as she was by his sudden movement. She opened her mouth to speak or perhaps to squeal again, but Chezzy was striding over to the other boys at such a rapid pace, that she didn't get a chance to, leaving her still seated on the rotted trunk. Chezzy drew up before the other boys. He stood a good half a head shorter than the shortest of them, but he knew it didn't matter. And he could see just how much it didn't matter on the faces of every one of them.

They had turned beaten brows to Chezzy, and, though none of them moved to leave, each swayed uncomfortably while casting shift heavy eyes to each other. Byron broke first, and he croaked, "What do you want?"

Chezzy squared up to Byron, then he jerked his hand back and pointed to Sarah, where she still sat, wide eyed with her mouth hung open. "You lay hands on her again, and I will come for you. I don't care what kind of trouble I get into. You think your arm hurts? I'll break your legs next time."

Byron's face flushed half with fear and half with anger. For a moment, Chezzy thought he was going to balk, but Byron started moving his broken arm in its sling and seemed to think better of it. The other boys had gone frightfully still except for their eyes, which drifted between Chezzy and the ground. Terry let out a slight sound. It was almost like a moan or a whimper. Chezzy's eyes flashed to him.

At that point, quite suddenly and directly in the middle of all of them, a hole opened up right in the air. A brilliant blue eye with hazel flecks appeared in it and scanned around in all degrees, as a woman's voice sounded. "Are you sure this is the right place? I can't believe you didn't even get the address."

"I'm sure I saw it at some point. Maybe I saw that I was going to see it. You know how it gets so muddled," came a man's voice somewhat distantly.

"Oh, there are children everywhere looking at me."

"At you?"

Byron screamed. He had fallen back and was scrambling away with his one good arm, to little effect. The scream had sprung the other boys into action, and they too took flight. The only one that stayed, was Chezzy, and the eye rested on him for the faintest of moments. They looked at each other, the eye and he, and then the eye popped out of existence, leaving Chezzy to look around, but all he saw were other children watching him and watching the panicked boys flee.

Chezzy glanced back at Sarah where she was still sitting. She seemed confused but hadn't gotten up from the tree trunk to investigate. She merely stared at Chezzy. But, before he could call out to her or anything, Ms. Shoemaker was yelling at the back door of Wutherford Home. Chezzy whirled around and saw her storming across the grounds towards him. Her face was pulsing purplish brown, and there were veins that almost glowed as they popped out from her forehead. However, despite the intimidating visage she made, Chezzy did not feel afraid. In fact, there was an entirely different emotion welling up within him.

"You better stay away from me," Chezzy screamed back, threateningly. He had made up his mind. He wasn't going to stay at Wutherford Home anymore. No matter how he had to get out.

Ms. Shoemaker narrowed her eyes. "I know what you did at the Smith home, Chester Nithercot." Everyone fell still in the yard, except for a small girl named Camilla, who was racing after Ms. Shoemaker. As she reached Ms. Shoemaker, she tugged on the woman's sleeve. Ms. Shoemaker had been gauging Chezzy, and he her. Then she turned and looked down at Camilla.

The girl dropped her hand at once and averted her eyes as she worked to pull the words out of herself. "Um, Miss, there's a, there's some, some, people, some people that are here. They're inside, and, and, they said, well, they said they were here to adopt. Yeah," she drifted off at this, and her brow had furrowed intensely as she moved from one foot to the other over and over again. After some moments of this, Camilla turned and ran back toward Wutherford Home. She looked to have some tears coursing down her cheeks.

Ms. Shoemaker turned back to Chezzy. "I'll be dealing with you shortly." Then she turned suddenly and stormed back toward Wutherford Home with heavy stomps that left actual footprints in the green grass. Chezzy watched her go with a mixture of anger and relief. The other children slowly went back to playing, although there was a heavy tone of fear with all of them. Even their voices were kept at a whisper as they ran and went about their various games.

Chezzy turned back to Sarah, walking over to her. She had shaken some of the shock from her face, but she still trembled. Her lips parted as she managed a word. "Why?"

"I'm not staying here anymore."

"What do you mean?"

Chezzy glassed over to the stone building. He had loved and hated this place his entire life, but there was nothing here for him anymore. "I mean, I'm leaving."

"But where will you go?"

Chezzy kicked a rock and thought of the Fieldmores again. "It doesn't matter. I'll find somewhere." He looked over to where the eye had appeared and something in his memory clicked. "One eyed ghost," he mumbled.

"What?" Sarah asked.

"Nothing. I got to go. Before she gets back."

"Oh." Her face fell, and Chezzy met the pleading, blackened eyes. "But you can't leave."

"I have to." Chezzy glanced back to Wutherford Home, then he looked at the woods near him. He could sneak through them and make his way around to the road. If he kept out of sight, maybe, just maybe, he could make it back to the Fieldmores. Even if he didn't remember exactly how to get there, he could find it. He had to. He glanced to Sarah once more then briskly jogged into the trees.

But Sarah followed after him. "I don't want something to happen to you too," Sarah called, catching up.

Chezzy chewed this as they moved deeper into the wood. "Nothing's going to happen to me," Chezzy replied at last, pausing and wheeling to meet her. But something like a meteor came down over them, and the force of it sent both tumbling across the ground. Sarah smacked against a tree as Chezzy was thrown into an assortment of weedy bushes. For just a moment, it was as if his own face was reflected in the fire, but Chezzy shook his dazed head, and it was gone. He looked over at Sarah. She wasn't moving, and Chezzy scrambled to her. A gash across her forehead was bleeding profusely, and she appeared to be unconscious.

"I've been looking for you," came a voice.

Chezzy sprang to his feet recognizing him instantly. It was the same man that Chezzy had seen near the Fieldmore's house. He had dirty blond hair that shot up in every direction, and he wore sweatpants and an unbuttoned, floral shirt. Stranger still, underneath his shirt, could be seen what appeared to be some kind of green leather shirt that reached in a V to near his neck and protruded like a hitched up collar.

A crooked grin struck the man's face. "Why are we hiding?"

"Hurt," Chezzy managed to mumble. He was looking at the man's eyes. They were blue and green and white ringed about the iris, and Chezzy felt his stomach lurch.

"Oh?" The man glanced down at Sarah and stepped forward frightfully fast, startling Chezzy. "Not so hurt." His smile deepened and he dug around in his pockets for a moment before pulling something out. "Do you know what this is, Chezzy?"

No one had ever called him that before, but it rung oddly in his ears. Chezzy examined the object. It was a weird pocket knife that had several buttons on it. He looked up at the man with dread. "It's a… a pocket knife, isn't it?"

"Yes and no," he bobbed his head side to side. "It is a knife and an unknife, you understand?"

"I… no?"

The man sighed, though not unhappily, then flicked the blade out with such speed that Chezzy gave a little start. The blade was sort of fuzzy looking as if it weren't quite real. "With a knife you can cut things, like this." And then he drew the blade across the back of his wrist letting out a flow of deep, red blood. He winced, sucking his teeth. "I forgot it hurt." Then he continued, "Okay, so, here," and he showed Chezzy a button before pressing it, "is how we switch on the unknife, you see?"

Chezzy gave a slight, uncertain nod as he stared at the man, attempting to figure out just how mad he was.

But the man drew the blade a second time across his skin, and the wound mended smartly, leaving only a faint trace of the cut that had been there underneath the blood on his wrist. "And here's for cleanup." He showed Chezzy another button that he pressed and then proceeded to slice the blade up and down his skin, which wiped or sucked or somehow removed all of the blood that had been there. "See?" and he showed his arm forward.

Chezzy could clearly make out where the cut had been, but he could not deny that it was healed. "Sarah?"

"Yes," said the man, and he was already drawing the unknife across Sarah's head, and the wound was mending.

Her eyes fluttered as she looked up at the two of them. "What happened?"

"You had a little knock on your head."

"Are you okay?" Chezzy asked.

"Yeah," Sarah said, sitting up.

"You're Sarah Cristobal, aren't you?"

"Yes," she replied in a half daze, reaching a hand to the bump where the cut had been.

"Very good. Could you please go join the others in the playground?" Sarah started to speak, but he interrupted her. "I assure you that, unquestionably, your Ms. Shoemaker will not be cross with you." And then, almost to Chezzy, he muttered, "Weird lady." Abruptly, he stiffened. Then his eyes turned glassy, and he continued to speak. "No, I'm not going to do that. You can try, but I assure you that I will crash this whole place down before I let you have it." Just as abruptly, the man was looking at Sarah again. "Well, go on. I need to speak with Mr. Nithercot here privately, you see."

Sarah nodded with a furrowed brow, and, after throwing Chezzy a wide eyed look, she tentatively got to her feet and headed through the trees back toward the grounds of Wutherford Home, one hand held still to the knot on her head.

The man turned back to Chezzy. "Now, I know who you are, but the people back home will insist that I test this on you. You know, due diligence and whatnot."

"Test? What?"

"The unknife. As I unknifed Sarah and myself. Unknifed? Unknifening?"

"No, but-"

"Antiknifening?" He shook his head. "Alessa was right."

"But test what?"

"This." Before Chezzy had a chance to react, the man had drawn the knife across Chezzy's arm. It split, red and bloody, and Chezzy flashed with anger. He screamed and lunged for the man, knocking the knife out of his hands. Entangled in a grapple, Chezzy's claw like nails scratched at the man, but the man wasn't angry. He was laughing. Laughing and holding Chezzy's cut arm.

"What?" Chezzy yelled.

"Just look at it. Great Heisenberg. Just look at it."

Chezzy looked down to the cut on his arm, but the cut was gone. Only a faint smear of blood remained. He looked at the unknife laying several feet away on the ground, then he looked back to the man. "How did you do that?"

"No, how did you do that? Do you ever get cuts? Or bruises? Broken bones? I bet not for long and the amount of time is only getting shorter." He had released Chezzy, and Chezzy had done likewise. "What about... have you ever been trapped in a burning car? You had any of that? No burns. No scars. No bruises." The man pointed over toward Wutherford Home. "I know you broke that kid's arm. Beat those other kids into colors. You did all that. And not a mark on you."

Chezzy scrunched his face. "Am I in trouble?"

The man laughed. "That's funny. But no. No. You aren't in trouble."

Chezzy was scanning the man, trying to put it all together. "Yeah, I did that. All that."

"Good," the man was nodding, "good." He took the unknife and began closing the scratches that Chezzy had given him. "Here's what it is, Chezzy. I'm here to give you a place to live. And," he shrugged slightly, "more. I guess."

"More?"

"Yeah. A lot more." He laughed again. "So, what do you say? Huh? You want to get out of here or what?"

VI.
Aris Kepler and Alessa Da Maxwell.
Dropped.
Boletare.

They walked back to the grounds of Wutherford Home together. All of the kids were situated in a line as Ms. Shoemaker led a woman with long, dark brunette hair to meet with each. She wore jeans, black leather heeled boots, a black leather jacket, and, just slightly visible underneath her jacket, was a similar, leather looking outfit like the man's, only hers was blood red. Like his, it had contours as if it were armored. She brightened when she saw the man and Chezzy approaching, but Ms. Shoemaker did exactly the opposite.

The strange woman took one glance at Chezzy, and he knew the hazel flecks in her blue eyes well. She was waving her hands to the other children. "Go play now, thank you. Thank you, go play." The kids dispersed in an uneasy migration back throughout the grounds. They gave Chezzy and the man quizzical looks, though none dared approach them. Ms. Shoemaker's face had paled a shade, and it had tensed to the point of disfigurement. She was shaking some where she stood next to the woman.

The man walked right up to both of them and smiled at Ms. Shoemaker. "Well, we will take this one." He gestured to Chezzy in a movement that was near like a bow as he beamed from Chezzy to Ms. Shoemaker.

"Take this one?" Ms. Shoemaker spoke as if she didn't understand what he meant. Her eyes, which were situated deep in her heavy face, shifted between the man and Chezzy incredulously.

"Is that not the correct phrasing? As I've heard, this is the kind of place that dispenses orphans. So, this one right here," and he waved his hands around Chezzy as if to display him, "we'd like to give a home to him."

"But, but," she sputtered. She was searching for the words, though she couldn't seem to find them. "But why?"

"Why?" The man was giving her a perturbed look.

"Well, I don't mean why. I mean, I mean…"

"Yes?"

"I think Ms. Shoemaker," the woman had interjected, "is taking ill in the heat is all. Isn't that right, dear?"

"I mean," Ms. Shoemaker continued, "but him?"

The man smiled. "Oh, yes. Him."

The man, the woman, Ms. Shoemaker, and Chezzy all sat in Ms. Shoemaker's office. It was still half Ms. Bartleby's office as only a portion of her things had been moved out. Guilt and discomfort rushed over Chezzy as he looked around, discerning between the two women's belongings. Ms. Shoemaker's decorations were easily distinguished as almost everything she had put up contained pictures of a boy band that couldn't've been older than Chezzy. She had posters, a painting, and even a clock with their faces instead of numbers. Oddest of all, was a woven blanket with a poorly done rendering displayed in the yarns.

The woman was conversing with Ms. Shoemaker and going over various bits of paperwork while the man was glancing around, somewhat bored. He met eyes with Chezzy and gave him a sly, half smile. The man dug around in his pocket and drew out a thick ring that he slipped over a finger then pressed a little button. Chezzy gasped as a sort of holographic ball formed in the man's hand. The woman and Ms. Shoemaker paused to look at Chezzy as the man hid his hand with the ball under his chair.

Chezzy and the women peered at each other before Ms. Shoemaker cleared her throat and continued. "And here, Mrs. Maxwell? Da Maxwell? What is that?"

Chezzy looked back to the man who was watching him. The man flicked his wrist and tossed the holographic ball to Chezzy who, startled, made to catch it. He was shocked when he felt the ball actually settle in his hands. Instinctively, Chezzy tossed the ball back, and the man caught it with a flash of a smile. The woman he had come with, however, shot the man a fierce glance, but he took the ball, gave her a wink, and then bounced it on the floor to Chezzy who caught it.

The ball actually thunked when it hit the floor. Ms. Shoemaker looked up, but the woman quickly directed her to another page with a question. Chezzy tried to hide his grin as he bounced the ball back to the man, but the man wasn't looking at Chezzy, and the ball went skipping around the room before settling near the corner. Instead, the man was staring straight ahead. His eyes were glazed, and his mouth was open. "Go ahead, stab him. You stab him as many times as you can." His eyes then refocused, and he looked around the room at everyone staring.

Ms. Shoemaker looked positively shocked. Her heavy jaw hung open slightly, and the color had drained from her face, though it was quickly remounting within her.

"Aris," said the woman.

"Hawk," responded the man as he threw his hands up in a shrug and nodded toward Ms. Shoemaker. "Might as well-"

"Yes. Yes. I know. Might as well do this." The woman cut back irritably before grabbing Ms. Shoemaker by the face and staring deep into her eyes. Ms. Shoemaker went slack.

"That's what I said. That was the plan I wanted." The man huffed and looked to Chezzy. "That was the plan I wanted," then he turned back to the woman, "but you wanted the paperwork to be right, so here we are. Besides, did you even look at the paperwork? She wants to do a home visit. That's not happening."

"What's happening?" Chezzy ventured fretfully. He hadn't a clue what he should do, and he was torn between wanting any way out of Wutherford Home and fear that Ms. Shoemaker was in some real danger.

"Oh, no, this part is good. Watch it," said the man.

Sweat was forming over the woman's face, and it ran down her cheeks. Then she spoke clearly. "Chester Nithercot was adopted by a lovely couple, the paperwork was filled out, you did a home visit and found the entire situation appeasing, and you don't worry about Chester at all."

"And be nicer to all of the, the other kids here," added the man with a twirl of his finger, then he winked over at Chezzy.

The woman sighed and licked her lips. She was trembling terribly. "And be nicer to all of the other children here."

"And wear more brown."

"Wear more brown? What?" The woman looked over at the man and then cracked a smile.

The man snapped and slapped his hands together in a funny way as he rose. "Great. Let's get. All of this real sun is getting to me."

"Get?" asked Chezzy, looking up at him.

"Yeah, get out of here. Do you need anything?"

His breath arrested while images of Ms. Vose and Ms. Bartleby kicked about in his mind. "I don't have anything."

The man and woman led Chezzy out of Wutherford Home and toward their car. Chezzy had a wary feeling as if he was being kidnapped. He glanced back to Wutherford Home and spied Sarah watching him from out one of the windows. He gave a slight wave and a last look at her and Wutherford, before getting into the car and shutting the door. He wasn't sure what he'd seen in Ms. Shoemaker's office, but he felt certain that he wouldn't be getting picked back up this time.

"I know you're wondering who we are," began the man as he climbed into the front, passenger seat.

"Yeah."

"Well, I'm Professor Aris Kepler, and this tall bag of brains," he motioned to the woman who was now driving them out of the paveway, "is Professor Alessa Da Maxwell, and we, well, we are the directors of Balefire. Which probably sounds like nonsense. But it's a kind of school for children like you. Or like us, I should say. More or less. You know, clades and… super scientists and all."

"But… I'm not a super scientist," Chezzy protested.

"Ever tried?" asked Professor Alessa Da Maxwell slyly.

Professor Kepler shot her an amused look. "Chezzy, what's important right now is that you're a clade. And that's good enough to get in." Then he chuckled to himself as he seemed to sink back into his thoughts.

Chezzy stared at the back of the man's head as the car bumped along. "Professor Kepler?" he asked.

Professor Kepler turned back to Chezzy with a funny expression. "Yes, Chezzy?"

"What… what is a clade?"

The man seemed to regain his bearings. "Well, that's you and all the others like you. Like me, well, like her. We're all clades or adjacent. You'll see when we get to the school."

Chezzy thought about this a moment before he responded. "So there really are other kids like me?"

"Well, no. But, also, yes. But mostly no. Or mostly yes, but no. Do you see what I'm saying?"

"No." And he didn't, but he was interested and excited despite his misgivings.

"Tell him about the everling lab," Professor Maxwell chimed in as on she drove. "He'll get to see-"

"What? No. Don't tell people about the things I tell you. It'll all get muddied. It's muddied enough once I know it."

"I just thought he'd be excited. I'm excited. I mean it'll explain a lot to him. Besides, it's not as if you hide it, talking in front of everyone."

"Talking? No. Listen, we're both excited. And I didn't mean to do that. It's not like I can help it. Why don't you try slipping and see how you like it?"

"And end up slobbering all over myself? Babbling incoherently. So embarrassing. How about, instead, you let me see the wedding that-"

"No, no, no. We aren't getting into that again." Professor Kepler turned back to Chezzy then sighed. "Listen, there's a lot to tell you. It really might be easier to just show you."

"Show him? You won't even show me and I…" she hesitated. "You might give him a heart attack."

"I, what? Then he'd be fine and it wouldn't matter."

"Oh, I suppose you're right. It's weird having one around again."

"Not really."

"Not really? It's different when you're visiting them every other day. It's been a lot longer for me."

"Yeah, I guess so."

Something dinged, and Professor Maxwell glanced at the odd bracelet on her wrist. "Penton found more acid."

"Did he…" Professor Kepler muttered, though it wasn't really a question. They sped along the avenues and streets, past buildings and bridges, and out into the countryside. Both Professor Kepler and Professor Maxwell had gone quiet, seemingly lost in their thoughts. After a while, Professor Kepler began mumbling to himself about a lightning storm. Chezzy watched him intently but could hardly make out any of the words at all. Still, an idea was forming. Suddenly, Professor Kepler straightened up and looked around outside again.

Chezzy chanced another question. "Where are we going?"

Professor Kepler peered back at him with his violent eyes, but it was Professor Maxwell that responded. "We are heading to a keyhole."

"A keyhole? Like in a door?" Chezzy posed back to her.

Professor Maxwell gave a slight frown. "Sort of. A keyhole is how we travel between here and there."

"Here and there?"

Professor Kepler interjected next. "Many, many years ago, well, there were people like us… well, or like you, I guess, and they wanted a place where they could live and do everything that they wanted or needed to do. So, they built this place for themselves… and us. But in order to get from here to there, you need a keyhole. And that's where we are driving to now. The nearest keyhole."

"What kind of place is it?"

"The keyhole?"

"The place we're going to."

"Uh, an underground place, I guess you could say. Kind of."

Chezzy felt his face fall. He had no idea what Professor Kepler meant, and, even though he was fond of his basement in Wutherford Home, he couldn't imagine living out the rest of his schooling, or maybe even more, in a basement. "You're… you're taking me to a school in a basement? To a, a what? A basement schoolhouse?"

Both of the professors let out riotous laughs at this while Chezzy stared at them, blanched. "I wouldn't call it a basement schoolhouse," Professor Kepler relented. "I mean, well, you'll see what it is soon enough."

They arrived at a rundown gas station some time later. The gas station looked like it was near to falling apart, so shabby its roof and walls were. The only service pump had a bright yellow, *Out of Order* sign. The station was sat in the center of a dead town, a place seemingly devoid of residents. Despite this, there were a number of vehicles parked in the lot outside, and the blinking open sign that rang welcome to any that might see it hung crookedly in the window, under the station's name. The name was scrawled in brown across a patchy white painted board. It read *Keyhole Petrol Station* and the words were quite a bit faded.

Professor Maxwell pulled in and parked the car on the side of the small building. All three of them exited the vehicle, then Chezzy eyed about cagily before following as Professor Kepler led the way around to the front door. As they walked, Professor Kepler lifted his wrist toward the side of the door. The bracelet he wore came more into view, and Chezzy saw that it was rather like some kind of a device than jewelry. He looked at Professor Maxwell's, and hers was much the same. The door swung open abruptly at Professor Kepler's motion to reveal a dusty, dim, and rather lacking, mini mart. It seemed near abandoned, except for a sports radio playing quietly somewhere.

"Oh, Directors. Didn't know you'd be back so soon," said a voice in the corner, startling Chezzy. A squat, balding man was sitting unmoving behind the register, listening to the sports announcer, which Chezzy saw was coming from the man's own bracelet device.

"Everything was easy enough, Pad."

"New student, then?" He was looking at Chezzy with mild curiosity.

"A new one."

"What sub is he going in? Do you know yet?"

"No?" said Chezzy.

"You know that kind of thing must wait for the Showing," scolded Professor Maxwell.

"Aw, yeah, I know. I just thought, you know, maybe a heads up would be nice is all. You know, for curiosity's sake."

"Curiosity's sake? Did you say curiosity's sake?" Professor Maxwell's voice was rising. "We know full well that you're placing bets. And now you're out to cheat it?"

"Hey, not cheat. Not cheat," Pad protested. "Just get a bit of an edge is all. Alright, alright. Just thought I'd ask. Hey, what about Minerocket?" But the look on Professor Maxwell's face told him she'd had enough, so the man waved them off with a grumble, turning his attention back to the sports announcer.

The three of them strode forward across the room and through a door marked *Restroom*, which turned out to be much more spacious than even the mini mart had been. Once inside, both Professor Kepler and Professor Maxwell began whipping off their outer clothes. Professor Maxwell, her jacket and jeans, and Professor Kepler, his sweats and floral shirt. It was then that Chezzy saw that the strange, leather undershirts actually stretched to clothe their entire bodies in different fashions. The discarded bits were gathered into a large purse that Professor Maxwell kept hung at her shoulder.

Chezzy looked up at Professor Kepler. Standing in the green outfit, he was entirely intimidating. It wasn't that he was particularly tall, but he was muscular and fierce, and when he grinned, there was something dangerous in it. Professor Maxwell stood equally impressive. She was tall, about the height of Professor Kepler, and her hair stretched down past the small of her back. She smiled coolly at the two of them as she typed something into her bracelet, and then she flung open a stall door to one of the toilets.

Inside, rising as the toilet pulled back into the wall, there was an egg shaped container, large enough to hold the three of them and then some. Chezzy's mouth hung slack as he looked at the whole thing. He gulped, heavily. "This is always here?"

"Always," said Professor Kepler as he clapped Chezzy on the back. "It's a portapod." He grinned mischievously. "That's what I call it anyway." And, as the egg opened, Professor Kepler laughed, leading them inside. Yet, Chezzy hesitated as the man turned a funny look on him. "You don't have to come if you're scared."

The everling looked back at Professor Kepler. "I'm not." Then he stepped into the egg, eyes steady to the man.

"Good. This is the keyhole to Inverkim near Saidbury."

Chezzy had no clue what those places were, but he felt excitement racing his limbs as the egg closed in around them and sealed. For a moment, it was dark, but tiny lights flickered on inside. Then, with a whoosh, the egg dropped. Chezzy's stomach gave a hurl as his feet lifted slightly off of the ground. He was certain that something had gone terribly, terribly wrong with the machine. They were hurtling down at such an extreme speed that Chezzy felt the skin of his face pulling away from him. His body was wild in the air, and his eyes had trouble with focusing, so wobbly was everything around him.

He searched frantically and then managed to settle his sights across Professor Maxwell and Professor Kepler, who were both holding on to handlebars that ran along the wall of the egg. They were both smiling pleasantly and watching Chezzy as he attempted to flail an arm over to grab one of the handles. Each swipe of his arm seemed to warp through the air as if he only half existed, and, each time, he failed to grab hold of it.

Then Professor Kepler reached out a hand and took Chezzy's arm. Chezzy felt himself pulled and drifting before his fingers gripped around metal. As he did so, he suddenly came out of the ferocity of the fall and was standing on even footing next to the two Professors, who both started chuckling. Chezzy looked around him as they laughed, his heart still mad in his chest. He could feel movement in the egg, but it was so subdued as to hardly be noticed at all.

"You should've seen yourself," Professor Kepler chuckled. "But really, it's a lot more fun when you let go."

Chezzy looked up at the smiling man. "Is it safe?"

Professor Kepler's grin stretched wider. "Oh, it's safe," then he let go himself, and his body rose and drifted, seemingly stuck in a slower state of time. His limbs moved lazily about, as did his face, which froze now and again in an expression of joy.

Chezzy, too, let go. He didn't know how long they drifted in that mad state, but he saw the professors both tumbling wildly alongside him. Then, without warning, everything was still, and the egg was opening back up. Professor Maxwell was out first, and she was standing on a cliff between two giant robots. They had spider like legs thick enough that a couple people could stand in them and whose length could've easily spanned over buildings. They converged in a windowed chassis accoutered with cannon like devices. But they stood immobile, their threat implicit.

"Welcome to Boletare," Kepler muttered.

"Boletare," Chezzy repeated.

"Well, Inverkim. But Boletare at large."

"Right," Chezzy gave, still staring around.

"So, I'll see you at the school?" Professor Maxwell was saying, checking something on her bracelet.

"If you're lucky," Professor Kepler replied.

"If you get into any trouble with him, I'm not coming to get you." She was giving Professor Kepler a suspicious look.

"We're just getting his school supplies."

"Well, I don't want you witsacking anyone or building anything atrocious. Like that thing last year. Oh, what was it?"

Professor Kepler gave a grunt. "It was an attachable, cybertronic, scorpion tail."

"Yeah, that. And you aren't even wearing it, are you?" Her hands were firm on her hips as she nodded, knowingly.

"It's hard to sit with. They don't make chairs for giant scorpion tails, you know. Besides, we were going up top. I can't even imagine the fit you would throw if I wore that up there."

Without batting an eye, she added, "I'm putting it in storage."

"What? Don't do that. I like it where it is. Go to the school. Do the schooling stuff, alright? And stop harassing me about my scorpion tail. We have stuff to do."

"And you're dealing with the Penton thing." Then Professor Maxwell pointed her wrist that had the bracelet device on it at a strange square of cement on the ground that bore a sign reading *Official Evestry Portal Zone*. A stringy abstract of purple electricity shot down. Within the area of the shape, there seemed to be a room, but before Chezzy could get a look at it, Professor Maxwell had leapt through the hole with her tongue stuck out, and the entire thing had disappeared with a tiny, electric buzz.

The ground smoked lightly where she had been, and Chezzy pointed at the spot with his mouth open, but Professor Kepler was already following a trail that led around the cliff and down the side.

Chezzy stumbled after him. "She just went through a… through a, a hole. Like a portal hole or something."

"Yeah, exactly like a portal hole or something. I see you've been reading. A little spoiler, we'll take one of those to the school when we're done too." Professor Kepler was looking down before them.

"Done?"

"Shopping. Didn't you hear? We have stuff to do. Don't you want to go shopping?"

"I guess." But Chezzy barely had pockets, let alone money to spend in them. He looked out at the small hamlet situated near a river that flowed through the center. It was picturesque except for the giant, multilegged robots, frozen and dirty, looming over everything. The legs came down over houses and sat in yards or the roads, and Chezzy wondered if they worked at all. The evening sun sent its shadows stretching far across the grounds.

Chezzy paused, looking towards the sun, wondering at where it came from so far underground. The light of it strange and visible in waves of stricken colors. And it wasn't just the sun. There was an entire sky spanning overhead. It even held faint cloud like formations that traversed above. "Professor Kepler?" Chezzy asked.

"Yes?"

"There's a sun underground? And a sky? A whole sky?"

"Yeah, not like a basement."

"No… but…"

"You wouldn't expect us to live in the dark and go about our nights and days without a sun or sky, would you?" They had arrived at a place in the road where several, hovering carts sat, and Professor Kepler was climbing into the seat of one.

"I guess not," Chezzy mumbled as he cautiously took the seat next to Professor Kepler in the bobbing, floating machine. "And these?"

"Hovercarts. What? You expect us to walk?"

"I guess not," Chezzy mumbled back, wondering what he'd gotten himself into and how to get himself out again if he needed to. Then the car sprung forward of a sudden, and they were zipping down the road at an incredible rate of speed.

VII.
Everling.
News breaking.
The Bankers.

Saidbury loomed and soon enveloped them. It was a full, rollicking city, bustling with people. They all wore colorful armors similar to those of the directors, though some had designs or images illuminated on theirs. Robots went around that ranged in size from tiny, bug like things that zoomed through the air, to masses of metal that towered above shops and homes. Many of the robots were old and creaking. They wandered the streets like vagrants, largely avoided by their human counterparts. The largest bots, on the other hand, were the same type of spider like bots he'd seen in Inverkim, and they were all completely inactive. Still, one tremendous machine ferrying people around the city skirts stepped right next to Chezzy and Professor Kepler, and the footprint it left was larger than the whole of their cart.

They went on, right for the center, where other carts were zipping about and parking around a large fountain. In the middle of the fountain, rose a statue of a shaggy sort of man. He was standing atop a machine of gears and cranks, and his hands were outstretched as water shot from his palms and fell lavishly into the pool below. Their cart pulled to a stop just in reach of the splashing, and Professor Kepler stepped out of the cart with Chezzy in tow. "Welcome to Saidbury and whatnot. Now, there are many stops to make, as there are a number of things you'll need for school."

The everling had been eyeing around, weighing running, doubt coursing him as another sensation crept at the back of his neck. He couldn't bring himself to look to Kepler. "I… can't buy anything. I haven't any money." He stared at the ground as he said this, and he nudged a rock with the toe of his battered shoe, feeling dizzy.

"You won't have to worry about that," Professor Kepler assured as they walked down one of the streets.

"Why not?"

"Well, there used to be many more like you, you see. But they're all gone now. So, Gotbew's Digital Finance, Loan, and Trust took their collective aureus-"

"Aureus?"

"Their money. And they lumped them into an account to be dispensed in the case of another coming forward. Your kind, you see, are very important here."

"My kind? Why?"

Professor Kepler grinned, and he began. "This entire place, this world we keep down here, it wasn't just founded by others like you. Yeah, they brought others down. Clades and the like. And they grew this world. Here, where we didn't have to hide what we are. And science could take focus. But they also oversaw this world. They were in charge of everything. So, one day, you'll be in charge of it, too."

Chezzy couldn't help but laugh, everything spinning around him. "What? Why would I be in charge?"

"Because, you… outlive us all."

"I, what?"

"You're an everling. That's what it's called. And you can't die."

"I can't die?" Chezzy felt his mind flare on fire, his steps sludging along.

"No. Not really. Have you noticed how slowly you age? You're smaller than other fourteen year olds. Younger looking."

"Yeah, but," Chezzy didn't know what to say, his mind clouding.

"It's part of it. You're aging slower, and sometime soon you'll stop aging altogether."

"I'll stop aging? When?" He could hardly see. The buildings around felt like they were falling on to him.

"I can't say. You know, some stopped aging very young, and they looked like children their entire lives. Others stopped very late."

"But, how?"

"It's what you are. It's how you're made. It's... genetic. And likely your children will inherit it too. Some at least. They'll be everlings."

"And my parents?" The words came out slurred, and Chezzy felt as if to faint. Professor Kepler's arm shot out and caught Chezzy, and the man steadied the everling against him.

"There, there. It'll pass. Try to focus. Keep walking and just listen to what I'm saying. There's a lot to tell you. Now, for the time being, don't go around telling people you're an everling. Don't tell them what you can do."

"What I can... do... Why?" Chezzy half murmured. Everything was blurry around him, and he struggled with feet barely responsive. But, slowly, sensation was returning.

"Because when our world finds out about you, there will be an uproar of sorts. People will do anything to get to you, to influence you, to gain for themselves. Others won't want you here at all. It's been a long while since someone like you has... been. The implications are staggering."

"Did you... do... something to me? What's... wrong with me?" Chezzy managed to ask. The world was coming back in around him.

"You're just adjusting, that's all."

"Adjusting to what?"

"The pyramid. But never mind about that. We've got a versolock to purchase and a bank to upset." Just then, Chezzy spied what appeared to be a mother and son, who were half cat and half human, coming down the walk. Their outfits were much like the others that Chezzy had seen down here, and they nodded politely to Professor Kepler as they passed.

"Kitty," Kepler greeted. She gave a curt nod back and hurried on.

"What are they?" Chezzy asked in a hushed whisper.

"They? They're people. Clades. Like you. Like me. Sort of."

"Professor. I know a kid like that. When I first saw you-"

"Yes, Stuart Fieldmore, Jr. I'm aware."

"Is he a clade?" He was beginning to stand on his own, and he tested his feet carefully.

But Professor Kepler wasn't paying attention, and he had stopped moving. He was mumbling, and his eyes were hazy. "Take it down. Get it to the portal."

Chezzy stabilized himself against a nearby wall as he looked around, still too weak to do anything but watch. He saw a toddler in a hovering stroller, and the kid seemed to be setting fire to her blankets while her father reprimanded her. Droids bustled around, and the father caught alight before stumbling through a couple of people who just up and popped out of existence, reappearing after he'd passed.

Some machines erupted from the wall of a nearby building, hosing the man in some kind of foam, which quelled the flames. He sat on the ground in resignation. A woman breezed around him with a hovering aquarium. It held a long snake with wings, and it leapt out to zip around the man, startling him anew, before plunging back in the glass box. The man grumbled, getting up and snatching the hovering stroller before going on down the way, still covered in foam.

He passed a shop that boasted a whole crowd of children clambering around, despite the occasional shockwaves that rolled out from the store, blowing dust on the passersby. One blast shucked the man of much foam, but he went on, indifferently. Chezzy squinted through the gritty air and spied the sign above the store, *My Minerocket and Me*. Another middle aged man, who glowed a soft, blue light, brushed the dust and foam off of him with an annoyed look before hurrying away. But the everling was watching a third man that rose into the air nearby and popped out of existence amongst a crackle of green electricity.

"What are we waiting for?" Professor Kepler asked, startling Chezzy as a girl came by riding a truck sized, elephantine robot, that she parked outside a shop before hopping down and rushing inside. Professor Kepler ducked under the trunk of the thing and went in after her. The wooden sign that hung above the door read *Mantuckit Porview's Versolock Express* in flashing, neon swirls. Chezzy tested his legs, their strength returning. Then he gauged the shop and moved in after the director.

The inside of the shop was like the Fieldmore's kitchen after startling Stuart. There were spine like poles shooting out from the walls, the floor, the various beams that were haphazardly placed about. Littering across these spines, were countless, electronic bracelets, much like the ones Chezzy had seen everyone down here wearing. A crooked, old man was rummaging around through the thousands of what Chezzy figured were versolocks. The girl who had been riding the elephant robot was standing in the center and waiting.

She had glasses and long, light brown hair. She wore the same sort of bodysuit as everyone, and hers were a reddish maroon. She turned with a gapped tooth grin to Chezzy and Professor Kepler. Then she reached out a thin arm and offered her hand to Professor Kepler, who took it, warmly. "Director Kepler, it's nice to meet you."

"Oh, please, call me Professor Kepler."

The girl giggled. "I'll be attending school at Balefire this year. My name is Fern Hudson, and I'm quite certain I'll be in Sciofall. I read that there was a big controversy with your placement, though they still put you in Phrenbook."

Professor Kepler smiled bemusedly. "Something like that. I'm sure you know with me it was… problematic, aside. But Sciofall? You seem rather certain."

"Yeah, well, both of my parents are in Sciofall."

"Lindle and Fell Hudson."

She nodded energetically. "You know them?"

"Your mother built that machine out there."

She nodded again. "But I helped. After my Zeta year, I plan to go to work for my parents' company instead of apprenticing somewhere else."

"Here you are, Miss." The crooked, old man came trudging back with a thin, gilded silver versolock, and he offered it to Fern while eyeing Professor Kepler warily. "A Bangle. Model 023. Just like you asked for. You know, most need to try on a few before they find the right one."

"Most don't know what they're doing. I do, and this is the right one." She slid the device over her wrist. It lit up and scanned her as the size of the thing seemed to adjust itself. An image projected above the device that was a hand comprised of mathematical symbols and unknown letters, building into possible words.

Then a voice, like that of a young girl's and very similar to Fern's, came out of the versolock. "Hello, are we going to stay together?"

Fern nodded, her smile wide so that you could see all of her teeth, the fore two gapped. "Oh, yeah. It's perfect." The versolock let out its own, excited giggle.

"Good," said the old, crooked shopkeeper, though he looked skeptical, nearly displeased, at the fading symbol. "You should get on out of here. Payment will pull from your account. You make sure there's enough in there. You don't want to see what happens when someone comes up short for a versolock payment."

"Do you know who I am?" she gave assuredly. Then she turned to Professor Kepler. "I'll see you at school, Professor." She glanced at Chezzy. "And you," then she hurried back out of the shop, her and the versolock both still giggling.

The shopkeeper turned to Professor Kepler and Chezzy. He looked the boy over before he spoke. "You hardly ever bring in a student yourself." He had a rough voice, and his small eyes were dark and searching.

"Yes, well, Mantuckit, we need an Eidolon. Model Zero."

Mantuckit Porview looked as if he had been struck. "You want what?" His eyes flashed to Professor Kepler's own versolock and then to Chezzy.

"An Eidolon. Model Zero. And I need you to keep to yourself that we got one. I don't want the news breaking just yet."

"News? What are you saying? What kind is he?" His eyes had widened as much as he could widen them, though they still seemed small.

"Just get the versolock, Mantuckit." Professor Kepler was staring piercingly at Mantuckit who seemed to have just noticed.

The old man gauged the professor, sullenly. "Scheming?"

"Never," Kepler gave.

Mantuckit turned an unimpressed look to Chezzy. "I keep the compact, you keep the compact?"

"That's right."

Mantuckit Porview looked again to Professor Kepler, studying, then he ambled to the back of the shop where he drew out a locked, brass box. His own versolock was accessing some kind of control with the box, and it opened as he returned to Chezzy and the director. Out from it, he pulled the versolock. It was the color of steel with blue and green swishing through it. Professor Kepler took it from Mantuckit in a snatch and slid the versolock over Chezzy's offered wrist.

It lit up and scanned Chezzy before projecting an image that looked sort of like a cracked skull. The cracks etched out in a double crisscross. Mantuckit Porview near fell back with a shudder. He had knocked several versolocks from their posts, and they were skidding over the floor. But Mantuckit did not care. "Heisenberg's fear, look at that," he exhaled.

Chezzy felt the versolock adjust to his wrist, and then it boomed in a coarse, deep, fearsome voice. "Are we going to stay together?"

Chezzy looked up at Professor Kepler. "Go on and answer him. It'd be rude not to."

"Ought I?"

"Oh, you should. This is the one, without doubt."

Chezzy looked back down at his versolock. "Yes." It was like an explosion inside of him. He felt an electric burst travel throughout the entirety of his body. Chezzy could have sworn he heard his fingers crackle. His eyes saw a brightness that drowned out everything else before fading. A faint visage of the symbol seemed to float in the air where it had been moments before.

Mantuckit Porview was still frozen and staring at the spot too. His eyes drifted slowly over to Chezzy and then to Professor Kepler. "What are you going to do? You can't keep him. I'll-"

"You're going to do what I told you to do. And that's the end of it. Your contract already decrees you are to maintain a student's anonymity. This is only more so, is all. Are we clear with that?"

Mantuckit swallowed again and nodded. "We're clear with it, yeah. We're clear, you and I, as daisies." He cleared his throat. "But I hear you've been having all kinds of problems at the school." Kepler didn't reply but only watched the man a moment, the pair of them glaring at one another. Mantuckit brushed his hands in the air dismissively. "What do I know that you wouldn't?" He waved his hands again.

Chezzy and Professor Kepler left the shop at a brisk pace. The elephant robot and Fern were gone, but Chezzy could make out the footprints of the machine amongst the dirt off of the paveway. He threw an eye to the professor. "That was kind of tense."

"I told you... Uproars and whatnot." Professor Kepler watched Chezzy as Chezzy looked to his new versolock.

He was examining it closely then turned back to Professor Kepler. "What does this do?"

Professor Kepler shifted as they walked. "Well, it's kind of like a personal aid. It monitors you, your belongings, and it performs certain... duties for you. They really are remarkable machines. But you'll have a lot of time learning how to operate them at school with Professor Sappmo. For right now, it's going to access your account and retrieve your coursework."

"My account and coursework?"

"Yes, your bank holdings, as well as all the books and lessons and homework and… everything will be accessed through that wrist bound buddy."

Chezzy looked down at the device again. "Professor? What was that symbol that it showed? He didn't seem to like it."

"Mantuckit Porview doesn't like much." Then Professor Kepler gave a side look at Chezzy and sighed. "Whenever a versolock is selected, it does a quick DNA analysis of you. Then it shows a… a speculation. A probability, of what sub you'll end up in at school."

"Sub?"

"Yes, well, students get placed into various subspecies depending on what sort of classification they are. The various clades. The girl we met, she's certainly going to be in Sciofall. I don't doubt that at all and neither did she. Of course, with Sciofall it's almost always clear, but we won't know for certain till the Showing."

"What is the Showing?"

"It's where a student demonstrates what they can do while our AI system analyzes them. It's nothing to worry about."

"So, my sub is everling?"

"Chiropa is the everling sub. But there hasn't been a Chiropa attending since I was in school. Now, we're going in here." Professor Kepler was gesturing up at a menacing looking structure built of carved stones, each higher than a man. Above the arched door it read *Gotbew's Digital Finance, Loan, and Trust.* The heavy doors, which were built of thick iron or some other metal, swished open for them to enter.

Arched ceilings fell about, demarking an array of richly painted murals. Marble floors, bright white and swirled with black, stretched across the massive room. There were silver pedestals with floating statues hovering above them and silver desks with projected screens. People were queued up and approaching these desks, which were manned by thin robots. Walking amongst the robots and monitoring their work, were things Chezzy had never seen before, except maybe in comic books or science fiction posters.

They had long, thin arms and thin bodies with bulbous heads about the size of a large cantaloupe. Their skin was the color of ash, and their eyes were large and some were blue and some were grey and some were purple. They stood about the height of Chezzy, and they wore draping robes of alabaster or obsidian. As he and Professor Kepler drew closer and joined the queue, Chezzy could see that the employees had no visible mouths and only four fingers to each hand. He gestured to them, open mouthed, and looked up at Professor Kepler, but then he noticed the paintings more clearly above them.

The paintings showed the creatures in a crashed ship or conversing with humans or spanning the galaxies. There were dozens of different depictions of them. "Professor, are those aliens?" Chezzy managed the question with a mighty crack in his voice.

"Yes. They wrecked here many decades ago and have since become the bankers of our world."

"Bankers?" Chezzy blurted incredulously as he glanced at the statue closest to them. It was that of an alien whose head was halved open, while a planet with circling moons bobbed up and down out of it. "What are they called?"

Professor Kepler let out a short laugh. "We don't really know what to call them and thought it'd be very presumptuous and rather rude of us to name them. You see, they have no mouths. Not like they've told us what to call them. So, we just call them Bankers, since they seem to have chosen that profession for themselves. They understand maths extraordinarily well, and we have managed to communicate somewhat through that… that and a few other ways.

"Seems they don't really have a way of getting back. Anyway, we gave them some land here in our underground world to live on. They could never live up top, you see. It'd be madness. Next thing you know, though, they had built this whole building, and, pretty soon, we realized that they had, well, sort of revamped our monetary system. Of course, they've helped in other ways as well. Their technology allowed a few scientists to harness clade abilities. Such as Mantuckit Porview and his former partner, Machina." Professor Kepler's face shifted wryly before becoming some expression that Chezzy couldn't recognize. "Anyway, Bankers."

"Bankers," Chezzy repeated, shook.

"It was either that or Painters," said Professor Kepler with an offhand gesture up at the ceiling, "or Sculptors?" he added, looking at the nearby statue. "But neither of those was really right. Mainly, they bank."

Just then, a desk had opened up, and Professor Kepler and Chezzy were beckoned forward by a vaguely humanoid android manning it. It hovered, having no legs, its torso sporting only a single arm. And its head had been reworked at some point, removing the human features of it. "Scan," the robot said through the remains of its mouth as they approached.

Professor Kepler took Chezzy's hand and brought his versolock forward to be scanned by the projected computer screen. The android froze for a long time, and then a light began to blink on the top left corner of the screen. A Banker with dark purple eyes rushed over and examined the projection, which was sorting through numbers and names. The alien glanced at Professor Kepler then eyed Chezzy before turning to another of the Bankers who then hurried over to join.

Soon, there were five of the Bankers all looking at the screen and making very small hand movements to each other as they traded looks. Occasionally, they would all pause and look at Professor Kepler or Chezzy before resuming this behavior. After a long while, the purple eyed Banker pressed a button on the screen, and then all of them dispersed. The purple eyed Banker glanced back at Chezzy a last time, then it, too, walked away.

"What just happened?" asked Chezzy.

"You just got the funds is what happened," replied Professor Kepler, then he took Chezzy and ushered him out of the bank.

Upon exiting, Chezzy glanced back up at the sign hung at the entrance of Gotbew's Digital Finance, Loan, and Trust. "Professor, how did they write that sign if they don't understand our language?"

"Don't need to read to write."

Chezzy walked on, weighing what he'd said. "Why's it called Gotbew's?"

Professor Kepler gave an offhand shrug. "Well, Gotbew's was our old bank. Gotbew, the younger of course, he was driven out of business once the Bankers set up shop. His old establishment is still sitting a few streets over, as are a few other closed locations. They haven't been used for anything in a number of years. I think Gotbew, himself, still… visits… them at times."

Chezzy thought about Gotbew standing outside the ruins of his bank. "That's kind of sad."

"Maybe…" There was a hint of bitterness in his tone, "but, that's also the way of it. Adapt, or…" Professor Kepler trailed off. He was leading them down the street and then between two buildings and on to a second street. Here, Chezzy bumped into a man the size of a watermelon, and very near the shape, who then cursed Chezzy for not looking. The small man had only one eye high up near the top of his head. Chezzy apologized, but the man was already waddling away, seeming to fume to himself. Professor Kepler, contrarily, had brightened and seemed rather amused by this. "He'll be kicking himself later when he realizes who you are."

VIII.
Menders.
Veronica.
Dates.

*T*hey crossed the road and entered another shop, *The Fine Menders Shop of Thaddeus Butterflew*. Displayed in the windows, were some of the armored outfits like what everyone was wearing down here. At entering, they were greeted by a petite man with a mouth full of blaring white teeth that matched his absolutely white hair and his cloud white attire. Chezzy thought about how much Mr. Fieldmore would love him.

"Welcome, welcome. Oh, my dear Professor Kepler, are you bringing a new student in? Wonderful. Just wonderful. Oh, I do love to see you touring them about when you do. Dear, it's been a while. How's that Emerald Honey Badger mender doing you?"

"Oh, it's very good," replied Professor Kepler, looking down at his armor. "I'm quite fond already."

"Well, you do tear through them, you know." The man looked over at Chezzy as he pointed at Professor Kepler. "This one here, I swear it, he comes in for a new mender every other week, don't you know? I about strain myself trying to keep up with him. But this, this," he was waving his arms around what Professor Kepler was wearing, "I've outdone myself with this one, mind you."

"So, that's a mender?" asked Chezzy. He looked around the shop but couldn't make out any other of the outfits, save those displayed on automaton mannequins in the windows. Instead, there were shelves lined with small boxes about the size of a large jewelry box. Each appeared to be made of carved wood, and there were several different tones.

"Oh, dear." The man's face had fallen. "Topper. I thought he was just making a statement in that get up. With that hair and, oh, look at those nails. I was certain he was an Oxenbor. But do look at those eyes. Oh, I apologize. Please, please do forgive me." He had taken Chezzy's hand and was shaking it vigorously, his teeth blindingly bright.

"It's fine?" Chezzy wasn't really sure what the man was apologizing for.

"Now, Thaddeus, I am in need of your discretion," Professor Kepler cut in, and the man at once straightened and peered into Professor Kepler's eyes.

"Of course, Director. Whatever you need." His eyes flitted for the briefest moment to Chezzy.

"I need a Black Tiger mender for him. Do you have any still?"

"My Zarathustra, a Black Tiger? Y-yes, yes, I think I do. It would, it would be in the back somewhere, though. I'm sure." His eyes were darting back and forth between Professor Kepler and Chezzy.

"Good." Professor Kepler took a seat on a nearby settee. He was watching Chezzy pleasantly as Thaddeus turned and bounded back through a doorway.

"So, menders are clothes?" Chezzy asked.

"It's what we wear. There are all different sorts that act differently based on what you need or what you can do. Thaddeus Butterflew, here, well, he invented the materials. You'll soon find that the sort of clothes you wore in their world won't last long here in ours. They can't hold up to the strain."

"The strain?"

Professor Kepler yawned then continued. "When you came out of that fire did any of your clothes come out with you?"

"I… don't know. I don't really remember when they pulled me out. I just woke up in a hospital bed."

"Well, do you think your clothes survived the fire?"

"No, not really."

"What Thaddeus Butterflew is bringing you would survive that fire. It would survive a great number of things, in fact."

Just then, the back door burst open, and Thaddeus was rushing forward with a dusty box the color of charcoal. He held the box forward. He was sweating heavily and breathing quite hard, but a faint smile was creeping on to his face. "Here, I found one."

Professor Kepler nodded. "Go ahead."

From inside, Thaddeus drew out a thick, circular chip, about the size of a large coin, that had been attached to the inside lid of the box. He held this out toward Chezzy. "Versolock."

Chezzy offered up his wrist, which immediately began analyzing the chip with a scan. Then the versolock boomed, "Black Tiger," startling Chezzy and Thaddeus.

But the mender maker quickly went back to work, setting the chip into the inside lid of the box and drawing out what looked like a folded length of nearly black cloth. He gave this to Chezzy to hold then pointed to a series of doors. "You may change in one of the cubicles."

"Okay," Chezzy returned uncertainly.

Thaddeus joined Kepler on the settee as Chezzy passed and entered the cubicle. He quickly slipped off his shoes, the dirty pants, and the ratty shirt he was wearing. Then he unfolded the cloth. It appeared to be a robe, which he pulled over himself. It hung loosely, and Chezzy glanced at his shoes and wondered if he should put them back on.

Just then, an electrical surge washed over him. The current tensed the cloth as it shifted and reformed. It covered his feet and formed legs right around his own. It kept spreading, and armor or padding or whatever all began springing up in places. Soon, it all was firm against him yet very pliable. Chezzy twisted his body, testing the fabric. It felt almost as though he wasn't wearing anything, but yet, he felt stronger with it, as if it was reinforcing his every movement.

"How is it?" Thaddeus asked nervously.

"It's… it's really good." Chezzy said, but it wasn't really good. It was absolutely excellent.

"Come out and let's test it," Professor Kepler added.

Chezzy exited the cubicle and stood before the both of them. "How do we test it?"

"Oh." Thaddeus exclaimed. "But it's a Black Tiger and you're, well, you. So how do you want to test it?" He was accessing something with his versolock, and a series of shelves came down from the ceiling. On the shelves were swords and guns and small machines that Chezzy had no clue what they did.

"What?" asked Chezzy, but Thaddeus had taken a flamethrower from one of the shelves and was pointing it at Chezzy. "Right, no. That's okay," Chezzy said nervously, backing away from the man. Thoughts of running rose as he eyed to the entrance.

"Thaddeus, why do you always have to jump to extremes?"

"You're one to talk," Thaddeus Butterflew replied, and with a little pop, a ball of fire shot towards Chezzy and engulfed him. From beyond the roar, he could hear Professor Kepler chastising Thaddeus Butterflew, before Thaddeus turned off the flamethrower with an impish giggle. The pair turned, silent and immobile, though, as Chezzy kept burning inexplicably. Chezzy felt his vision go wobbly, and the smoke seemed to penetrate deep into him. He couldn't breathe, but he didn't hurt. He didn't understand what was happening.

He opened his eyes what seemed like a moment later. Professor Kepler was standing over him with a concerned face. Thaddeus Butterflew stood several paces back with his hands to his face and his mouth awap. "Well, the mender worked," said Professor Kepler.

Chezzy lolled around in a haze, unable to think straight. His belly wrenched in a sudden spasm as he looked down at himself. He was completely undamaged, his mender unscorched. He absently felt for his hair, finding it completely intact. He looked back at Professor Kepler, a mix of distrust and fever sweeping over him. He wanted to bolt, to fight, but his stomach was letting out wild calls. "I'm really hungry."

"We'll go get something," replied Professor Kepler as he reached down and helped Chezzy to his feet. He turned to Thaddeus. "Not a word."

Thaddeus was nodding emphatically, but he said nothing more as Professor Kepler and Chezzy departed his shop.

They ate at *Gavvy's Eatery, Drinkery, Dinery, and Dishevelry* down the way, and Chezzy's strength and caution grew. He had ate quietly, the professor at ease across from him. Then they played a card game for a bit after the meal, where holographic images of monsters would project out over the cards and fight each other. All without having to sit through a Crattleboards length lecture beforehand. Kepler won every round, though he insisted that he had let Chezzy have the better cards. But Chezzy didn't care that he was losing.

He was torn. Overwhelmed. Uncertain. But unhurt. He didn't know what to make of Boletare. Of everything he had seen. Of what had been done to him and told to him. Of Professor Kepler. The everling remained quiet through the game, and Professor Kepler was keenly aware of him. He felt the man's unblinking study as he sifted through the events of the day.

"What are you thinking?" Professor Kepler asked as he gathered the cards back.

Chezzy shifted awkwardly. "It's a lot. I don't know."

"Disappointed?"

Chezzy almost shivered. "It's not that. It's..." He glanced around at the other tables, the other people wrapped up in conversations with curiously concerned, occasional eyes for Professor Kepler and Chezzy.

"Go on," Professor Kepler urged.

"It's not real," Chezzy answered, unsure of how much he wanted to voice.

"Not real?"

Chezzy hesitated but went on. "I've been to a lot of homes... It never lasts." He gestured around.

Professor Kepler smiled. "This is your home, Chezzy." He rose and scanned his versolock across a sensor next to the electric candle on the table. Then he winked and said, "Tab's settled," before languidly leading the way. "We have to get your course work." Chezzy watched the confidence of the man, despite the nervous notings of those around. He could go. Walk away. Run away. Maybe leave this place and find the Fieldmores. But he rose and followed after Kepler.

They came to an area of the village that was bustling with families who all had children about Chezzy's age or a little older. Many were lined up on a moving sidewalk, whose surface appeared to be a liquid that was somewhere between dark metallic and a brilliant white in color. The sidewalk fed into a towering building with a sign that read *Ye Olde Book Machine.*

More interesting yet, was the parking lot of Ye Olde Book Machine. There were an assortment of odd vehicles and robots parked there. Among them, Chezzy could make out the large elephant robot which had belonged to Fern Hudson, the girl from Mantuckit Porview's Versolock Express. He looked up and down the line on the moving sidewalk, but he couldn't see her with any of the people there.

Professor Kepler stepped on to the liquid looking walkway and held out his hand. Chezzy was surprised when he didn't move forward or sink into the metal, and Chezzy took his hand before tentatively stepping on, himself. Chezzy immediately felt unbalanced and would have fallen if it hadn't been for Kepler's hand. He soon found that by leaning any which way, he would immediately and effortlessly slide in that direction, as if across ice. Within seconds of practice, he felt stable and in total control of his movements.

Kepler had been watching Chezzy amusedly. "It's called a slipstream."

They glided along towards the shop at a leisurely pace, and Chezzy became very aware of the family in front of them. The family was made up of a thin mother and two children, a boy and a girl. The girl looked to be near the same age as Chezzy and the boy a little younger. But the thing that caught Chezzy's eye was that the entirety of their skin and hair was constantly fluctuating between colors. What's more, their menders seemed to do the same.

At first, he thought it might be a trick of the light, but as he watched them, he became more and more certain of it. Now and again, their hues would return to something normal, and Chezzy could see that the girl and mother had strawberry blonde hair, with the boy's being several shades redder. The girl's color was currently grey, but then it quickly shifted to pale purple. Very near to the purple color that her mender would reset to when her skin normalized. The mother was fussing with the son who was arguing about something he had wanted to buy.

"You know we can't. We already had to go on payments for Fair's new menders, and I still have to save up for your versolock."

"Oh, come on, mom. We can ask grandma and grandpa. I bet we still could." The boy pressed on while the girl looked away. Her eyes met with Chezzy's but immediately averted. Her color suddenly shifted into many different hues that caused her to almost blend into her surroundings. With a deep breath, she reset to her strawberry blonde hair and lavender mender, though her eyes continued to rainbow, averted from him.

"I said no," chastised the mother, her tone turning hard.

Abruptly, the family popped into the entrance of Ye Olde Book Machine as the slipstream took them through some heavily draped curtains. Chezzy was sure the family went almost as black as the curtains when they passed through. He glanced up at Professor Kepler to see if he noticed, but Kepler was mumbling to himself and staring off into the distance. A moment more, and Professor Kepler was looking down at Chezzy. "You were very close with Lenna Vose, weren't you?"

Chezzy's stomach plummeted. The question sent an eruption through Chezzy's mind that left him stunned. All of Wutherford Home came rushing back to him, dousing the dazzlement of Boletare. Ms. Vose, Ms. Bartleby, Sarah, everyone who had been there and everyone who was still there. For a moment, the feeling came again. The end. Like he was about to be dragged back. He cleared his throat as if to speak but then only managed to nod awkwardly.

"Yes, well," said Professor Kepler.

Chezzy thought that he was going to say more, but, just at that moment, the thick, dark curtain swept over them. They were awash in the black, and the fabric felt like dry, warm water running over Chezzy. The warmth pumped into his skin, and it was really very cozy. Chezzy felt Professor Kepler's hand on his shoulder. It gave him a tight squeeze and then was gone. Light broke in golden rays as they jostled out into a large, multistoried room.

The slipstream wound around and up the several floors of the room, before twisting back down again. All around, there were little landings where you could pop off of the conveyor. Each nook had plentifully cushioned seats or overlarge bean bag chairs and couches sat around tables. Lining near every bit of wall, were little screens with ports and wires coming out. Kids with their parents were strewn about, and some were scanning codes on the walls with their versolocks, while others had the machines connected to the screens.

There was a general burble of talk, and a small, hardened woman was bustling around and bossing about several flying bots that looked like orbs of varying sizes. The bots were comprised of bisected spheres, the top halves of which were metal, and whose bottom halves appeared to be some kind of golden colored energy fields. In many of these energy fields, floated strange, self frothing drinks, that came in odd metal mugs, and bizarre looking pastries. The bots were zooming around delivering the food and drinks to the various nooks or picking up abandoned cups and plates. Chezzy looked up to Professor Kepler uneasily. "Is this, like, a library?"

"Very like. Very much like. It's a café. It's a bookstore. It's a place that holds such an immense wealth of knowledge, of learning. Come. Here," and he gestured to an empty nook off to their right. They were somewhere near where a second or third story would be if the building had been arranged in such a fashion. Much as it was, there didn't seem to be any distinguishable levels but only sections at all varied heights and orientations. The nook had three separate sitting areas fetched off in different corners of the outcropping. Professor Kepler took a seat in a very large chair, large enough to hold three people. He put his feet up on an ottoman and gestured to a nearby stool next to one of the monitors and cords.

"What should I do?"

"Scan or plug in your versolock. It will begin downloading your coursework for you. And feel free to browse and get anything else you might want."

Chezzy approached the stool. He glanced back to Professor Kepler to see that the hardened woman had come up almost out of nowhere and was talking with him. Her face had softened, and she was grinning eagerly at Professor Kepler.

"Griselda, oh, yes, yes. I think we'd both have a Tizzy Froth. And pick out your favorite pastry. That's the one that I want," Professor Kepler was telling her.

Griselda blushed heavily. "Sure, Aris. I'll have that right out for you."

A girl and her father had gotten off on their landing and were talking as they moved to one of the other little stations next to Chezzy. The girl had short, black hair and very dark eyes. Her father was much the same, and both of them wore burnt yellow menders. As the girl sat at a chair near a monitor, her father turned and went back down the moving sidewalk to the little bar at the bottom. He seemed to shoot Professor Kepler a hard glare on his way.

Chezzy watched the girl plug in her versolock and scroll through the touch screen of the monitor. She had a bored look about her, and she gave a bored sort of sigh, before she noticed that Chezzy was watching what she was doing.

"Alpha year?" she threw to him.

Chezzy swallowed. "I guess, yeah."

"Pretty mild for an Oxenbor. A Sciofall mother. Nothing wrong with that."

"Right." Chezzy had no idea what she meant by this. "What… what will you be?"

"Sciofall, of course. Father was in Sciofall. I am sure I will be as well, even though mother was in Phrenbook. Not that Oxenbor, or even Faxowl, is totally without merit. It is just…" she trailed off with a frowning look.

Chezzy waited a beat. "Just what?" But then he noticed that she was no longer looking at him. Rather, she was glancing behind him.

"Is that Professor Kepler there?"

"Yeah."

"You know he is the only Phrenbook student to ever beat out every single Sciofall student in DATAs? He even beat the scores of Maze Bledshire, and Maze is the only person Midifen Shells ever took on as an apprentice. He and Professor Kepler were same year and all. Of course, Professor Kepler is… well, Father has told me plenty about him. And my father would know, being the head of the Bureau of Formerly Everling Affairs." She paused a moment. "Did he bring you?" She was giving Chezzy a more interested look now. Her eyes peeling over him as if in study.

"Yes? He… he did." Chezzy felt heat rising into his face, though he wasn't exactly sure why.

"I have it that Professor Kepler never brings students for precourse. Unless it is a very special case. He is rarely seen doing it. So why is he bringing you?" Her eyes had narrowed as if squinting would help her see through Chezzy.

Chezzy shrugged. "There was no one else to bring me."

The girl cocked her head. "I doubt that. Plenty of parents request escorts at times. They are always provided, but almost never is he one of them. So, what makes you so special?"

Chezzy gave a kind of half shrug. "I don't know. I'm not from here."

"Are you from above?"

"I guess so."

"What do you mean you guess so? You either are or you are not. Nothing to guess about it." A pastel pink had crept into her pale face. She was giving Chezzy an incredulous look that was somewhat tinted with her inquisitiveness.

She didn't even seem to notice that her versolock was saying, "Would you like any other courses, books, or special lectures added?" on repeat.

"Yeah. I came from up there," Chezzy said, though he was feeling increasingly apprehensive about sharing anything with her.

"Enough, Pierson." Her versolock quieted. She was looking at Professor Kepler again, and her face seemed to calm a bit before she turned back to Chezzy. "I apologize. That was rude of me."

Chezzy glanced back at Professor Kepler, who had received his tea and pastry, and he was sliding a somber side eye Chezzy's way. The girl had turned back to her monitor and was punching something in. She unplugged the cord hastily then offered her hand to Chezzy. "My name is Veronica Fayette. And you are?"

Chezzy reached his hand to meet hers, but her father had just returned carrying a blue liquid in a small glass, and her hand dropped before Chezzy had the chance to shake it.

"Veronica, I hope you are done. The arbiter just called and wants me to give a statement to Hoolihow. Again." He took a sip of the blue liquid and made a disgusted face. "This Eye Bright is awful." He held the small glass up in the air, and immediately one of the flying droids snatched it from his hand and carried it off.

"I am not finished," and she gave a quick glance to Chezzy.

"Why do you insist on coming here? We can get all of this at home."

"We talked about this already." Her tone had turned to match his.

"For all the good it did." Veronica's father was eyeing Professor Kepler with evident disdain, and Chezzy watched as his irises suddenly illuminated into a bright amber. He took Veronica's hand and pulled her. "Come along." Then he led them both to the liquid metal walkway. Veronica and Chezzy shared a last look before her and her father sunk down on the slipstream, out of view. Chezzy turned from them to the director.

Professor Kepler was indicating one of the metal mugs for Chezzy, so he hopped off of the stool and headed over. He glanced down the conveyer, and, as Veronica and her father slipped through a curtained area below, Chezzy spied Fern Hudson again, in a nook near the bar. She was raptly focused on the screen in front of her, though she seemed rather frustrated, and after a bit, she pulled the cord and began looking around the building.

She grabbed a bot abruptly, causing the liquid in the mug it was carrying to slosh out and start drifting around inside the energy field. She appeared to be interrogating it when she suddenly looked up, directly at Chezzy. Chezzy was startled and made as if to hide, but Fern was looking right at him. She bolted for the rising slipstream, making a direct path to him. Chezzy looked over at Professor Kepler, who was minding his drink. They met eyes. "Aren't you going to have yours?" asked Professor Kepler.

"Yeah," said Chezzy, and he took a quick sip that burned his tongue.

Noticing this, Professor Kepler reached over and traced his finger down the side of Chezzy's mug. "Here, try this."

The mug felt slightly cooler in Chezzy's hand, and he took another sip, finding it to now be the perfect temperature. It was frothy, sweet, and spicy. "This is really good, Professor, but…"

"Oh, I know. Griselda does wonders. You ought to try this pastry," and he held out the plate for Chezzy. The pastry on it was decorated to look like a golden monster with wild hair, long, clawed hands, and glowing eyes. The eyes were some kind of a gas that appeared like fire and smoke. After a reassuring nod from Kepler, Chezzy took a small bite and found that the eyes popped with a fruity flavored gel.

He swallowed quickly and said, pointing with the pastry in his hand, "Professor, Fern Huds-" but just then, a bot swooped down, grabbing his pastry and carrying it away, just as Fern stepped off onto their landing.

She took one look at Chezzy then scanned around till her eyes settled on Professor Kepler, and she marched directly to him. Professor Kepler lowered the plate and spoke in a pleasant tone, "Fern Hudson, are you stalking me now?"

Fern brushed this aside. "Professor, I have all the Alpha coursework, but it won't allow me to download the Beta coursework without a professor's approval. So, since you're the professor, you know, the director, I thought it best that I ask you."

"No time for nonsense, eh?"

"None, sir."

Professor Kepler gave her a curious look. "Shouldn't you be focused on your first year work first and worry about your second year work second?"

"Professor, I believe I am fully capable of handling my Alpha coursework while getting a more than ample jumpstart on my Beta coursework. If you doubt me, I'm prepared to-"

"I don't," he interrupted.

"P-pardon?" His interruption seemed to have thrown her, and an uncertainty crept into her voice for the first time.

"I don't doubt you."

"Oh. Yeah, well," she was attempting to shift back into her flow, "I suppose you would approve, well, for me to have access to the Beta downloads then? The full course and supplementary material?"

"Without doubt." He was giving her a half smile. Chezzy could see that his versolock had lit up and seemed to be operating on its own. "And I believe you can check here on Chezzy's monitor and you'll see that it's all available to you."

Fern turned to look at Chezzy. He wasn't sure, but he felt like this was the first time she had truly looked at him. Her light eyes were fixed behind her glasses, and she seemed rather pleased to find him there. Chezzy gazed back and managed a smile, but she brushed past him to his monitor and plugged her versolock into it. She seemed to melt slightly.

A few moments on, and her versolock told her that the download was complete in its almost identical voice to hers. Fern turned as she unplugged and gave the happiest, most grateful smile Chezzy had ever seen. "Oh, thank you so much. Thank you, thank you Professor. And you, um, Chezzy. Thank you."

"My pleasure," replied Professor Kepler.

Fern was already hurrying down the moving sidewalk as Professor Kepler looked to Chezzy. "Take a girl like that to a place like this," he clicked his teeth, "there's a proper date for you."

Chezzy gave a nervous laugh.

He could see that Professor Kepler's versolock was lit up again, and then he said, "There, now you can give her both the alternate sub specific coursework and Gamma course work, if you want to. Why break ice when you can melt it?"

Chezzy knew he was red. Nothing like a date had ever occurred to him before. He wouldn't even know where to start.

Professor Kepler seemed to be reading Chezzy's thoughts, though. "You keep it simple. But there will be time for dates yet. For now, I guess you'll be needing another pastry." Then he took another sip of his drink as his versolock dinged. He glanced to it. "Acid, acid."

IX.
A Milclade.
Melts.
Raven.

They walked along the streets while Chezzy watched the fake sun in the distance, which was refracting purples and blues and pinks in pulsing patterns, wholly unlike anything he'd ever seen the real sun do. He had mentioned this again to Professor Kepler, who had only responded, "That's mostly why I like this one better. That and the controller system. You know, Chezzy," he had turned to Chezzy and was looking serious, "things aren't going to be easy at school."

"Why?"

Professor Kepler had started to walk again as he spoke, and Chezzy was following with him. "It's complicated in that we're in a world that just recently had to redefine how it operated, since all of the other everlings are gone now."

"What happened to all of them?"

Professor Kepler sighed. "They're out there, here and there. But they aren't themselves anymore. Not really."

"What do you mean?"

Professor Kepler ran his hands through his hair and rubbed his temples before he began to speak. "Many years ago, there was a clade... a milclade. You see, he was unlike any other clade we had ever encountered. He could modify molecules and atoms and, well, people never really fully understood the extent of his ability. They tried. But they never really did. There are a whole slew of laws governing marriage and children for exactly that reason. Sometimes, when certain clades have children together, the abilities that come out can be… unmanageable. It can be a very tricky thing. A dangerous thing.

"So this clade, his name was Greyire Phren, he began taking the everlings and changing the way their brains worked. And he took other people too. He changed them." Professor Kepler took a deep breath, and he exhaled slowly before he continued. "He made thousands of nearly braindead servants and killed many hundreds more. Others were just lost. We don't really know how many are still out there."

"And he's still out there?"

"Yes. I see him. Sometimes."

"You see him? What do you mean?"

Professor Kepler took another, deep breath. "My mind is not fixed in time, like yours, you see. I move sometimes into the future and sometimes into the past. I see and interact there, and then I come back. You've already seen me at it several times. It's not something I can really, fully control. But I've slipped many times and had little talks with Greyire. I'm sure there will be more."

Chezzy thought about this and then asked, "So does that mean he'll want me too?"

"Who won't?" Kepler grinned. Then he pointed his versolock at another official evestry portal zone square on the ground, exactly like the one through which Professor Maxwell had travelled. A blast of purple electricity shot from his versolock and opened a hole on the block.

"Are we evestry?" Chezzy asked.

Professor Kepler let out a laugh, then he jumped through the hole. Chezzy could see him standing upside down on the other side of the portal. The everling eyed the hole then decided to step through, carefully, with one foot. He felt a tremendous yank, and he tumbled through. He flipped over and landed on his side, coughing, in the middle of a snowy field. The sun was still setting, and the white of the snow seemed to reflect the colors of the sky and cloud cover. Chezzy sat up as large flakes were falling all around him, dampening his skin and giving him gooseflesh.

"Every time. Supposed to be set to summer." Professor Kepler was looking at a small, projected screen from his versolock. Suddenly the clouds in the sky sped away, and heat seeped back through the air. Professor Kepler was looking at the snow on the ground. "It's going to take a bit for this to melt." Then he laughed. "That Alessa. I swear."

"What? She did this?"

"Oh, yeah. Loves a good joke, that one. Knows I like to keep the grounds at summer all year round. I told her if she wants winter, she ought to go to Bandelmount. I mean, even Saidbury or Sidelight do snow days for special occasions. But she just likes to irk me. Anyway, come on now. We can go up to the Keris."

"What's the Keris?" asked Chezzy.

"That is," Professor Kepler was pointing ahead.

Chezzy whipped his neck around, and his jaw dropped. In the sky, sat what looked like a space station. A huge, outer ring was rotating in a circle, and there were many towers and sections shooting up from inside that spinning circle. The bottom of the station connected to towers of stone and metal that were rising the ground below, out of, what appeared to be, the remains of a very old castle. "What is that?"

"That is Balefire. You have the old castle there below and then the Keris. That's the upper portion of the school. You'll have full run of the place until classes start."

Down by the old castle, there were a series of rivers and bridges that stretched all around its base. Most of the rivers fed over to a large lake, and the little islands they created were uncovering in the melt. They revealed mini forests and sandy beaches and high outcroppings. Some of the islands were isolated as their bridges had collapsed, or perhaps they'd been torn down. Between Chezzy and the archipelago, hills rolled and stretched far around them. And encircling the entire campus, were still, towering robots. He could also make out some kind of stadium in the distance and more forest and even dunes of sand erupting from the abating ice that stretched out to one side, past the robotic towers.

"Best get to the Keris. It'll be dark soon. If I let it be." He gave Chezzy a wink then strode happily through the hastily melting snow. Chezzy clambered to his feet and followed. They walked down across the hills then over bridges, and, rather soon, they came to the large entrance of the old castle. They went in and passed over stone flooring. The grounds had seemed completely deserted, such that Chezzy was startled when they came across a waifish man with amber skin who was wearing a near matching color mender. He was approaching with a tired gait from out one of the many hallways nearby.

The man had given a little wave to Professor Kepler and growled, "Director, your pick up and fetchin' went well?" He was scrutinizing Chezzy, and Chezzy saw that his eyes near matched his skin and mender as well.

Chezzy was struck. "Ms. Shoemaker would love him," he mumbled.

Professor Kepler shot Chezzy a mischievous look. "Oh, it went fine."

"Eh, I saw Director Maxwell got back o'while now. She turnt the 'ole place into winter. Scaret the animals and the trees all t'death. Near scaret me t'death as well." He let out a gruff laugh as he scratched himself. "Anywho, we had our sup up in the mess lab already. Director Maxwell said you'd be eatin' at Saidbury, but that ain't the point. Tech McGeehee said that Copernicus was at it again. Said he'd want a word with you and for you both t'look at the thing. 'Cept that ain't the point either. Point bein', McGeehee also said his droids been findin' 'em odd pots again o' yellow stuff. Said he got two o' 'em what was lain about. I don't rightly know who a'been leavin' 'em out." He gave a rumbling cough that ended with him sucking his teeth.

"He get hurt again?"

"No."

Professor Kepler thought about this a moment. "Thank you, Penton. You have a good night, now."

"Yessir, Director. Oh, and another thing. That dog has been got out again. Flying round somewhere. Bound to plop in a pot at some point," and then the man turned and continued down the same hall he had come from. There were torches of some kind down that way, and they seemed to bob and move, but Chezzy couldn't see them well enough to know why.

"Penton Fulcrank. He's the ecologist here," Professor Kepler explained, pulling his attention.

"Penton," came the shout of a small man who wore menders in shades of dark pearl. He stormed over to the ecologist. "I've seen two of them wandering around the Keris this week. The students will be here soon, and they're going to trample all over them. How are they managing to get inside?" The man paused as he spied Chezzy next to Professor Kepler. He was staring at Chezzy, his mouth hung open.

"Tampago," nodded Professor Kepler as he took Chezzy on into the castle, through a great hall. Chezzy glanced back at the small man and Penton as he neared a series of what looked like large elevators made of glass. The door of one opened automatically upon approach, and they entered the spacious compartment. With a great shift, they were flying upward, erupting from the old castle, and Chezzy could see out across the grounds from their little glass vantage. It shot up and into the center of the Keris, whereupon its doors opened, and the pair spilled into a large hallway encircling the elevator rises.

"That was excellent," said Chezzy, breathing hard.

"Always a good ride," added Professor Kepler. "Now, to your quarters, which have sat rather unused for a long time. No mind, though. Raven's had cleaning bots scouring it to bare."

"My quarters?" Chezzy hadn't really thought much about where he'd be staying. He supposed he'd just sleep wherever there was space, which had always kind of been the case, anyway.

"Yes, typically new students don't find out what dorm they're staying in until the Showing, but we already know what sub you're in, so there's no real point in waiting for that. Also, you're going to be an Alpha, which is a first year student."

"I… know." This last statement had caught him off guard.

"What I mean to say, is that you'll be a year older than the others in Alpha. It happens sometimes, especially with those from up top."

"Oh. I don't mind," and his thoughts turned to what Mr. Fieldmore had said about putting him in Patty's grade.

"Good, because your year won't matter. Nor your age."

They went on in silence for a while, taking many passages and many slipstreams, all of which had no railing. Chezzy kicked a small stick over the side of one. They went higher in the Keris, the windows evidencing the breadth of Boletare beyond. Then they rode up another elevator, past several floors to the very top. "This is really high up," Chezzy commented.

"Well, it is the tallest tower. That's where your dormitory is. Most of this entire tower has been in disuse for a long time, as it was largely the area for the everlings. Not that there were ever very many of them, but still. They were anticipating a new generation." The doors spread open, and they stepped off. They followed the passageway, and in a tucked away corner, stood a man in a thick coat with large lapels. He scrutinized Chezzy and Professor Kepler before throwing out some words in a foreign language.

Professor Kepler responded in the same language calmly. The man seemed to protest, but Professor Kepler flicked his versolock, and the man vanished, startling Chezzy.

"Professor? Who-"

"Good evening Director Kepler," spoke a voice, cutting Chezzy off. They had arrived at a great, gear shaped door. At the center of the gear was a small glass dome. It was dark in color, but it had lit up a slight red when they approached. The feminine voice spoke again, presumably to Chezzy. "Good evening."

"Why, hello," boomed Chezzy's versolock, frightening Chezzy as he jumped.

Chezzy looked to Professor Kepler, and they both laughed. The woman's voice was laughing too, and Chezzy wondered where she was. "Hello," he offered to her. Lights flashed between Chezzy's versolock and the door as they both seemed to be scanning one another.

"Good evening, Raven. As you can see, we have an everling for the dorms," said Professor Kepler in a pleased tone.

"Director, I, I, well, I don't know what to say. I almost thought you were fibbing. This is wonderful, just wonderful. Really." She sounded as if she was choking up.

"Is Raven a person?" asked Chezzy in a whisper to Professor Kepler, keeping his eyes to the little dome.

"No, no," replied Professor Kepler. "Raven is your dormitory AI. Each of the dorms has one. She manages all aspects of your dorm as well as monitoring the entry. You can also link up with her on your versolock." He looked back to the door and the glass dome. "Raven, this is Chezzy."

"Of course, of course," Raven went on, and Chezzy was certain he heard tears in her voice. "Come in, please." The gear began to turn, and it wheeled to one side revealing a circular entryway.

Professor Kepler gestured. "Well, I'll let you get settled. Breakfast will be served in the morning. Raven will fill you in on all of the details, of course, so have a good night now," then he turned and walked away.

Chezzy regarded the dorm. The common room before him was a large, circular chamber, littered with fluffed couches and tables. In the center, sat a fire pit with no flue system or fireguard, which made Chezzy uneasy. High windows filtered in the last of the evening light and tinted the dark upholstery a shade of blue. The walls themselves possessed several screens, though all of them were powered down at this moment. Chezzy wandered through. Upon closer inspection, he found that the fireplace was really a sort of lavaplace as a strange, molten material bubbled within it. He felt hot of a sudden and tried not to think of the Smiths as he went on.

In several chambers off to the sides of the common room, he found large beds that projected privacy curtains up to the ceiling when he activated them. Near to the chambers, he found a few bathrooms, which held massive, sunken tubs with multiple spouts inlaid in the floor. The bathrooms also had large windows that looked out the sides of the tower, so that he could see far across the grounds and over the Keris. He stood and looked out them for a while. He could just spy a strange creature flying around and doing loops a ways away in the falling light.

Most interestingly, Chezzy found a spiral slipstream that led up to a massive chamber, which stretched over the entire top of the tower. It was like a large observatory, and the room had many cushions and seats that went across the floor, as well as desks and screens of some kind. But the remarkable part was that where walls should start, there was, instead, a massive, clear dome that stretched over the entire room. The whole thing allowed Chezzy to look around at every part of the sky above. He could see millions of stars appearing at the cease of the sun. Billions, even. And the view gave him a full scope of the skyline.

He could hardly make out the horizons, except for one stretch of sky in the very far distance that appeared to still have sunlight there. And not even receding sunlight, but full on, day time sunlight. Chezzy strained to see more, certain it was a trick of his eyes, but there it was. Somehow the light was remarkably localized and hardly affected the neighboring areas, such that the demarcation was quite evident. Other than the strange patch of light, he could see that there were twinkling lights on the ground to one direction, and he thought it must be a town or a village nearby, though he didn't know for certain.

Chezzy plopped down on a cushion in the observatory. It was all his, he realized. This entire section was all his. He hardly knew what to do with it. Glancing around at the false sky above, he couldn't believe his luck. It was only this morning that he had been at Wutherford Home, yet it seemed so long now. He wondered if he could bring one of the beds up here into the observatory.

"Do you like it?"

Chezzy jumped with such a start that he knocked into a desk, toppling a screen to the floor. "What?"

"Do you like it?" she asked again.

He had completely forgotten about Raven, and he gave a huge sigh of relief before he spoke. "Yes. I do. Very much so."

"There are other themes if you wish to try any of them."

"Themes? What sort of themes? What do you mean?" Chezzy picked up the screen machine, finding it broken. With a wince, he set it back on the desk.

"If you would like, we could run through the sampler, and you could choose the one most suited for your needs."

He didn't know what she meant. "I guess, but…"

"But what?"

"Well, Raven, is it possible to put a bed up here?"

"Of course it is. Tomorrow, I can summon the droids to rearrange everything, and we can run the simulations. Unless you would prefer to do it tonight."

"Well, no. I mean, tomorrow is fine. I think. Really, I don't know what I'll be doing, but we can wait."

"Excellent," and she did sound really pleased.

"Sorry about the… computer thing."

"You can break more if you want to."

"Right," Chezzy chuckled as he fell back across the cushion and closed his eyes. He was drifting very quickly and only woke slightly to catch a bit of the flirtatious conversation between his versolock and Raven. She was asking his versolock what its name was. He wondered about this, but then sleep took him completely.

Chezzy's versolock navigation had brought him down through the Keris and into the dining lab. It was a massive chamber with walls of inlaid metal. What appeared at first glance to Chezzy to be windows rising the sides, were actually gigantic screens that alternated between images of outside and informationals. Winding in the center of the hall, was a massive, zagging table, which possessed a moving slipstream running through the center. It held plates, bowls, and flagons with all sorts of unfamiliar breakfast foods and drinks that were conveying along. Each end of the slipstream met with tiny portals, seeming to zap food in and out of existence.

Chezzy's stomach grumbled, and he rubbed his groggy eyes. He had been roused that morning by a half dozen small droids that were attempting to work a bed up the winding slipstream and into the observatory. Unable to go back to sleep, he had followed the lines and arrows his versolock projected to the dining lab. He looked over to where Professor Kepler sat, eating his breakfast while chatting with Professor Maxwell. It was a raised section of the table and appeared to be the starting point of the slipstream.

Really, the entire table was rather empty. On the other side of Professor Kepler, was a heavyset man whom Chezzy had not seen yet. He wore light grey menders and goggles, and he appeared to be droning on about something to the amber skinned Penton Fulcrank next to him. The only other person there was the small man in the pearl menders, and he was watching Chezzy as the everling approached the table. He had sort of hazel eyes and dark hair, and his attention caught the eye of Professor Kepler who, upon spying Chezzy, beckoned him over. "Please, have a seat and help yourself."

Chezzy did, sitting next to Professor Maxwell, and he took a plate and began serving himself a yellow pudding, which he soon found tasted like eggs.

"Director Kepler, really," it was the heavyset man next to Penton Fulcrank. "We must go and see Copernicus today. The whole thing is odd at best and bizarre at worst. I've been sorting the uploads, thereby isolating when the issue occurred, but I really need your eyes on it. Penton said that he told you already, but I must reiterate," he paused, "and so I am."

"We'll look at him, Gee. I told you. Those cauldrons, have you checked into what they're made of?"

"Oh, yeah. I've been running tests. It's some kind of polymer. Something I haven't seen before. I think I can replicate it, though."

The director pondered this. "After breakfast, we can- Ah." Professor Kepler had interrupted himself with a small cry.

"What is it?" asked Professor Maxwell.

"He did it. He did it." Professor Kepler was looking at a little projection on his versolock. He pressed something on the versolock, and the image shot up and across the air in front of them in a screen that stretched the width of the entire dining lab. It looked like a newspaper to Chezzy, and the heading read *EVERLING ENROLLED AT BALEFIRE FOR THE FIRST TIME IN DECADES! By Bag Hoolihow.*

X.
Bug.
Rippling.
Bogey.

"Source in Saidbury," read Professor Maxwell aloud from the article, a heavy note of what sounded like offense in her voice. Chezzy turned his attention to the body of the piece and began to read to himself.

Jumping mad and roving Heisenberg are the words of the day in all of Boletare. I've just had a report and firsthand account that the newest student enrolling at Balefire is an everling, the first everling to attend the school since before the Greyire years. What's more, this is the only known, unafflicted everling since the end of the Greyire movement, now some thirteen years past.

A source buried in the heart of Saidbury has said that they have met the everling and witnessed a testing that proved that the student would be in the, before now, defunct sub Chiropa at Balefire. Further details, at this point, are that the everling is a boy of about twelve years old, said our source. Which could mean that Directors Kepler and Maxwell are initiating an early enrollment for the everling. Something rarely done at Balefire. But rarity is all around.

We've reached out to the arbiter's office for comment, but Arbiter Bakehour only had this to say: "What? What do you mean? No. Hold on." (Four hundred and thirty two point four billion cesium ticks of silence.) "Every department in the evestry is well aware of what is happening and is looking into the details as we speak and is very well informed of the situation at hand as well as the ramifications of this... this thing... were this thing a thing, or... yes."

The Everling and the Acid King

Correspondents have reached out to Balefire for further comment on the matter, but thus far, we've received only the usual, automated response from Kepler's office AI, Saida. We will be bringing you further details as this story continues to break.
Special Report, Bag Hoolihow.

As Chezzy finished reading, he heard Professor Maxwell let out a soft, annoyed scoff. Turning, he saw that she and Professor Kepler were staring at each other calmly. It was as if they were having an entire conversation without words or movement. The rest of the people there were watching them, except for the small man. He was watching Chezzy, and Chezzy met his gaze then quickly looked back to his plate of food.

Professor Kepler's voice rang out of a sudden. "Tech McGeehee, we will go down to look at Copernicus before lunch. Professor Tampago Brown, as to your request, well, we don't really have space on the staff for Bop currently, but she can check back in later. Chezzy Nithercot."

Chezzy gave a start at the mention of his own name. He looked to Professor Kepler. "Yes, Professor?"

"You will be going on a little trip with me as soon as we finish with Copernicus. I trust you'll be ready for that." He was giving a keen eye, and there was a hint of something dangerous in them.

"Yes, Professor." Chezzy hadn't a clue what they were doing, but he felt the start of excitement welling in his stomach. "I just... Raven wanted me for something. Should I skip it?"

"Not at all. Find me once you're finished." Then he rose and strode out of the dining lab.

Chezzy hurried through breakfast, then he rushed off to his dormitory. Raven was already rolling it open for him when he got there, and he was surprised to find dozens of droids bustling about the dorm. They were cleaning and rearranging the furniture and crawling over every visible surface. They were even on the walls and the ceiling, riding around as if gravity had never occurred to them. Chezzy came to a stumbling halt when he saw the sheer number of the machines, and then he called out uncertainly, "Raven?"

"Oh, don't mind, don't mind," she said. "They'll get out of your way if you need through. They're built to avoid feet."

"Yeah, but what are they doing?"

"Just preparing, that's all. Are you ready?"

"I guess so." He stepped forward, careful of the droids that rushed away from his feet.

"Well, have a seat." A couple of the droids were bringing a plush chair for Chezzy, and they set it before him.

He kept forward and sat down then watched as the droids paraded around in a sort of dance until they were positioned, encircling the room. "Now what?"

"Now this," replied Raven.

Thousands of projections shot from all of the tiny droids. Chezzy gave a slight gasp as he watched the lights rake across everything. The room shifted from a lounge to the stone walls of an ancient fortress. Chezzy knew this because Raven began speaking as the projections changed every couple of seconds.

"Fortress, 1363. Club, 1967. Dungeon, 1744. Playhouse, 1991. Mansion, 2002. King's quarters, 1555. Cave dwelling, 533. Laser grounds, 2084. Dragon's nest, 3022. First office, 1884. Lab, 2015." She went on and on for several hundred or even thousands of different styles. She covered styles from movies and books and from life and from every corner of the imagination.

In the end, Chezzy was so overwhelmed he told her to stop and just chose Pillowtown and Blanketsburg, 2012. Then he asked, "Raven? How often can I change it?"

"Well, these are just samplings of what I'll be doing and not the full scope, but we can have it changed every day if you want to."

"Every single day?" he asked.

"Yes."

"Well, why not just keep changing them every day then?"

"A splendid choice," and she really did sound pleased about it. "It's been so long since I've gotten to do anything to the dorm. It'll be so much fun." All of the droids sprang into life, and they moved about the room, working. "And let me know if you have any other wants or commands."

"Right… well, I've got to get going, you know. Professor Kepler wanted me to, to… help with something. I think."

"Of course," she exclaimed. "I've already tracked where he is, and your cute little friend there will bring navigation up for you whenever you're ready."

"Oh, you," boomed Chezzy's versolock.

Chezzy gave a start. "Sure… thanks? And… bye. I guess."

"Good bye," she chimed.

"Good bye," Chezzy's versolock added.

Chezzy stood, feeling almost embarrassed for his writs, but he had other things to be focused on, so he hurried out of the dormitory. His eyes were dancing, and he felt a little dizzy from all of the shifting images he had just watched. Beneath him, arrows and lines popped into existence, and he quickly followed them as they led the way through the Keris. They took him very low in the structure, almost, he was sure, to the bottom of it. Though not quite to the old castle. Chezzy came to a cracked door that led into a massive lab.

Circling the upper parts of the walls inside, were little, camera like devices, and they were interspersed with monitors and computers, many of which were on and seemed to be running diagnostics of some kind. The lab was filled with tables, which were all littered with bits of robots and all kinds of parts and tools. Piled haphazardly on one table, were dozens of metallic, buzzing boxes, about the size of a deck of cards. The table practically rattled, but it didn't seem to bother Professor Kepler or Tech McGeehee. They were both sat at it, examining a man who had darkly curled, sort of bobbed hair, and who was wearing what looked like a very long robe. The man was staring straight ahead, and he was speaking, as if on repeat. "To know what we know what we know to know what we know what we know to know."

Tech's goggles pulled up from his eyes and back up over his forehead without him even touching them. "He's the third one. I did Tesla and Bohr just last week. No telling how long Tesla was like how he was. I don't think anyone has been down to that area in a good, couple years anyway. It's all storage… I only went down there because Bohr kept walking off that way. That's how I found him. Took me right to him. Both were babbling mad. Hadn't the faintest idea when the last time they uploaded either, but when I got to their uploads, I saw they had begun doing them at odd times. They were completely off schedule. It was a mess." Tech McGeehee sighed as Chezzy took a careful step into the room, but none of them seemed to notice him.

"Right," gave Professor Kepler as he watched Tech McGeehee, unblinking.

Tech McGeehee rubbed his eyes before he went on. "So, uh, then I started trying out the uploads, just working my way back. Sometimes they didn't know who they were. Other times, they came out screaming. Like they were being attacked. Mind you, I don't know what would've, but if they've been hacked, then I don't know how. Or who. Last time we had one go funny was," he stared up and scratched his neck, "gee, over a decade back, I'd say. Around the time we had that series of system failures. It's funny is all. Real funny. Thought you'd want to see him before I went to reloading him."

On the table, the man droned on. "To know what we know what we know the king-"

"Yes." Professor Kepler cut him off with a small flick of his wrist, and the babbling man vanished. Chezzy was startled a moment. "Well, Chezzy, what do you make of it?" Professor Kepler hadn't even looked Chezzy's way, and Chezzy wondered how the director had known he was there. Tech McGeehee, on the other hand, whirled around with a shocked expression.

"I-I don't know, Professor."

Professor Kepler looked over to Chezzy. "And if you had to guess at it? Then what would you say?"

Chezzy shrugged. "He looked possessed."

Tech McGeehee gave out a large laugh, but Professor Kepler kept watching Chezzy, his face giving nothing away. Another moment, and he rose, turning to Tech McGeehee. "Go ahead and reupload him. And Gee, do you know if we have any footage of the area that Tesla was found in?"

"I… uh… well, I can look into it."

"Do," then he turned back to Chezzy and said, "come on," and they left Tech McGeehee sitting in his lab.

Professor Kepler was walking very quickly, but he paused, slinking against a wall. He was mumbling to himself, though Chezzy could hardly make it out. "But they aren't static. And the ripples…" Professor Kepler's versolock dinged and for a moment it illuminated. Chezzy could see the many missed messages from someone named Saida and another named Kid.

"He might be a moment," Professor Kepler's versolock said.

"What… what is he seeing?"

An image projected out of the versolock. A pyramid sat in the middle of a city. "He's seeing this."

"What is it?" Chezzy moved nearer, but the image vanished.

"What was that, Chezzy?" Professor Kepler asked, coming back to himself.

Chezzy stepped back, startled. "I… sorry, I was just asking where we are going."

The director was straightening himself. "Oh, well, I made a promise and I intend to keep it. And you're coming with me."

"But, what? Why?"

Professor Kepler stretched his neck then began moving on down the way. "Honestly, Chezzy, if I have to teach you why you should keep your promises, then maybe I should hold you back another year."

Chezzy felt his face flush as he followed. They turned down another hallway, and they saw two men talking who were both wearing rather normal looking clothes. They waved to Professor Kepler, and one of them said, "Good morning, Director."

"Good morning, Doctor Tyson, Doctor Hawking," replied Professor Kepler as he gave them a cheery wave. They turned back to exchange a word, and then one of them disappeared as Professor Kepler passed directly through the other one. Chezzy stepped around him just as he disappeared as well.

Soon, Chezzy found himself and Professor Kepler on a sky elevator that dropped them into the old castle. From there, they made their way out and across the little archipelago section with all of the bridges and islands. Chezzy spied Penton Fulcrank as they crossed over. The man seemed to be herding what looked like three large, bearded pigs that were at least the height of a grown adult and whose beards trailed all the way down to the ground. Circling above Penton, was a winged animal that Chezzy couldn't quite make out, though it was chittering down at the ecologist.

One pig, the biggest of the lot, was grunting at Penton, and Penton was scolding it right back and gesturing over to another island, which was quite muddy and housed several other pigs like it. The bridge between the island they were on and the pig island was sloshed with mud and had several holes punched through it, presumably from the weight of the animals. Penton's voice was growing louder, but Chezzy couldn't make out what it was that he was saying to the pigs.

Professor Kepler gave a little laugh, and they continued on and away from Balefire. They appeared to be heading towards the area where they had come from yesterday, though it was harder to tell now that all the snow had melted. Glancing back, Chezzy could see the giant, bearded pigs walking slowly over the bridge to the muddy island while Penton was still throwing his hands in the air. He seemed to be yelling up at the flying animal, who was now just a blurry speck above him from where Chezzy was.

The everling and the director reached the cement square. Professor Kepler shot at the cement with his versolock, and, again, a purple, electric portal formed there. "Are these the only places we can use the portals?"

"Not at all. But Kid… the bureaus, they don't look as closely when I use the official zones. So, come on," he said, before he jumped through the opening on the cement.

Chezzy frowned down at the portal. Then he readied himself and leapt. He swished through his side and found himself landing on his feet on the other, his eyes going a bit dizzy as he did. Professor Kepler caught him and helped steady Chezzy, who mumbled a thanks as his footing stabilized.

"Better," Professor Kepler commented, though he was focused directly ahead.

Looking around, Chezzy saw that they were back in Saidbury on the same street and the same cement square that they had departed from just yesterday. Professor Kepler was already walking down the road, and Chezzy had to sprint to catch up with him, despite a slight dizziness creeping into the everling. "Are we…?"

"Yes. We are."

Chezzy wasn't sure if Professor Kepler knew what he was about to ask, but very soon, he found that they were, indeed, standing outside of Mantuckit Porview's Versolock Express. Professor Kepler turned to Chezzy and gave him a rather serious look. "Professor?"

"I'm not real worried about you," began Professor Kepler. "I will tell you this. Mantuckit Porview may be a Sciofall, but that doesn't mean he should be taken lightly." Then Professor Kepler threw open the shop door and entered.

It was dark inside. Every light sat extinguished, save the sun behind them, which cast their shadows far across the room and dimmed as the door swung shut. The thousands upon thousands of versolocks all hung on their poles that stuck out at every which angle. Everything was still, and no one was immediately visible within the littered shop. Mantuckit Porview seemed to not be in there at all.

Professor Kepler moved forward carefully then stopped in the middle of the room. His eyes were fixed, and Chezzy followed his gaze but saw nothing there, save an empty stool stowed in a corner. Kepler's versolock illuminated with a soft glow, giving dimension to the room about them. Chezzy took another, round about gander but caught nothing while Professor Kepler watched only that same spot. After some time, he spoke. "Mantuckit. Is this because of Pubby?"

"You fool milclade. You bogey and fiend," the voice rang with strain, seeming to come from the corner, and it gave Chezzy a start.

"You think you aren't the same?" Professor Kepler was grinning. "There was a time…"

"Time," spat the disembodied voice of Mantuckit Porview. "You think you own time, but not everyone sees it that way." Chezzy could hear a rising mix of anger and fear in the man's voice.

"You don't know time," replied Professor Kepler softly.

"Yeah, but I know you, Aris Kepler. You're a thief, pretending that you merely borrow time."

"No, I merely bend to it."

Many things happened at once. Professor Kepler bolted forward. Mantuckit Porview appeared in the corner for the flash of an eye, hooded over in a bolt of menders. The thousands of versolocks in the shop lit up and shone blinding lights that blotted out everything else. A thousand voices went up at once in a babble of indistinguishable sounds. Chezzy felt a shock of electricity that knocked him down to the ground and left him slightly woozy.

His eyes began to readjust as the lights from the versolocks had all faded. He heard Professor Kepler's voice first as the versolock babble died out. "You rigged them all? Has it been all you've ever sold?" He lay on the floor, mostly immobile, a few paces away from Mantuckit Porview, who still stood motionless in the corner.

"Not all, no." The old shopkeeper bared his teeth in what was almost a threat. "Maybe I've made some that sit outside of the system. Some you can't track. Some even you will never see coming, bogey."

"You think I won't get yours?"

Mantuckit Porview took careful steps up to Professor Kepler. His old and crooked body seemed to weigh him down to one side. "You know, I know what you'll do to me. But Pubby didn't deserve being witsacked."

Professor Kepler was talking, but he wasn't talking to anyone there. "Don't worry about the yellow. Smell. Smell."

Chezzy realized then that his limbs could move. He watched as Mantuckit Porview circled around Professor Kepler towards Chezzy, his small eyes never leaving the director as he spoke to Chezzy. "I'll be having the evestry come to get you. They'll figure out what's best. Not the bogey here. I'll not have him hurting you as he has others."

"What do you mean?" Something was sweeping him. His muscles seemed to truly come alive as if the electricity had pumped him full, and he was fit to burst.

"The evestry, they're going to do what's best for you. That monster there," he was pointing at Professor Kepler, and he had edged closer just slightly, "he's always been a horror. Always thought he was better than the law. It's astounding they gave him that school to run with what he's done. But they're afraid of him. So now he's been infecting the children of Boletare. It's astounding, everling. You don't know the crimes he's committed. The little lives he's ruined." His eyes were jerking back and forth violently between Chezzy and Professor Kepler. "There's no telling what all he's ruined in other times too. Absolutely no telling. He shouldn't even have been born. He's a milclade and someone had to stop him." Mantuckit had stepped just a little bit closer when he said this.

"But what has he done?"

"Oh, child. Terrible things." Chezzy could tell that Mantuckit Porview was fighting back tears. "But don't you worry, everling. The evestry has folks for you. They'll know what's best."

Chezzy caught a glance of Professor Kepler behind Mantuckit Porview. He was watching Chezzy. But Mantuckit must have seen Chezzy look, because he whirled his head. Chezzy didn't know why he did it, but he took hold of Mantuckit Porview's versolock arm. Electricity shot through Chezzy again, and it fed back into Mantuckit as the man screamed. Then, all at once, the lights went out and plunged them into darkness.

Chezzy was startled, but he could still feel Mantuckit's thin arm and the man's versolock gripped in his hands, so Chezzy held on to the tangible nothingness. He could hear Mantuckit as he continued crying out. It was right in Chezzy's ear. Chezzy fought, and he tried to pry at Mantuckit's versolock, his nails digging into the man's skin. His fingers were clawed around the rim of the versolock, and he pulled with all his strength. He could feel Mantuckit batting at him as he struggled.

Then it cracked under his hands as Mantuckit's versolock broke apart. Chezzy looked back up at the face of the old man as his own versolock illuminated the room as its voice boomed out. "What was that?" In the sudden confusion he had lost sight of Professor Kepler, but the director was standing behind Mantuckit Porview with his hands clasped to either side of Mantuckit's head.

Mantuckit let out a cry. "Witsack me, you Bohr bogey. The Acid King is coming for you. Your head will split the same as-" His words caught in his throat, and then he let out a horrible scream.

Chezzy fell back, staring at the pair of them. They were jerking oddly, and it seemed as if they weren't truly there. Like they were some kind of horror house trick of the eye. Undeniable though, was the scream of Mantuckit, which stretched for what seemed like an eternity. It only died out when Professor Kepler appeared to reenter himself and drop Mantuckit to the ground. Yet, even then, it rang in Chezzy.

XI.
Kid.
Milclades.
On a little outing.

"What did you do to him?" asked Chezzy as soon as his voice came back, and he could breathe again.

Professor Kepler was taking the versolock pieces from Mantuckit's wrist. "They call it witsacking."

"What?"

Professor Kepler looked up from the broken versolock for a moment. "He's in another time now."

Chezzy stared at Mantuckit Porview. He could still hear the sound of his scream. "But, but what will happen to him?"

Mantuckit began muttering at that moment, which gave Chezzy a fright. The words, though, weren't really words, just a tangle of nonsense. Professor Kepler managed to pull the versolock free, and he was examining it. "He will lose some time, I suppose. Right now, he's there. Later on... you know, I could bring him back to here. But which here will be not really here. Course, at the moment it will certainly seem like here to you and I. Or to you. More so to you."

Chezzy stood in shock, trying to parse out what he meant. "What? But... Professor?"

"Don't worry. He'll catch up with himself eventually." Professor Kepler was smiling at Chezzy, but it gave the everling an uneasy feeling. "We should be getting back to the school, now, shouldn't we?"

"I... No? Wait. This isn't right. We can't just leave him like this," Chezzy said, looking at Mantuckit. He was drooling, and his incessant babble was blowing spit bubbles out of his mouth.

But Professor Kepler was already heading toward the door and simply called over his shoulder without stopping. "Someone will be along." Chezzy hesitated another moment before collecting himself and following after. Outside, some people had gathered. Clearly, they had heard the scream, and Chezzy wondered what Professor Kepler was going to do about it, but the professor merely waved to them. "Good day," he gave as he passed them by. Chezzy followed with his head down. The people were staring at them.

Professor Kepler didn't seem to mind, and he had his attention tied to Mantuckit's versolock as they walked. Chezzy feared that the authorities would be coming to get them, but no one followed after. And the crowd who had gathered outside of the shop soon disappeared as they rounded corners. Chezzy was feeling sick, and he steadied himself against the shopfronts, tripping along after. "Professor?" Chezzy managed to ask.

"It must be why he isn't showing up in the maps," Professor Kepler said, not hearing, or outright ignoring, Chezzy.

Chezzy eyed him warily. "Professor, what did we do?"

Professor Kepler turned to Chezzy as they ambled on. "We removed a man who, at whim, could have electrocuted every person wearing a versolock. Or worse. He could've blown all of Boletare into single handedness."

"What's going to happen to him then?"

"They'll put him in Kellogg's Sanitorium."

"And us?"

"What of us?"

"Will they come for us?" They had reached the cement block, and still, no one was around, though the evestry sign loomed ominously. Professor Kepler fired the portal and jumped through. Chezzy followed, his legs still feeling weak as he fell forward. He rolled on to the outskirts of Balefire, breathing easier as he sat up and looked down across the grounds. Chezzy could see the giant, bearded pigs in the distance. They were all wallowing on their muddy island, except for the largest one. That one was staring across the bridge where Penton Fulcrank was working, attempting to repair the holes in it. The everling's eyes went on over to the director. "Professor? Will they come for us?" he repeated.

"No. Well, not yet."

Chezzy watched Professor Kepler a moment as he got back to his feet. The man seemed unbothered by this, totally, going on down towards the old castle. Chezzy cleared his throat and ventured another question. "Have you, well, he said that you've done that to a lot of people. Have you?"

"Oh, yes. Several. And I'm going to do it to several more before it's all over." Professor Kepler gave a wave to Penton as they passed, and Penton waved back.

"Before what's all over, Professor?"

Professor Kepler gave Chezzy a strange smile. "There's a person hiding in the Keris."

"A what?"

"A person. A clade. Hiding in the school."

"What for?"

"What for, indeed. You remember the cauldron that was left here? This so called Acid King left it. In fact, he has been leaving them all over. Yet, none of the artificial intelligences, the simulated intelligences, the droids, or the staff have been able to find this person. We have, on our versolocks, layouts of the school, and it even tracks the versolocks, such that you and I can see where everyone is. But, this person has not appeared. Why hasn't he appeared? Because Mantuckit Porview made it so. He has a maliciousness out for me and perhaps a great deal more."

"I wonder why," Chezzy mumbled.

Professor Kepler paused and regarded him. "You won't wonder for long."

"What do you mean?" They had reached the old castle and were heading through it.

"I mean, you're going to find this person."

"Me?"

"Oh yes, you. And you mustn't go blabbing about it to the staff and all."

"But how?" He could hardly dress himself and Patty wouldn't be here to help this time.

"You can't track this clade's versolock, but you can track the SIs at the school."

"The SIs?"

"Yes, the projected people around the school. As you saw just earlier in Tech's lab. For some reason, this clade has been tampering with them. And though you might not be able to see his hidden versolock, you can track the SIs."

"But what would I even look for?"

"Irregularities." They had stepped into a sky elevator, and it went zipping up.

"But, isn't there someone better for this?"

"No."

Chezzy looked out across Balefire, exasperated. But the view vanished as they rose into the Keris proper and resolve was slipping into the everling. The doors whooshed open, whereupon they were accosted by a short man with a very bushy mustache and dark brown menders. The man wore a matching top hat as well, and Chezzy noted that his menders were shaped much like a tuxedo or suit. The man gave one look to Chezzy and fumbled his words, the lot dropping right out of his mouth, and he looking for where they landed.

"Oh, mighty Heisenberg, it is true," he finally managed to groan. Then, recomposing himself, he looked to Professor Kepler. "You should've contacted me immediately. Even if it were just a suspicion."

"Not at all," said Professor Kepler coolly.

"Not at all? I've had messages and calls pouring in all the way from Saphill Wedd to Loegria and parents and, and, well, I'm certain you saw the article by Bag Hoolihow." He glared accusingly then gave a scoff. "Not at all? I should have been the very first call you made as soon as you suspected that there was," he gave a disquieting glance to Chezzy, and his voice dropped to a whisper, "an everling alive."

"I wouldn't say the everlings are dead. I just saw one at Everdine recently."

The man's lips twitched a little. "Oh, you know what I mean. Why didn't you tell me?"

"A new student coming to attend Balefire doesn't really necessitate the evestry's involvement."

"A new student?" The man was sputtering as he yelled. His face flushed with a wave of anger as his eyes darted around. He appeared to be looking for the right words to scream, though there weren't any posted.

"Chezzy," Professor Kepler began, robbing the man of the opportunity to yell further, "this is Arbiter Kid Bakehour. Kid, this is Chezzy."

Arbiter Bakehour was looking down at Chezzy. His eyes were bulging as he examined the boy, and there was something very much like fear stretched over his entire face. He was breathing hard, and then he began to mumble. "Needed to figure out protections, a statement, the implications for the evestry." He was slowly turning back to Professor Kepler as he spoke. "A, a, a, plan in place in case Greyire... Greyire... What have the molers been doing? They could come... What do we do? What do we do, Aris?"

"I'm already doing it, Kid. Go back to the evestry. I'll meet with you later this week, and then I'll fill you in on what you need to know."

"Need to know? I'm the arbiter of all Boletare. I need to know everything. Everything that you know. Everything you're doing. I need to know it all." His voice had gradually risen, and when he finished, he was near yelling again.

Professor Kepler had a bitter smile. "You think these casual years have made me something different than what I am, Kid? You... will know what you need to know."

The man huffed, throwing an outlandish look to Chezzy then back to Professor Kepler. "Milclades," Arbiter Bakehour muttered as he backed a little, allowing them out of the sky elevator before taking their place inside.

"I'll be sure to pass along your well wishes," Kepler called just before the doors zipped shut and the elevator dropped. He turned to Chezzy. "You don't have to worry about him."

"He said the same thing Mantuckit Porview said." Chezzy was standing uneasily.

"He did."

"You've mentioned it too. What does it mean?"

"Milclades?" Kepler shifted, watching Chezzy closely. "We can't help what we're born as. Milclades... or orphans."

Chezzy chewed the hurt of that. "But what are they?"

Kepler's teeth were set firmly. "I told you there are laws governing what clades can have children. Sometimes those laws are broken, and a child is produced with an ability that is beyond reason. Those children are called milclades."

A short silence stretched between the two of them. "And you're one?"

"I am. But I'm not the only one."

Dinner in the dining lab that night was especially quiet. The few other teachers hardly said anything, but all seemed aware. Chezzy ate as quickly as he could then made his way up to the everling dormitory. There, Raven greeted him enthusiastically, but Chezzy wasn't feeling very talkative. He crawled through the maze of pillows and blankets and readied himself for bed before braving the maze again to the observatory. There, he found most of the chairs and tables relegated to the sides, while centroid to all sat an overlarge bed. "Thanks, Raven," he said to her with a yawn.

"Oh, it's my pleasure, Chezzy. You just wait to see what I have in store for the dormitory. Every day, Chezzy. Every day. Multiple times a day. Who knows?"

Chezzy slipped under the covers and looked up at the false sky above, the billions of stars alit in their make believe worlds beyond. He was slipping into dreams, the stars fading to darkness. There was something against the window of the dome, an animal of some kind, maybe, that was tapping its little claws rhythmically. Chezzy thought that he should see what it was doing, but then, quite suddenly, he was asleep, and when he awoke the following morning, he had forgotten all about the animal.

The week ahead unfolded with strange tediums. Kepler had many meetings with the evestry, encouraging the everling to investigate alone. Chezzy spent much of his time following the map on his versolock as it led him all over the Keris and old castle in pursuit of rogue SIs. Half the time though, they would pop out of being, only to reappear in an entirely different part of the school as soon as he neared. And twice, he had spied tiny people, none higher than his knee, running away from him. But he hadn't managed to catch them either, though Chezzy wasn't positive if they were SIs or not.

Confused, he visited Tech and asked him if there were any miniature SIs in the school, but Tech outright laughed at him. He explained that the SIs were only modelled off of famous figures from history, most of whom were scientists, artists, or pop stars. "You know, the important ones," Tech explained. Chezzy had laughed at this and asked which Bogdanov had been. The SI seemed to have taken up residence in the everling tower and spent his time following Chezzy around, scoffing while whispering small insults. Chezzy hadn't a clue as to how he had upset the holographic man so much. "He was a scientist. And he's just mad that you have what he wanted, is all. Fool spent years trying to get it, so," Tech McGeehee had shrugged and laughed. "Not all great men get to figure out something like that. Takes someone truly different."

Oftentimes, Chezzy would wander down to the grounds to break from his peculiar quest. He'd find Penton Fulcrank down there, who never seemed to mind showing Chezzy the various wildlife that was kept at the school. Within three days, Chezzy had seen a dozen animals that had never existed above. These included a lion with two heads, a bear with skin like an elephant, an elephant with a shell like a massive tortoise, and a whole slew of winged honey badgers. These last were the most interesting by far, since they were constantly escaping and wreaking havoc around the grounds.

Really, Chezzy had enjoyed nearly all of the staff currently at the school. The only exception was the small man in the white mender, Professor Tampago Brown. Evidently, he taught Gene Production, Maths, Chemics, Biochemics, something called Thought Over All, and a myriad of other courses at the school that made him totally inescapable. Yet any time they were in the same room, Chezzy would catch Professor Tampago Brown staring at him in a flat, expressionless sort of way. Chezzy had even gone so far as to ask Professor Kepler about this before the director rushed out one morning after breakfast.

"There's going to be a lot of people that stare at you. Most of the students will have never seen an everling in their entire lives."

Despite what had happened at Mantuckit Porview's Versolock Express, no one ever came to take Chezzy away. Nor did they apprehend Professor Kepler. Still, the words of Mantuckit Porview stayed with Chezzy, and he found himself up late at night thinking about what had been done to the man. And not just him. Professor Kepler himself had said there had been others and there would be more. The whole thing made Chezzy uneasy. This unease only grew worse when, two weeks before the school break ended, he spied Professor Kepler receiving somewhat heated words from a man that Chezzy had never seen before.

He wore beige menders in the fashion of a robe, and his accent was wholly unfamiliar to Chezzy. "I've already spoken with Director Adskis, and she agrees. We must hold it this year. If you had informed us, we would have begun preparations already, but it must be."

For a moment, Chezzy feared Professor Kepler might grab the man and witsack him, but instead, the director remained calm. "The Pyriphlegethon is every four years. That's always been the way, and it hasn't yet been four years. So, no, it won't be this year. You can tell that to Mare Adskis too."

The man had eventually left, rather deflated, and though Chezzy had meant to ask Professor Kepler about it, it wasn't until several days later that he saw him again. Chezzy had been snacking in the observatory when Kepler's head had popped through a portal directly next to Chezzy, surprising him such that he dropped his entire plate.

"You startled me," Chezzy said, recomposing himself and looking down at the droids already moving in to clean up the mess.

"We found three more of those tubs. I'll be pinging you the locations. I need you to keep after it, but we will have the chance to talk more soon." Then he was gone before Chezzy had a chance to respond. But he wasn't the only strange visitor Chezzy had. That very night, a flying honey badger came tapping at the glass top of the observatory dome.

Chezzy was awoken by the scratching and nail scrapes, and he sat bolt upright to look at the thing. The flying honey badger was dark and had scars all over him. Seeing Chezzy, the creature crawled to one side and began motioning to something far below them, over the edge of the dome. Then quite suddenly, the animal dove down and disappeared in the darkness below. Chezzy had tried to look for the flying honey badger, but he could not see where the thing had got to.

Later that same week, the teachers began arriving at Balefire. They came in flying vehicles, or atop robots, or riding strange animals. Chezzy had run down through the Keris while still attempting to relearn his days of the week. He was finding that almost everything in Boletare was new. "Ahmesday, Mayday, Tuesday, Oax'aday, Fersday, Fahberday, Seyerday," he chanted, reading off a projection from his versolock. "Never going to remember this."

"I remember them," his versolock boomed.

"Very helpful."

He spent most of the day watching for the teachers, but any time one of them caught sight of Chezzy, their expression would completely change. To what, Chezzy wasn't certain. Eventually, Professor Kepler came outside to fetch Chezzy, and he was brought in for introductions in the dining lab.

There was Professor Benhearst who taught Mind Over All and Controlled Physics. Professor Gunby who taught History of Everything and Pioneer Tech. Professor Clyster who taught Realized Vivisection, Cryptozoology Made Manifest, and Crossbreed Handling. Professor Camfell who taught Body Over All, Structural Strictures, and Above Ground Blending and Studies. Professor Kettlewack who taught Projection Over All, Finite Reasoning, and Purported Proportional Projection and Handling. Professor Sappmo who taught Versolock Unveiled and Mastering Menders. And there was Professor Shi who taught Defense Style and Execution and who was apparently the Minerocket referee.

After that, they began to blend together, and Chezzy wasn't altogether certain what the others taught or what their names were, exactly. What he did know, was that he felt thoroughly exhausted at just meeting each of them, and it made him wonder how their classes would be. The only classes or teachers he had ever had were Ms. Bartleby and Ms. Vose, and that was just one class that they called school. Of course, Chezzy had spent the majority of his class time sequestered, and both Ms. Bartleby and Ms. Vose had been fine with that.

After everyone had arrived, dinner commenced in the dining lab with even Chef Scasbor in attendance. He rarely ventured out from the kitchen but was there now, watching the hubbub, silently munching. Chezzy was the sole student present. Very few of the teachers and staff addressed him, but he could pick out the various, hushed conversations that the teachers were having. Amidst the burble, Chezzy could see Professor Kepler, who was giving Chezzy a peculiarly empathetic look. It was dashed as rounds of salted sugar floats came trundling across the great table.

As Chezzy took one of the glasses, Professor Kepler appeared at his side, leaning over with a whisper. "Tomorrow, I am going on a little outing. I'd like for you to join me."

Chezzy nodded, feeling the rumbling of apprehension that continued into the following morning as he bathed and dressed before making his way through the horror campground woods of the common room. Professor Kepler was waiting outside his dorm, and Chezzy gave him a grim look. "Good morning."

"Morning. Are you ready?"

"I think so." Chezzy caught a glimpse of Bogdanov who was spying at them from the tucked back corner in the hall.

"This shouldn't be dangerous," Professor Kepler said, as if reading his mind. But then he repeated, "Shouldn't be," in a way that told Chezzy that it very well could be. They went on in silence, the Professor seeming to be deep in thought. Chezzy had attempted to talk about his search, but Professor Kepler had brushed it off. "This is not the time for that. We have one chore today, and we must focus on it."

Chezzy had held his tongue after that, though his ominous feeling only deepened when they reached Saidbury. He felt sick and dizzy and the director watched him for a moment, as if in study. Then he sequestered a hovercart, zooming their way towards the hamlet, Inverkim, that sat next to the portapod that had dropped them down into the underground world of what Chezzy now understood was called Boletare. Sure enough, they arrived at the portapod, and Professor Kepler had used his versolock to summon the egg, and up they rode.

Chezzy had held tight the entire ride, as he watched Professor Kepler who was let loose in the capsule, twisting slowly in that mad fashion. They popped out in the bathroom at Pad's Keyhole Petrol Station. Pad had come in to the back to see them, and though he gave Professor Kepler a rather cold greeting, he couldn't help but stare at Chezzy.

A car awaited them in the parking lot, and they got in and drove through the countryside, largely quiet. But a rising suspicion was coming over Chezzy. He knew this road, this neighborhood, these yards. He felt almost queasy with recognition, right up until they pulled to a stop in front of 1121 Morrel Drive.

Chezzy shot an uncertain look to Professor Kepler who winked back and exited the car. Together, they walked up and rang the doorbell. Stuart Fieldmore Sr. answered with a broad, toothy smile that dropped when he laid eyes on Chezzy. "Why, Chester." He looked between Chezzy and Professor Kepler and hardly noticed their menders, which were quite out of place, especially on this block and in this neighborhood.

"Mr. Fieldmore," greeted Professor Kepler.

"Oh, dear," replied Mr. Fieldmore.

"Oh, don't be silly. You can call me Professor Kepler or Director or Professor. One of those will do just fine." He was smiling wryly.

"Professor?" asked Mr. Fieldmore, as if he'd never heard the word before and hadn't the slightest clue what it meant.

"Exactly. You're doing very well."

"I am?" Bafflement had spread across Mr. Fieldmore's face, and he kept looking to Chezzy for answers.

"Yes, you are."

"Oh."

"We're here about your son, Stuart Jr."

"Oh, dear," exclaimed Mr. Fieldmore.

"Professor," corrected Professor Kepler.

"Professor?" Mr. Fieldmore was staring blankly at the strange attire that Professor Kepler was wearing, having just noticed.

"Why don't you invite us in?" suggested Professor Kepler.

"Invite you in?" replied Mr. Fieldmore quizzically. But Kepler was already ushering Chezzy through the door, right across Mr. Fieldmore's decorative rug.

XII.
The needles.
Curie.
Subs.

Mr. Fieldmore took them into the parlor, and as they passed the stairwell to the second story, Chezzy caught sight of Mrs. Fieldmore who was standing, stricken, at the top.

"Children's Services?" Mrs. Fieldmore asked, but Mr. Fieldmore did not respond to her.

Instead, he addressed Professor Kepler with a great croak of his throat. "Have a seat." Then he gestured to the couches in the parlor.

Chezzy and Professor Kepler took their seats. Mrs. Fieldmore entered then and said, "Doesn't look like-"

"Dear," Mr. Fieldmore interrupted. He cleared his throat and looked at Chezzy and Professor Kepler. "We've been expecting you for, well, quite some time now so," with a broad gesture of his arms he went on, "please, make yourself at home. Can we get you anything? Anything at all?"

"Yes," replied Professor Kepler. "You can bring up your son, Stuart Jr. I think it best if he joins us."

Mr. Fieldmore gave a great, audible gulp. Mrs. Fieldmore turned a violent shade of yellow. "My, uh," he fought to clear his throat as there seemed to be a large bubble in it, "my son?" He was giving a worried look to Mrs. Fieldmore.

Patty had appeared behind Mrs. Fieldmore, and Chezzy gave her a friendly wave that she didn't return. Her face was just as stricken as her parents' faces. "Oh, yes." Professor Kepler continued, "I think he'd be interested in hearing all about our school and what we can offer him there."

"School?" repeated Mr. Fieldmore.

"Yes," said Professor Kepler, then, "professor," and he pointed to himself.

"Professor," repeated Mr. Fieldmore.

"Yes, very good. Again, I think you're really getting the hang of it."

"You… Professor," Mrs. Fieldmore managed.

"It's really going around now. Yes, I run a school for children like your son."

"Like, like, Little Stuart?" There was something dawning on Mr. Fieldmore's face, and it was spreading to his wife and child. Patty was looking at Chezzy with something similar to hope or suppressed joy.

"Yes, Chezzy here has confirmed to me that he possesses evolved physical manifestations of some kind or another, which is something very common where we live."

"Where you live?"

Professor Kepler gave Mr. Fieldmore a very sympathetic look before he continued, "Really Mr. Fieldmore, Stuart should join us. I do need to see Stuart to make certain that his physicality is enough to secure him a spot at my school, Balefire. Though, from what I know and what Chezzy has told me, he will fit right in there without difficulty."

Mr. Fieldmore blinked. He stood still for several seconds, and then he called out, "Stuart, would you come here, please?"

Another minute passed, and they could hear the unlocking of a door and the heavy, shuffling steps of Little Stuart as he approached the parlor. He entered and gave a frightened smile at Chezzy and Professor Kepler. His spines stretched so far that he had to turn to work them through the large entryway around his mother and Patty as he entered. Then he stood with a nervous look about him, the muscles under the spines twitching.

Professor Kepler thought for a moment, eyeing Stuart contemplatively. "Splendid," he said at last, in a strange tone. "And Chezzy tells me that your needles can shoot out. Right?"

Little Stuart gave a slight nod. "Uh huh."

"Yes, and can you control that? Can you dislodge the needles individually? How long does it take for them to grow back?" Kepler's tone was soft, the words slow.

"I, I…" he began. He was giving his father a look, who seemed, almost imperceptibly, to nod. "I can't really control it. Just happens when I get scared. Takes a couple days for them to grow back, though." Little Stuart gave a shrug.

Professor Kepler stood abruptly, so fast that Chezzy feared Little Stuart's needles would indeed shoot out again, but they didn't. "I'm going to give you an address and tomorrow you will go to that address. There, you will meet with Professor Maxwell. Professor Maxwell will fill you in on all the questions you may have as well as show you to where you can purchase school supplies for Little Stuart. She will also provide you with an Irma Contract for you to sign."

"An Irma contract?" It was Mrs. Fieldmore who ventured this question.

"Well, we can't have you telling people about our school, can we? It's no big deal, of course, just notes that you understand that if you break confidence with the school to anyone who lives, well, up here, we have the right to erase your memories." Each of the Fieldmores looked as if Professor Kepler were about to erase their memories right then and there. "I expect to see him on the ninth when students move in. Good day Mr. Fieldmore, Mrs. Fieldmore, Patricia, Stuart," then Professor Kepler strode out of the parlor and out of the house with Chezzy quick to his heels. And though Professor Kepler had been pensive, by the time they parked outside of Pad's, the both of them were joking about the shocked faces of the Fieldmores.

Raven had begun helping Chezzy with the mapping of the Keris as they tracked the SIs throughout it. They were attempting to isolate erratic behavior in the SIs as well as sort out the unused sections of the Keris where this person might be hiding. His map was a three dimensional model of the school that Raven had marked with labels that would help organize, highlight, and color coordinate explored and unexplored areas or other sections of interest. With a motion, the map would project out of his versolock. The machine would also project pathways for him to navigate and follow. To Chezzy, it was extraordinary.

Despite the ominous nature of what he was doing, though, Chezzy rather enjoyed exploring the school. The only other drawback seeming to be that Chezzy had to listen to the flirty conversation between his versolock and Raven. Of course, Raven interspersed this with everything useful Chezzy needed to know. And, on the day the rest of the students would arrive at Balefire, she had directed Chezzy to an irregular SI that appeared stuck in the lower levels.

The arrows and lines had led him to a darkened hall on the lower east side of the Keris. This was unusual, since most of the Keris was lit by floating lanterns that drifted about, but here, there were only a few of them scattered on the floor. Two of the lanterns managed to flicker with a little light that illuminated the *Hudbot* brand name and logo. Chezzy stepped carefully around the dirty floor. It was sprent with stone rubble and sticks. The hall, itself, was mostly metal, but there was a section where stone and metal met.

It seemed this was where the Keris met with the old castle, and the corridor Chezzy was in whipped around in a big U shape. As he came around the corner, despite his map forewarning, he gave a start as there was a woman standing, facing the wall opposite him. She was staring at the wall, frighteningly still. Chezzy held his breath, surprised she hadn't disappeared yet, and then he chanced a few steps forward. The ground beneath him was dusty, and there was an acrid smell in the air.

"Hello?" Chezzy ventured, but the woman did not react. "Hello?"

Of a sudden, she began trembling, and she turned to look at Chezzy, her mouth hung wide as she screeched. "No fear of... acid... will fall... king will fall..."

Chezzy stumbled back in a panic, slipping over the gravel and crashing into the floor. He looked up at her encroaching in a jitter twitch frenzy, but then she popped out of existence. Chezzy gave a huge sigh as he got back to his feet, noticing that he had fallen into a dark, sticky substance. He groaned and tried to scrape it from his menders. Whatever it was, it had run down from a section of the wall where she had stood.

He could see that the metal had been eroded, and, upon further inspection, it wasn't just the metal that had been destroyed by something caustic, but also the stone. "No wonder it's such a mess down here. Where are the cleaning droids?"

"I've filed a report with Tech McGeehee," Raven chimed.

"Can you file a report for this gunk on my menders?" But a glimpse of something small darting across the floor caught Chezzy's eye.

"They are arriving," boomed his versolock.

Chezzy's heart near stopped. "Okay." Then he looked around once more. There was nothing there. Just broken lanterns, stone, and branches. Chezzy checked the map one more time, finding nothing, before dashing back down the corridor.

When he reached the entryway of the old castle, he saw hundreds of kids pouring through. Evidently, they had all arrived by means of what looked like some sort of massive aeroship that sat hovering in the air. Out of the sides of the aeroship, were slipstreams that touched to the ground. And it was upon these, that other kids wearing every shade of mender were riding down. There was a buzz of talk that filled the air and, hollering over that buzz, were the voices of the teachers that were ushering students into the old castle. All, except for the Alphas, which they were gathering together just outside the main entrance.

The everling eyed them but couldn't see Stuart there. A worry slipped across his brow. He hadn't noticed, but Professor Kepler was standing right next to him, and he gave a small start when the professor began to speak. "You ought to join the Alphas. You may not be like them, but you are one of them." Chezzy thought about this. There was something strange in the tone of Professor Kepler, but he nodded and walked over to the group of Alphas. They were all gathered around Professor Maxwell.

She was giving them a discerning look when she noticed Chezzy. "What is on you?"

"I don't know," Chezzy shrugged. "I fell in it."

"Looks like sap. Here," she was accessing something on her versolock. "It's not a lot so we can probably get it off." A strange, vibrating sensation ran over Chezzy's body as his menders began to clean themselves before it stopped. Professor Maxwell squinted. "Good enough. At least they're black." Then she turned to the crowd, her versolock projecting out a list of alphabetized names. Chezzy saw his own name. At least he saw the name Chezzy Nithercot, and he thought that curious.

The versolock began cycling through the names, Stuart's whipping by in the scroll. When it reached Nebulous Zee'han, it stopped. "All here, except, you know," the versolock said to Professor Maxwell who gave an approving nod as the list vanished.

"Right. If you would all follow me, please." Then Professor Maxwell turned and walked briskly down a wide hallway and veered into a doorway. They followed her in, and Chezzy could hear the others talking loudly around him. Many were asking each other if the rumors were true. If there really was an everling at Balefire. Chezzy felt his body tense. What Professor Kepler had said became all the more real to him in that moment.

After going through several more passages, they found themselves in stands circling a strange sort of arena. The arena itself was surrounded by a thick glass, and the ground of it looked to be stone, battered into sand. In the center of the arena, stood Professor Tampago Brown next to a device with many wires and a large display that stretched up to the high ceiling. Around the stands, there were other sections where other students in other years were filing in and sitting down.

Chezzy saw one student who looked like a grand, stone statue next to a red haired boy with an extra set of arms. Chezzy realized that all of the students in that section were different. Not different in the way that all of them were supposedly different, but they looked very different. There were kids who looked animal or who had abnormal limbs or who had extra limbs. In fact, more than half of them didn't even look human at all. Most of the kids in neighboring sections didn't appear to have anything odd about them. Save a beautiful girl whose entire skin illuminated in amber light.

Sat next to Chezzy, was a girl with curly, dark hair and dark skin. She gave him a smile that he returned awkwardly. On his other side, was a boy that was sort of doughy looking and who had jet black hair and a milky tone. Several rows down from him and another ten seats away, Chezzy spied Stuart. Stuart gave a wave and gestured to the empty chair next to him. As he rose, Chezzy caught a glimpse of Veronica who, sole amongst those around her, was watching Chezzy with a calculating look. He looked down, squeezing past people until he plopped down into the empty chair, trying to eye Veronica surreptitiously through Stuart's needles.

"Good day," beamed Stuart. "It'd be a great day if my stomach weren't in shambles. But hey, I didn't really get a chance to thank you. Mother and father and Patty are delighted about this place. Father says I can have a real life here, and that maybe the walls will be able to survive longer than a couple weeks if I can gain some measure of control over, well, you know." His eyes flitted to Chezzy's chest.

"Yeah. No, I'm fine," and Chezzy pulled his mender down to show Stuart his chest where one of the needles had struck him. Chezzy looked at Stuart's own mender, which was a shade of light blue and barely covered what a pair of shorts might.

"Oh, that's excellent. Did they do that? How did you even end up here anyway? Sounds like you have to be like me or have some kind of super brain or something. Is it because of how you look? Mother said that you did look a lot like an animal too, so maybe that's it?"

"Not exactly," murmured Chezzy. He wasn't sure what to tell Stuart about it all, though surely Stuart knew nothing about everlings.

"I heard that we are going to find out what everyone can do today. That that's what the Showing is," Stuart went on excitedly, not really paying attention to what Chezzy had said.

"They're going to find out a lot more than that," came a familiar voice to Chezzy's left side.

He turned and saw Fern Hudson as she plopped down next to him. "Fern," he said, surprised.

She gave him a curious scan before she went on. "They'll know what you can do, if anything, what you're composed of, what your possible and current intelligences are, and what sub you'll end up in."

"Sub?" asked Stuart.

"Mhmm," said Fern. "See the other kids in the other seats on the other sides? They're all sat with their subs. It's really very simple. They do it so that subs can learn together when they have similar abilities. Like you," she gestured a slight hand at Stuart.

"Me?" he asked.

"You'll be in Oxenbor, just like them," and she pointed to the kids in the section with the large, stone student. "Oxenbors have physical evolutions. Like you. It's really nothing to be worried about. I'll be with them," and she pointed to a group of students who were sat together and were, quite likely, the calmest and best behaved. All of them were raptly attentive, except for two near the top row who had some sort of flying drone that they were controlling as it zoomed around above them.

"Who are they?" asked Stuart.

"That's Sciofall." She said it with relish. "We aren't clades with abilities like you. Just a couple brain leaps ahead, is all."

Chezzy was looking at the other sets of seats now. There was another section of relatively normal looking students who were lounged about. He couldn't discern anything particularly noteworthy about them. But in the next section of students, there were two girls who were throwing what looked like balls of ice at each other. And near them, was a boy who was spouting out of his mouth what must've been a bathtubful of water, drenching another boy sat next to him. Everyone laughed, including the drenched boy, and then the first boy began reabsorbing all of the water. And in the first row, sat the glowing girl.

Fern caught Chezzy's gaze. "That's Faxowl, with the lightning feather." She indicated the symbol above their section of the stands. Chezzy glanced back to the girl. She was glowing brighter than Mr. Fieldmore's smile, and Chezzy met eyes with her briefly before turning back to Fern. "They don't have physical traits like the Oxenbors, but they manifest physical things. And those kids, there, with the odd eye," she was pointing over to the normal looking students lounging, "that's Phrenbook. Don't let their looks fool you. They're a scary lot."

"That's where Professor Kepler was, right?" Chezzy asked. He gave them a look, and his eyes flitted over to another section where the teachers and staff were all sat, save those that were down in the arena. Next to the staff seating, though, there was a smaller, empty section of bleachers, and Chezzy had a sinking feeling he knew who went there. His eyes flitted up to the familiar symbol above them.

"Yes, and Professor Maxwell." Fern was nodding knowingly.

Chezzy snapped back to her, just barely hearing her, and hastily added, "Right, and Professor Maxwell."

"What do they do?" asked Stuart.

"Mind stuff," said Fern.

"Mind stuff?" parroted Stuart. "What does that mean?"

"It's different for each. Some of them can move things with their minds or read minds or," she shrugged, "other things. Mom said she knew a boy named Odel Pammy that could blink people out of existence with just his thoughts."

"Whoa," said Stuart, "that's amazing."

"A milclade," Chezzy mumbled. Fern caught it, and she studied him thoughtfully.

"What happened to him?" Stuart asked.

"No idea. She said he disappeared one day. Maybe he blinked himself out of existence in his sleep or something. Some people are just too dangerous. That's why they regulate those kinds of things. Can't go having a clade that can accidently destroy the whole world, can we? Or even intentionally."

"Wicked," said Stuart. He was giving Chezzy an impressed look with his mouth hung open in a weird smile, baring his many, sharp teeth. Chezzy was suddenly struck with how peculiar it all was.

"Wicked is right," continued Fern. "Breaking the law like that is how Greyire came into being." She gave another knowing look to Chezzy.

"Greyire?" asked Stuart, but Fern shushed him and pointed. "Look, they're starting."

Professor Kepler had joined Professor Maxwell and Professor Tampago Brown in the arena. He was holding his hands up to the students, and a hush fell over the stadium as every eye turned to him. "I give you Director Maxwell with the list," he gestured to Professor Maxwell who smiled up at the students, "and Professor Tampago Brown with the Showing device." Again, he gestured, though this time to Professor Tampago Brown before his large, glass screen and machine. Professor Tampago Brown gave a slight bow.

Professor Kepler took a seat at a plush chair to one side of the arena. Then he said, "Let the Showing begin."

XIII.
Showing.
Fair.
Feen.

*P*rofessor Maxwell stood forward from the great screen, and she called out in an amplified voice, "Arlene Aberfor."

All of the students were looking around when a tall girl was sucked through her chair and vanished from sight. The older students all gave a laugh as she was spat out into the arena from a portal hole that had opened at one side. Arlene Aberfor looked around at the closing hole, and grumbling, she got up and stepped forward to Professor Maxwell who guided her over to Professor Tampago Brown.

The small man began situating scanning devices around Arlene before nodding to Professor Maxwell who stepped forward and spoke with the girl a moment. Then the two professors backed away, giving Arlene plenty of room. The students around were watching excitedly. Some were jeering while others clapped. It seemed like some were even placing bets on where she would end up.

Chezzy felt Fern grip his arm in a fit of excitement, and he turned to look at her. Whatever happened, Chezzy missed it, but the whole crowd gave an ooh sound and then broke out in applause. When Chezzy looked back to where Arlene had stood, in her place now was a ball of dark brown hair, the size of a small car. Above, the screen was flashing, and rows of stats spouted out, followed by the large lightning feather and the word *Faxowl* over it. The Faxowl students gave up a cheer, which died out as Professor Kepler and Professor Maxwell set their versolocks to zapping at the hair, burning it away.

The smell of burnt hair and grousing filled the stadium, and a short while later, Arlene Aberfor emerged from the wad as the last strands were singed off of her. Even from the stands, Chezzy could see that the lightning feather symbol had appeared on her menders. Professor Maxwell was already directing Arlene, and she went up to be greeted by the other students in her section with high fives and back pats. The stadium fell silent, though, as Professor Maxwell called out a second name.

"What are your last names? Both of you," Fern whispered.

"Fieldmore," said Stuart.

"Nithercot," added Chezzy.

"Nithercot?" She was looking between them. "Well, I'm Hudson so that will put you, uh," she was pointing at Stuart.

"Stuart."

"Yeah, Stuart, before me and then you, Chezzy, after me. Ooh," and she gave a shiver, "what if I don't get in?"

"Nervous?" Chezzy asked, for he was certain that she was certain that she was going into Sciofall.

Fern let out a laugh. "No. But, sometimes, and it doesn't happen often, but, just sometimes, people get, well, rejected."

"They what?" spurted Stuart just as Professor Maxwell called out, "Tan Beauford," and a dark haired boy four seats over was sucked down through his chair. Stuart's eyes had gone wide, his mouth shrinking small, the color fleeing his furred face.

Fern was nodding solemnly, gritting against a grin that broke. "Nah, you'll be fine. Look at you. Oxenbors pretty much always get in. It's just the Sciofalls that have to worry." Her face fell just a little.

Stuart gave a heaping sigh that almost sounded like a growl and shook his needles. "Well, that's a relief, then."

Fern flashed him an annoyed look.

"Well, I'm sure you will be fine too," Stuart added hastily.

The great screen was showing Phrenbook over their symbol, a finely lined eye with a strange, cloud like iris. Cheers of

"Minerocket. Minerocket," were bellowing from the Phrenbook section.

Fern gave the slightest notice to this result then continued. "Are you nervous?" She was looking at Chezzy. "Probably not. You did get pulled in by Professor Kepler. I doubt he'd go getting someone that he wasn't positive belonged here."

"No," replied Chezzy. "I'm not nervous about that, really." He stared down at a boy who was standing proudly before the machine as it read off of him. Stats poured over the screen, followed by Sciofall and their symbol, a mix of math marks and maybe words that shifted around in the pattern of a hand. Chezzy became suddenly aware of Fern's discerning stare, and he avoided her gaze.

"Metwell Chase," called out Professor Maxwell. The boy that was sucked into the arena had almost scale like skin, though the tone was much the same as Chezzy's. Metwell stood and was prepped, and soon the screen flashed Oxenbor to the, quite literal, roars of the Oxenbor sub. The Oxenbor symbol faded above, two whipping tails intertwined, one of them spiked. The symbol appeared on Metwell's menders just as it ceased to be above. Then the boy ran to join the Oxenbors and was soon lost amongst them. "Marsle Chin," reverberated Professor Maxwell's voice.

Students looked around as a boy was sucked down and spat out in a tumble of navy menders. Chezzy saw that it was the doughy boy with jet black hair that he had sat next to earlier. Professor Kepler had actually come forward to greet Marsle, and they were exchanging rather urgent words. Excited whispers had taken over the audience, and Chezzy could make out the word everling being tossed around. And while all attention seemed to have gone to Marsle, Chezzy could still feel Fern's eyes boring into him.

The speculations only rose as the boy kept shaking his head at Professor Kepler, as if he didn't want to be tested. Even Professor Maxwell made to intervene, but Professor Kepler motioned for her to stay. The only one that seemed uninterested was Tampago Brown, who was keying in to his machine and checking it thoroughly. This went on until Marsle Chin seemed to agree, moving on to be hooked up by Professor Tampago Brown as Professor Kepler walked away.

Chezzy watched Professor Kepler put something in his ears while Professor Maxwell attempted to get his attention. But the man sat back down without giving her a glance, his focus entirely devoted to Marsle. Professor Maxwell looked alarmed of a sudden. She whirled toward Marsle who was sweating with his eyes squeezed tight, the scan already begun. She rushed forward but was too late to stop it.

Marsle pressed his hands to his ears and made a loud, flat sound. Chezzy felt his stomach turn and gurgle, and unable to stop it, he lost control of his bowels. Horrified and looking around, he realized he wasn't the only one. Professor Maxwell had lurched, mid stride, her hands over her belly, her mouth wide in shock. There was a mass drawing of alarmed faces all across the stands followed by a terrible stench. A collective groan swept the arena. "Oh, not again," Stuart groaned at Chezzy's side.

Marsle Chin looked around apologetically. Above him, the screen came alive and placed him in Phrenbook, but there was no applause except that of Professor Kepler. The director was laughing hysterically and chanting, "Minerocket, Minerocket." He removed the earplugs and turned to Professor Maxwell who stormed towards him sporting a very uncomfortable gait.

"Everyone?" she was shouting, which was amplified over the sound system. She looked up to the staff and teachers, whose disgusted faces matched hers.

"Oh, I've been concealing him forever for that," Professor Kepler was saying, his voice getting caught by Professor Maxwell's hidden microphone. "Completely worth it." His smile was unstoppable.

Professor Maxwell looked angry for just a moment more, and then she broke into a laughing fit. Professor Kepler had accessed his versolock, and suddenly the menders and versolocks of every student and teacher began interacting. Chezzy's own even lit up, and he felt that strange sensation again as his mender cleaned itself and him. The knowledge of this ability appeared new to most everyone else, though.

Professor Maxwell composed herself as she escorted the embarrassed Marsle Chin to the Phrenbook section then called out for Minny Deerwink, who went on to put on a fabulous display of lights up in the air before being sent to Faxowl. She was followed by Frige Denhauer, who made everyone slightly sleepy and was sent to Phrenbook. It was only a few more students before Professor Maxwell called out for Veronica Fayette. Like those before her, she was sucked down and spat out in the arena. Only Veronica's gaze kept drifting back to Chezzy, her eyes fetching him out of the crowd. The machine ran, and Sciofall appeared without hesitation. The students chanted for Minerocket, and she was cheered so loudly that Chezzy felt certain he must have missed something in the feed of information on the screen. But still she watched him.

"Stuart Fieldmore," came the cry of Professor Maxwell. Chezzy turned to tell Stuart good luck, but they only managed to share an odd look before Stuart was sucked through a portal on his chair. He popped out at the bottom and did a small roll, skidding sand, before he rose. The Oxenbors were already chanting, and, sure enough, the screen soon lit up with the Oxenbor symbol to thunderous applause and a relieved Stuart.

Fern was gripping Chezzy's arm. Her focus had turned from him to herself. There were only a few more students before her own name was called, and she was pulled from Chezzy's reach. In the arena, she stood from her tumble and straightened herself out before approaching Professor Maxwell and Professor Tampago Brown. She appeared to be looking over at Professor Kepler, though, and the man gave her an encouraging nod. Her eyes darted back around to look up at Chezzy just as the screen lit up, and Sciofall spelled out above her.

Fern beamed for a moment and then sprinted to the Sciofall section where she was welcomed by the others. She took a seat just a few down from Veronica Fayette, who eyed her then turned back to Chezzy with her same, contemplative look. Chezzy pretended not to notice her and looked to Professor Maxwell who called out with a cracking voice, "Turod Ingleward." Then a boy with dirty blond hair was portaled into the arena.

His demonstration required a table, on which sat an apple. The boy looked at the apple before picking it up. The fruit rotted instantly in his hand. Professor Maxwell stared at him, her expression odd. The screen above them flashed Phrenbook, and Professor Tampago Brown regarded the boy gravely before seeing him off to join his sub. Chezzy looked to Professor Kepler who only stared at the floor.

"Fair Jekyll," Professor Maxwell called, and a rather pretty girl popped into the arena. Chezzy instantly recognized her as the girl who was in line with her mother and brother outside Ye Olde Book Machine. Her long, strawberry blonde hair flared in a rainbow as her skin and menders went shifting through many colors before settling into a timid and flushed pink. She approached Professor Tampago Brown, who adjusted the sensors, and then she flashed through hundreds of shades.

The screen above shone Faxowl, and she smiled politely to the burst of applause and cheers that continued while she turned crimson. Not the crimson of a blush but a pure and absolute crimson. It held and only changed after she had sat down with the other Faxowl students and attentions finally shifted back to the arena, to a girl whose name Chezzy had missed. But after her, came a boy who was apparently her brother, and both of them had some kind of tail, and they both went to Oxenbor to no one's surprise.

Afterwards, was Fever May, whose ability required a great deal of set up. A wall divider was brought in and placed in front of Professor Kepler. Fever walked over and looked at the director before positioning herself on the opposite side of the wall. Then Professor Kepler did a series of faces while Fever talked with Professor Maxwell. Without anyone being entirely certain what happened, Phrenbook appeared on the screen, to mostly scattered applause.

Then came a dark haired and dark skinned girl named Pey Nag who went to Sciofall. Chezzy had stared at her name, and the first bit of nervousness finally crept into his skin. He braced himself and watched Professor Maxwell belt out, "Mag Owen," and a boy some four rows behind Chezzy was sucked down and into the arena. For a moment, Chezzy was struck, his body frozen. He looked to the Oxenbor and Sciofall sections and saw Stuart and Fern with quizzical looks on their faces, but he averted his eyes and settled them on Professor Kepler.

The man held his gaze as they watched each other from across the arena all through Mag Owen's showing, which Chezzy caught none of. Professor Kepler gave Chezzy a comforting nod as the next student was brought down. All of the Showings after that passed in a haze. One in Faxowl, two in Phrenbook, one in Sciofall, one in Oxenbor, another for Sciofall, two more for Oxenbor, and another for Phrenbook. Chezzy's mind had withdrawn. The names, the applause, and the chanting all blended in the distance as they went on.

Fern's expression of concern had grown into a brow furrowed worry. Stuart kept looking around with his mouth open as if he didn't quite know who to ask what happened, but certain there was someone he was supposed to ask. Professor Kepler watched Chezzy calmly as each student was swallowed and spat and shown. Chezzy felt some kind of mirrored emotion with the man. Then, at long last, Nebulous Zee'han was called, and Chezzy was the last person left in the seats in his section.

Nebulous was a pretty girl with long, cascading, dark hair, a dusky complexion, and a prominent nose. She approached Professor Maxwell and Tampago Brown somewhat timidly. When Professor Tampago Brown signaled he was ready, the girl shut her eyes, and her hair swirled around her in a dark cloud. At once, Professor Maxwell, Professor Tampago Brown, Nebulous, and all of the nearby machinery that wasn't bolted down, lifted into the air. The crowd gave a riotous cheer, and a rather disgruntled looking Professor Tampago Brown was forced to kick off the large screen and away from the girl. He soared for a short bit and then crashed to the ground.

The professor looked up, alarmed, and Professor Kepler laughed, which earned him a further annoyed look from Professor Tampago Brown. Then Nebulous, Professor Maxwell, and the machinery all drifted back down and settled on the arena floor. The screen behind was already alight with the symbol and name of Phrenbook. Professor Maxwell had gone over to help Professor Tampago Brown up as the cheers broke out from the stands. Nebulous thanked them in an embarrassed manner then hurried to join the other Phrenbooks.

"Chezzy Nithercot," came Professor Maxwell's voice, and the cheering for Nebulous died and was replaced by an unnatural silence. All eyes flitted to where Chezzy sat just as a great sucking pressure opened beneath him, and he warped through and out into the arena. Voices started, a jumble of whispered speculation, as Chezzy looked up to Professor Maxwell above him. She reached down and took his hand to help him up. "It'll be fine," she whispered.

Tampago Brown was fiddling with the sensors, and he kept his eyes averted from Chezzy the whole while he was attaching them. There was something tense and very deliberate in his avoidance. Professor Kepler had come forward, and he leaned in. "I thought a blade would be best, you know, to demonstrate. Is that alright with you, Chezzy?"

"A blade?" Chezzy asked, alarmed.

"Yes, to show how you heal. Would that be alright with you? I don't suppose you'd like fire again, would you? Or perhaps we could blow you up or something?" Professor Kepler was smiling casually as if the conversation they were having was positively normal.

Doubt swept through Chezzy. None of this was real, and it had all been a fluke. He was just an orphan kid from Wutherford Home, and he didn't belong here at all. He should go back. Back to Sarah and Byron and his cronies. He knew how to deal with them. He looked up at Professor Kepler in a terrified silence, which the man must have taken for confirmation, because Professor Kepler was pointing his versolock at the ground and drawing a portal with it.

Through the purple beam of light, a rapier cut up into the air. The man caught it out as Chezzy went woozy. He spied Professor Maxwell and wanted to say something, but no words came. All around, was a smear of leering students beyond the glass. And as Professor Kepler lifted the sword, students were standing, crowding closer. There was something animal in Chezzy, desperate and dangerous, and he felt the sweat start all over him. But then a hand rested on his shoulder.

Chezzy looked up into the eyes of Professor Kepler, the one eyed ghost. His hand squeezed gently on Chezzy's shoulder, and the two of them were linked in just that moment. Chezzy opened his mouth to ask him to stop, but Professor Kepler didn't wait. He drove the rapier directly through Chezzy's chest and out his back. It exited with a spit of blood, and the whole stadium gave a gasp followed by several screams from students.

Chezzy stared at Professor Kepler as he withdrew the sword with a nod, then he dropped it to the ground, where it promptly vanished through another portal. Chezzy looked around. He could make out Fern's excited face and Stuart's confusion in the crowd. And he could see Veronica with her cool calculation. Everyone was silent now, but the crackling and sparking of the machines behind him drew his attention. Above shone Chiropa and its symbol, a skull with a multi cross crack.

The hole in Chezzy's mender closed up as he reached for it absently. His chest soon followed. But the screen glitched wildly as erratic sparks shot out. Smoke jumped from this device and that one, and Chezzy felt himself being pulled away by Professor Kepler. The data bits on the screen ran and were joined with other sub symbols, names, and other stats. But the whole thing was going haywire. Tampago Brown was running around trying to shut it all down, while Professor Maxwell screamed at him to leave it as she retreated with Professor Kepler and Chezzy. At last, the screen gave a final crack and died.

Chezzy felt Professor Maxwell's hand in his. She was leading him over to an empty section of the bleachers. He looked down at his menders. The Chiropa symbol had etched itself on his chest, though something about the image looked somewhat off, as if the machine's breakdown had affected it. Professor Maxwell opened a door in the wall and nudged him in. He took a seat in the empty section and looked back out. There was no cheering. Only murmurs spreading like wildfire. He spied Veronica Fayette, who sat still and ponderous, ever looking upon him. And he spied Fern Hudson who seemed to be trying to convey something to him, though he could not make it out. And then he spied Fair Jekyll, sat with a pained look of understanding.

At long last, Professor Maxwell spoke, and her voice boomed. "Please follow your versolocks to the dining lab for dinner." The students began to rise, and they filed out of the stands, the talk mounting amongst them.

Professor Kepler opened the door into Chezzy's section. "How are you?"

Chezzy shrugged. "I'm alright."

Professor Kepler seemed to understand this wasn't entirely the case. "I'll show you on."

Together, they walked up the stairs and into a hallway lit with the floating lanterns that drifted around the entire school. "What happens now?"

"What happens now is there are going to be a lot of eyes on you. That part will be hard in many ways and nice in others. Either way, you must keep doing what I've asked you to do. Nothing with that has changed."

"Find the Acid King."

"Exactly. Tonight even. After dinner."

Chezzy chewed this. "Did I break the Showing machine?"

They had drawn up to the end of the hall where a purple portal shifted on the wall. "It seems that way."

"How?"

Professor Kepler looked down at Chezzy. "It needed an overhaul anyway."

Chezzy's eyes went to the warped symbol on his menders. "I am an everling, though?"

Professor Kepler chuckled. "Without doubt. Now, go on. I'm sure you're starved."

Chezzy was, and he turned and stepped through the portal. He and Professor Kepler exited into a chamber right outside of the dining lab. They were joined by a mass of teachers and students filing through several other portals and halls. Upon seeing him, there was a general murmur and a sense that all were afraid to speak too loudly, lest Chezzy hear. They gave him a wide berth all the way to the large, zagging table of the dining lab.

Chezzy looked on as students quickly took seats and began spooning out heaps from the serving dishes on the table's slipstream. Professor Kepler gave Chezzy a nudge. "Go on and join them." Then he departed for his seat at the teacher and staff section. Chezzy looked over to the opposite end of the table which was largely avoided, so he headed for that and sat down.

"I swear it was one of them. It looked just like a branch, but it was running around," said a boy that Chezzy recognized as Metwell Chase.

"You're totally lying," added another Oxenbor whose name Chezzy couldn't remember, but he had a long, prehensile tail that flicked around. Both boys paused when they saw Chezzy, and their voices dropped. "Let's sit over here."

"Yeah," Metwell added as they moved away down the table.

Chezzy dropped his head and pretended to fiddle with something on his versolock.

"I know what it's like." The voice was light and warm and bubbling with a sort of trembling compassion. For a moment, he was reminded of Sarah.

"What?" Chezzy looked up and saw it was the strawberry blonde girl, whose hues were shifting from a normal color to a pale pink.

"I... Mm, I think everyone is just being really rude. That's what I mean. And it's just... I don't like the way they are reacting to this. Sorry." Her eyes went down embarrassedly, her tone running dark. "I don't know what to say about it. Is it okay if I sit with you?"

"Sure," Chezzy hastily drew out the chair next to him.

"Thank you." She sat down and took a roll from the conveyor then began nibbling nervously. She chanced a furtive look to Chezzy and saw that he was watching her. "I'm Fair."

"Do what?"

"Fair, mm," she giggled. "Fair Jekyll."

"Right. That's what Professor Maxwell called you. For the Showing."

"Right, she did call me by my name." She gave Chezzy another embarrassed look. "Not a made up one." But a group of students who were set nearest to them were mumbling to each other and shooting scrutinizing scans to Chezzy with their versolocks. Fair looked mortified, and she shook her head. "They're just scared, you know?"

"Yeah. Right."

"Really, they are. Most of them have never seen one of, of, mm, you, before. So, it's," she shrugged, "it's silly. Isn't it?"

"Have you seen one of me before?"

"Sure, at... well..."

"There you are," Stuart exhaled as he appeared across from them and plopped down opposite at the table. "I was looking all over the other side for you. That girl, what was her name? Feen? Anyway, she was over there looking for you too." Stuart suddenly realized that Fair was there, and he hesitated, going wide eyed at her. "Hello, Miss. I'm Stuart. Stuart Fieldmore Jr."

"Hi," she ventured back. "Fair Jekyll."

"Wicked name. Everyone from here has wicked names. Don't they?" Stuart scratched his face then grabbed a whole platter of toasted breads from the conveyor. "How come, do you suppose?"

"It was because of the first people down here," said Fern, coming out of nowhere as she sat on the other side of Chezzy.

"Feen," Stuart greeted gregariously, his arms extended and the word, likewise.

"Fern," she corrected with a frown but barely acknowledged Stuart or Fair outside of that. "Part of the reconstruction of commonality. But, more importantly, are you doing alright?" She had spoken almost harshly to Stuart, but her voice softened and slowed when she redirected to Chezzy.

"Yeah, I'm fine."

"Did you know?" She adjusted her glasses with a roll of her eyes. "Of course, you knew. This will cause havoc. You know, everyone thought it was some silly rumor, but it's real. Really real. Do you need anything?"

"No. I'm fine." Chezzy looked across the dining lab to Professor Kepler. He followed the man's gaze which rested on the boy, Turod, where he ate with Minny Deerwink. When Chezzy looked back to Professor Kepler, the man was staring right at him. They shared a brief moment, then Professor Kepler gave a wink and returned to his meal.

"The Sciofalls are all upset," Fern was saying, "but they're being ridiculous. You want to do something after the feasting?"

"I'm…" Chezzy thought of what Professor Kepler had said to him. "I've been sort of exploring the Keris, so I thought I'd keep doing that."

"Mm, we could come with you," Fair chimed in.

"I mean, so long as we don't get into trouble, you know," Stuart cautioned. "I don't want to break any rules or anything. Oh, my, I haven't even seen a rule list or, or, oh." He gave a little start as his versolock squeaked up in a high pitched voice and projected out a list of rules, expellable offenses, and other pertinent information. "Oh, I have to look this over. No one told me. Honest."

"Oh, leave it," snapped Fern, and Stuart looked rather stricken. "Classes don't even start till tomorrow. Let's do it." She nudged Chezzy with her elbow.

"Yeah?" Chezzy wasn't certain if it was a good idea to bring them along or not.

"Yay," Fair exclaimed and then giggled again.

Stuart, who had been attempting to surreptitiously read the list from his versolock, realized that the others were looking at him. "Oh, all right," he surrendered.

XIV.
Map.
The bot room.
With Acres androids.

*P*rofessor Maxwell rose from the table and addressed the students. "I know we've had a very exciting first day. I'm equally certain you're now feeling extremely stuffed, and classes are the furthest things from your minds. However, they do begin tomorrow, so I suggest you make your way to your dormitories and get a good night's rest. Please review any rules on your versolocks, and if you have any questions, consult your dorm AI." She sat back down and fell into a private conversation with Professor Kepler.

Students were rising and filtering out of the dining lab, following their projected directions to their respective sections of the Keris. "Come on," ushered Fern.

"Hold up," said Stuart. "It says here we have a curfew." He shoved his versolock forward for Fern to see.

She didn't look at it. "I know what it says. I'm sure she knows what it says too," and she jerked a thumb towards Fair.

"I do," added Fair with a nod.

"But who cares?"

"I mean I do, a little," added Fair timidly.

Fern shot her a stern look. "Yeah, well, we have plenty of time before curfew. Besides, are you going to spend all school year following the rules?"

"I thought I was," said Stuart. He was looking back and forth between each of them. Every time he paused over Chezzy as if to ask for help.

"No, no. Stop that," Fern went on. "You realize what a maze this place is? I doubt anyone has explored the entire layout."

"What if we get lost?" Stuart asked.

"What?" Fern shot back. "We have versolocks."

"And I have a map," piped in Chezzy.

"You what?" asked both Fair and Fern in unison.

"I have a map? Of the Keris. It's on my versolock."

"No one is supposed to have access to a map of the Keris. They're very strict about that," said Fern disbelievingly.

"What? Why not? Doesn't every versolock have it to navigate?"

"Our navigations are accessed through routers in the Keris. The routers tell our versolocks where to go. They don't just know or have their own map. I don't think they're supposed to remember either. And even if they were to remember, the Keris changes its layout regularly. It was a safety precaution instituted when it was first built," Fair explained. "You see, it does randomized resets and layouts throughout the year. And only certain operating systems know what the layout is at any given moment. And, only versolocks that are tied to the Keris, those belonging to students and faculty, are able to access the routers and their nav programs in order to navigate through it. No one should have access to an actual map." Fair shrugged.

Chezzy looked from her to Fern who nodded. "She's right."

"Well, what's this then?" Chezzy brought up his versolock, and the Keris map projected out.

Fern and Fair's eyes went big, and Fern quickly gripped her hands around Chezzy's versolock to block the projection. She was looking around in a panic. "You can't... don't..." She took a deep breath. "Don't show that to people." She loosened her grip to see that the map was gone, then she grinned at Chezzy. "Oh, this is excellent." She patted Chezzy's versolock fondly. "This is really good," she laughed. "Come on, let's go."

They slipped out of the dining lab and managed to sneak down a hallway where they stowed away in a storage closet of some kind, while they listened to the dying babble of students and teachers. "Did you see what time it is?" hissed Stuart.

"Shh," admonished Fern.

"It's going to be okay," added Fair, and she patted Stuart's arm comfortingly. He stared at her dumbfounded, and Chezzy wondered if Stuart had ever really spent any time with anyone outside of his family.

"Hey, let's see it again," Fern said to Chezzy.

"Yeah, sure," and he lifted his versolock and projected the map.

"How did you get that?" Fair asked.

"My dorm AI gave it to me."

"Really?" Fair seemed to be processing this new bit of information.

"Professor, uh, Maxy whatever said something about that too. What is it?" Stuart asked.

"Toppers," muttered Fern. "Every school sub has an Artificial Intelligence that runs their dorms and helps with all kinds of things. You'll have one in Oxenbor too. It'll link up with your versolock when you get there. You'll see."

"Oh," replied Stuart, but he was shaking his head at Chezzy and mouthing "What?" to him.

"There's no way they're just giving these out now."

"No," added Fair.

"I mean, it must be because you're you. I guess."

Chezzy shrugged. "It could be. I still don't really understand what, you know, being me means." He felt a pang of panic as he wondered if Professor Kepler had given him the map just to look for whoever was hiding here, and maybe he'd be upset that he showed it to other students.

Fair gave a little laugh. "I'm not sure anyone does yet."

"Do you hear that?" asked Fern.

"Is it a teacher?" Stuart's spines flexed out.

Fern frowned. "No. It's silence. I think they're all gone now. So, where to, Chezzy?"

Despite what he was feeling, Chezzy grinned. "Well, there's this weird bot room and then there was a hallway with-"

"What do you mean bot room?" Fern interrupted.

"It, well, it had a bunch of androids or something in it. It was right here." Chezzy pointed to a room on his projected map. He couldn't see any SIs near it, and he felt relieved.

"Bot room?" Fern looked around.

"Bot room," Fair returned with a shrug.

"Bot room," Fern said decidedly. "We're doing bot room."

The floating lanterns in the hallway were dimmed low for the evening. Normally, when you bumped into them, they would excuse themselves, but when you did it in the evening, they would whisper their pardons. They bobbed along as the four of them made their way through the Keris. They were following the projected arrows on the floor that came from Chezzy's versolock. They were mostly quiet, too, though Stuart kept getting nervously close to walls or lanterns, and he would scrape his spines, which would screech against the metal. The girls did their best to corral him while Chezzy marched them along.

Inwardly, Chezzy hoped they didn't come anywhere near whoever was hiding down here. Not while they were with him. But every time his versolock toggled the directions off because someone was nearby, Chezzy's heart leapt. The group would scramble to hide until they could look back at the map. Chezzy eyed the dots, and Fern scooted in close. "Roving Heisenberg, I think those are other versolocks," she mumbled. "See, that's us. You're the black dot. I'm the maroon dot. Stuart is the blue dot. And Fair is that purply dot that keeps changing color. They're just like our menders."

"Can we be done with this already, guys?" Stuart glanced back at his own versolock to check the time, then he let out an oddly animal sigh.

"Would you calm down already? Look at this thing. We aren't going to get caught. We can see everyone that's coming our way. Right?" She looked to Chezzy, but Chezzy was watching a yellow dot that was lingering somewhere behind them.

"We should go," Chezzy said.

"Thank you," exclaimed Stuart in a voice that was at once quiet and loud.

"No, not to the dorms. We need to keep moving, though." Chezzy looked at the yellow dot again and thought of what Kepler had said about the Acid King not appearing on the map. Then, with a jolt, he realized that may no longer be the case with Mantuckit Porview in the sanitorium.

"Oh." The disappointment in Stuart's voice was immeasurable.

Chezzy hurried ahead, and the other three were quick to follow. They took a turn and then another before going down a slipstream. As they slid down the walkway, Chezzy popped the map up again. The dot had been keeping pace. Chezzy clenched his mouth. "Come on, the bot room is right over here."

He took them down another hall and around a corner before accessing the door to the bot room. It was near all dark inside, but the chamber was massive, featuring what appeared to be hundreds of androids and assorted piles of electronics. Chezzy's versolock lit up of its own accord, shining a great beam across the huddled mass of lookalike bots. The other versolocks lit up likewise.

"Oh, man," exclaimed Fern. "These are decommissioned Acres androids. What are they still doing with Acres androids?"

"I can't believe they kept them," muttered Fair somberly. Chezzy brought back out his map just as Stuart bumped his spines into one of the bots, toppling it over and sending pieces of the thing scattering across the floor.

"Could you keep quiet for five ticks?" Fern scolded.

"Look at that," said Fair as she approached a pile of burnt electronics and robots stuffed in one corner. They were mostly in bits. "This is weird. The damage isn't… mm, I wonder what happened."

"Hard to say. It's all burnt." Fern kicked through bits with the toe of her menders.

Fair picked up a discolored metal and glass tube. "What do you think, Chezzy?"

Chezzy looked up from the map, deactivating it as he did. The yellow dot had gone into another room back up the hall a ways. "What's that?"

"What do you think it is?" Fair asked again.

Chezzy stepped forward and reached a hand out to take the tube, but as soon as his fingers touched it, a green spark let out. "Whoa."

"What was that?" Stuart near yelled.

"Could you keep it down?" Fern shook her head. "Unbelievable."

Fair had set the tube back down, wary of being shocked herself as she looked over Chezzy. "Are you okay?"

"Yeah."

"Oh, of course you are," then she smacked herself in the head lightly, her skin swirling red. "Forgot."

"I forget too."

"You forget to die?" Fern asked. She had cracked open the head of a bot and was looking inside. They laughed. Even Stuart managed a nervous chuckle as he huddled against a wall, afraid to touch anything.

"I forget I can't die."

"I guess you'll outlive us all. It's strange to think about. Like, you'll be around when my children are grown and my children's children. And on," Fair mused. "You know, I messaged my mom about you when everyone found out for sure. She was pretty excited."

"I saw your mom," Chezzy revealed.

"Really?"

"I saw you and her and your brother at Saidbury. I didn't see your dad, though."

Fair, who had gone from shadow dimness to neon shifts of colors now drifted back into a dark hue. "My dad's gone."

"Oh, no," Stuart whispered.

"Sorry. My dad's gone too. I guess," Chezzy added.

Fair let out a small laugh, despite her disposition. "I'm sorry. That isn't funny. I shouldn't laugh," but she was smiling all the same. "Do you know who they were?"

Just then, a scurrying drew their attention as a little figure ran nearby. Fair whirled then let out a nervous laugh.

"What is that?" Stuart screamed.

"Shh," Chezzy cautioned him.

"It's one of those twig folk. I know they have them on the grounds somewhere," Fair giggled in relief.

"Are they dangerous?" Stuart's voice had dropped overtly low.

"Not when we have big, scary you around," Fern scoffed. She had pulled the innards of the android head out, and she twirled them in her hand as she scrutinized it all closely.

"They're fine," Fair assured. "They're just little humanoid animals. Little guy probably just got lost."

Just then, Chezzy's versolock burst out with the map again, and Chezzy's eyes flitted to it. The yellow dot was right outside the bot room door. "No," he gasped.

"What is it?" Stuart quaked.

"I think we're being followed," Chezzy said.

"What?" Stuart's voice rose.

"By who?" Fern asked, turning from the android she was deconstructing. She looked to have pocketed some bits of it.

"Hide," Chezzy ordered. In unison, their versolock lights went out just as the door to the room opened, letting in a new light. It crossed the four of them, and Stuart's eyes flashed with animal brightness, his needles flexing and relaxing over and over. Chezzy felt Fair's hand on him. She was pushing him back toward the corner with her finger across her lips. Fern and Stuart followed at a painstakingly slow rate. Chezzy could see a shadowy figure across the room moving through the androids, but it didn't appear to have seen them, yet.

Fair had taken ahold of Stuart, and she positioned him behind Chezzy and told him to huddle down and curl up. "Keep your eyes closed," she added. Chezzy felt the rise and fall of Stuart's breath by the prick of needles against his back. A clank of metal sounded off from somewhere in the room, but Chezzy could no longer see the figure. Fair froze for a moment, then she moved Fern against the front of Chezzy. After that, she leaned back against Fern, all of them positioned in this weird line. She was there a moment, and then she was not.

She had blended completely, but she was still there. Chezzy could just make out the sound of her soft breaths. Stuart trembled behind him, his needles pressed further into Chezzy's back. He was certain they were breaking the skin. Fern let out an almost annoyed sigh, and for a moment, Chezzy had to fight the urge to laugh. But then there were footsteps nearby, and Chezzy wondered if this was, indeed, the one who was hiding down here.

"I know you are here." The voice was familiar and Chezzy could see that whoever it was, was not ten paces away. Slight and small, the figure went on, meandering the bots. "I am going to report you. I already submitted a message to Professor Maxwell. She should be here any moment. If you do not turn yourselves in, you will probably get expelled."

Stuart's body tensed violently against Chezzy's back then fell to terrible shakes. The needles were working deep into his skin, and he tried to nudge his elbow back at Stuart, but it returned, likewise pricked. It occurred to Chezzy that Stuart's needles could possibly go right through him and maybe into or through Fern too. Chezzy shuddered, and Fern flashed him back a quizzical look, but the figure had drawn closer, shining forth a sporadic strobe of lights.

The lights glinted right across the group of them with Fair completely unseen. The figure paced right to left and back again, stopping here and there to flash out those lights, and then there

162

was nothing but the soft sound of steps somewhere unseen. Chezzy held his breath and listened to the movement. A straight beam shot out far to his right, and he watched it wave around and then settle on a panel near the door. The light clicked off, and there were more steps.

Chezzy could just almost make out the figure at the panel doing something. Lights around the room flashed on of a sudden. It was like daylight, but cast as they were, Chezzy still could not see Fair. He did, however, see Veronica Fayette turn from the opened panel, a tangle of reconfigured wires visibly spliced. She scanned, her eyes, roving slowly. They looked directly at Chezzy, where he held Fern, huddled against the back of Stuart, and then they went on. She passed them over several times, in fact, but never actually saw them.

Veronica sighed angrily, and she kicked over a nearby android. Mumbling, she kicked over another and another. Then she picked up broken parts and began throwing them about the room in a fit. Chezzy glanced back to Stuart who was cradling his face in his hands as he shook. He looked as if his fear was building into a frenzy, and Chezzy tried to nudge him as he whispered. "Stuart?" He felt Fern jab an elbow into his stomach. "Something's wrong," he whispered to her.

"She's going to hear you," she hissed back.

Veronica was still storming around, lobbing android heads. She was talking to herself or perhaps to her versolock as the device was talking too, the both of them overlapping one another. She picked up a shoe, or perhaps a foot, and hurled it, flying right for them. Chezzy reached his hand out to catch it, but Fern grabbed his arm back down.

The foot smacked across Stuart's back as Chezzy wriggled free and threw his arms out, not for the shoe, but to cover as much of Fern and Fair as he could. Stuart gave a yelp as a jolt of spines shot out with impaling force. Chezzy felt his back break out in pricks, but he clutched his mouth against the pain, with only a whimper escaping.

J. Christie

Veronica Fayette had stopped and was looking to where they were hidden. Then she headed over, her pace quickening. Chezzy was sliding to the floor, and Fern turned to ease him down quietly. Chezzy couldn't see any needles that had hit her, but he didn't yet know about Fair. All he could see was Veronica as she pushed another android out of her way.

It crashed into a little vat of some kind, which cracked and leaked out a noxious liquid that sizzled against the android. Chezzy felt a chill run through him, and he wondered if it was the same type that Penton Fulcrank had found. Veronica had paused, having knelt, and was hovering the back of her hand over the chemical. Smoke was coming up, and the android's skin was melting right off of it. But the door at the far side slid open, and Veronica whirled around.

"What do you think you're doing?" Professor Tampago Brown asked, standing in the door with a keen look.

"Professor," Veronica began, "there is someone here. I, I followed Chezzy Nithercot down here with his friends. I think they are in here, and I found this. Look." She was gesturing at the spilt chemical.

Professor Tampago Brown took weighted steps forward, a curious talent given his small size. He glanced an eye to the acid then back to Veronica. Then he lifted his wrist and did something on his versolock. "With me," he said to Veronica.

"What?"

Professor Tampago Brown raised an eyebrow. "Come with me."

"Professor, I think they are still in here. Hiding or, or, listen, they are in here. I know it."

He lifted a hand and motioned his fingers at her. "And the room will be checked. Now, mind the spill."

"But Professor-"

"It wasn't a suggestion, Miss Fayette. You will come with me, and we will discuss a fitting length for your detention." He turned and strode to the door.

164

Chezzy could see that Veronica was shaking with anger, but she followed after the man without further argument before the door zipped shut behind them.

"We have to get out of here," said Fern. She was already yanking the needles out of Chezzy, heedless of their barbs. Chezzy grunted with pain at each one.

"I'm sorry, guys," Stuart was saying in a wheeze. Fair appeared before them, startling the others. She was sinking to the ground, though, with one of Stuart's needles protruding out of her arm. Stuart turned a sickly color.

"I'm fine," Chezzy was saying to Fern. "Get to her. I'll be just fine."

Fern spun over to Fair and looked at her arm. "Can I just yank it like yours, Chezzy?"

"No. The hooks." Chezzy stopped. His versolock lit up with the map automatically. He could see the dots of Veronica and Tampago Brown far down the hall and leaving. He glared at the yellow dot, but there was another, unknown versolock right outside the bot room door. A green dot. "Shh," Chezzy cautioned, and all looked to the map.

Fair was rising again, tears in her eyes, and she was shaking all over, but she vanished. Chezzy's map slipped away as the door opened, and the group of them rearranged themselves to hide behind Fair. Chezzy peered through her, and he watched as Professor Kepler stepped into the room. The man's eyes automatically fixed on the corner, and he gave a sort of grim smile. Chezzy felt the color drain from his face.

"It's alright," he said. "They've gone. Fair, you can relax now."

Fair appeared once more, the colors pumping back into her face. Her legs were pressed against Fern's front as she collapsed back. Her arm was bleeding even more, and she was covered in sweat and looks of apology.

"Fair?" asked Stuart as he stood up behind Chezzy. He was breaking down, and he didn't seem to care that Kepler was there. "Oh, no. Oh, dear. What have I... what have I done?"

J. Christie

"It's quite alright, Fieldmore." Professor Kepler sounded cold, and he knelt down next to Fair when he reached her. He worked the needle out expertly then produced something in his hand. Chezzy recognized the unknife, and Professor Kepler was drawing it across Fair's arm. It healed neatly, and he began clearing out the blood that was on her colorful skin before her mender moved back over the spot. "That's some trick you got there, little bit."

Fair was nodding her head. "It's hard to… to…"

"I know. I know," said Professor Kepler. "Here," he offered her the unknife, "it'd be better for you to hold on to that."

Fair took it in her near delirious exhaustion. "Am I in trouble?"

"No." Professor Kepler stood. "Stuart Fieldmore?"

"Yes, sir?"

"Can you lift her?"

"I, yes. Yes, I can."

"Good. Then could you and Miss Hudson here take Fair to her dorm before reporting to your own? You'll find a route uploaded to your versolocks that I assure you is entirely devoid of," he cleared his throat, "obstacles."

"Yes, sir," said Stuart, then he lifted Fair easily from the ground. He looked down at Fair and then up at Professor Kepler. "Are the rest of us in terribly bad trouble, sir?"

Professor Kepler relaxed and chuckled to himself. "No. No, you aren't in any trouble. Not yet, anyway. Though I wouldn't let Brown catch you out." He was watching Chezzy.

"Oh," replied Stuart.

Fern was studying Professor Kepler. "But we broke curfew. It's against the rules."

"Yes, the rules, well," and he opened his hands in a half shrug, and then he chuckled again. "You really ought to get her back. She did a lot tonight, though you might not really realize it, and I need to have a word with Chezzy here."

"Okay," said Fern as she shot Chezzy a concerned look.

"Yes, sir," added Stuart. He paused and looked at Chezzy then spoke through near gritting teeth. "Thanks for, for blocking them."

Chezzy nodded to Stuart. "Done it before."

XV.
Eidolon.
Slipped by.
A hole in my head.

Chezzy rose and watched as the others carried Fair out of the bot room, but as soon as the door whooshed shut, he whipped back to Kepler with a blurt. "I didn't tell them what I was really doing."

Professor Kepler paused a beat. "You can tell them what you're doing. But I'd keep it between you lot and not go spreading it around any further."

"Really?"

He nodded.

"But, why can I tell them? Isn't that… well, wouldn't that be bad?"

"Why? You don't think they could be helpful?"

Chezzy shrugged. "Just seems dangerous."

Professor Kepler near laughed. "You know what's dangerous? Brown. He won't care for this little treasonous action."

"He'll know?"

"Oh, he'll find out."

"What will he do then?"

Professor Kepler leaned closer to Chezzy. "It doesn't matter, really." Then he laughed quite loudly before his face sort of turned sad.

"Professor?"

"Yes?" He leveled his eyes back to Chezzy.

"How did you know we were here?"

"Maybe yours isn't the only versolock that tells him extra things. Or maybe I always knew, you know?" He tapped his head suggestively.

"Is that why we aren't in trouble? Do you want me to mind the curfew?"

"Oh, no. What's a curfew? Chezzy, the task I gave you takes a heavy priority. And, not only that, but I want you to learn everything you can. Everything about this place. Everything this place has. I want only the world resting in your mind... The rules... don't matter. But for right now, you should be off. Tampago Brown is on his way back here, and it's better if you aren't here when he arrives, you know."

Chezzy nodded, but he felt uneasy. He didn't really understand what Professor Kepler was up to. He pointed to the tipped vat and the chemical. "Is that..."

"The Acid King?"

"Yes."

"No, that's just his acid."

Chezzy stifled a laugh. "So, the Acid King was here?"

"Perhaps." Professor Kepler regarded the vat for a moment. "Who knows what Acid Kings get up to."

Chezzy left the director amongst the old androids and followed the arrows lighting his way back to the everling tower. There, he trudged through the beachfront that was his dorm, though he paused to look at the ocean waves crashing against the back of the lavaplace. He was hungry and thought to ask Raven if he could get anything from Chef Scasbor in the kitchen, but he decided against it and instead, rode up the slipstream to crawl into his bed. It was a fitful night of sleep, and it stayed with him into the morning, worsened by the sandstorm in the common room.

He spent forever trying to navigate through the storm, blindly searching for the exit, before he finally made it out. He shook sand off of him while Bogdanov cackled from his nearby corner. He wished he knew how to do the cleanup thing that Professor Kepler had done as it took forever to remove the grit from his menders. Eventually, he raced down, realizing he didn't even have time for breakfast, which pained him as he had woken with an aching belly.

Chezzy chased the lit up lines and positively flew into the classroom where Professor Sappmo was projecting a list of students for Versolock Unveiled. Professor Sappmo looked from his list to Chezzy. "Right, we have you today." He sported a rather flat countenance that betrayed nothing.

"Right," Chezzy mumbled back as he looked around the room. He had this lesson with the Phrenbooks and Sciofalls, and he was relieved to see Fern waving him over to an empty seat beside her. He rushed past the Phrenbook students, who were isolating themselves as best they could, and sat with her. "Is Fair okay?" he asked Fern in a whisper. His eyes caught sight of a glaring Veronica Fayette, who was turned around from near the front of the class.

"Yeah. She was fine. She was talking loads by the time we got her to the Faxowl dorms."

"That's really good. I was worried."

"Yeah, but what happened with Professor Kepler?"

Another wave of dread swept over him at the prospect of telling her and the others about the Acid King. Professor Sappmo cleared his throat and stared directly at Fern and Chezzy.

"Tell me about it later," mumbled Fern.

Other students turned to look at them both, but Chezzy held the man's gaze. The professor was older with the thinning sides and back of his greying hair cropped close. His face was mostly hidden by a large, grey beard, and he sported some many pocketed menders over his heavyset frame that were in a shade of light green. "I am Professor Sappmo, and this is Versolock Unveiled," he went on in a drawling voice.

"Oh, this is very exciting," Fern whispered.

"Now, while I go through this list of names, please ping my versolock and let me know what model you have. You do remember what models you have, don't you?" There was a general babble of affirmation, and Professor Sappmo held up his hand for silence. "That's good, that's good. If you don't, then ask the machine and the machine will tell you. But before-"

Several students had just asked their versolocks, and there was a sudden, loud mix of voices as all of the versolocks answered at once. Professor Sappmo gave a mildly exasperated look, took a deep breath, then continued, "before you all ask at once, I want all of your versolocks on whisper mode, and I want you to wait your turn. That way, when you ask, you can hear what it has to say. If you don't want it said aloud then have the machine message it to you, and you can forward that to me. If you don't know how to do these things," he was accessing something on his own versolock, "here's the little tutorial to walk you through your settings mode. But don't touch anything that we aren't talking about yet. I don't want another student exploding."

A round of nervous laughter swept through the room but died quickly as Professor Sappmo stared out at the students without smiling. "Speaking of blowing up," Professor Sappmo went on, "if you are having issues with your versolock, do not, I repeat, do not contact Mantuckit Porview for assistance. Mantuckit Porview, who I'm sure all of you purchased your versolocks from, is no longer in business as I understand. So, if there is an issue, please come to me or to Tech McGeehee. But probably me."

Professor Sappmo noticed there was a hand up in the front row. He gestured and Veronica Fayette spoke in a very clear voice. "Is it true that Mantuckit Porview is now at Kellogg's Sanitorium?"

Professor Sappmo gave her a steady gaze before proceeding in his slow, drawn tone. "I am not privy as to Mantuckit Porview's current living situation. Nor do I care where Mantuckit Porview's living situation is. I am here for one thing and one thing only and that is to teach you how to operate your versolock. So, when I call your name, you tell me your model. Understood?"

The class mumbled an affirmation.

"Good." Professor Sappmo began calling out the names.

It became very quickly clear that almost every student in the class had a Bangle or a Cuff, though the models were all slightly different. But when Professor Sappmo called out Chezzy's name, and he responded with, "Eidolon... Model Zero," the class gave a start, and Professor Sappmo paused notably before proceeding.

"You have an Eidolon, Model Zero?" hissed Fern when she was certain that Professor Sappmo wasn't watching.

"I... yeah?" replied Chezzy. "Is that really good or something? I don't really know what the differences are."

"Really good or something?" Her voice had raised an octave, and a few students nearby glanced around at her. "Mantuckit Porview only made a couple of Eidolons. Just a couple. I'm not sure anyone has ever even had one. Maybe that's why-"

"Miss Hudson, would you like to teach the class?"

Both Fern and Chezzy's heads whipped over to Professor Sappmo, and Fern gave an astute, "No, do you need me to?" in return. Her voice was more frank than worried.

A brief smile slipped across the man's face, buried in his beard, before he continued in a serious tone. "Alright, then, well, as I was saying," but Professor Sappmo paused as he caught sight of Chezzy's hand stuck in the air. "Nithercot?"

"What makes my versolock so different from the other versolocks?" He was thinking back to the night before and wondering if he and Fern were thinking the same thing.

"How long have you had your versolock? Two weeks? Three? Something like that, I bet. How long have you been interacting with other versolocks? Days? If that. I assure, as the class continues, you'll learn full well the difference between yours and everyone else's. As will everyone in the class."

"But can't you just tell me the differences now?" Everyone went still, and it was completely silent in the classroom. It seemed like the other students were eager to hear what the Eidolon could do too.

Professor Sappmo let out a strange chuckle that went on for just a little too long. "It's going to take a lot longer than a few pointed sentences to explain the full capabilities of the device on yours or anyone else's wrist. Especially yours, as I believe there may well be only two or three people left in the entire world that know exactly what they can do. And even those people might not know the entire extent of it. Were they not mad from vagrancy or... disputes with other people."

"I see," said Chezzy.

"Now, might I continue with the class, or do you have any other questions that you would like to ask?"

Chezzy opened his mouth, but Fern near laughed next to him, and he thought better of it. "Go ahead," he said instead, mimicking Fern's earlier tone. Then he exchanged a smile with Fern before noticing that Veronica Fayette was still turned around and staring at him. Her eyes were black ice, and she didn't waiver until Professor Sappmo began speaking again.

He spent the rest of the class briefing the students with an overview of the lessons to come as well as how to access their versolock menus, options, and settings, which included an area where you could name your versolock.

"Name them?" Tan Beauford had blurted out. "I'm calling mine Bad Boy Beef, no doubt."

"Toppers," mumbled another Phrenbook.

"Careful," Professor Sappmo had warned, "once you name them, it is permanent, and individuals are seldomly issued a completely new versolock."

"What?" Tan Beauford asked. "You mean I can't just go and buy a new one if I want to? That's daft."

"You can, or you could... either way, the profile of your first will come with it. So, think about that before you go with Bad Boy Beef or something else like that. I, in fact, know a grown man whose versolock is named Farts McBlow." All of the students had a fair laugh at this, but, when they quieted down, Professor Sappmo continued. "Yes, but imagine how difficult it is for him in the workplace or in his social circles. The name comes up more than you think. But by all means," he gestured at Tan, "go with Bad Boy Beef."

As they left the class, Fern was playing with her versolock, and suddenly Chezzy's own versolock lit up. "There," she said, "that's my schedule. Sync it up with yours, and we can see what other classes we have together. I have to run off to my maths class right now, but when I see you at lunch, we can compare. And you can tell me all about what happened with Professor Kepler. Or just message me during class. It's an easy one, so I can spare to be a little distracted." Then, with a flashing smile, she ran off to join the rest of the Sciofalls filtering down a slipstream.

As he watched her go, Veronica Fayette bumped into him. "Excuse me," she mumbled curtly.

"It's fine," said Chezzy feeling very cold of a sudden and noticing that she wasn't exactly moving on.

"I know you were in that room last night. Out past curfew. I am going to be scrubbing tanks in the genetics lab for weeks. Do you realize how many detentions I received for getting caught?"

"No. How many?"

She made a disgusted face. "You are going to be sorry about that."

"For you being out past curfew?" For a moment, Chezzy was sure she was going to spit on him, but the flush in her face seemed to dissipate before she spoke again.

"How is it you came to be?"

"Do what?"

"Who are your parents? Mother and father said your kind had not been having children for years. They said they are uncertain how one managed to slip by." The look on her face wasn't exactly mean anymore, but it was cold.

"Slip by?"

"If one slipped by then how many others might have? Well, I am sure the molers will come for you or any others. They did for all of the rest, now, right?" Then she pushed on past Chezzy and continued after the rest of Sciofall sub.

"Molers." Chezzy repeated as he looked down to his versolock in order to access his navigation to his next class. He looked at the device a moment. "I bet Raven would like it if I named you," he said to the versolock.

"Yes," boomed the versolock, frightening a straggling Phrenbook student who flinched, wide eyed, and hurried away down the hall.

"Oh, I would," came the voice of Raven, also from his versolock.

Chezzy gave his wrist an annoyed look. "You're always in there. Shouldn't you be in the dorm?"

"I can be in both," she said, indignantly, and Chezzy gave a sigh. He went about accessing Fern's schedule and trying to sync up both of theirs before hurrying after the lights and lines leading him to Controlled Physics.

He had this class with the Faxowl and Phrenbook students, which he was really pleased about as he was eager to check on Fair. He found her milling around the classroom with the other students, and she turned nearly purple when she saw him before sidling up. "Sit with me, will you?"

"Yeah. Of course. But are you okay?" Chezzy asked.

"Oh, I'm fine. See?" she whispered and showed him the faint mark where Stuart's needle had pierced. "We were more worried about you. I mean, they can't really suspend you, but what kind of trouble did you get into?"

"None, really."

"None? And Professor Kepler?"

"He wasn't mad at all. He just told me to watch out for Professor Tampago Brown and…" Chezzy caught his tongue before spilling anything about the Acid King. He just wasn't ready for that yet. "And that's it."

"That's really curious." Fair seemed to be chewing this over before brushing it aside. "We should grab a table. Come on." The classroom was surrounded by descending rows of chairs and metal tables that went down to a stage of sorts. Chezzy and Fair took seats near the top row and looked around but didn't see Professor Benhearst. "This is exciting. I've been looking forward to Controlled Physics. Maybe you haven't, though. Anyways, I'm glad we're in here together."

"I'm glad too, but I really don't know what this class is for."

"Oh," Fair laughed. "In here, we learn more about how we affect other things or even how they affect us. It'll be fun." She was beaming, twisting shades of gold. "Might not be the most useful class for you, but I guess that's what your Practicum is for."

Chezzy found himself feeling very fond of her shade shifts as she spoke. Her emotions, words, even nuanced movements seemed to add or detract colors and cause changes. She was a constantly evolving painting. And every now and again, she would become self aware, and her color would shift back to a more natural one, if only briefly. "What's my Practicum?"

"Each sub has a Practicum. It's where you, as an individual, really get to experiment with what you can do with your abilities. So, our Practicum, that is, the Faxowl Practicum, is the class Projection Over All with Professor Kettlewack. But that's not till Fahberday. Oh," Fair's colors went in a bright flourish. "I just remembered. A bunch of students were talking about the Sidelight trip this weekend. Do you want to…?"

"Want to what?"

"Want to go together?"

"Sure. What is it?

"Oh, it's a fair town nearby. It's loads of fun. So long as we don't have too much homework, I'm sure we could go and check it out."

"Yeah."

Just then, Chezzy's versolock lit up and said in its bone shaking voice, "You have a message," which startled many of the nearby students.

"Sorry," said Chezzy, checking it. "Any chance you can be quieter?" he grumbled to the versolock.

"I can," it boomed back.

"Right," murmured Chezzy. He pulled up the message and saw that it was from Fern confirming that she got his sync. "Hey," he looked up to Fair. "Fern and I synced up our schedules so we would know which classes we have together. Do you... do you want to do that too? You know, so we know."

She went a shade of scarlet and nodded. "Sure. You know, so we know."

Students nearby became distracted by a disturbance on the stage below, drawing the attention of Chezzy and Fair. Darkness, like smoke, was drifting across the platform, eating away at the visible light there. There was a collective intake of air as everyone held their breath and watched the darkness spread out to the edges of the stage, across the floor, billowing to the first row of desks. The students that were sat there leapt to their feet and backed up to the second row, where those students were already rising to flee.

The darkness stopped, though, and it pulled back until it seemed to suck onto the body of a very petite woman wearing goggles who stood in the center of the stage. She had a black, sleeveless mender, and the receding darkness had come to rest in swirls etched across her pale arms. The undulating darkness traced up to her neck and fed out to her hair, which itself was merely a mass of twisting black smoke.

Professor Benhearst raised the goggles to her forehead and pointed a long finger at a spot on the stage. The students' heads turned in unison, and Chezzy spied a palm sized gathering of darkness. When she spoke, it was in a hissing and halting cadence that was painful for Chezzy to follow. "How... we... interact... with... the world... changes... the world. What... we... put forth... may... modify... permanently. May...

destroy… absolutely. May… create… unapologetically. We must… be… deliberate… in our… actions. We must… weigh… our… actions… accordingly. We… owe… our… consideration… to society… to nature… to the world… at large. You," she was pointing to a student that was still standing in the second row, "come… forward. Take this," and she picked up the darkness in her hand as if it were a solid object.

The student, who Chezzy quickly recognized as Nebulous Zee'han from the Showing the day prior, took tentative steps up on to the stage. Professor Benhearst held out the darkness to her, and Nebulous took it in her hands. "It feels like glass. Like a glass ball," said Nebulous with a relieved look washing over her.

"Now… use… your… ability," Professor Benhearst said to her, though she was looking out at the classroom. Professor Benhearst closed her eyes and lifted her arms into the air while her head slunk down on her neck.

Nebulous glanced around at the other students, and a few of them nodded to her. She seemed to concentrate, and then her, Professor Benhearst, and the darkness all rose into the air and floated there, weightless. Professor Benhearst's eyes opened in surprise for a moment before she closed them again, feigning calmness. Nebulous hovered, uncertain of what to do next. It was several moments before Professor Benhearst reopened her eyes and looked back up from where she hung.

"Now… set… us… down."

Nebulous obliged, and she and Professor Benhearst sunk back to the floor. The darkness, however, continued to hang in the air. Nebulous looked up at it quizzically.

Professor Benhearst was pointing at the floating darkness. "Today… I… will hand… out… these… retainers. You… will pair… up. You… will… cast yourselves… thusly. You will… make notes… on… the effects… you… have. This… shall… serve… as your… guide… moving forward… in… this… class." Abruptly she turned and walked back to a hidden area behind the stage. She returned with a box and beckoned the students. "Come… down… in… your pairs."

Chezzy and Fair made their way down together to line up. When they took the small, glass orb that Professor Benhearst handed them, she regarded Chezzy skeptically. As they went back for their chairs, another orb was spouting small, indiscernible objects on the desk of a bored looking boy as he poked it. His partner pushed the boy aside and tried to poke it himself, causing the objects to vanish as the orb began spouting the thoughts of Nebulous Zee'han. "Quit it, Tan, he's going to hear," she gave with a blush. Her ball was floating around the room now while another orb was gushing a strange liquid, which drenched several students, including Nebulous and a somber looking Marsle Chin. He hardly reacted as he stared at his orb next to a rather alarmed Turod.

"Mm, I'm not sure. Am I supposed to just shift colors at it? Will that do it? Oh, I'm not sure," Fair said as they took their seats.

"That's easy for you," Chezzy replied. "Am I supposed to just die on it?" A ball a few seats down exploded with a growth of hair that spilt out over several people who said rude things to an embarrassed Arlene Aberfor. The girl apologized profusely as she tried to untangle the other people while Fever May sat laughing, shrouded in the hair.

"Oh, that's true," Fair was saying. "I mean, you could try it." She took the glass ball and held it against her skin as she went completely translucent.

"Whoa, just like last night." He could make out her outline but just barely.

"Oh, well, not exactly but sort of. I can turn to blend in with most things, I guess. It's hard, but if I really concentrate, I can kind of cover other people like a blanket. I've never seen how far I can take it, but my mother once hid our whole warehouse from my brother." Fair giggled, and the orb blushed pink. "Here, you try something." She handed it to Chezzy.

"Right." He took it, fiddling with the thing as he tried putting his nails in and even biting it, but nothing changed. "I don't know," he said. "I mean, I don't think I work like the rest of you do. I don't really modify… the… world… around… me," he added, mimicking Professor Benhearst's rhythmic tone.

Fair giggled again. "Well, they put you in this class for a reason, didn't they?"

Chezzy glanced at Fair, and he tried to look for the mark again, where Stuart's needle had pierced her. "I was put in here because they don't know what to do with me."

"Oh, that's not true," Fair reached a hand to Chezzy.

"I think there's something I should tell you." He was squeezing the orb as he pressed it harder and harder into the desk. He hadn't noticed the thing turn blood red.

"What is it?"

A crack rang out, and the orb in Chezzy's hand split, startling both of them. Immediately, it mended itself, and Chezzy cracked a smile. "Hold on." He lifted the orb and smashed it on the desk. Again, it repaired itself.

"Oh, that's really excellent," said Fair. "Do it again." Chezzy did as he was bade, but as soon as the orb and desk collided, the ball burst into flames, sending fiery shrapnel around, scorching Chezzy's hand. Fair cried out as she fell back barely dodging a piece. Then she looked to Chezzy, a pale blue. "Could've burned a hole in my head."

XVI.
Chisket.
Harbors.
No fear of perfection.

Chezzy watched the burns heal across his hand, then he turned to help Fair back to her feet. Professor Benhearst was already at their side, and she scowled before speaking in a low hiss. "Just… what… do… the two… of you… think… you… are… playing… at?"

"Professor, it just blew up," said Fair.

"Childish," replied Professor Benhearst as she looked down at the burning bits of ball, bubbling like lava on the desk. She turned and moved along down the aisle.

"Childish?" questioned Fair. She gave Chezzy an affronted look then said, "Foolish," in the same voice as Professor Benhearst. Chezzy laughed. They spent the rest of the class with Chezzy gathering the burning, glass bits. His hands would scorch and then heal, but the orb never stopped burning. Eventually, the metal desk was searing hot and Professor Benhearst was forced to summon Tech McGeehee to come see what he thought of the situation.

But as they left the class, Tech Mcgeehee still hadn't come, and Professor Benhearst was brooding, mumbling. "Cannot… replace. Acres Androids… is… gone…"

"Sorry you didn't get to work with the retainer more," Chezzy said to Fair, but Fair didn't seem to be listening. "You alright?"

"What?" Fair asked, snapping from her daze. "Oh, mm, yeah. I'm fine."

"Are you sure?" She didn't look fine.

"Mm, yes. Just hungry."

"Dining lab, then?"

"Yes." They walked down to lunch, and Chezzy realized he was weak with hunger. His feet struggled to drag him into the dining lab, but he rallied when he caught sight of Fern and Stuart waving them over to the same place where they had sat before. Immediately, Fern set about syncing up everyone else's versolocks as Chezzy and Fair took seats. Chezzy crammed ample helpings of some sort of grilled chicken into his mouth between a rushed recounting of what happened with Professor Kepler, while still amending anything said about the Acid King. He knew he couldn't keep putting off the conversation, but this wasn't the right place for it.

Stuart had sat tensely through the tale, but he cheered when Fair patted his hand and assured him that she was fine. Emboldened by her gesture, he piped up and regaled them with his morning. Apparently, he'd run into Marsle Chin in the bathroom earlier, and Marsle had made his weird sound, which, of course, made everyone go and startled Stuart so badly that he had pierced the toilet wall with one of his lingering needles. "It was fretful is all I'm saying."

Fair nodded with wide rainbowing eyes.

Stuart looked around at the others, but they didn't meet his gaze. His cheeks flushed as he picked at the food on his plate. "You know, this is probably the best chicken I ever had," he added, nervously.

"Chicken?" Fern asked.

"Yeah, the chicken," Stuart repeated, wielding it on his fork.

"That's not chicken, you oafenbor," Fern chortled.

"What do you mean?" Stuart asked, regarding his fork with newfound distrust.

"All bioproteins in Boletare are lab grown," Fair interjected. "And over the years, they've been redesigned, and couldn't really be considered chicken, or beef, or whatever toppers eat."

"That one's called chisket," Fern added.

"Oh… swell," Stuart replied, and he set his fork down apprehensively.

"What's wrong with you?" Fern asked, noticing Chezzy's detachment.

"I," Chezzy began but faltered. "I need to talk to all of you tonight."

"About chisket?" Stuart ventured, eyeing out other dishes on the conveyor.

Chezzy shook his head.

The everling waited nervously for them that evening. He had never had friends over before, and he didn't know how to tell them what Professor Kepler had asked of Chezzy. He felt so anxious, that when Raven finally announced Fern at the door, Chezzy nearly choked on his own tongue as he sprang up to tell Raven to let her in. He gave a last look around the common room, while the door wheeled over to reveal Fern.

The whole of the everling tower was in the style of a spaceship, whose windows revealed the common room to be in the midst of a battle deep in space. Other ships zipped to and fro in an exchange of phaser fire. Occasionally, there would be a hit, and the entire room would appear to tremble. Fern bounded in, unsteadily, just as one direct hit took place. "Oh," she said as she looked around. "This is really different from mine."

"Yours?" Chezzy asked.

"The Sciofall common room. I mean, I never thought I'd see in here. So few have."

"How's it different?"

"The theme and, and, everything. Basically. It hadn't even occurred to me that yours would be so different. Ours is just a wall of reminders and helpful tidbits for each class and things like that. And here… are we fighting in a space war?"

"Yeah. Raven said that the subs normally voted on dorm theme or something like that. Does Sciofall not?"

"Who's Raven?"

"I am," Raven chimed in.

"Oh, right. Dorm AI. Well, ours is called Kingdom Fallire," she said in a matter of fact tone.

"Kingdom Fallire?" scoffed Chezzy.

"Oh, King," said Raven with a note of annoyance in her voice.

"How do you know him?" Chezzy's versolock boomed.

"Oh, he's nobody," Raven replied airily.

"He's beautiful," piped Fern's own versolock, to which Fern blushed slightly. It might've been the first time Chezzy had seen her blush.

"Cool it down, Cradle."

"Cradle?" Chezzy asked.

"Yes. Cradle," Fern spat back defensively. "It's short for Cradle of Knowledge. I thought it was cute." She was looking at Cradle and holding her other hand to the versolock as if to defend it.

"Alright, alright. I get it."

"Well, what did you name yours?" Fern came back with. She bit her lip and puffed her chest out.

"I haven't named mine yet," he admitted.

"Yeah, well, that's pretty rude. He's helping you out with everything, and you haven't even given him a name? I'm surprised he doesn't pop off your wrist and leave."

"He can't do that," Chezzy laughed. "Can he?"

"Well, not without an attachment, but he can power down and disengage." Chezzy could see that Fern appeared entirely serious, but just then, Raven announced the arrival of Fair and Stuart. Chezzy's stomach plummeted again.

"Whoa," gave Stuart as he walked in. "This is so cool. This is much better than our dorm."

"Oh, it's excellent," breathed Fair. "Ours is just a demo reel of all the former Faxowl students showing off their abilities. But this, this is really excellent."

"Showing off their abilities?" Stuart seemed offended. "When we voted, all of the Betas and above voted for the forest theme. They said they'd kept it as forest theme for the past nineteen years or something, like it's a tradition. It's lunacy."

"So, you got to vote?" Fern asked.

Stuart and Fair both nodded, then Fair added, "But the rotating exhibit is always up. I guess it's supposed to help us realize our potential. But the theme this year, technically, is a tech training course."

"That's neat. I mean, Raven changes mine at least every day, but I haven't seen that yet."

"This changes every day?" Stuart shouted.

"Yeah."

"That's really not fair," he said then glanced to Fair before going on. "I guess the forest is fine, but we have fake bugs everywhere, and the rain gets on everything. Honestly, it's like the other Oxenbors are determined to be animals. To actually be animals. It's mental. Can't keep anything clean. Even our beds are little hovels. Like nests with brambles for a roof and everything. Totally mental. Honestly, what I wouldn't give for a real bed." Stuart was looking around at the passages that trailed off from the common room. "Which dorm do you sleep in?"

"Neither," replied Chezzy.

"What?"

Fair was giving Chezzy a strange look, and Fern added, "Do you mean that you sleep in the common room?"

"No, I sleep in the observatory. Raven had them put a bed up there for me and everything." Chezzy stared back at their slightly stricken faces. A few ticks later, they were all in the observatory, staring up at the false stars appearing above them.

"I tell you," Stuart was telling Chezzy, "this is really something. Really. Maybe we should all move in here."

"No, you should not," Raven replied, affronted. "No one stays in here but the everling."

The girls chuckled nervously, and Fair kindly asked, "So what did you want to talk to us about, Chezzy?"

Chezzy breathed deeply and launched into it, much to the increasingly horrified faces of his friends. When he finished, they all three began to speak at once, and it continued this way, them talking over one another, until Stuart huffed, "I should ask my parents about this."

Fern and Fair froze for a moment, before Fern shouted, "If this Acid King guy knows we know, then what will he do? We can't have every parent storming over here to pull students out of Balefire."

"They'd close down the school. We might end up in Saphill Wedd. Or maybe no other schools would take us," Fair added pensively.

Something in what she said struck Stuart. All he said was, "Oh."

"I think we should help," determined Fern.

"I, mm, I agree. I think," Fair gave in.

"And we should start right away. Tonight even," Fern added as the group of them looked to Stuart.

Stuart shook his head but said, "Okay. So long as we don't break any rules or anything."

"We aren't breaking the rules if Professor Kepler said it's okay," Fern reminded.

"It could still be dangerous. Some homeless man hiding buckets of acid and calling himself a king?" Stuart shivered. "We could get hurt... with acid."

"It's going to be fine, Stuart," comforted Fair, though even she seemed concerned. She had her hand on Stuart's arm, which wasn't lost on him.

"But what kind of person hides in a school?" Stuart asked.

"Whoever it is, must not be that dangerous if Professor Kepler wants us to find them," Fern reasoned.

"Then what kind of school harbors a... an Acid King?" he returned defiantly.

"I guess this one," Fern snapped. "You can go back up top if you don't like it."

Stuart's mouth clapped shut, and he kept it shut while the group of them gathered up to head down into the lower Keris. As the everling tower door wheeled back, Chezzy hurried right through Bogdanov who gave a glowering look as he glitched weirdly before storming off in a rant. Something Bogdanov was oft to do.

"I don't know what the deal with some of these projected people is," Chezzy muttered.

"They prefer to be called SIs," interjected Fern.

"How do you know that?" asked Stuart.

"You ever tried talking to one?" she snapped back.

"Well, if I ever want to learn about mermaids," Stuart replied, sardonically, "I'll be sure to ask Linnaeus." He looked over at Fair. "Seriously, that guy is always on about them."

"I wish Bogdanov just talked about mermaids," Chezzy said as he led them to the elevator. "I'm pretty sure he wants to kill me."

Stuart laughed at this. "At least he isn't trying to take notes on your tail. Linnaeus, I'm telling you, that's another thing about him."

"He's got a thing for weirdoes, does he?" Fern shot.

"No, just me," Stuart replied.

Fern gave a little sigh in return.

"Why do they prefer to be called SIs anyway?" Chezzy cut in.

"Mm, at one point they were trying to shift into android counterparts, called post humans. SIs were for their digital formats." Fair's voice dipped a little. "They abandoned the android attempts. Basically all Simulated Intelligences of past peoples are digital now." Her colors flourished and changed rapidly as she spoke.

"Well, Professor Kepler wanted me to try to track any that might be hacked," Chezzy said.

"Hacked?" Fern exclaimed. "Have you found any?"

"One. It was like she was stuck to this broken up wall. Then she lunged at me before vanishing."

"That's not scary at all," Stuart trembled, and his versolock let out a high pitched whimper.

"Yeah, well, it's not like she could do anything," Fern said with a tone of annoyance as she rolled her eyes at Stuart.

Chezzy brought out his map and looked at where the SI had been. The little dot was still in the same area and wandering around.

"B-but she went after him," Stuart stuttered back to Fern.

"We'll be fine," Fair comforted him. "They can't actually touch anything. Chezzy just ran right through one and nothing happened."

"Maybe sometimes they can turn it on and off," Stuart suggested fretfully.

"Turn it on and off?" Fern returned incredulously.

"Yeah. Whether or not they can touch things." Stuart glanced around for support but found none.

The elevator opened as Fern and Chezzy exchanged a look. She rolled her eyes again. "Can't imagine what you'd do if you had to deal with Porta. That SI was outside our dorm trying to measure the heads of students to see which one of us has a criminal future. The things he said about me…" She went about accessing something on her versolock as Stuart mumbled in shock.

Chezzy was taking them all deeper into the Keris, his lines retracing his steps back to the place where he had seen the glitching SI. Fern's versolock pinged, and a short while later, a small, robotic butterfly caught up to the four of them and landed on Fern's versolock with another ping. "What is that?" Stuart hissed. He had jumped when the butterflybot whizzed past him, his spines flexing rapidly.

"It's a little scout bot I made. Aren't you?" she asked tenderly to the butterflybot whose wings fluttered back to her. "I can send this ahead to make sure no SIs attack you," she added, her voice turned mocking.

"Oh, well, that's good thinking, that," Stuart replied, the sarcasm lost on him.

"That storage room was a trove of old Acres robotics and parts. Give me a couple days in there, and who knows what I might be able to build," Fern added.

"I don't want to go back in there," Stuart replied, though he did seem to relax a little.

"Me either," Fair smiled at him.

"Yeah, well, neither of you have to."

As they went deeper into the Keris, Stuart's paranoia seemed to resurface as a jittery hold sort of took over him. It was commonly known that the Keris was largely lit by floating lights that wandered up and down the halls and bobbed around the ceilings of classrooms. But as they got down to the lower Keris, they saw that many rested on the ground with flickering lights or floated around emitting no light at all. Bumping into many of them prompted broken, robotic apologies as the group made their way through the castabout darkness.

"Odd," said Fern.

"An SI?" Stuart had added, but no one bothered to answer. They were looking at the damaged wall.

"It looks corroded," said Fern as she held her versolock to scan. She looked down at the readings. "It's chemical," she mumbled to herself. "Like acid." She looked up, wide eyed, at Chezzy.

"Mm," replied Fair as she paced around, kicking small sticks and bits of rubble out of her way. She stopped at a broken lantern and nudged it aside. "That and the lights down here." The lantern at her foot sprang to life and popped into the air. Both she and Stuart gave a start.

"Pardon… Par… Par… Pardon," gave the light as it only managed to hop again and again down the hall, the words coming with each clank on the floor.

"I don't think anyone else comes down here, really," Chezzy said. "I heard Professor Kepler and Tech McGeehee talking, and it sounded like there were a lot of problems." Chezzy flicked on his map to check for anyone near but saw no one.

"That's weird," murmured Fern.

"What is?" he asked back.

"That Tech McGeehee can't get this all running. I mean, with the system it's operating on, it would only take him a few hours or maybe a day. I mean, these lights," and Fern kicked one of the resting lights, which gave off the barest glimmer of a glow for a moment, "they're programmed to travel back to the tech office at the first hint of an issue. Even if one went down with a full system failure, it would send out a mayday to the tech office immediately. At worst, there's droid retrieval and everything."

"How do you know all of this?" asked Stuart.

"Most larger facilities run on something like what Balefire has," Fair quickly explained.

Fern gave Fair a studious look. "That's right." Fair blushed a shade of shifting pink, which lit up her skin from the previous shades of shadow. "So it doesn't make sense that he hasn't been fixing any of these," Fern continued, resolutely.

"Maybe Tech has been busy," offered Chezzy.

"Busy with what? The system is so streamlined," Fern added, dusting off a logo from a crashed lantern.

"I don't know. Maybe the Acid King guy did something to them?" Stuart offered.

"Maybe," muttered Fern. "But how is he accessing them?"

"Fern." Chezzy had come to a stop. "There's something over there." He had caught a glimpse of movement down the hall that had disappeared around the corner. All eyes turned in the direction he indicated. For all his size, Stuart stepped behind Fair as if to have her shield him. His remaining needles trembled high above her. With a ping, Fern's butterflybot flew up ahead of them toward the turn in the hall while her versolock projected out a live feed. It showed the bobbing progression and the wings, which flashed into view before centering on two huddled figures.

One was the SI woman that Chezzy had seen before. She was stuck to the wall and speaking, though Chezzy couldn't make out what she was saying. The other figure was a man who seemed not to be wearing any menders at all. Though, he did appear to have something around his head, which was held close to the wall where the SI was stuck. He was extremely thin and spoke in a low, broken tone.

Stuart shuddered as Fair held her hand to her face. Fern turned to Chezzy with a skeptical raising of her eyebrows. "What do you think?"

"That's the SI I saw." Chezzy flicked out his map and looked at the hall, but he didn't see any dots to indicate the man, so he closed it and looked up. "I'll go first. Not like anything can happen to me, right?"

"What's going to happen?" Stuart managed to ask to no response.

Fern was nodding at Chezzy with understanding all through her face. She motioned him on, and the group crept forward, allowing Chezzy to take the lead. But the man's voice erupted with a low cracking. "For the forsaken, why?" They paused and looked to Fern's feed again. He was focused on the wall, but the SI woman was blocking the view of the butterflybot. Fern went to direct it over, but the man turned, slightly, seeming to hear the flutter. In a panic, she recalled it. The bot came around the corner and flew right at Chezzy who ducked, narrowly avoiding a collision. It came to rest on Fern's versolock with a ping.

Stuart outright screamed, and the very last few of his needles shot out behind them. One pierced a floating lantern, which went forever dark as shattered glass tinked across the floor. The lantern crashed down, where it smoked and apologized. Footsteps sounded around the corner of the hall, and Chezzy whirled back and hurried along, but when he reached the corner and looked, he only saw the SI woman. Chezzy turned back to the others and shook his head.

"I am so glad you stayed in the back," Fern turned and angrily whisper shouted at Stuart who managed a simpering nod.

Fair had come forward to Chezzy, and she gripped his hand as he looked back to the SI. "Don't," she whispered. She was the color of ash and quickly paling.

"It's okay. It's not like she can…" Chezzy shrugged and walked forward. He felt Fair's hand tighten around his as she followed with him.

"No fear of perfection, you'll never reach it. No fear of perfection, you'll never reach it. No fear of perfection, you'll never reach it." The SI woman repeated it over and over as she tried to push her way through the wall but was unable to pass.

"What is wrong with her?"

"I don't know," said Fair.

Fern came up behind with her versolock ready to scan. Chezzy looked over at Stuart who had stayed down the hall a bit. "There's a piece of the wall missing," Fern said. Chezzy looked around and saw the melted metal that revealed a series of circuits and wires, some of which had been spliced open.

"What is it?" Fair asked.

"Could be part of the hardwire for the SIs," Fern shrugged. "Could be a number of things."

"What are you saying?" Stuart called down the hall.

Fern looked over and snapped, "Would you get over here?"

Stuart gave a little jump then took fretful steps forward. "Who is she talking to?"

"Her?" Fern indicated the SI. "To no one. She's just talking." Fern had reached into the metal hole and was messing with the wires inside.

Quite suddenly, the SI glitched around and was facing the group, startling all. She marched forward. "Do not… perfection… Fern… Stuart Fieldmore." She bumped into the opposite wall then flipped backwards again. "Fair Jekyll, your name is… Fair Jekyll, your name is…"

Fair quickly flattened against the wall as she let go of Chezzy's hand and faded out of sight. The SI's face popped over to Chezzy. "No fear of Chezzy Nithercot. Your data is corrupted. The acid will-" A light blasted out, illuminating the entire corridor where the four of them stood with the SI. They froze in the blinding light with their hands up to shield as a figure moved at its source.

XVII.
Caught.
The Greywatch.
Hand.

"What do you think you're doing?" The light slowly dimmed, revealing its emanation from the wrist of Professor Tampago Brown. He looked around at the three visible students, though none dared answer. With a heavy breath, he typed something into his versolock then added, "Follow me," before whipping around.

Stuart let out a soft moan, but trailed all the same. They each glanced back, uncertain if Fair was with them or not. No one spoke, but they exchanged subtle glances of communal concern, though Fern looked more annoyed than anything else. He led them through many halls and up into the rotating ring of the Keris where his office was. Tampago Brown paused a moment at a lab, neighboring the office. Chezzy could make out pieces of the showing machine scattered all within in various states of repair. But then Tampago Brown locked up the room and proceeded next door into his office.

Chezzy stepped after the man and immediately flung his arms out to stop the others, but then he saw that the floors were actually made of glass. Below in all the dark, the shifting landscape of the grounds spread beneath them. The islands and the lake were visible as well as tiny dots, which must have been animals milling in the separate lands of the archipelago. "In," Tampago Brown ordered, and they tentatively ventured into the office, Stuart gripping a nearby table as he closed his eyes tightly. But Professor Tampago Brown didn't appear to notice as he sat at his desk. "Anything you'd like to say about all this?"

"There was," Chezzy hesitated, "something down there. We need-"

"Curie is an SI." Professor Tampago Brown interjected, but he had just taken note of Stuart. "Fieldmore, are you going to dirty my floor and offend my nose?"

Stuart opened his eyes to shake his head, but just then, a wave of vomit cascaded from his mouth and splattered on the floor.

"Very well, Fieldmore." Professor Tampago Brown went back to his versolock and shortly after, several droids entered the room and began suctioning up the vomit. Stuart couldn't help but stare down at the droids as they cleaned, and then he threw up again right on the nearest of them. The droid froze for a moment then zoomed off trailing the vomit behind while another followed, attempting to clean the mess.

"Sorry," Stuart managed to say.

"I suppose Miss Fayette might have been right about the lot of you. No mind, though. Caught this time. I've gone ahead and notified the directors and Tech McGeehee on what you've been up to and the damage."

"Damage?" Chezzy balked. "You think we did that?"

Professor Tampago Brown gave what Chezzy thought was a rather dispassionate look. "It doesn't matter what I think. The director will decide."

As if on cue, a purple portal opened, and Professor Kepler came flipping through it. He looked around at the students before saying directly to Chezzy, "Is this some kind of double date? I can't tell if Stuart back there is playing fourth wheel or not." Stuart seemed to shrink, as hard as that was for someone his size.

"Fourth?" Professor Tampago Brown questioned.

"Oh, yes. A rather strained Miss Jekyll is hiding there."

"Surely not," he exclaimed, but just then, Fair came back into visibility near the doorway.

She was panting and slumped to the wall, barely holding herself up. "Sorry," she puffed.

"Not at all," replied Professor Kepler. "You're getting better at that."

"Not… good enough… yet…" she whispered between breaths, sounding almost like Professor Benhearst.

"Well, keep practicing," Professor Kepler encouraged.

"Director." There was a tone of anger in Professor Tampago Brown's voice.

Professor Kepler looked to him, unbothered. "Oh, you're quite right. That's enough for today. You three, back to your dorms. Chezzy, with me."

"What?" Professor Tampago Brown near hissed.

"Oh, yes, and you contacted Gee. So, when he gets here, you should head down to see about Curie. I'll join you there when I'm finished." Professor Kepler turned back to the students, coolly, as Professor Tampago Brown turned a dark red.

They left him stewing there as Professor Kepler escorted them into the hall. The director strode leisurely towards the central structure of the Keris, which was connected by a series of spokes to the outer ring. At an indicative glance from Professor Kepler, the other students hurried off on their own paths, while the director pulled Chezzy through a door and into some sort of massive gymnasium.

"You saw him."

"Yes," began Chezzy. "How did you know?"

Professor Kepler didn't seem to be listening as he lifted Chezzy's arm. "I'm going to look at this." He accessed something on Chezzy's versolock. "Still no name I see," he mumbled before Chezzy's versolock lit up. It projected out a three dimensional image of the hallway with Chezzy, his friends, the SI, and the figure they had seen.

Chezzy marveled at it. "Is that watching all the time?"

"Of course he is. How else do you think he interacts with you? Though very few versolocks can access this sort of thing." He winked at Chezzy with a devilish grin as he cycled through the footage before pausing it. He paced around the perimeter trying to find a better angle, even going so far as to squat, before laying down and sliding under the projection then crawling back out and sitting on the floor.

"Well?" Chezzy asked.

"No," replied Professor Kepler. "Not well. Not really. You must keep this to yourself, Chezzy. You and your friends."

"Why?"

Professor Kepler's demeanor seemed to have fallen. "The evestry would be furious. They're always looking for a reason to sack me."

"Sack you?"

"Yes. But they can't now."

"Why's that? Aren't they in charge of everything?" Chezzy didn't actually know anything about the evestry.

"I suppose they are in charge of some things, but not Balefire. No. Not me and definitely not you. But we can laugh about the evestry later. I need to see to Professor Tampago Brown and Tech McGeehee. But, Chezzy?"

"Yes?"

"Keep at it."

Chezzy nodded, and Professor Kepler returned the gesture as he rose and portaled through the wall. Then Chezzy turned to the door and walked the long path back to the everling tower. The lines stretched out in front of him, and he was so deep in thought on his walk that he ran smack into Tech McGeehee who was nearly running in the opposite direction. "Oh," Tech exclaimed through a jubilant face. "What are you doing out at this hour?" Then he giggled.

"I was-" Chezzy began.

"Oh, right. Right. Of course. The down there thing. Yes, with, uh, the SI or whatever else. I'm on my way now, you know."

"I thought you were supposed to be there already." Chezzy felt annoyed at how elated Tech appeared to be.

"You know, science can wait for any man, but not just any man can wait for science." Tech burst into a roaring laugh as he excused himself past and hurried down the corridor, singing as he went. "And everybody is aware of what you got…"

The Everling and the Acid King

"Everybody's mad here," Chezzy mumbled before continuing to follow the lines and arrows back to the everling tower. Twice, he caught his versolock humming the same song that Tech McGeehee was, and Chezzy chastised it before pondering aloud just what to name the thing.

"Prince Watermane," offered Raven.

"Prince Watermane?" both Chezzy and his versolock exclaimed at once.

"It sounds romantic," Raven rebutted. "Oh, Prince Watermane, I dearly need your help," Raven feigned in a dramatic tone. "Doesn't it sound fitting?"

"Midnight Arrow," boomed the versolock back.

"Both of you are mental," Chezzy sighed.

"Well, I like Prince," Raven retorted.

"Because you want to be called Princess," Chezzy went on.

"Well, it would be nice." Raven's voice was etched with offense.

"Yeah. Nice and embarrassing."

"Well, if I'm so embarrassing, then I guess you'd also be too embarrassed for me to welcome your guests at the door."

"Wait, what?" Chezzy hurried ahead.

"I'm sure you'll figure it out Mr. Big I Can Name Everyone Whatever I Want."

Chezzy pulled around into the last stretch of hall, where he spied Fern and Fair sat outside of his dorm with bewildered looks. "What are you doing here?" he asked as he drew up to them, panting.

"We wanted to make sure you were okay," said Fair.

"What's going on, exactly?" Fern nodded to Chezzy's versolock, which was begging Raven to talk to him.

"Raven wants me to name my versolock Prince... Prince Watermane or something. So, then she can be Princess Raven, I guess."

Fern gave Chezzy a look of exasperation as Fair smiled and stifled a laugh. "Ridiculous," Fern was murmuring.

"Tell me about it. Where's Stuart at?"

Fern let out an annoyed sigh as Fair explained. "He didn't want to get caught being out after hours. Again. Said he was lucky enough he didn't get in trouble already."

"He was too scared to come here," Fern corrected. "So, what happened with Professor Kepler?"

Chezzy looked around for Bogdanov. He didn't want the SI to overhear. "Let's try to get inside first."

It took forever consoling Raven before she finally agreed to open the door, and that was only after each of them referred to her as Princess Raven. Despite this, they were greeted by a drastically changed common room. Earlier, it had been a spaceship in the midst of a battle, but the battle was long over. The ship floated in black space, the windows cracked, the consoles damaged, sparking, flickering with faint lights. Debris bits blew by and sucked out into the void where they drifted. There was a suppressive silence as if there wasn't enough air to carry their voices to one another. And the room had been chilled such that their teeth chattered. Rather put off, they went up to the observatory.

"Guess we lost the battle," Fern muttered as they rode the slipstream. In the observatory, they took seats at a side table, and Chezzy recounted for them what had happened between him and Professor Kepler. When he reached the part about the three dimensional image popping out, Fern looked somewhat outraged, and Fair's lips got very tight as she turned a darker shade of night. Chezzy kept on until he had told them everything else Professor Kepler had said and done.

"I can't believe he can access those," blurted Fern.

"Well, you know what they say," offered Fair.

"No, what do they say?" Chezzy asked.

"They say," but Fair gave a worried look to Fern.

Fern sighed and continued for her, "They say that Professor Kepler doesn't believe in laws. Of any kind. I mean his history itself is pretty incriminating as it is."

"What do you mean?" Chezzy felt a knot in his stomach, but something in his head was clicking together.

"I mean," went on Fern, "that he's done a lot of things that people would call wrong, like Invention Day."

"Invention Day?"

"Yeah, well, one day he dropped a bunch of gadgets and, I don't know, creatures he made and all. Some people think he stole them from scientists in the future. So," Fern shrugged.

"Could be ridiculous. Could be why Maze Bledshire quit his apprenticeship and… dropped out of the public eye," Fair added, her colors muddying.

Fern canted her head a little. "Maybe. But that stuff's microscopic. Worse, people say he was in league with Greyire." At the mention of Greyire, both of the girls unconsciously looked to Chezzy and then away.

"The milclade who killed all of the everlings?" Chezzy confirmed, weightily.

"He didn't kill them," Fern corrected. "He made them molers."

Fair was nodding beside her.

"I don't really know what a moler is." Chezzy responded, recalling Veronica using the term before.

"It's someone whose brain has been tampered with by Greyire. It makes them his slave," Fair said the last word at a whisper.

Chezzy thought about this for a moment. "Do you think that's why Professor Tampago Brown was so mad at Professor Kepler? Because he thinks that Professor Kepler helped Greyire or something?"

"Tampago Brown was in the Greywatch," said Fair. "And there were all those claims about what Kepler did before most of them died."

"What do you mean? What did he do?" The uneasy feeling that he'd had after his and Professor Kepler's visit to Mantuckit Porview was creeping back into him.

"Well," Fern cut in, "you know about the Greywatch, right? They were a load of clades and scientists who were trying to hunt down Greyire. And then at Eldefool, there was this big battle between the Greywatch and a bunch of Greyire's molers. And the rumor is that Professor Kepler showed up out of nowhere. He grabbed one of the Greywatch people, and, well, he witsacked her, and the entire battle went sideways."

"The Greywatch was never the same after that," mumbled Fair.

Fern tossed a look to Fair. "Never the same? They weren't even alive except for like two people."

"Mm, there's Tampago Brown. And the one that was put into Kellogg's Sanitorium. That's what I heard about that."

"I heard that, too," said Fern, while she nodded.

"But there were a couple others that made it out of the massacre, I think."

Fern shrugged as she looked back to Chezzy. "Yeah, well, a lot of people think that what happened to the Greywatch was because of Professor Kepler. The massacre and all. Anyway, after Greyire disappeared, there were a lot of people found that were either witsackers or molers, but no one really knew if it was Professor Kepler or Greyire that did it, or what happened. Many think that Professor Kepler has been helping Greyire from the start." She gave Chezzy a grave look.

"Witsackers?" Chezzy managed as he recalled the scream of Mantuckit Porview.

The girls nodded solemnly. "He took their minds away. However he does it," Fair shrugged.

"Then why did you both come to school here?" Chezzy asked.

"Well, not everyone thinks like that," Fern said laughingly. "My parents don't, and they gave me a choice."

"Of what?"

"Saphill Wedd started because of Professor Kepler. And a lot of students have gone to Loegria over the years because of him. Or Albion," Fair clarified. "I mean, my dad trusted him. I know my mom doesn't think he did it, but I got, mm, Balefire helped pay for a lot of my coursework and… Not that…" Fair blushed in a twist of black and red before slipping translucent. "I mean, either way, this is the best school," Fair rushed out, nervously. "Loegria's good and so is Albion. And Saphill Wedd… well, it's fine."

"Saphill Wedd does have Tocques Habrocomes," Fern conceded.

"Mm, yeah, but Balefire is still the best."

"Unquestionably."

"So, I would have come, regardless. But that's not the point. The point is, no one has seen Greyire in ages."

"Oh, a long time," agreed Fern.

Chezzy weighed their words. "What happened to him?"

"Nothing really, I guess. I mean, he just sort of vanished," Fair replied.

"Or someone hid him," Chezzy suggested darkly.

Fern scoffed. "I doubt Professor Kepler has been hiding him away this whole time."

"But what if he has been?"

Neither seemed to have an answer to that. When they left, he sat in the observatory alone and looked up at the stars while his versolock illuminated the various constellations above or pointed out any oddities in the fabricated night sky. Its booming voice seemed to shake the glass around him, and Chezzy found himself wondering if the dome had ever cracked before and how dangerous it would be if the whole thing came falling down on top of him.

"I guess not very dangerous," he whispered to himself. He stayed up very late, so late, in fact, that the sky was seeming to lighten in the distance when he finally drifted off. But, before he managed to go to sleep at long last, he told his versolock, "Midnight." The versolock had lit up, and the settings menu popped out with the option to enter in the name, but Chezzy had already drifted away.

The morning came too soon, and Chezzy found himself hurrying to breakfast with just enough time to scarf down some toast and setters jam before dashing to his first class of the day. He had Mastering Menders with Professor Sappmo along with the Phrenbook and Sciofall students. The bell had only just rung before Chezzy came falling into the classroom, startling several of the nearby students. Professor Sappmo had given him a curious expression, and as he climbed to his feet, Chezzy spied Fern who was pulling out a seat next to her, which he quickly took.

"Did you see the message?" Fern asked.

"The message?"

"Read it."

But Chezzy was distracted by Veronica Fayette's hand firing up like lightning. Professor Sappmo nodded to her. "Do you not think it is rude of him to be late like that? If we have to spend every class waiting for him to barge in, that would be detrimental to our education, correct? Not all of us have as much time to waste as he does."

"Miss Fayette, if you want to tug on his pigtail, please do it after class." He looked back to the room. Veronica flushed a deep red but jabbed her hand back into the air. Impassively, he gave her a slight wave.

"Professor Sappmo, I heard that several students were caught out after curfew last night. Is that true?" She threw back an almost nasty look to Chezzy.

"I haven't heard of any students being caught out late, Miss Fayette, but I did hear that a Sciofall girl was worried about interruptions in class being detrimental to her learning." Several students began to snicker, but Veronica Fayette shot them a violent look. Her eyes went back to Chezzy, and they held him for several moments before she turned back around.

"I swear she hates me," Chezzy whispered over to Fern. Professor Sappmo had projected from his own versolock a video titled *The Anatomy of a Mender*. The man yawned as an exuberant anthropomorphized mender began addressing the class. "That's why she's trying to get us in trouble. She hates me."

"Sciofall has always hated Chiropa," Fern said, not taking her eyes from the video.

"What?" Chezzy said, rather shocked by this reveal.

Fern glanced to Chezzy and went a shade of crimson as she adjusted her glasses. "Well, it's not like it's a rule or anything. It's just, well, it's always been like that."

"But why?" Chezzy was looking back and forth between Fern and Veronica.

"Well, Chiropa, they have everything Sciofall wants, don't they? I mean, it's what they've always sort of worked towards, right?" Fern went on.

"Towards what?" Chezzy felt heat rising in his neck, though he wasn't entirely certain as to why.

"Well, immortality. I mean, man has always worked towards that in some way or another. And you, well, you just have it while every Sciofall ever has tried to get it. It's, you know, not fair is all. You have an eternity to learn, to experience, to… everything. You'll get to see our society through every turn and development. Everyone else will only be here for a moment."

"Tell that to the other everlings."

Fern rolled her pale eyes. "Yeah, well, that's a fluke. A blip. Whatever. There's an eternity ahead of you. You probably won't even remember us a few hundred years from now."

Chezzy felt as if something had been wrenched from his chest. The heat drained away from him, and he looked carefully at Fern. "You're mental. Really, you're completely mental."

"Am I?" Fern asked. "I already saw you get stabbed like nothing."

"No. I'm not going to forget you. You're the only friends I have." Something about the word friends stuck in Chezzy's throat, and he felt it crack slightly when he said it.

Fern nodded, her face tense and flushed, her eyes bright. Chezzy looked down, accessing Fair's message. *I know who the Acid King is.*

Before he could say anything about it, the class was prompted by Professor Sappmo to pull up their basics tutorial in their versolocks. Soon, dozens of projections erupted into the air, and they were all listening as every versolock spoke at once and detailed the basics of menders as well as highlighting certain specialty aspects of their own personal versions of menders.

Midnight spoke louder than any of the others, and Chezzy was frequently thrown bitter looks as neighboring students struggled to listen to their own versolocks, often encouraging them to speak louder. "Can you quiet down some?" Chezzy hissed at Midnight.

"I can't access the volume control," Midnight boomed back.

"I thought you were supposed to be the fanciest versolock," Chezzy mumbled, noticing that Fern hadn't pulled up her tutorial. He nudged her foot and gave her a questioning look.

She had been watching Chezzy's tutorial despite Midnight's interruption but then looked at Chezzy. "I already watched mine. Twice. Yours is more interesting anyway. Look at these options," and she pointed to something in the projection.

Chezzy turned to see what she had pointed at, but the projection changed to a sort of three dimensional demonstration. It showcased an everling's menders mending themselves as the character sustained various types of injuries. The whole thing played out in a cartoonish fashion as the everling was run over by a train or had a boulder drop on him. Each time, the everling would pop up and crawl over to his various body parts and they would reattach themselves.

"See?" Fern said with an offhand motion.

"Can I actually do that?" Chezzy asked her.

"Do what?"

"Put my limbs back on if they get cut off."

Fern shrugged. "I don't know, but I never heard of an everling that was missing any limbs. As far as I know, they always healed everything. Do you want to try it or something?" There was a note of excited curiosity in Fern's voice.

"No," Chezzy started, "well, maybe. I don't know. I certainly don't want to do it if I can't be put back together."

"You could be the first everling with a hook hand or something." She was grinning broadly.

"A hand?" Chezzy's voice had risen. "I'm not starting off with a hand. A finger, maybe, but even then…" he trailed off looking down at his fingers and trying to figure out which of them was the least important. "This is ridiculous," he mumbled.

"I'd cut off that one," said Fern, and she pointed to one of his pinkies.

"I'm not cutting off that one."

"Suit yourself," she said with a shrug.

The everling shook his head, lowering his voice. "Do you think she really figured it out?"

Fern shrugged. "Later. I'm picking out the finger I want."

He glanced back down to his fingers as they finished the demos. Then Professor Sappmo had them divide into pairs so they could test out the various, basic mender abilities. "Just the basics," Professor Sappmo was saying. "I don't want y'all trying anything too advanced and getting hurt," his eyes reached Chezzy, "or making a mess all over the floor. None of that."

Testing the basics for Chezzy meant that, along with the standard shielding tech, the settings demo, and the quick mending function that the other students were trying out, he also had to test the mending heal aid, anesthetizers, and blood cleanup. This meant that Fern got to shoot a laser from her versolock at Chezzy, which burnt into him several times, much to Fern's amusement. Each time, he healed back, and his menders repaired themselves.

"You sure you don't want to try a limb?" she asked him again. "I could turn the power up on this thing."

"I'm sure. Maybe that's what my Practicum is for anyway. I haven't the slightest idea what that'll be about."

"That's not till Fahberday. Do you really think you can go till Fahberday without knowing if you can lose limbs or not?" She was laughing gleefully.

"I've gone this long. I think I can stand to go a little longer before I know for sure."

"That's too bad," said Fern.

But just then, a blast of laser tore through Chezzy's arm and narrowly missed hitting Fern herself as it burnt a hole in the wall. Chezzy looked down to see his hand falling to the floor, and then, instinctively, he wheeled around, his teeth set to their edges. With a look of intense curiosity and terrible disdain, Veronica Fayette stood only a few feet away with her versolock held up. Chezzy took a step towards her, and she backed away, suddenly frightened.

He took another step, and he could feel the syncope swelling inside of him and reaching for his head and his eyes. Another step, and he slipped some as he was bleeding so badly that there was a puddle beneath him, his mender desperately trying to suck it back up as it moved to close over his stump. His eyes shifted focus. He could still see Veronica, but she was crying and hyperventilating.

Professor Sappmo had come up, though from where, Chezzy couldn't say. He put a heavy hand to Chezzy, and the professor was talking to him, but Chezzy couldn't make out what he was saying. Another step, only this time, Professor Sappmo was pressing back against Chezzy. Several Sciofall girls had flocked over to Veronica, and they were consoling her. She kept crying and waving her hands, but Chezzy couldn't hear any of that. He could only hear his heart beating, and the beating hearts of everyone else around him.

Veronica flashed a surreptitious look towards Chezzy, and he met it angrily as a sweat started at his brow. She was sinking to the floor while another girl threw her arms around her. But Chezzy was sinking too, and a terrible heat was coming over him. He pointed his stump at her accusingly. Blood spurted from the wound, and sprayed across the girls before his menders sealed over the end. Another student let out a shriek, but Veronica didn't flinch.

Other hands took ahold of Chezzy, but he could hardly feel them through the heat. He couldn't see anymore either, but he could hear Fern. "It's okay, I have your hand. It's going to be okay," she was saying, but then her voice was gone too.

XVIII.
A spare.
Gauntlet.
Box.

*H*e awoke with a jolt and found himself in some kind of hospital. He looked around and saw Fern and Professor Kepler at his bedside. Hovering next to them, was the most beautiful and horrifying woman Chezzy had ever seen. She had long, dark hair and delicate features, and her large, doleful eyes were striking against her candy red menders. Chezzy couldn't imagine what had happened to her.

She had neither arms, nor legs, but her torso rested on a hovering craft, arrayed with a multitude of robotic arms. Each arm seemed to work of its own accord, reminiscent of an octopus. He was staring at them as two of the appendages reached for Chezzy and lifted his arm for her to examine, her big eyes narrowing, her full lips pulled into a slight grimace. The memory of Veronica and his spurting stump hit him violently, but now, where his hand should have been, there was instead a slippery, elongated growth.

"Looking for this?" Professor Kepler asked as he held up Chezzy's severed hand sat on a platter.

"My hand," Chezzy cried out, incidentally ripping his stumpy growth free of the appendages' grip.

"Oh, it doesn't matter. You're growing a new one. Now you have a spare." He handed the severed hand on the platter to the woman who took it carefully with two of her tentacular limbs, her breath quickening.

"Ought we keep it here, Director?" she asked with a rather feigned disinterest.

"Yes. Keep it. Store it. But don't forget to shut the freezer door this time, Doctor Tiz'n. I don't want a repeat of last Everling Day. Smell was unbearable." He gave her a little smile, which she returned, though it dropped away rather quickly. Her craft whirred and whirled, then, with a fretful glance back, she glided quickly out of the room. Professor Kepler turned to Chezzy. "I bet you're starved."

"I am," Chezzy admitted as he watched his new hand reforming. Fern was equally entranced.

"I thought as much. It's not too long till lunch, but you can skip your next class while I have something delivered up. Medilab is kind of an odd date, though."

Chezzy felt his face flush, and he dared not look at Fern while he changed the subject. "Professor, what happened with Veronica?"

"Oh, she's in Tampago Brown's office, terribly distraught. She said she set it off accidentally, and that she was just beside herself with anguish."

"She wasn't," grumbled Chezzy.

Professor Kepler looked directly at Chezzy and paused a moment before saying, "Yes, I know."

"You know?" This time it was Fern who spoke up, and Chezzy chanced a look at her. She was staring open mouthed at Professor Kepler.

Professor Kepler looked to Fern. "Of course I do. Would you rather I was the sort of director that didn't know such things?"

"Well, no," said Fern.

"Then we are in agreement that it is good that I know these things, and that I should go on knowing these things. Even if I'm not the one the Sciofalls typically confide in. With a few exceptions," he said, giving Fern a wink.

Fern gave a hesitant nod as Doctor Tiz'n reappeared at the doorway. She was drifting over to them when Professor Kepler said to her, "Tizmerelda, could you please have something brought up from the kitchens for them? Our dear, sick boy here is quite starved it seems."

"Of course, Director." Her voice rolled out like a low hum. "Are you off then?" she asked him.

"I am. Many things to see," and with a flick of his wrist, there was a portal that he was stepping through, and he was gone.

Doctor Tiz'n smiled after him, but her demeanor seemed to change the moment he vanished. She looked back at the two of them with a face that was almost surly, which only accented her pretty features. Chezzy was suddenly reminded of Ms. Bartleby, and he felt a pang in his gut, which was swiftly followed by a wave of guilt. He was in a hospital again. Chezzy felt a sweat start at his temple.

His breathing seemed to quicken a moment, and he was staring at Doctor Tiz'n as she busied herself with her versolock, which was mounted on her craft, before gliding into the other room. A cool hand gripped his new one, and he looked down at it and saw that it was nearly completely reformed. Then he met eyes with Fern. "Are you alright?" she mouthed, and Chezzy nodded to her. She smiled, her glasses cocked crookedly across her face. "You know you have a green eye and a blue eye, don't you?"

Chezzy nodded again. "Yeah."

"Yeah, well, that's really, very rare. Do you think they see in different shades?" She was grinning goofily.

"This one sees everything that's there, and the other sees everything that isn't," he said, indicating with his old hand.

"How do you tell them apart?"

"I don't," and they both laughed as the door nearby whooshed open to reveal a little train of droids carrying breakfast cake and Teague sausages left over from the morning meal.

They ate together, joking and laughing, and got so loud that Doctor Tiz'n zoomed in at one point in a scold. "Do you mind? Some of us have work to do."

Fern took a swift look around. "But we're the only ones here."

Doctor Tiz'n's chest swelled as her craft rose to tower over them. "My duties extend beyond tending to students who don't need tending to." Then she veered around and sped out.

Fern and Chezzy burst back into hushed laughter, and it wasn't long before lunch began to arrive via another train of droids bringing Schrödinger sliders and Fibonacci fries. As they ate, Chezzy opened another of the slider boxes. "Are there not any more of the spicy ones? I keep getting the sweet sliders," Chezzy complained.

"They're all spicy," Fern replied.

"Well, no. The first one I had was spicy, but the last three were sweet."

Fern giggled. "That's the point. They're spicy and sweet until you open the box."

"Seems like they could just label them," Chezzy grumbled, and Fern laughed again.

They stuffed themselves silly, as the fries kept multiplying, and found themselves still groaning long after lunch was over. Fern's versolock had been politely urging them to get to class, but they missed it anyway. Finally, Chezzy looked at his own versolock. Both he and Fern had several messages from Fair and Stuart. News of Chezzy's injury had spread throughout the entire school, and exaggerations were saying Chezzy had been split completely in half.

"Absolutely ridiculous," Chezzy had mumbled as he sent quick messages back assuring them that he wouldn't be needing to borrow Doctor Tiz'n's hovercraft.

"Oh, I know. It'd be faster for you to grow your legs back than it would to convince Doctor Tiz'n to scooch over," Fern added as she picked herself up and readied to leave. They looked to each other, and Fern gave Chezzy a quick smile. "I should get to my last class, at least."

"I guess I should too."

"You'd think getting your hand cut off would give you a full day pass."

Chezzy held up his new fully formed hand and quipped, "We'll go for a leg next time."

"Don't tempt me," Fern winked then hurried out of the medilab.

Chezzy did likewise, following the lines and arrows that took him down to Defense Style and Execution, and he wondered how much more damaging it would be compared to his Mastering Menders class. When Chezzy reached the class, he found that it was being held in the gymnasium where Professor Kepler had brought him before.

He had this class with the Phrenbooks and Oxenbors, and when he entered, he watched a wave of relief wash over Stuart. Everyone else, however, was watching him with grotesque curiosity. Professor Shi had just entered, though, and he began immediately talking over the syllabus. Chezzy watched as eyes went back and forth between the professor and himself but soon found himself rather captivated by Professor Shi.

He was a small man with dark hair and dark eyes that seemed to read everything around him. But the truly striking thing about the man was his face, which didn't quite seem real and put all of the students on edge. He wore menders in a shade of darkest blue that were nearly black, and he moved with a deft speed that seemed like a trick of the eye. When he spoke, his voice came softly but clearly, and the students seemed to hang on his words.

"Did Fair tell you anything about her message?" Chezzy muttered to Stuart.

"No, nothing. I can't tell what he's saying." Stuart was fixated on Professor Shi as well, squinting his animal eyes. "So, what happened with you? Wait. I think he's talking about Minerocket tryouts, and I'm still trying to figure out what that is. Do you know? Oh, I think he's looking right at us."

Chezzy couldn't really tell if Professor Shi was watching them or not. The man maintained an unblinking gaze from his unnatural face as he continued to speak before splitting the class by sub. Upon doing so, he looked at Chezzy for a long time before motioning to the Oxenbors, saying "You work with them today."

Chezzy nodded and hurried back over to Stuart who was near a sort of obstacle course that the Phrenbooks were lined up at. What proceeded was largely a cringeworthy affair as most of the Phrenbook students struggled with each obstacle. Nebulous Zee'han, however, did breeze through, though, floating across most of it. But when Marsle Chin attempted the course, the rest of the class had held back, with their hands clamped over their ears, and no one spoke a word until the Phrenbook huffed past the finish line.

"So, what happened?" Stuart finally managed to ask. He was shifting nervously, and Chezzy could see the new spines growing back across him.

"Veronica Fayette cut off my hand with a laser beam in class."

"She did not." His eyes moved to Chezzy's hand.

"Right off. Smacked on the floor."

"Geez. Wait, is that the Sciofall girl who followed us?"

"Yeah. Her. And she was pretending to cry and apologize."

"She was pretending?" He looked doubtful.

"Definitely. When no one was watching her, she'd stop so she could get a better look at me before I passed out."

"Passed out?"

"Yeah. Woke up in the medilab and my hand was growing back."

"Growing back? That's mental."

"Yeah," Chezzy lifted up his hand. "This hand is entirely new. They kept the old one in the medilab storage."

"Honestly, that's unbelievable. Even for a place like this."

"It happened."

Stuart looked down at his own hand. "You can really lose a hand and just grow it back, just like my needles."

"Well, it's not like my hand shot off and stabbed someone."

Stuart gave a short laugh, but then his face grew serious. "Why do you think she did that?"

"Veronica? I don't know. She's been weirdly interested in me ever since I met her in Ye Olde Book Machine. She's always staring at me."

"Had to be an accident. Or maybe she has a crush on you."

"Fat chance."

"I don't know. Maybe that's how you ask someone out here. I don't even know how to do that, you know," Stuart pointed to the ceiling, "up there. It's not like I knew any girls other than Patty. Mother and father never thought I'd leave the house. You should've seen the construction plans they had for the basement. Of course, now they keep talking about moving down here."

The last of the Phrenbook students struggled his way across the finish, and Professor Shi looked over, calling the Oxenbor students forward. Chezzy watched as they began the gauntlet, and he could immediately tell that they were a lot more adept at this sort of thing than the Phrenbook students. A student with a prehensile tail went through some monkey bars doing cartwheels across. Another student with strange legs just sort of leapt over everything without any difficulty at all, then she gave a little bow at the end.

The only Oxenbor that seemed to have any trouble with it was Stuart. Stuart was a lot bigger than the other kids in his year. Chezzy was sure he had to weigh about as much as a hovercart already, and he wondered if he could just push over all of the obstacles. Professor Shi followed along offering advice. "Vault. No, use both arms there." Stuart struggled all the same, and when he got across the last part, there were scattered sighs of relief from the Oxenbors while the Phrenbooks looked on empathetically.

Stuart returned to the others burnt and bruised but mostly embarrassed. "Honestly, I can do better than that. I know I can."

Professor Shi then turned his unsettling gaze to Chezzy. "You are up."

The beginning of the course had a series of ropes where Stuart had gotten tangled up before falling to the bottom and crawling under to the other side. Chezzy looked over to Stuart who shrugged, but Chezzy wasn't worried. He had spent so much time climbing through the trees by Wutherford Home that a lot of it looked rather easy to him. Professor Shi called for Chezzy to go, and, at once, he was flying through the gauntlet.

He swung like mad across the ropes and climbed up a platform. Then he climbed across a pole, careful of the oscillating fire, before dropping to some monkey bars. These led to some rotating platforms that would lean side to side. Chezzy jumped across seven of them before clambering up a mesh web. At the top, he looked down at three different platforms, the lowest resting at least the length of seven people below. He didn't even hesitate, he just dropped to the lowest, slamming with a crack, his leg broken at an odd angle.

A gasp went around the room. Chezzy looked up at Professor Shi who only watched. Then he looked to a fretful Stuart. Chezzy lifted his leg and kicked it outward. It snapped back into place, and Chezzy tested it with gritted teeth, his menders helping to compensate. He took a step and then another, and he began to run before jumping across another gap. Clapping and cheers came from the other students. But he still had the floating islands, the fire blowers, the trick ropes, swinging beams, the shift bridge, and the laser maze, which actually would burn you a little if you touched it, and through which Stuart had merely barreled.

Professor Shi looked at Chezzy when he reached the end. Chezzy thought the man might've been pleased, but he couldn't be certain. The professor turned to address the class. "You'll be running obstacles every week, after which we will address defense styles. Your personal style will be addressed later." The Phrenbooks groaned, but Professor Shi silenced them with a look before dismissing the class. Stuart and Chezzy hurried down to dinner where he finally saw Fair.

"So, who is he?" Chezzy hissed to her as he took his seat.

"First, I'm so glad you're okay," Fair started.

"What? Right, of course. I'm okay." Chezzy looked around at Stuart and Fern to hide his embarrassment.

"I was just so worried, and everyone was saying you had no legs, and they were going to ship you off to Shivweigh's so they could attach robot legs to you and-"

"And I'm fine. I'm fine," Chezzy cut in. He looked to Stuart who was watching Fair uncomfortably. "You said you know who the Acid King is?"

"Yeah, but she won't say who," Fern scoffed.

"Because I don't know who it is," Fair said, her voice rising, her colors running white. She quickly recomposed herself and looked around. "I remembered. The first night in my dorm, I saw someone that came up who had acid for blood. I just remembered it earlier, but I haven't been able to find him. So, this weekend I want to sneak you all in so we can try and look through the profiles to find him."

"We can't sneak in," Stuart near shouted.

"Keep your voice down. Besides, everyone is going to be at Sidelight." Fern reached for a biscuit zooming by on the conveyor.

"I just barely got my needles back," Stuart moaned unhappily.

As the week went on, students began finding many more of the acid cauldrons around school. Arlene Aberfor even tripped into one and burned her hand badly enough that she ended up in the medilab for a few days. There was a rush of rumors, and the whole school was debating if the Keris systems had a virus or a rogue AI. Chezzy overheard many speculating as he made his way down to Cryptozoology Made Manifest with the Oxenbors and Faxowls.

The class was milling around on the grassy grounds, and he found Fair and Stuart huddled together near the back. "What's going on?" Chezzy asked.

"Oh," Stuart said, seeing Chezzy. "Fair was just telling me. She got here a little early." Stuart's face was sometimes difficult to read, but Chezzy felt certain that he was blushing.

"I don't know much. Professor Clyster ran by a little while ago," Fair began, "but all he said was that there has been a little problem with his other class, and that he might have to cancel this one."

"Excellent. We have other things to deal with."

Both Stuart and Fair looked slightly offended. "And miss class?" Stuart asked.

"You heard about Arlene, right? We need to find him."

"Yeah, yeah, I heard about Arlene," Stuart scoffed. "But listen, we've been out every night. Now you want days too?"

"If we're missing class anyway, why not?" Chezzy countered.

"Well," Fair shaded in a bloom of vibrant hues. There was something pleasantly warm about the way she'd color towards people. Certain emotions and certain people sparked more specific colors, and it wasn't lost on Chezzy. But just then, Professor Clyster appeared in the crowd. He was a very thin man, but his arms nearly grazed the ground. His skin had a bark like texture, and his mender, which snaked over him in a web like pattern, made it so he could've easily blended in any wood.

He lifted his long arms to silence the students, and his high voice sounded like sandpaper being rubbed together. "Our normal class will have to be tabled as during the prior class, the flying honey badgers, once again, escaped and are terrorizing the other species. So, it is our duty, today, to help Ecologist Penton Fulcrank to corral them. Unfortunately, the city of twig folk, which, if you will reference your syllabus, was to be part of this week's lesson, has fallen."

"Fallen?" asked Fair, a look of worry had come across her face, which had been in shades of leaf and grass before.

Metwell Chase rolled his eyes at her concern. "No wonder they can't keep the bloody pests out of the Keris."

"Yes, uh, Miss," he glanced down to his versolock, which was very slim and also the color of his skin, "um, Jekyll. Now, we will go over the twig folk another day, but if you would all follow me, and, well, be ready, we will join Mr. Fulcrank and some of the Phrenbook students that stayed behind on the, um, battlefield, as they say and, um, deal with this." With that, he turned and led them all across several of the islands.

The twig city was really a small castle that was maybe twice the height of a very tall man, resting on a large island. It was nestled against one of the old castle towers that stretched up to connect with the Keris. Zooming around in the air, were dozens of flying honey badgers. Penton Fulcrank was on the ground shouting and occasionally blasted one with orbs of electricity from a large device he was carrying around. When hit, the flying honey badger would fall in a dive and crash down, unconscious, causing more destruction and mayhem to the city below.

Down in the city, running amok, were what looked like sticks with little branch arms and legs. They were all different sizes, from as small as a retainer, to others that reached up to Chezzy's knees. Some among them were wide like swathes of bark that had been peeled from a tree, while most were thin branches swishing around. Flying honey badgers were swooping down and snatching many into the air, where the little sticks cried out strangely. Penton Fulcrank had several cages stacked around him, and the Phrenbook students were frantically attempting to corral the flying honey badgers.

Directly next to the cages, was Fern. Only she was absolutely covered in something that looked like a dark candy coating. Pey Nag and Fever May were breaking off the substance, which cracked, glasslike. Chezzy looked around, but he couldn't see any other Sciofalls from the class before. It seemed Fern and Pey were the only ones still there, which he thought odd. But he and Fair hurried over to Fern, cautious of the fleeing twig folk at their feet.

"Are you okay? What happened?" Fair asked as they reached her.

"I don't know, something terrible," Fern sputtered. The hard flakes breaking around her mouth. "I can't move my legs. It's pretty neat, though."

"Will it come out of your hair?" Chezzy asked.

Fern's eyes went big behind her glasses, which were iced over by the substance. "I hadn't thought of that." She frowned, which cracked the bits around her mouth further.

"Put them badgers in there," Professor Clyster hollered as he pointed to Chezzy and Fair.

"Go ahead. I'll be there in a bit," Fern encouraged as Fever May gave Chezzy a doubtful look. Still, he and Fair turned back to the fray and went in. They found themselves climbing through the city with the other students and gathering up the unconscious flying honey badgers. Many of the students, however, were just as destructive as the flying honey badgers, since they trampled over everything and would occasionally trip and fall.

Marsle Chin stepped on an actual twig person and snapped off the little thing's leg. Marsle had lifted it up and let out a wail, and suddenly everyone in the area had a little bathroom accident. The little twig person in his hand even squirted out a tiny amount of sap, which he tried to wipe off, but it stuck to everything. Meanwhile, the battle with the flying honey badgers came to a smelly, groaning halt. Professor Clyster and Penton Fulcrank argued with each other about how to activate the cleanup protocol for a painfully embarrassing amount of time before they finally called for help.

The whole lot of students had sat, sort of avoiding each other, spaced out around the islands with their heads down. Marsle Chin sat furthest of all, still trying to get the sap off his hand. Eventually, a portal opened and Professor Maxwell stepped through with a bemused smile on her face. She went into her versolock, and a sigh swept across the islands as their menders cleaned themselves up. Then Professor Clyster said something heated to Professor Maxwell.

"Keep the sawdust in your menders," Professor Maxwell gave back as the man clenched his mouth shut. He glared at her for a moment then burst out laughing. It was like the sound of studded wooden planks sawing against each other. Professor Maxwell flashed her smile around and looked to Turod Ingleward who was stood nearby with Minny Deerwink. Professor Maxwell ran a hand into his hair and tousled it before blasting a portal on to the wall. "Have fun," she added, then she stepped through and was gone. Professor Clyster composed himself as he looked to the students and gestured back at the twig folk castle.

"Oh, no, it's doing something," Fern commented, her mender having slipped up over her head, covering her hair and her face while the two girls were still working at removing the rest of the substance. "Please, work."

"Back to it, back to it," Professor Clyster was calling out. Soon, Penton Fulcrank was blasting flying honey badgers out of the sky again while everyone else tried to retrieve badger and twig person alike. Many students, Stuart included, were stacking cages on hoverdollies. Fair was sneaking around, blending casually into the havoc to escort twig folk to safety. Marsle Chin, however, had hid to one side, his face buried in his hands. Only Chezzy could see him from where he had clambered up on the castle itself. Twig folk were climbing over Chezzy's legs to better jump to safety, but Chezzy had his eyes on a particularly scarred looking flying honey badger, who had landed atop the stone roof of the castle.

This flying honey badger had darker fur than all the others, and its scars were like little rivers tracing all over the creature. Chezzy neared, and he strained his hand out to reach while balanced over the crenelated tops of two turrets, but the badger was just out of his grasp. He gave a little lunge and felt his fingers grip around the claw, but his foot slipped and hit the roof. A loud crack, and Chezzy's stomach gave an unruly dip as the entire roof came crashing down.

Whatever Chezzy crashed into cracked and splashed and burned all at once, and Chezzy released the flying honey badger, which went skidding across the chamber. Chezzy wrestled himself out of the largest piece of the cauldron he found himself in and slipped across the caustic liquid that had spilled out of it. He looked down at his stinging body as his menders attempted to cover back over his ate away skin. Then his eyes drifted to the honey badger unconscious across the room. Light was spilling in from above, and dust was swirling around. Faintly, Chezzy could hear the others outside.

He looked up at the light and a drip of acid struck his face. Chezzy flinched back, sucking air, as a hole singed through his cheek. Someone else called out for him as a chunk of the roof crumbled off and crashed into the half cracked cauldron next to him. It spun, slinging acid, and Chezzy threw an arm up. Something glinted in the light, and as the vat came to a stop, Chezzy spied the metal box attached to the side. He could hear it buzzing, and he scooted closer and wrenched it from the cauldron. It peeled off, affixed by some adhesive, and Chezzy held the box up to the light.

A second droplet of acid dripped down and hit the box. It exploded, and Chezzy let out a scream as his hand vanished in a burst of blood and bits. He bit his teeth together as he looked at the nub where his hand had been. "You've got to be kidding me," Chezzy said, his mouth gritted together. Suddenly, everything lifted into the air, and he looked out as the walls crumbled. The rubble all around rose with Chezzy, as did the acid.

He found himself drifting in the sky with the castle remains directly across from a floating Nebulous Zee'han. The other students stood outside her field and were trying to pluck rocks and debris and twig folk from the field without getting caught in it. Nebulous gave Chezzy a nervous, but friendly, wave. Chezzy twisted around, a handless nub waving back until he saw it. The students were attempting to retrieve the flying honey badger, but the acid was inching through the air and blocking them.

Chezzy kicked out with his foot and managed to nudge the little creature to him. He twisted around to Nebulous and pushed the scarred badger across the field to her. She caught it with confusion and watched as Chezzy attempted to claw through the debris. "You got to keep this up," Chezzy called back to her. "The acid, we can't let it splash back down."

He looked around him and saw several students helping to retrieve pieces of the vat. Turod was mending them back together as Minny Deerwink directed the others about him, but Turod didn't have every piece. A large part of the cauldron still floated near Chezzy, within the swimming acid. "Is it safe to grab that, Midnight?"

"It should be."

"Should?"

"Everything is safe for you."

With a groan, Chezzy put his remaining hand through the acid and felt the burn tear through his fingers and up to the edge of his versolock as he struggled against the pain. "Midnight?"

"Yes?" boomed Midnight.

"Help?"

Chezzy's menders shifted, sliding up over his hand, fighting at the acid. He felt his skin numb a little, but the acid was still eating through, biting into him. The everling let out a frustrated cry as he clamped his fingers around the largest cauldron piece then pushed it over towards Turod. He watched it soar in the drift, but Nebulous let out a scream, and Chezzy whipped around just as gravity returned. The ground came fast, and Chezzy's feet hit hard, the acid splashing there as he tumbled sideways before collapsing in the rocks with one ankle twisted around backwards.

XIX.
A blow up bomb.
Greyire.
Built.

*C*hezzy sat in a medilab bed while Doctor Tiz'n fussed over Nebulous, who flailed hazily. The doctor zipped around the girl, taking readings with her versolock and rambling to herself. "It's only the first week." She flashed an almost accusatory look at Chezzy. "Hand cut off. Now hand blown off. It's a right mess." Professor Maxwell, who was sat at the bedside of Chezzy, asked again if he was alright. She had been taking notes on everything he told her, and she was sending them on to Professor Kepler.

"It's basically healed," Chezzy replied, holding up the malformed growth where his hand used to be. Professor Maxwell stifled a giggle as Chezzy looked down at his leg and menders. He couldn't see under his menders, but he could still feel the burns there. On the bed next, Nebulous Zee'han was trying to rub the rather sizable knot on her head while bots dabbed gel over the acid burns on her skin.

Doctor Tiz'n was huffing, attempting to get Nebulous to stay still. She flashed Chezzy a frustrated look. "Next time you want a hand gone, just come straight here and I'll cut it off. Save us all the trouble. What'd you do with the pieces?"

Chezzy shrugged. "I think the acid ate them."

Doctor Tiz'n's head rolled back as she groaned.

That evening, he was released, and he found a newly clean Fern with Fair, and even Stuart, huddled outside of his dormitory waiting for him. Doctor Tiz'n had run an assortment of tests on Chezzy, and, while it didn't seem like there'd be any lingering effects, he was still bothered by just how long it took to heal. Nebulous had left earlier than he, but, before she left, Chezzy had thanked her for pulling him out of the rubble. Nervously, Nebulous didn't get a chance to respond as Doctor Tiz'n went around hovering and moaning again about all the students interrupting her work. The doctor continued to groan and complain until Chezzy left.

"Raven said he was fine. I don't know why you wouldn't believe her." Fern was saying it to herself almost as much as she was saying it to Stuart.

"Well, I don't know. Maybe we shouldn't believe what every robot tells us or does. Right, Fair?" Stuart threw back as his versolock gave an offended scoff.

"Right," Fair mumbled, her eyes uncomfortably to the floor. Stuart hadn't noticed her demeanor though, as he became enmeshed in an argument with Stanley, his versolock.

"Oh, come on, Stanley. Of course, I trust you. You've had my back for days now, at least."

"Does it hurt?" Fair asked Chezzy, trying to ignore the argument as she wiped her face.

"No, it's fine." Chezzy held up the weirdly formed fingers that weren't quite complete. "The acid slowed me down a little, but it's fine," he assured her. She had been a deep black but now was shifting between shades of blue and purple before turning suddenly pale. Chezzy turned to Fern, whose hair was stuck out in different directions. "You got to keep your hair."

"Yeah, well, it's pretty much stuck like this for a while. Hair bots about broke down trying to sort it out."

The others laughed, but then Chezzy noticed Bogdanov lurking in his corner. "Here, let's go inside."

Raven opened the door as Bogdanov gave a displeased sneer. The group stepped in, finding no floor in the dorm. Only open sky. Still, clouds floated around the common room, and even the chairs and tables were done up like little tuffs of cumulous that casually moved about. They plopped down in separate puffs before laughing again.

"This one is excellent," Fair exclaimed.

"Fully," agreed Fern, who seemed to be anxiously checking that the cloud wouldn't stick to her.

"It's alright," Stuart added, cautiously poking the floor with his toes from the cloud nearest the door. "I don't know why this keeps happening."

"Don't go throwing up again," Fern scolded. "Here, everyone, see if you can drift your clouds together." They did and Fern nodded to Chezzy. "So, how did you lose your hand this time?"

"A bomb."

"What?" the other three exclaimed.

"A what? A what is that?" Stuart sputtered. "You said a bomb? A bomb bomb? Like a blow up bomb?"

"Yeah," said Chezzy. "A blow up bomb. There was a metal box strapped to the acid vat, and it exploded when the acid touched it."

"Well, you don't still have it, do you? Are we going to blow up? Did you bring it here to blow us up?" Stuart was spiraling towards pure panic, and it took Fair's soft voice to calm him down.

"How would he-" Fern began but was cut off by Fair's raised hand.

"Stuart, he didn't bring the bomb. It exploded already. So, the bomb isn't here."

"Yeah, but... but... they're around. People keep finding them and all. It's like a... a... epidemic or something."

"An epidemic of acid bombs?" Fern repeated shaking her head. "You don't know what you're talking about."

"I can't believe the twig folk just had it there," Chezzy mused.

"They're twigs. What do they know?" Stuart snapped. "Honestly, they have like, uh, sawdust for brains or... or..."

"Sap," Fern finished, though she seemed deep in thought.

"That," Stuart agreed, pointing to Fern with a pointy arm.

"Where was the box?" Fern asked.

"Pasted to the outside of the vat," Chezzy answered.

Fern turned pensive again. "The outside of the box must be a sensor, but there has to be a receiver inside. If he's in the system, he might be using the routers to signal their explosion."

"Oh," said Fair.

"So, he can just blow us up?" began Stuart again.

"Keep your menders on," Fern gave disregardingly.

Chezzy pulled out his map. "Midnight, can you highlight all of the areas where we know that the acid cauldrons have been found?"

"Yes," Midnight boomed, and he did.

"Stuart's right," Chezzy said, looking over the map as Fern's eyes grew wide. There were several notable areas and a few where cauldrons had been found multiple times.

"Bad precedent," Fern muttered.

"He's going to…" Chezzy went on, "he's going to bring down the Keris."

"He can't do that." Stuart near shouted. "Can he?" He looked to Fern.

She had turned down to her versolock and was looking over some analysis there. "Theoretically, yes. But this," she motioned to the map, "this isn't enough. Everything he put down got collected already. And he'd need something massive near the central supports. There's been nothing there. I don't even know how he could sneak it in."

Stuart gave a huff. "Well, we need to evacuate either way."

"Professor Kepler knows about the boxes," Chezzy mused. "I told Professor Maxwell about them, but they aren't evacuating, so there must be a good reason they aren't. And I've seen those boxes before."

"You have?" Fern's eyes squinted from behind her glasses.

"Yes. Tech McGeehee has loads of them in a crate in his office."

"That's lunacy. He wouldn't be keeping loads of bombs in his office," Stuart balked.

"Unless it's him," Fern reasoned. "You know, if we got ahold of one of those boxes, I could maybe track the signal. Maybe we could confirm if it's Tech or not."

"We need to break into my dorm," Fair whispered, and everyone turned to her. Stuart nearly slipped off of his cloud.

The next morning, Chezzy awoke to the scarred, flying honey badger scratching around atop the dome of the everling tower. Excitedly, the creature had gestured and clawed at the glass, and Chezzy had waved back. But soon, Penton Fulcrank came zooming up sporting some kind of hover pack and hollering at the badger. They seemed to argue, and the flying honey badger took flight with Penton in pursuit.

Chezzy puzzled after the two then rushed to get ready. Today was his first Practicum class. Every student at Balefire had their Practicum today, each with their own subs. But since Chezzy was the only one in his sub, he'd be the only one in the Chiropa Practicum. The class was to be held in the everling lab on level three, which was hidden in the Keris and whose entrance was disguised by a memorial statue. The statue was that of a young everling named Sannyrion who had to be poked in the bellybutton to access the lab. At least, that's what Chezzy had been told by Professor Kepler, the instructor of his Practicum.

After scarfing down his breakfast, hollering bye to his friends, and noting that Professor Kepler wasn't even in the dining lab, he raced for the everling tower, somewhat anxious. Chezzy came to the giant statue and looked up at it. Sannyrion was sat in a pensive pose, and Chezzy had to climb up his leg and on to his lap in order to even reach his bellybutton. Chezzy got to the spot and looked awkwardly at the little hole. He reached forward to put his finger in, and a tiny laser zapped him.

He yanked back, a scanner emitting from the bellybutton already.

"Midnight?" Chezzy asked, but Midnight was already scanning it back. The everling statue gave a jolt and then shifted to one side as lines formed in the wall behind it. The door had been wholly invisible before, but now it slid open as Chezzy slipped off of the statue and peered through. The lab was empty, and it lit up as he entered. Cautiously, he stepped forward, but the doorway sealed shut behind him, startling Chezzy. He could hear the statue beyond sliding back into place. He looked around the lab.

The lab consisted of several chambers and all kinds of equipment. There were even a few half built robots, which Midnight scanned. "I prefer my server form," Raven chimed.

"Android, all the way," Midnight boomed back. This sparked an argument over preferred robot forms between the two of them.

In the next room Chezzy found, the area was completely white and completely bare and covered in a sort of polymer glass coating. It was slick, and he was able to slide around in it. Where the walls and the floor met, it was curved together in such a way that he could run and slide up before sliding back down again, as if he were wearing skates on a ramp. Chezzy ran around playing at this when a sudden sound made him slip, and he found himself falling down on to the floor of a chamber in the old castle.

He looked up and saw three men stood around him. "Sorry," he said, fairly confused about where he was and how he got there, but none of the men seemed to notice him.

One man, who was bald and wore clear menders that showed lined markings that ran over his entire body, was speaking. "Are you sure this is what you want then?"

"Yes," growled a second man who, upon looking at him, didn't seem to have a natural structure to his face. Everything felt slightly off center. When Chezzy looked at the rest of his body, it appeared the same. This arm was longer, this hand was larger, this eye was higher. Everything about him was asymmetrical.

The third man was silent, but tears were running down his face. The first man spoke again, drawing Chezzy's attention. "Alright." He was accessing something on his versolock, and Chezzy saw the asymmetrical man's versolock light up as well. "Then you have it." The first man gave a rather harsh look to the other two men then simply faded out of existence. The asymmetrical man pulled up his versolock, and a long list of names shone into the air before him. There was a grim smile across his face.

"What do you think of him?" Chezzy whirled around to see who had spoken.

He found Professor Kepler was standing behind him. "Think of who, Professor?"

Professor Kepler motioned to the asymmetrical man. "Of Greyire."

Chezzy turned to take another look at the man, but the world was dissolving around him, and he found himself standing back in the white room with Professor Kepler. "That... that was Greyire?"

"Yes, it was," replied Professor Kepler.

"And who were those other men?"

"One of them was named Ahmes. He was one of the oldest everlings that we knew of. Greyire molered him."

"And the other man?"

"That man..." Kepler turned a pensive eye to the spot where he had been. "That man is Alessa's father. She never knew him. Vanished long, long ago after a spat of crimes."

Chezzy thought about this. An odd link formed between he and Professor Maxwell, but he pushed the thought aside. "What did he give to Greyire?"

"It was a Showing registry. It had the names of all the clades and their recorded abilities... everything. Not easy to get. They're only stored in a few places, you know. But you're here for your Practicum. Unfortunately, I have to tend to some other business, so you can take the rest of the day off."

"But… are you going to evacuate the school?"

Professor Kepler paused, taking the measure of Chezzy. "Why would I do that?"

"Because of the explosives and the acid. You know about it. He's going to blow this place up, isn't he?" Chezzy's voice rose a little, and he fought to steady his breathing.

Professor Kepler's face remained calm. "No. I'm not going to evacuate the school. I have the utmost trust in you. You'll figure it out."

"Figure it out? What if he's Tech?" Chezzy spurted.

"Tech? You think the Acid King is Tech?"

Chezzy scrunched his face up. "He has all those explosive boxes in his office, and he's already in the system, so it'd be easier for him to hide. And maybe the figure we saw is just an SI he's made to distract us or… or…"

"Or maybe Tech is just bad at his job," Professor Kepler said.

"Or that," Chezzy conceded.

Professor Kepler glanced to his versolock. "If you want to look through the recorded database or hook up any drives to the projector room, you can. I have to get going."

"You don't want me to come with you?"

Professor Kepler gave a sly smile. "No, not for this one. Do what you see fit to. I won't be able to help much as I've some important things to take care of." Then, with a purple flash, he was gone.

"More important than acid bombs?" Chezzy managed to the empty lab. He wandered back out, unsure of what to do. He meandered down towards the grounds. Along the way, he passed by several classrooms where he could hear other students in different years doing their own Practicums, but he marched on and wondered what else Professor Kepler knew.

Chezzy rode an elevator down and walked out of the old castle before heading back around to the remains of the twig folk castle. He sat on a rock and watched as the little twig folk jabbered to each other. They were all working to rebuild, and some sailed on boats carrying loads of supplies from the forest nearby. Chezzy looked over to the flying honey badger island, where a large, electric bubble reached shore to shore.

Chezzy could see the flying honey badgers within, watching the twig folk boats as they passed. Others flew at the bubble's edge, only to be shocked and drop down before rising to try again once they woke. Chezzy got up from the rock and approached the enclosure. Stood apart from the rest was the same scarred badger, watching Chezzy. Suddenly, the thing turned and looked behind Chezzy, and Chezzy whirled to see Penton Fulcrank walking up.

"Hey now," said Penton Fulcrank, and he looked over at the flying honey badger. "Put that o'dome on t'day. Keep 'em in. Ah. There he is. That one there, with the scars, that's D.O.G."

"That's what?" Chezzy asked.

"That's D.O.G. He the first one t'get made by the director's own direction. An' he's the favorite still. There's something awful smart about that fella there. He go'n t'get out of that cage he in. Surely he will."

"Professor Kepler made them?"

"He… I think he were lonely," Penton cleared his throat.

"And he named that one D.O.G.?"

"He did." Penton Fulcrank gave a sigh and looked up over the bubble before looking back down at D.O.G. and gesturing at him. "I think he knowed who you 'as. He lookin' at you like that. Anyhoo." Penton Fulcrank continued across another bridge to another island as Chezzy turned back to D.O.G., but the flying honey badger wasn't looking at him anymore. Instead, he was staring at the twig folk, baring his teeth angrily. Chezzy turned to look at the little stick people as he rubbed his newly grown hand.

At lunch, Fern, Fair, and Stuart were excitedly talking about their Practicums when Chezzy arrived. "What about yours?" Fern asked as Chezzy missed grabbing a plate that went by on the slipstream.

"He... couldn't be there."

"What do you mean?"

"Professor Kepler was busy, so I didn't have my Practicum," Chezzy explained as he snatched a plate off the next batch that passed by.

"Oh, Chezzy," commiserated Fair.

"Is that bad?" Stuart asked.

"It's fine," Fern shrugged. "Lay off him, both of you." She gave a half smile to Chezzy.

"Mm, you're right," Fair nodded, more to herself than to Chezzy. "Listen, we can't stay too late tomorrow at Sidelight. Oh, should we just skip it?" Fair grimaced.

"Can't skip," Fern replied flatly. "We'll get into the registry afterward."

Chezzy's stomach sank. "Wait. Registry? What registry?" Chezzy asked.

"The Showing registry. In the Faxowl dorm," Fair said. Fern grinned alongside her.

"Why does she look like that?" Stuart asked.

"Because we're going to hack it, you loaf," Fern laughed. "At least, I am."

"How long will it take?" asked Fair.

"Cradle?" Fern looked down to her versolock.

Cradle chimed in. "With a locapter scanner, you could probably locate the drive, cut into the chassis, and remove the data file in under thirty-three trillion ticks."

"Guess who has a locapter scanner," Fern smirked.

"Cut? Won't we get in trouble for that?" Stuart asked, suddenly shaking.

"Not any more trouble than we would for sneaking into Tech's office tonight," Chezzy quietly interjected.

"Wait, what?" Stuart spat.

"Professor Kepler said I should do what I see fit to do," Chezzy added.

"I don't think Professor Kepler meant to damage school property or," his voice lowered, "sneak into a staff office. Maybe we should ask first. I mean, maybe the director was preparing to evacuate the school, and that's why he missed your Practicum."

"He's not going to evacuate. It's up to us, Stuart. We need a box so that Fern can track the Acid King. And if Fair has found out who he is, then we need to know that too," Chezzy explained.

"But," Stuart began.

"Listen, Stuart. I'll take the blame," Chezzy countered.

"You what?"

"Anything goes wrong. We get caught. It was all me."

"You can't do that," Stuart said, but it was obvious the idea appealed to him.

"It's like what Professor Kepler said," Chezzy added.

Stuart's eyes grew large. "What did he say?"

"The rules don't matter. And this is a priority. So, the office tonight and Faxowl dorm tomorrow during the Sidelight trip." He turned to Fern. "A locapter?"

Fern sent around a sly look. "I just have to pick it up from Mail Warp. I'm not letting Tech's crummy system take forever to sort it and bring it to me. Besides, if he is the Acid King, I think it's better to avoid his oversight."

"So, we can still show them around Sidelight a little?" Fair asked eagerly.

"Fine," Chezzy conceded, concealing his own excitement about the town. "But how does your scanner thing work?"

"It's used to locate specific devices in large structure robotics for diagnostic and repair purposes," Fern explained. "We'll find the registry and rip it right out."

"Ohhh," Stuart groaned, turning a sickly color.

Fern brushed him off. "As for how we break into Tech's office, I think I have a plan."

"I can't believe the door just opened up," Fern repeated, shaking her head.

"I didn't even have to go invisible," Fair agreed.

"What a waste of a good plan." She was eyeing a paper slip she had taken from Tech's office before pocketing it.

Both of them seemed somewhat disappointed, but Chezzy was relieved how easy it had been to get the box. Tech's door had opened right up for him. There wasn't even an AI monitoring the room, which the girls had said was odd. But Chezzy was able to walk right in and take one of the boxes without anything preventing him. He looked down to the humming metal in his hand as they reached the Chiropa door, and it began to wheel aside. He scanned for Bogdanov, but didn't see the SI around. "I'm just glad we got it," Chezzy said.

"Well, yeah, but…" Fern seemed at a loss for words.

Stuart appeared in the everling common room. He was huddled up in a shiver amongst the snowscape of the room. "Is it… done?"

"It's done, you big wimp," Fern threw out as she stomped forward into the snow. "Wasn't even locked."

"Oh," Stuart responded with a note of relief that left the instant his eyes settled on the metal box in Chezzy's hand. "Shouldn't it be in a… in a… like a bomb box?"

"We're going to deactivate it, Stuart," Fern rolled her eyes and turned to Fair. "Can you deal with him?"

They spent the night in the everling dorm together, much to Raven's disapproval. Chezzy had been in charge of the deactivation under Fern's instructions. Fair had escorted Stuart up to the observatory and distracted him by playing a game on their versolocks. The game involved projecting little figures to fight with one another, which elicited squeals from Stuart, to Fern's increasing annoyance. But she gave a satisfied huff and bounded forward when Chezzy unhooked the last chip, and the humming of the box died. She snatched up the box, twiddling it in her fingers as she made notes in her versolock.

"Careful," Chezzy cautioned.

"What? It's off. No hum," Fern gave as she trudged through the snow to the slipstream up into the observatory. Chezzy sighed and followed after.

"Honestly, I bet you'd love Crattleboards," Stuart was saying to Fair as they entered.

The group wound up talking about Sidelight until Fair and Stuart passed out. Fern seemed to never tire, and eventually Chezzy crashed as well. When Chezzy awoke, he noticed the box on the chest of a sleeping Fern. She had some sort of headset on, but he could tell she was asleep by the slight snores she made. Chezzy crept close and took the box off of her then set it aside. It still made him uneasy.

He roused the others, and they raced down to the old castle, where students were amassing to go to Sidelight. Professor Maxwell was trying to bring order as students lined up to file out to the waiting hovercarts. Each could hold six students, and the group ran forward to grab one together. The cart bobbed around as they clambered into the seats that ran around the inner edge. Stuart took up two seats by himself, and he nearly toppled everyone when he plopped down, all of them giggling as they fought to hold on until the hovercart settled.

Chezzy turned, scanning the other carts filling until almost none were available. Marsle Chin was ambling back and forth along the rows, asking if there was room, but students kept turning him away. With his head hung, he didn't even bother to ask Chezzy's group, but Chezzy called out to him. "Marsle, hey."

Marsle looked alarmed by this. "You... you know my name?"

"Well, yeah," said Chezzy.

"How could anyone forget the name of the person that made you use the bathroom on yourself?" asked Stuart, grinning his animal teeth to the others with an air of superiority.

"Be nice," chastised Fair, and Stuart's mouth clamped shut.

Marsle looked mortified, and the color drained from his face. "Yeah, s-sorry, about that, you know," he said, and he began to turn.

"You can ride with us if you want to," Chezzy added, though Fern nudged his side.

Marsle looked back, astonished. "Really?"

"Sure," Chezzy replied.

Marsle climbed on. It was crowded, and they had to have him sit opposite of Stuart since Marsle was the next biggest kid, and Stuart was already making the hovercart dip down threateningly to one side. Marsle beamed around. "Really, wait till my mom hears. Really, she won't believe it at all."

"Believe what?" asked Chezzy, though he noticed that Fern and Fair were giving him an odd look.

"That I got to ride to Sidelight with you. She'll be so proud. You know, she asks about you every message she sends me, almost."

"She does?" Chezzy had an uneasy feeling.

"You mean she asks about all of the students?" asked Stuart.

Fern had set her face in her hand, and Fair was shaking her head from side to side at Stuart, coloring dark.

"What?" asked Stuart. "What is it?"

Marsle had turned pink himself, and he was looking at Chezzy apologetically. "I'm sorry. I didn't mean to… to… you know."

"What?" blurted Stuart again, but Chezzy understood.

"Stuart, every one of our parents ask about him every time we talk to them," answered Fern in an annoyed voice.

"Really?" he asked and looked over to Fair who was nodding in agreement. "Really," repeated Stuart again, though this time it wasn't exactly a question.

"Y-yeah," added Marsle.

"Oh, because you're one of those, uh, yeah. That's right," said Stuart, and he nudged Chezzy's arm. "Must be weird." He looked to Fair hoping for her to agree, but she was looking down now, blending into the seats of the hovercart.

"It's alright," said Chezzy, turning to look away from his friends. Several carts over, he spied Vivi Halflight, the pretty Faxowl whose glowing skin left Chezzy blinking.

"I just forget is all," explained Stuart, who now was sounding dejected. "Honestly, it's not that big of a deal. Everyone here is special in some way. Even Fern."

Fern rolled her eyes as she snapped. "You don't get it. His parents or grandparents or something probably built this whole place. None of us would be here if it wasn't for them. He is basically royalty."

"But not really, right?" Stuart asked, hopefully.

"Really," Fair corrected. "Why do you think the evestry is having a fit?"

"What's an evestry?" Stuart asked.

"Mm, they run things now that the everlings are..." She shaded darkly.

"And they're having a fit?" Stuart went on, not noticing.

Fair was evening her colors out. "Haven't you been reading the articles from Bag Hoolihow?"

"What bag?" Stuart asked.

"Heisenberg, help him," Fern muttered.

"I don't really read the news either," Marsle chimed in helpfully.

Fair shot Marsle a look. "It's more than Bag Hoolihow or Djinni Arrappa or whatever. It's everyone."

"Well, yeah," Marsle conceded.

Chezzy realized that Stuart was staring at him. "What?"

"I just don't see what the big deal is," Stuart shrugged.

Before anyone could reply, though, the cart jolted forward, and they looked around as a cry went out from nearby. A couple of Epsilon girls in another cart were rocking theirs from side to side as the younger boys they were riding with gave out little cries. The hovercart tilted wildly and threatened to buck them all out of their seats. Neighboring students were laughing, but that didn't hide the look of unease they had, lest one of the boys was thrown out and crashed into their own hovercart. Chezzy turned back to Stuart who was still giving him an odd look, but he didn't say anything else. Instead, he looked in the distance where Sidelight would slowly grow from.

XX.
Sneaking.
Nik Daedle.
Out of the bomb.

Chezzy couldn't imagine why people would want to live anywhere else. The buildings were all lit up and flashing, and there were shops of every kind on every road. Arching overhead, were rides and rollercoasters that spun and twisted people around. Patrons walked about talking joyously as they snacked on treats from the many shops and roving carts. Some carried drinks that were the size of a bucket, and everyone was wearing an array of oddities that were strapped over their menders.

One man walked by sporting a solar system that actually circled around him. And Chezzy spotted a woman draped in a fur that would periodically come to life and resituate over her menders. A man riding a tortoise the size of a truck came cantering past. The man, himself, wore a twin shell to his tortoise, and he threw little candies from buckets that were stacked around him. Each candy had a little note tied to its wrapper.

Stuart picked up one of the candies as they disembarked their hovercart and read the note aloud. "'Don't be a prat?' What? That's all it says?" He looked around at the other students before picking up another one. "'Use the passing lane for passing?' What?" He looked up to the tortoise man, but he was already far down the street and still throwing his candy and notes.

"Come on," Fair was saying to them, and she and Fern led them further into the village. Marsle followed along, a hopeful look on his face.

"What is this place?" asked Chezzy.

"Mm, people live here and all, but it's just a big playground. A lot of younger scientists move here and work on their starter projects and the like, so you see a lot of new things popping up here first. And, also, there are rides." Fair added the last part with a short laugh.

"Whoa," said Stuart.

"Yeah, whoa and whatnot," Fern cut in lowly. "I have to run by Mail Warp. We can meet up at The Sugar and Salt Research Station." She flashed a meaningful look to the others before setting her eyes on Marsle indicatively.

"Nice," breathed Fair, trying to see if Marsle had noticed, but he was still fixated on Chezzy. "Well, let's try a ride."

"Sure," Chezzy chimed in, all too aware. Soon, they were on a rollercoaster, which zoomed around the village, between and over buildings. There were no rails, really, but the cart followed a very specific path. The others laughed and screamed, and Marsle threatened to yell. He was looking pretty sickly but was laughing again by the time they got off.

Afterwards, Fair led them on to The Sugar and Salt Research Station, which was just a little pop shop with snacks, custom ice creams, and its very own in house salted sugar floats. Chezzy ordered a round of floats for everyone and topped it off with a sweetbreads platter. Fair had nervously watched Chezzy pay before he passed a float to her. A little relief crept into her color, and they wound up snacking around a table as they waited for Fern to arrive.

"My mom's not going to believe this," said Marsle.

"I can't believe this place either," added Stuart.

Chezzy could tell that Sidelight wasn't what Marsle was talking about, but he didn't correct Stuart and neither did Fair or Marsle. It didn't matter though, because, just then, Fern appeared and snatched up her own float. "I love these."

"Well?" Chezzy asked suggestively, trying to eye the thing bulging at her mender side.

Fern flashed him a wink, straw in mouth. "Did you see what's going on outside?"

"No? What?"

"We have to move." Then Fern gave herself a brain freeze trying to down the rest of her float before hurrying out, the others in tow. In the streets nearby, thousands of water balloons were rolling out of dispensers at varying points. At once, the war broke out with indiscriminate volleys, and the five of them rushed to join. It seemed like the entire school was there. Chezzy even spied Veronica Fayette running through the explosions of water, seeming to have fun. He edged away nervously and looked around for his friends.

Fern was baiting students into chasing her so that Fair could lob balloons from chameleoned places, only becoming visible for bursts. Stuart was so big he couldn't hide, and Chezzy ran over to Stuart, pelting Metwell Chase who lunged and attached himself to a wall, raining balloons back at Chezzy. The balloons broke apart on the needles of Stuart, and soon they looked like little bowties at the ends of Stuart's spines. Marsle sped by, being chased by Beta year students. He was laughing and threatening to yell again, but they kept after him.

Something stabbed into Chezzy's back, and he reached back and found blood there. He looked up at Stuart. "You poked me."

"Oh, it'll heal," Stuart called as he began running at the wall underneath where Metwell was attached. Stuart took one big bound up and managed to hit Metwell in the face with a particularly large balloon that served to get Stuart just as wet as it got Metwell. Chezzy laughed at them both but stopped when he saw Veronica again. She was watching him with that strange look she always had.

"We need to get moving."

Chezzy jumped and turned to see Fern with Fair lingering behind her. "Right."

"I want to stop by the science district, but we should hurry back," Fern added.

"Science district?" Chezzy looked back to where Veronica was again, but she had disappeared.

"I'm pretty sure Tech's going to be there," Fern commented. "He had some notes about it in his office."

Soon, they were sneaking away from the melee and into the science district. They passed a number of breakfastries and shops along the way. Chezzy struggled to make mental notes of each for future trips. But that was soon overshadowed. The science district was abuzz, and most notable there, was the Burroughs Brothers Power Borrower Shop. The shop promised that they could provide people with the abilities of certain clades for a limited amount of time.

One of the brothers, a heavyset man, was calling, answering someone. "That's right. Five and a half quadrillion ticks. Perhaps soon we can make them permanent."

"And how close are you to that?" The voice was familiar, and Chezzy turned to see Tech McGeehee. Chezzy exchanged a look with Fern.

"Quite close. Quite. Quite," the one brother nodded his heavy face.

"These fools are no more innovators than you are, Tech." Chezzy spied Professor Tampago Brown in the throng. "They're pulling a sham. Finally cracked grandmother's safe, did you both?" He leveled the words accusingly at the brother.

"Let's get out of here," Chezzy mumbled to the others who nodded in agreement before slinking out of the crowd. They tucked away through alleys and byways, and Chezzy noticed that the water balloon bows on Stuart had disintegrated to nothing. At one point, they spied Marsle Chin asking Fever May if she had seen Chezzy. She shook her head to a dejected looking Marsle, but Chezzy couldn't make out what she was saying. On they snuck.

When they reached the carts, they guiltily boarded one and took off back for Balefire. "I feel pretty bad about that," Fair mumbled.

"Can't be helped," Fern replied.

"You think I'm bad when I'm scared? Imagine what would happen with him," Stuart's eyes were big, and he nudged Chezzy.

"Yeah," Chezzy said.

Sidelight slipped away, and Chezzy could see that Fair was feeling more nervous now about the Faxowl dormitory. At least with Tech's office, there wasn't an AI monitoring them. He looked at the Keris in the distance as the school grew. Before long, they were riding up an elevator then navigating to the central, lower section of the Keris, near the dining lab and close to where the Keris met the old castle. There, they came upon a strange field with a swirl of lightning and lava just beyond.

Fern poked the field quizzically but was interrupted as the dome above lit up and spoke with a severe voice. "And what is it you've got here? I know you don't expect me to let your friends inside. I need not remind you of the rules." Before the AI even finished, she projected out a rule list governing who could enter which dorm.

"Ma Berravere, I only need to show them something we have on file in the Faxowl histories. You know, the Showing registry and all. I couldn't find it anywhere else, so I thought maybe you would let them see it. It's just a small thing," Fair protested.

"A small thing, Fair Jekyll? A small thing? Letting in a, we have an Oxenbor and a Sciofall and a, a…" The dorm AI trailed off. "A Chiropa? Is that… is that Chezzy Nithercot with you?"

Fair glanced back at Chezzy. "Yes."

"Oh, forgive me." The AI's voice had flipped and sounded almost nervous. "You may enter."

"I can?" Chezzy asked.

"Yes, of course. Do forgive me. Director Kepler made it explicitly clear that you're to have access to anything you need."

"Right," Chezzy replied. The others flashed him a look.

"Guess I won't have to walk you through it," Fern mumbled to Fair as they watched the lava and lightning drain away before the field fell, revealing a chasm. A small bridge descended down and they crossed into the Faxowl common room. It was filled with desks, chairs, and monitors, and it looked more like a study hall than a common room. Chezzy scanned the numerous scorch marks and other damage from the experimental rough housing of the Faxowls. Even the desks, their headsets, and screened eye gear were notably marked up.

Of greater note, though, were the great cylindrical screens around the center of the room, some scratched or singed, but all operational. Various students from various years were rotating around the screens, and they were melting from one to the next in a continuous stream. They showcased the students exhibiting their abilities while listing off various things about them. The four drew up before the cylinders. "We really shouldn't be here," Stuart muttered.

"Oh, can it. You heard what Ma Berrawhat's her face said about Chezzy," Fern slapped back.

"Ma Berravere," Ma Berravere corrected, but Fern ignored her as she drew out a tube shaped device that had four arms with sort of magnetized legs. "Oh, no," Ma Berravere muttered.

"Whatever the everling wants," Fern parroted as she swept the locapter scanner across the room before centering it on one of the consoles near the series of screens. She walked forward and pressed the device to the chassis. Of its own accord, it moved around before situating and lighting up a section of the console. "I can get into that," Fern asserted before kneeling down with her versolock. A laser shot out and cut into the metal. The dorm AI let out a groan, as did Stuart. Chezzy's hand twitched absently.

Fern cut a neat square from the metal then brandished some tools and went to tinkering inside. Before too long, she drew out some kind of drive, and the cylindrical screens all went blank, an error message appearing. She turned a sweet smile to Chezzy before situating the square back to the console, welding it shut, and grabbing her locapter scanner. Fern felt over the rough weld spots. "I don't really have anything to buff that out."

"Everyone's going to notice that," Stuart gestured.

"Doesn't matter," Chezzy said. "Ma Berravere?"

"Yes?"

"Do you have to listen to me too?"

"Yes."

"Good. Don't tell anyone what happened here. Understand?"

"I do."

Chezzy nodded and looked to the others. "Good enough?"

Fern shrugged, looking over the drive. "Good enough for me."

"Yes, but how are we going to read that thing?" Fair asked.

"I think we can in my lab," Chezzy remarked.

Fern looked up, alert. "Your what?"

They stood in the everling lab as Fern twirled around. "I cannot believe you were keeping this from us."

"I only just got it yesterday," Chezzy protested.

"We could've used this yesterday." Fern was walking around in the white room area.

"For what?" Stuart asked, seemingly unimpressed.

"Well, I could've used this yesterday," Fern corrected. "Let's fire this thing up."

"Fire which part, exactly?" Chezzy asked. "It's not like it came with instructions."

"Since when do I need instructions?"

"Just a room with some old junk behind a statue, right Fair?" Stuart asked.

"No," Fair replied. She had been quiet as she looked around, but now she turned to Chezzy. "Chezzy, do you realize what you could do with this place? What you could build?"

"Not really. Like I said, I didn't have much of a Practicum."

"This is some of the most advanced equipment to come out of Acres Corporation," Fair added, her voice near a whisper.

"And Hudbot," gave Fern.

Chezzy looked around and saw both names stamped on much of the equipment. "Is that good?"

Fern snorted. "A lot better than the Acres droids we found, but look at this." She had taken control of a console, and she pressed a button. Suddenly, the white room was filled with the profiles of dozens of former students. "Cradle, you know my criteria. See what you can find." The profiles went zooming by, so fast it almost made Chezzy dizzy. He and the others backed out of the room and closer to where Fern was lounging, sat atop some other unknown piece of equipment.

Suddenly, the white room filled with a single profile. There, stood a sickly looking boy. His pale yellow menders had tubes coming off of them, and he was grinning shyly while holding one of the tubes over one of the retainers from Controlled Physics. The orb ate its way through the table before it clunked down to the floor below. The sound startled the boy, and he gave a timid shrug. Writing was flashing around, detailing his interests in materials development, Boletare histories, SI programming, and music theory. Then it flashed symbols and numbers that Chezzy didn't understand. "Nik Daedle," Chezzy mumbled, looking at the name. He turned to Fair. "Is that the one you saw?"

Fair nodded. "Yes."

For the next several days, they scoured through documents, informationals, Bag Hoolihow articles, and everything else they could get ahold of. All of their excess time was spent in the everling lab trying to find anything at all. But there was no mention of Nik Daedle anywhere else. Chezzy had started to take nightly strolls down to the flying honey badger pen so as to give his eyes a break. D.O.G. would greet him through the bubble, and the animal would gesture towards the twig folk with evident hatred. The twig folk had been hard at work, attempting to rebuild their castle.

During all this, Fern had managed to hack into the box, only to find the signal had been disconnected from the school routers. "It'll come back on, I swear," she had assured them.

"What? When the school blows up?" Stuart argued back.

"These things run on cycles. It'll sync up eventually."

"Eventually, when the school blows up," Stuart looked around at the others for help.

"Yeah, or that. But really, it'll take some time for the entire system to come back on if that's what he's trying to do. He might be using an external router that's tapped into the school system, and that's why we can't see it. Either way, if it connects, we'll be able to find him or the router."

"What good is a router?" Stuart scoffed.

"The boxes might be cycling, but the router is going to have a constant signal from him. It'll take us right to him," Fern smirked. This did little to comfort Stuart, but Fern had rigged the box up with the locapter scanner and some other things she had put together. Supposedly, she'd get a notification if things came back online in any way. But, so far, there hadn't been a beep out of the bomb.

The box was still quiet when their next Practicum came around, and Professor Kepler didn't show up. It was the same the week after that. The director hadn't even been seen at meal times either, nor around the school at all. So, during each Practicum lesson, Chezzy found himself sitting in the everling lab, scouring video files for Nik Daedle. The everling lab had morphed into a somber sit in where they took turns poring through everything they could think of. Chezzy felt like he was losing his mind to all the boredom. All while the box sat nearby, completely unconnected.

The only lead had been found a couple evenings earlier while they all sat around in the everling lab with takeaways from the dining lab. Fern had stood and shouted, "I knew it. I found you, I knew it."

"Is it Nik Daedle?" Chezzy asked, scrambling out of his chair, despite his numb backside, and dropping his utensils to the floor.

"Yeah, well, no. Not exactly. I was thinking, get Shivweigh records and Fieldmyre records and all that. They aren't kept in the same places and can be a bit, uh, trickier to get ahold of. But I figured it might give us something."

"And did it?" Fair asked, making no effort to hide her displeasure. She was palely hued and, as she rubbed her tired eyes, waves of color rippled across her face. She glanced over to Stuart who was snoring in the corner, face down on a desk that was visibly covered in drool.

"No. But Kellogg's Sanitorium has this." She projected up an image and file of a man.

"Trick Daedle?" Chezzy asked, scratching his back, absently.

"He's a Sciofall," Fair pointed out.

"Yeah, well, he's the only Daedle we've found. Looking at his age and all, I'm thinking dad."

"There's no family listed or anything?" Fair went on.

"No. Nothing. Nothing else I can find on him at all, except this. But maybe we can pop over and ask him," Fern lifted her eyebrows suggestively.

"Kellogg's has pretty restricted visitations. We wouldn't be able to get in for a long time," Fair replied.

Fern's face scrunched up as she looked to Fair. "I didn't know that."

"Mm, it's a dead end," Fair said flatly.

Fern sighed. "I bet the Acid King scrubbed everything he could from the systems."

After another week, four additional students had stumbled into acid cauldrons. The pressure to figure out what was going on was mounting as teachers struggled to respond to inquiries from students and parents alike. Professor Kepler had been mute on the matter, as had Professor Maxwell. But Chezzy knew it was really up to him. Unlike the rest of the staff, Tech McGeehee was frequently seen about in a rather chipper mood. Chezzy and his friends had mostly abandoned the file search on Nik Daedle and instead had been tailing Tech in their free time.

"It's boring. Worse than the files," Stuart moaned during breakfast. "He just sits in his lab. Honestly, if he's the Acid King, then I'm Arbiter Kid Bakehour."

"Did you hear Professor Kettlewack and Professor Clyster talking about the Faxowl break in again?" Fair asked.

Stuart went terribly pale. "No?"

"It's nothing bad," Fair assured him. "They decided it must have been the Acid King."

"Who's spreading that name around?" Chezzy asked, suspiciously. Fair shook her head.

"Didn't learn a lot. Professor Kettlewack spent most of the conversation complaining about some SI she has a crush on," Fern threw in, her mouth full as she chewed. "Said the SI's been so glitchy she can't ever tell where it's going to be. Has her all flustered, I guess." Fern glanced to her versolock. "Oh, we got to go." She grabbed a few more things from the slipstream and her plate and popped up. The Practicums today involved some sort of off campus trip for each sub. Except for Chezzy's. He sighed, thinking of Wutherford Home, as he continued to eat alone while everyone filed out of the dining lab.

After he ate, Chezzy wandered back to the everling lab alone with little to do as Tech had gone out with the Sciofalls. He paced around, scratching his back as he looked over his projected map. His back had been itching for weeks, and he wasn't sure what was wrong with him. As he stared at the map, the little dots seemed to blur. He put the map away and plopped down in a chair. The all night searches, trailing, and research sessions were starting to take a toll on him. Twice, he'd passed out in hallways, only to have Midnight wake him before he was late to class.

Chezzy awoke that evening to Fern shaking him. "What is it?" he asked groggily as he looked around the lab.

"Signal just connected," Fern said as she looked back down to her versolock. Chezzy turned to Fair and Stuart who were stood nearby, nervously.

Chezzy straightened up, reaching for his back.

"Why are you scratching again?" Fair asked.

"Please, Fair," Fern cut in, and they gave each other a momentary look. The two had been inseparable the last few weeks and had taken to some sort of unspoken communication that often left Chezzy and Stuart exchanging their own uncertain looks. Fern turned back to her versolock and concentrated.

They watched her silently as Stuart fidgeted uncomfortably. "Where is it?" he ventured.

"It's… It's…" Fern looked back to Chezzy. "Let me see your map." Chezzy lifted his versolock and projected it forward. Fern glanced between the map and her versolock multiple times and shook her head.

"Fern?" Fair asked.

Fern looked around at the others. "It's coming from the twig folk castle."

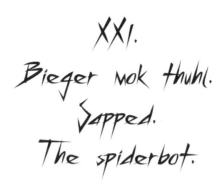

XXI.
Bieger mok thuhl.
Sapped.
The spiderbot.

"What if the twig folk won't let us in?" Chezzy asked as he hurried through the passageways.

"We might have to ask them nicely," Fern huffed as she trotted after him.

"I don't speak twig folk," Stuart protested at the rear. His thudding footfalls echoed around the hallway heavily.

"It is an elective," chimed Fair as she panted. She was shifting pale with notes of pink or red in her cheeks and around her eyes.

"Is it? Do you speak it?" Stuart looked impressed. Fair shook her head, and Fern did likewise.

"Never mind," Chezzy cut in. "We'll figure it out."

"I speak Twigliss," boomed Midnight. They all gave a start but kept moving.

"You do?" asked Chezzy as he recomposed himself and covered his versolock with his other hand.

"Yes," Midnight responded, somewhat muffled.

Chezzy looked back to Fern who nodded with a grin. "Let's get down there."

Stuart's groaning continued all the way down to the grounds, which they found empty of students. The evening sun was descending in a mad hurry, and the sky was already deeply purple above. The four of them ran across bridge after bridge in the low, undulating light until they got to the island with the flying honey badgers. The animals had piled dirt going up a fourth of the security bubble, and it was blocking the view to the center. Around the rim, there were many flying honey badgers standing guard, and they peered down at the four students, imperiously.

Puzzled, Chezzy called out. "D.O.G.?" Two of the flying honey badgers were chittering to one another before one disappeared, only to reappear shortly with a visibly dirty D.O.G. He looked at Chezzy then looked over to the twig folk with a snarl. Chezzy followed his gaze. The twig folk had made a lot of progress since the castle's destruction. Walls were up, as were two towers and a main hall of sorts. Even at this late hour, they labored away. Atop the walls, Chezzy could see that they had mounted tiny scorpions, which pointed menacingly at the flying honey badger bubble.

"Aw," said Fair, "they're mastering defensive siege engines."

An eyebrow lifted above Fern's glasses. "And that's a good thing?"

"Well, it's cute," defended Fair.

"It is cute," Stuart added. "And scary."

"Won't be so cute if we have to break in," Fern went on.

"Something isn't right," said Chezzy. The other three looked to him. "I'll go talk to them."

"By yourself?" Fern asked.

Chezzy eyed her back, trying to sort out how to keep them safe. "Yeah, what's a scorpion next to Stuart's barbs? You guys hang back in case… well, in case anything happens. If it does, you go get Professor Kepler, okay?" He said it, but he felt a wave of apprehension, so he added, "Or Professor Maxwell or Professor Tampago Brown. Just, someone," he relented.

Stuart groaned. "Why don't I call them now?" But Chezzy was already crossing over the bridge to the island of the twig folk. Many of them quit their work to look up at his approach. They jabbered to one another in the squeaky, reedy sounds they made, and soon, from the great hall, came the heaviest of them that Chezzy had seen.

The Twig Queen was nearly up to Chezzy's knee and looked like the old root of a long dead plant. She was thick and aided in her walking by a number of small twig folk who held on to her many, sporadic arms. They helped her up to the fore wall, where a small throne was being placed for her to sit at. Then she looked at Chezzy with the dark holes that marked her eyes.

"I'm… I'm looking for the Acid King," Chezzy hesitated, "or maybe a machine he installed here."

Midnight immediately translated what he said in his tremendous tone. This sent a wave of jabbers that ran across the many, amassed ranks who were watching on. When the queen spoke, sawdust emitted from her mouth, and her voice sounded like the husky creak of old wood in tall trees. She spoke slowly and clearly, and the other voices of her followers died out when they heard hers. She said three simple words, which sounded like, "Bieger mok thuhl." Chezzy didn't understand her at all.

"What'd she say, Midnight?" But Midnight did not reply as there was an uproar of small voices from the gathered twig folk as they rushed around. The Twig Queen had stood up, quite abruptly, and she was being helped back down into the great hall while others took up arms around the outer walls. They carried small, wooden spears and little bows with arrows. The triggerfish were all manned and aimed at Chezzy, and Chezzy held up his hands. "Whoa, what just happened? You need to calm down a little."

Midnight began to translate, but screams were erupting from one side of the tiny castle as a wall caved over and crumbled down into the river, sending the twig folk who were atop it scattering out. Burrowing up, came D.O.G. first. He was followed by a streaming line of other flying honey badgers who crawled out and took flight. They speared their way into the tiny castle and began wreaking upon the twig folk a vicious onslaught. "Wait, no," Chezzy called, but the badgers did not listen.

He glanced back to his friends on the bridge behind him, their mouths all hung slack. Fern stiffened her lips together and gave Chezzy a nod. In a moment of absolute determination, he turned and leapt over the crumbled wall. He had to find where the signal was coming from. Immediately, a cry went up from the twig folk that were on the battlements, and Chezzy felt something pierce his arm. Looking over, it was one of the bolts from a scorpion. Already, the twig folk around that scorpion were fitting it with a second bolt and taking aim at Chezzy again.

He charged at them and felt the bolt skid across his cheek bone as he grabbed the scorpion and ripped it up before tossing it to the river. Several twig folk flew with it, and he felt a pang of guilt rush inside of him, but he didn't have time for that. He could see D.O.G. divebombing, trying to break into the great hall area of the castle. The twig folk had largely taken up defensive positions around the great hall, and they were lobbing their spears at the flying honey badgers who swooped in close to them.

Chezzy bolted forward and felt a piercing in his foot that tripped him over and sent him flying into the building. The great entrance gave in as Chezzy crashed through like a giant. He landed face first in a little explosion of dust and rubble. He coughed against the dirt as he rubbed his eyes, so he could peer around the inside of the chamber. It was large enough for him to stoop and walk through, though he could only go maybe four or five steps before he'd hit the other side.

In the center, sat the Twig Queen in a throne that seemed to be made of the bodies of twig folk who had died and hardened into such a shape. She was staring at Chezzy, her knotted mouth frozen in angry shock, but he wasn't looking at her. He was looking past her. Back behind the throne, were multiple acid vats, strapped with humming, metal boxes. Chezzy scrambled to his feet, smacking his head on the ceiling as he did, then looked down at his throbbing foot.

A little spear stuck out from it, and he leaned down and drew it just as a horde of angry twig folk swarmed in around him. The spears flew, many stabbing through his menders and sticking his skin. He swung his arms around, swiping at the nearest of the little figures and knocking them back, but there were hundreds, maybe thousands, attacking him. He knew that soon they would skewer him down and claw their way over his entire body.

D.O.G. stormed in, soon joined by other flying honey badgers. They fought with the twig folk, and some were so stuck full of spears that they looked like Stuart. "Stuart," Chezzy gasped, hoping they'd hear. Hoping the others could help. But, regardless of whether they'd come or not, Chezzy barged forward to the queen and the vats of acid. She rose, the Twig Queen, and was stretching out her many arms in what looked like an attempt to block Chezzy in some way. But something dark suddenly exploded from her gaped mouth and from every knotted hole on her body.

It flung over everything, and Chezzy found himself bound in the dark, sticky substance. It brought him to a stop right before her. Peeping around, he could see the flying honey badgers and twig folk were all stuck too, their eyes, likewise, darting around as their limbs moved in near slow motion. The few free twig folk began swarming, and Chezzy could hear the dull padding as they climbed up him and the others. The substance continued to harden, but Chezzy kept pushing forward, desperately.

The Twig Queen beheld Chezzy, and she lifted her arms again threateningly while her dark eyes watched. She spoke a long series of words as she watched Chezzy then lifted her arms even higher. The little branches seemed to grow and break out with new sections as she did so. Outside, the cries of his friends signaled the arrival of more twig folk, but from where, Chezzy couldn't say.

"Don't," Chezzy managed to mutter, but she shook her head. Just then, a wooden bolt pierced right through her side, and she gave out a great wail. Chezzy struggled to speak as his eyes looked around for the source of the bolt.

The Twig Queen cackled as a trail of words came. This time, Chezzy could hear the muffled translations of Midnight from beneath the sap. "You're too late. He's already begun."

Large hands wrapped around Chezzy's sides and pulled him up. In a panic, Chezzy tried to turn his head, which moved painfully slow. But Chezzy was whipped around as he fell to the floor. He could see Fair and Fern positioned at either side of the torn up entrance of the twig castle, with a scorpion each and firing shots. Their own versolocks were shooting out lasers at bolts incoming and burning the bits before they could impale the girls. An angry looking Fern fitted her scorpion with another bolt before giving Chezzy a concerning look. "You got sapped."

Chezzy's head turned further, and he saw that it was Stuart who was trying to break up the solid sap while swatting away at the oncoming twig folk. They were coming in through various entrances but could do little against Stuart's immensity. Stuart began beating at the sap, which had hardened like candy. It cracked, and Stuart peeled large chunks away which clung to Chezzy, leaving a glue like residue. Chezzy watched as some of the unaffected flying honey badgers took up a perimeter and were keeping the twig folk at bay as they attempted to storm in.

"We have to get out of here," Stuart was panting as he tore the sap away. "Did you see the acid over there? I think he's hiding in here."

"We can't, Stuart," Chezzy managed as the sap cracked around his mouth. He could feel it falling away from his face. His hands were free now, and he was helping to peel it off.

"Honestly, we can see the vats. That's all we need," Stuart added. Chezzy's legs broke free, and he worked to his feet.

"Midnight?" Chezzy shouted, and the map projected up in front of him. He turned while Stuart was still ripping sap from his menders. He looked from the map to the corner where the signal seemed to be coming from.

"Chester?" But Chezzy pulled himself from the pleading Stuart and marched towards the back of the hall. Some of the twig folk had broken past the flying honey badgers and were swarming at his feet. "Chester?" Stuart called again, but just then, Fair let out a cry. Several twig folk had come in through the upper walkways and leapt into Fair's hair. She went wild with color as she tried to fight them off. Stuart whipped back towards her and bounded forward.

He lunged after the twig folk as he tore them away from Fair and crushed them in his bare hands. He turned around, menace in his eyes, and put himself between Fair and the oncoming band. The twig folk were attacking at his legs, but he was swiping at them and crushing them before hurling them out through the holes, far into the dark night. He didn't seem to care about hurting them or about getting into trouble anymore. He was fighting to save Fair.

Chezzy stormed on through the hall, kicking at twig folk and dodging around as he approached the queen and the acid. He stepped right over her and reached down to the side of the cauldron, but there was nothing there. He turned to say something to the queen, but then he saw it. Faintly, in the dim light, a line on the wall. He traced his hand in the square and then pushed it. The wall gave and opened, revealing a dark passageway, large enough for Chezzy to squeeze through. He couldn't see where it ended but tucked to one side, was a blinking machine. Chezzy looked back around for Fern.

She and Fair had regrouped to one side of the broken fortifications. Fern had a fistful of arrows and twig limbs that she set to loading and firing, stout determination in her face. Her versolock was lasering independently, dropping bolts and twig folk alike. The whole thing would have been comical were it not altogether horrifying. Her and Fair, both, were edging away from Stuart who was roaring nearby, collapsing entire walls and towers as dust enveloped him. A turret had fallen near the water's edge, and twig folk reinforcements could be spotted in the current, floating over to the back of Fern and Fair.

"The honey badgers in the sap," Chezzy called to Stuart through the dust. Stuart appeared with teeth bared and eyes flashing with a menacing glow. It was as if the nights sleeping in the Oxenbor dorm had finally turned him feral. He had one of the sapped badgers in his hand, and already, he was tearing it free, unconcerned of the fur that ripped out with the sap. The badger didn't seem to care either, as soon it hurried back into the fight. "Fern," Chezzy called to her. "I have the router." He couldn't even see her anymore in the haze.

Through a swirl of particles, she came light stepping forward with Fair at her heels. They trampled over the queen and collapsed next to Chezzy. Fern was looking into the secret passage, her eyes nestling to the machine. "External router. I knew it." She wiped the dust from her glasses with her menders before reaching out and wiring the machine to her versolock. She scrutinized her versolock closely, her lips moving absently. She looked up to Chezzy of a sudden. "No," she breathed, barely audible in the shouting and destruction. Fair was firing next to her and didn't even register that Fern had said anything at all.

"The walls are coming down," Fair called, but Chezzy didn't respond. He was focusing on Fern.

"What is it, Fern?"

"He's in the dining lab. We have to get there now," Fern replied, this time louder.

"The walls are coming down," Fair repeated, and Chezzy looked up. They were already starting to topple, and he could clearly see they were about to come down atop of them and atop of the explosive acid next to them.

"Get out now, Stuart," Chezzy shouted as he pushed Fern and Fair into the passageway and started frantically crawling through after them. He could hear the crashing behind them and the sound of the subsequent explosion as the passage entrance vanished. The Oxenbor was lost somewhere behind them, and Chezzy felt his stomach plummet as the girls dragged him on. They reached a wall and pushed against it. The wall opened, and the three of them spilled into the old castle's main chamber. Chezzy scrambled around to help Fern and Fair up. "Are you okay?"

"I'm fine," Fern spat, dust in her mouth.

"I'm okay, I'm okay," Fair added.

Chezzy looked around the entrance to the old castle. "You've got to check on Stuart. I need to call Professor Kepler and... and get to the dining lab." Chezzy looked down to his versolock. "Call Professor Kepler, Midnight. Call everyone."

"I can't reach them," Midnight boomed. "I can't reach anyone. Something is wrong."

Chezzy looked to Fern and Fair. A dark figure had loomed up behind them near the entrance, and Chezzy's breath caught in his throat. The figure was lifting something as twig folk came storming towards it. A sudden illumination bore out as lightning orbs fired across the twig folk. It was Penton Fulcrank, who held a rageful look on his face. "Get on o'er," he called off to someone unseen. He wasn't alone. A group of the giant bearded pigs trampled past him, stomping the little twigs.

"We got this," Fern said to Chezzy. "You get up there."

"What?" Chezzy asked, shaking his head and looking back to her. "They're trying to kill you. I can't leave you with the twig folk."

"Yeah, well, I think you're getting the short end of the twig but someone has to stop the Acid King," Fern replied.

Fair was already slipping out of sight. "And he said you could do it." Both girls were turning, running for the entrance of the old castle.

Chezzy swelled for a moment as he looked after them. Then he took a breath as he whipped around and barreled forward. He crashed into a sky elevator. It shot up, then stopped halfway with a clunking thud. Chezzy looked above him, alarmed, and examined the Keris. The ring had drifted to a stop, and every window was dark. Chezzy thought back to what the Twig Queen had said. He shook his head and looked at the ceiling of the elevator where a hatch door sat.

He struggled to climb up the walls, grateful his arm was nearly completely healed, and reached for the hatch. It was too high, but Chezzy wasn't about to give up. He jumped, knocking the access door open before slamming to the floor of the elevator, which gave a threatening lurch. Chezzy breathed. "You can't get hurt." He got back up looking at the plummet beneath him. "Okay, you can get hurt. But you can't die. Probably." Chezzy readied himself then jumped again, his hands gripped at the edges of the hatch door, and he scrambled, kicking his legs and slowly pulling himself up and through.

Chezzy bolted up, looking around at the clear polymer, and his eyes found what he hoped would be there, a clear ladder running all the way up to the Keris. Without hesitation, he ascended, though he constantly misjudged the rungs, which were nearly impossible to see. Still, he reached the top and prised his fingers into the door, which popped open with surprising ease. Chezzy climbed up and on to visible ground.

"Raven?" Chezzy called, but no answer came. "What's happening?"

"She's not responding," boomed Midnight with a hint of panic. "They've all been… shut off."

"Where's everyone? I need to find Professor Kepler."

"Everyone is locked up. You still have access to the monitoring equipment, which is currently operational. But the other versolocks, the AIs, I can't connect to them."

"Show me Professor Kepler," Chezzy demanded. Instantly, a projection shot out that showed Professor Kepler sitting in an office with the Phrenbook student, Turod Ingleward. The director seemed calm and was staring at the camera, as if to look at Chezzy.

"There's something else," Midnight boomed.

"What?"

Midnight shot out another series of projections that showed the various SIs roaming the corridors and passing through walls all over the Keris. "Where are they going?"

"It looks like they're heading to the dining lab."

"Show me what's happening in there," Chezzy commanded, but just then, something exploded out of his back and landed with a clink behind him. Chezzy scrambled around on his hands and knees to see what happened. The thing that had come out of him was a small, stylus shaped piece of metal. Several legs were unfolding as it lifted itself up and went scurrying away. Without thinking, Chezzy lunged for it, missing and slamming chin first into the metal floor.

It ran across the hall, and Chezzy took after. A far door opened just a crack, as if for the thing. But Chezzy hurled himself after the little robotic spider and crashed down with his hands, flattening the machine outright. He lifted it by one of the broken legs as it struggled to get free, pricking at Chezzy's fingers. The door next to Chezzy slid open, and standing in the entryway, was Veronica Fayette. She had mad and frightened eyes that flashed to the spiderbot.

"Give it to me," she spat.

"What? No way. It's… it came out of me."

"It is mine," she spat again. "Give it to me."

"It's yours?" threw back Chezzy. "What's your little spider robot doing inside of my back?" His temper was rising as the memory of Mastering Menders came to him.

"Nothing. But I… just, I need it, is all."

Chezzy tried to calm himself. "For what?"

"I was just tracking you is all. I knew you were up to something. I suppose you did all of this, did you not?"

"She's lying," Midnight's voice boomed so loudly that both Chezzy and Veronica jumped, and Chezzy dropped the robotic spider, which again began sprinting over towards Veronica.

She reached down a hand to grab it, when it was instantly blasted into dust by a laser from Midnight. Veronica gave a scream of rage. "You destroyed it. You ruined everything. How could you do that?"

"You're crazy. Why did you put that inside of me?" But Veronica was beyond words. She took a step forward and struck Chezzy right across the face. Midnight lit up, and Veronica's face washed over with fear. "Wait, Midnight," Chezzy panted as he rubbed the spot on his face where she had hit him. Almost instantly, it had stopped hurting. "What is the matter with you, Veronica?"

"I... I... I just," but words seemed to fail her.

Chezzy shook his head in disbelief as tears began to well in Veronica's eyes, and she let out a soft sob. He started to say something, but just then, he spied someone else across the room and rose quickly, his eyes wide. "Something you need to see," Midnight boomed again, but Chezzy was watching the figure.

Veronica looked around too as the figure lumbered closer to them. It was one of the SIs, and it didn't even seem to see them. It just walked right through one of the walls and was gone again. Chezzy cleared his throat. "Midnight?" he asked.

Midnight shot out an image of the dining lab. Pacing up and down on top of the table, was the Acid King. Chezzy could see the pale yellow of his menders, almost the same color as his skin, torn so badly they barely covered as much of the man as Stuart's did of him. But, unlike Stuart's, tubes ran from the man's mender and connected in and out at various parts of his sallow looking skin.

There were half healed cuts all over him, and there was something wrong with the man's face. He looked both familiar to Chezzy and altogether unknown at the same time. It was Nik Daedle, and yet it wasn't anymore. Atop the man's scantly balding and scabbed head, sat a crown of metal and wires, some of which plugged directly through his skin. Worse yet, there were dozens of bubbling vats stacked around the dining lab. Chezzy had to stop him, or something terrible was going to happen.

Chezzy tore through the door without hesitation, but Veronica Fayette was fast to his heels. Midnight was tracing out a path for him, and Chezzy was following it at breakneck speeds. Unfortunately, the further he got, the more difficult it became to follow the lines as SIs were flooding the hallways. Chezzy spied Bogdanov amongst them, but the usually volatile SI didn't give Chezzy a second look. The SIs became a blur of muted colors, and soon, Chezzy was smacking right into walls.

Veronica Fayette didn't seem to be fairing much better. He could hear her grunting and crying out as she tripped or smacked a wall. "You wait for me," she kept crying to Chezzy.

"Just go back. You're getting hurt," Chezzy called.

"Well, so are you," she hollered dementedly. Her face appeared for a moment and was contorted madly.

"I'm not going to stay hurt, though."

"Neither am I," came her response through gritted teeth.

Chezzy whirled around. "I mean it. This guy is dangerous, and I don't think anyone is coming to help us. You shouldn't be doing this. You just… can't."

Veronica gave Chezzy a look like he'd slapped her. Her chin shook, and her lips were pursed in anger. Then she lifted up a fist and struck him in the eye. "You do not decide what I am capable of."

Chezzy's hand went to his eye, where the ache quickly subsided. He looked back at Veronica in shock. "What?"

She hit him again, harder this time and in the teeth, then turned and sprinted ahead, getting lost amongst the many projected bodies. Chezzy stretched his mouth and plowed after her. The SIs were getting denser, and they blended into each other such that Chezzy could barely make out his next step, let alone the projected path. Still, he spied the entrance to the dining lab, where the SIs all moved to congregate.

Chezzy stumbled in and collided with a vat, which rocked, spilling acid over the floor. It sent up toxic plumes that burnt his nostrils, and Chezzy realized the skin of his hand sizzled. He sucked his teeth and grinted against the pain before looking around. The SIs were gathering about the zagging dining table, upon which, stood Nik Daedle. Many of his tubes stretched out to nearby vats wherein they dripped. The man had taken up one of the tubes, though, and he was dragging it across the wall. *The Acid King shall fall. Come and fall, come and fall,* spelled the script he etched there.

XXII.
The Acid King.
Reflected.
In the crown.

Chezzy glanced down at the vat next to him and spied the humming box strapped to it. Then he looked around to the vast number of them strewn throughout the dining lab as they momentarily came into view from between the SIs. The Acid King gave a sudden, trembling, coughing laugh. His thin arms shook as he held them out before he spoke. When his voice came, it sounded as if he had not spoken much in a very long time. It was heavy and croaked. "Hark, come you into here looking? Looking for what? What now is the final throne room of the Acid King. Is that what you've come here to see?"

Chezzy looked at the metal and wire crown of the man, plugged and pocked into his head. Some of the wires that ran off it were clearly spliced into wires that had been revealed through a burn in the wall. Chezzy thought of the boy Nik Daedle, now the Acid King. He didn't know how to respond, but he didn't have to. Already, the man was whimpering and clearing his throat in order to speak again.

"You tremble, you know? Is this your first time with royalty? Hah," his short laugh ended in a series of coughs. "Come as my subjects, you have. Come fore to see the marvel. The only moler to know himself a moler and more beyond. And here, all my years of work. You see them? These in here and the hundreds like them. They're hidden o'er the rest. Such painstaking drippage. And so many stole. I might transcend to something higher for the sacrifice I have made. Mayhaps, I'll rise from the fall. It has been done before."

The Everling and the Acid King

The man had not turned around, but yet still he etched the words on the wall deeper and deeper. Chezzy reached out for the humming box and tugged it loose from the vat of acid. He pocketed it then edged forward, lightly. There was no sign of Veronica, but, through the throng, he could spy more of the vats nearby. The SIs concealed much, though they stood still upon taking, each, their individual place to look upon the Acid King.

"Oh, my dear, my sweet dear. How you tremble so. Do you quiver? Are you chilled? Or are you just, so, awed?" The Acid King had crooked his head to look behind him, but he did not look in Chezzy's direction. The man turned around and grinned. His one eye carried a large plug from his crown in it, and both sockets were terribly sunken. Chezzy could still see hints of the boy that he once was, though the boy himself was long lost. All that really remained, was the Acid King. His dark and stained teeth seemed to shake as the man spoke on. "Have you not an answer? Mm? Speak to me, little girl, for you might be the only living witness to my last act. Bask so, in the glory of my grant. You may bare it." He coughed again through his gravel ridden throat.

"I am not," came a reply. It was Veronica. She was standing near the table, just barely in sight.

"You are not what, little thing?"

Veronica was stirring up her courage, but even Chezzy could make out her shaking legs. "I am not here to be your witness."

"Is it so? Even so, it isn't so, isn't that so?"

"No," there were tears on her face, and Chezzy knew he had to do something, anything. He had to at least draw the Acid King's attention to himself.

"If it is not, then it still will be. Shall I melt you into the floor, and you can spend your last moments with me, seeing the great fall?"

"No," she shouted this time, but it came with a slight cry.

"Child, oh, child, I fear, brave as you try to be, and king though I am, we are both slaves to this moment. Truly slaves."

"I am no slave," Veronica was saying as Chezzy began edging forward again.

"Hah," the Acid King gave in his short, laughing way, "are we not bound, you and I, right now to this moment? To this time? Are we not drawn in to our place by those lines that define? You, you of Sciofall, I'm sure. Me, look at me. Look at what I am." He was holding some of the tubes up, which were dripping on to the table. It smoked where the drops landed. "Given o'er, I was. Given o'er as a child. Oh, but the years went on, and I saw for what it was. No, I was not given, I merely was. And here, now, are we not both caught by what must happen? You in your place, and I in mine. Examine, you will, the puppets that surround. See here," and every single one of the SIs looked over at Veronica in unison. "Do you see how they must bend to their, situation?"

Veronica was looking back at all of the projected people, but she didn't respond to the Acid King. He bent them this way and that, and had them all, in unison, gesture for him and bow. "Do you? Ohhh," the Acid King cut himself off with a moaning sigh. "It seems, then, that I must amend. I was wrong, though only a bit."

"What are you saying?" Veronica spat back, frightfully.

"You are not so singular as you might have been."

"What do you mean?" Her anger was bubbling back now at the perceived slight.

"You may have come to bear witness, but so has another." The heads of all the SIs swiveled around to look at Chezzy. "Come you, too, to be the testament to my will?" The Acid King was addressing the everling.

Chezzy cleared his throat, looking around at the hundreds of eyes. "No."

"No?"

"Maybe you're here to be the testament to mine," Chezzy gave back.

"Hah," laughed the Acid King, "then we shall witness each other's wills, and we will see which will wins out. Is that not the ultimate way of it?" He was giving a saddened grin to Chezzy that revealed the murky colors in his teeth. The Acid King didn't even seem to notice that Veronica was raising her versolock and aiming it at him.

Something shot from her versolock, and it struck the Acid King high in his chest. The man lurched back as something sparked and sizzled under his skin, and he sank to his knees with a loud cry. Chezzy was running toward Veronica as fast as he could. From the corner of his eyes, he saw the Acid King rising back up. "You think your machine can live inside of me? Nothing can live inside of me but this sacred acid that I bleed."

Chezzy had his hand on Veronica's, and he pulled her hard as the nearest cauldron exploded. They fell under the winding table, and Chezzy covered himself over Veronica, but it only served to halfway protect her as the acid splashed over them. He felt it searing into his back as he held her tight, but still so much had run down over her, and she screamed out. The table was sizzling and smoking, and some of the acid had eaten through it already and was dripping across them.

Chezzy felt the humming in his pocket. "Come on," Chezzy yelled as he pushed Veronica along the path of the table, away from the acid.

"It matters not if you crawl away. There's nowhere to crawl to. Everywhere you go, I will remain. I will linger, and we will fall, each of us. I will eat this machine down into the ruins beneath us. There will be nothing but that smoldering pile to reckon. Do you not see the sums?"

The SIs peered under the table at Chezzy and Veronica before swarming. They blurred out all sight, and other vats of nearby acid exploded at Nik's will. Veronica was hurt terribly, but there was nowhere safer to hide than under the table, which only grew ricketier by the moment. The acid ate through everything. Even Veronica's versolock was heard to be crying out.

"My children, do come out and sit with me a while. This is not how I want it to be. With agony and despair. It's only a moment I ask of you. Give me only this moment, and I'll rob not, of you, your joy."

Veronica collapsed. She curled and held herself as she cried. Chezzy tried to see her through the twisting legs of the SIs, but there were too many. Desperately, Chezzy scrambled away from her across the acid drenched floor. He exited the king rat of SIs. He was badly burnt, but he could feel that whatever Midnight was doing was numbing his skin. The Acid King stood atop the dining table, the slipstream at his feet broken and warped and leaking something strange around a cauldron that sat with him.

Nik looked at Chezzy with mild surprise. "Are you not hurting child? I cannot imagine the pain you experience. Truly," and he dipped his hand into the cauldron next to him then pulled it out. The acid merely dripped off of him. "We are, each of us, such marvelous things. I remember my own time here, short as it was. Of course, the other children feared to touch me or to be... too near. They were oft to tease. Perhaps they knew but did not yet understand what I would become. They could not yet know that I was a king. A king made for the fall."

Chezzy climbed up on to the table and faced the Acid King, his friends below flashing in his rattled mind. Balefire was his home now. And it was filled with animals, with students, and teachers. Even Veronica sprawled and damaged nearby. He couldn't let anything else happen to them, and there was no one else coming to help. "You don't have to do this. Please, you don't."

"Of course, I do. I remember, as a boy, I would get sick, and I would lose my bed or eat a hole through the floor or the wall. It is what I was made for. Don't you see that? Can you not see what you were made for?"

Chezzy felt the hum, and he watched the drip on the Acid King's hand. "I think I see," he whispered.

"Yes. And you see how it ends here?"

Chezzy shook his head. "It won't for me."

The Acid King gave another sad smile. "But of course it will. There's no other way for you to go."

"No," said Chezzy as he walked forward and reached his hand into the acid of the vat. He felt the numbed pain as he lifted it back for the Acid King to see.

Nik's eyes went wide as he watched the hand slowly try to heal itself. "Oh, my." He gave Chezzy a sympathetic look. "You will have, very much, the hardest time of all, it seems."

Chezzy paused. "What do you mean?"

The Acid King moved closer to Chezzy, careful of the cord coming out of his crown. "You will be the true witness of the fall. Weeks from now, they will pull you from the wreckage, and you will recount in your own words what happened here. Not images from my machines alone. No. Joined with the words of a child." There were tears in his eyes. They ran down his face and fell to the table where they burned small holes.

"That's not how it's going to be."

"Then how will it be?" The Acid King's one eye twitched and a cauldron exploded, sending fresh droplets across Chezzy, but Chezzy didn't even flinch. The numbing in his skin took the acid, and the man watched the cycle of eating and healing.

"How you wrote it. The Acid King shall fall. Just the Acid King." Chezzy dipped his hand back into the acid and held it there.

The man let out a laugh. "Mayhaps. And who will he give you to when it is done? Do you wonder?"

"What do you mean?" He pulled his soaked hand free and felt it running and burning.

Suddenly, the Acid King gripped his hands around Chezzy's face. "Do you not fear him? I should have feared him."

"Who?" Chezzy struggled against the man's grip, but he could not break free.

"I'll show you just what was done. And we will crash this all."

Chezzy saw the determination in the man's eye, and he reached his acid soaked hand into his pocket, feeling the humming, metal box. There was a momentary flash of light, and Chezzy saw his own face there reflected again as the explosion rocked through both of them. Chezzy's hip dislodged as his mender fought to hold him together. He and Nik were both thrown in opposite directions. Chezzy hit the floor and tried to scramble up, his abdomen in pieces, and his hand gone again. He found his mender moving for him, forming an exoskeleton that compensated for the busted bits beneath. It moved up over his new stump, too, and formed a rudimentary claw that opened and closed at the twitch of his reforming muscles. He turned back to Nik Daedle.

The Acid King was sprawled on the remains of the table against the far wall. His head was held up slightly by the crown, which was still connected to the wires in the wall. The cable was pulled taut and tangled around the legs and arms of the man. Chezzy could only see him briefly, though, because the SIs were swarming to him. "The cord," Chezzy screamed, and Midnight understood. The laser flashed from his versolock, severing the connection to the wall. SIs flickered around Chezzy. Some disappeared, others went glitching wildly. They walked in the air or shot through walls or juddered in place.

The Acid King let out his short laugh as his head popped down from where it hung and smacked against a bit of the broken table. He pushed himself up, and Chezzy could see the man was bleeding acid from a severe wound across his abdomen and legs, which trembled terribly. "Hah. No. It's already happening, you see. It cannot be stopped."

Without thinking, Chezzy charged toward the Acid King and tackled into him. They crashed back against the wall as the Acid King's body strained to leak more acid from the tubes, and even his wounds, on to Chezzy. It came at a faster and faster rate, which weakened the man terribly as it drove Chezzy back again, allowing the Acid King to rise once more. His versolock fired out blasts of laser, which Midnight combated with shots of his own. The blasts struck together in the air, leaving a burnt, plasma scent that stung Chezzy's nostrils.

Nik Daedle grabbed up a few of his tubes and slung them at Chezzy. The acid splattered across the everling. Already, it was eating through the shielding and the numbing effects of Chezzy's mender. Chezzy could feel it getting through his skin and reaching for the bone. A nearby vat exploded, and Chezzy instinctively covered his versolock with the mender claw. He didn't want Midnight to melt right off of him, if that was at all possible. He didn't know how much Midnight could take.

The Acid King laughed through the smell of scorched air and toxic fumes. But Chezzy barreled forward and slammed into him. They skidded across the floor and splashed down in a thick acid puddle. The Acid King did not mind, as it had no effect on him, but Chezzy felt the burn. Chezzy cried out and tried to hit the man, but, despite his wiry appearance and noticeable injuries, the Acid King wrestled Chezzy right off and held him to the floor. "It will be more than I ever could have dreamed."

Chezzy screamed, his face buried deep into the puddle. The acid was in his eye and in his mouth, and his scream came out garbled. "Midnight?"

"My child. My sweet child. The things you do not yet know. I will show you them. I can see it, you know. I have it right here."

The pain was searing, and Chezzy cried for Midnight again. Electricity pumped from his versolock, zapping through Chezzy and the Acid King. For a moment, they were bound and quaking together, until Chezzy absolutely erupted into flames. In the fury of it, the Acid King's own versolock exploded, letting out the briefest cry of an electric voice before doing so. The Acid King himself howled as he fell back, his hand completely gone, mirroring the everling.

The flames of Chezzy drew back and vanished, leaving only smoke in their wake as Chezzy scrambled, completely blind in one eye, to grab the crown from the Acid King, which he wrenched from the man's head. "No, please. You do not yet know the horror," the Acid King pleaded, but Chezzy gripped the cord that ran into the Acid King's eye, and he jerked it out. It tore free, a long, multi wired connector. The Acid King fell back limply, and a wave of horror swept Chezzy. The Acid King was dead.

Chezzy looked back down at the crown. "What do I do?"

"Put it in," boomed Midnight.

"In what?" Chezzy asked, but he already knew.

"Put it in your eye," Midnight answered anyway.

"This is the worst," Chezzy shouted to no one in particular. Still, he drew up the connector and jabbed it into what remained of his acid soaked eye. Pain exploded in his head as Chezzy's whole world cracked. He was no longer in the dining lab of the Keris. He didn't seem to be in Balefire at all. He was in the crown. There, a young and nervous looking Nik Daedle was recording himself as he sat in a metal room, huddled near a toilet.

"Dad," Nik said. "I want you to know that I love you. I'm going to be…" Nik trailed off before giving a half shrug, "not around. But worry not. Really. Professor Kepler has a job for me. An important job. He says I'm to be a hero. And I could make you so proud, were you only not upset. Keep safe, this secret for me. And worry not, because I know you tend to worry."

Just then, a door opened behind Nik, and the silhouette of Professor Kepler was stood there. Professor Kepler stepped inside, and Chezzy could see others behind him. Professor Kepler knelt down next to Nik Daedle as the boy began to tremble. "Is it time yet?"

"No, Nik. Not yet," Professor Kepler replied.

"But he's here?"

Professor Kepler paused before responding. "Yes. He is." He nodded back, and Nik looked over at a lumbering man with asymmetrical features. For all his size, the man was almost childlike in appearance, despite the warping of his face. One eye was bigger than the other and one cheek near caved in. One of his ears was shrunk near to extinction, and he seemed to be perpetually winking with a pained, half grimace, though this emotion, if it was one, never reached the larger eye. Chezzy recognized him immediately. It was Greyire.

Nik shuddered and struggled not to cry. "Will it hurt?"

Professor Kepler's breath caught in his throat. "In so many ways." The video ended abruptly, and Chezzy saw nothing at first. Then, shooting through his mind, came the visions of every SI at Balefire. They were scattered all around and difficult to decipher as images came and fled in seemingly random import. But Chezzy could see Veronica. She was hurt, and Chezzy was hurt, and everything was falling apart. "What do I do?" Chezzy called for Midnight.

"Connect it back to the wall."

"We already blasted through the cord," Chezzy screamed in a panic.

"I can fix it."

Chezzy clambered up, but his new vision disoriented him. Still, he grabbed the ends of the cables and held the two pieces together. Midnight fused them with a series of beams. An overwhelming sensation bathed Chezzy. The erratic visions of the SIs came into focus, and he felt his control sweep through the Keris. He could feel the doors, the SIs, even the metal, humming boxes across the various vats of acid. Chezzy swooned and feared he'd pass out, but he gripped the wall. "Now what?"

"Shut down the explosives," Midnight boomed.

"How do I do that?"

"Think through it."

"Right, just think through it," Chezzy shot back sarcastically.

"Think through what you want to happen," Midnight offered again.

Chezzy thought about how he wanted the buzzing boxes to stop. Miraculously, he felt them all power down. He could hear the nearby ones fall silent. He thought of the SIs for a moment, and, immediately, they began flooding back into the dining lab. "No, no," Chezzy struggled, then he managed to shut them all off. Like that, they vanished. "Not bad," he mumbled, then he unlocked all of the doors and turned back on the AIs. After that, he wanted the droids to come in and do something about the acid, and soon he heard some of them come zooming into the dining lab.

"Midnight, Chezzy," came the ring of Raven's voice. "What happened?" Midnight and Raven fell into conversation as

Chezzy watched the video feeds of people exiting their dorms and offices. He could see Professor Kepler rising up from his chair, alongside Turod. Already, the director was firing a portal, which showed into the dining lab.

Chezzy ripped the cord from the wall, which brought him back into the dining lab proper. He looked around. "Veronica?" He spied her, curled up with droids zooming around her and attempting to clean the acid there. Chezzy ran forward and managed to lift her up with his wrecked body, largely due to his menders. The everling clung to her mutilated form, the injuries bled out from the burns that glazed her. And he looked up for help, seeing the portal where Professor Kepler was passing through. Chezzy regarded the director uneasily, but there was no one else. "We need to get her to Doctor Tiz'n," he panted.

Professor Kepler took a short glance over the crown on Chezzy's head before nodding. Then he opened a new portal on a nearby wall. Together, they passed into the medilab where Doctor Tiz'n was already fussing around and piling up the needed supplies for her various bots. She took one look at Chezzy and Veronica and gave a small yip. "Place her there. Just right there," she added, indicating a bed as her many robotic tentacles slipped on some very thick, strange coverings that looked like gloves.

As Chezzy set Veronica down, Dr. Tiz'n moved him back, sealing off Veronica's bed area. Chezzy turned and looked up at Professor Kepler who had said nothing until this moment. "I need to know everything." He sunk into a chair, expressionless, and waited while Chezzy burned and healed and regarded the man with his one eye. Chezzy looked at his footsteps across the floor where they had left burn marks. "Chezzy?"

"Yes?" Chezzy said, looking back to Professor Kepler.

"Are you okay?"

"Yeah," Chezzy replied, but all he could think of was Nik Daedle. Just then, the medilab door whooshed open, and in rushed Fern, Fair, and Stuart. They bore an array of minor injuries and worried expressions that weren't assuaged by the crown on Chezzy's head or the connector jabbed into his eye.

"Oh," Fair blurted while Stuart turned away with a dry heave.

"That is something," Fern added.

"Do you mind?" Doctor Tiz'n hollered from the secluded operating bed.

The three of them looked embarrassed, but Professor Kepler sprang up from his seat. "I guess we'll get this out of you."

"Yeah," Chezzy almost whispered.

"Tizmerelda, is she stable?"

"Yes, Director."

"Good. Could you spare your gloved self long enough to remove this from Chezzy?"

"Erm, yes." The barricade parted, giving just a short glimpse of several bots working around a bedbound Veronica. Doctor Tiz'n zoomed forward, swapping gloves as she looked over the crown on Chezzy's head. She gripped one robotic claw to the connector and braced against Chezzy's forehead before yanking it out. It hurt worse coming out than it did going in, and Chezzy bit his lip, letting out only the slightest of sounds. Stuart downright fainted, collapsing in a terrible thunk as Fair covered her horrorstruck face.

"Did you get it in… in the same way?" Fern asked.

Chezzy nodded, covering his eye with his stump. "Yes, I did." He watched as Doctor Tiz'n eyed the stump disapprovingly then took the crown over and dipped it in some unknown solution before drying it in a strange machine.

"Is it safe, Tizmerelda?" Professor Kepler asked.

"It is." Doctor Tiz'n was already heading back to Veronica, glove swapping once more.

Professor Kepler drew the device from out of the machine and looked it over. "The crown of the Acid King," he mumbled to himself. He turned to Chezzy. "Heal quickly. We will be talking very soon." The director then portaled out of the medilab as the students looked on. Chezzy turned to the others as Fern and Fair attempted to step closer.

"Stay back. I still have acid on me."

They paused, uneasily. "But are you okay?" Fair asked, her colors resetting, though her eyes remained as rainbowed as ever.

"I... don't know."

Fern nodded. "What happened?"

Chezzy just shook his head.

XXIII.
Setters fruit.
Killed.
The token.

Chezzy plucked the fruit from the twisting branches of the tree. The fruit was weighty and bore the color of the setting sun. The little island had multiple such trees, and as Chezzy bit into the fruit, the sweet juice ran down his new hand. Fern had told him that setters fruit was a special hybrid that had been made several decades earlier. They were the best fruit Chezzy had ever had. He turned back to his friends and sat in the thick grass while they looked on at another island several islands away. They had been watching Professor Kepler, who was hosting a meeting of sorts between himself and the twig folk.

"How much longer till classes start back?" Stuart asked.

"A better question is when can we go back to Sidelight," Fern retorted.

"Did you end up trying to see Veronica again, Chezzy?" Fair asked.

"Yeah, I did."

"And?"

"Doctor Tiz'n still isn't letting any visitors in."

"Mm, it can't be that bad, can it?" she asked, nervously.

"Maybe she just doesn't want to see you," Fern shrugged.

"Yeah, maybe." Chezzy took another bite and watched Professor Kepler uneasily. He hadn't told any of them about the video of Nik Daedle, and he was still trying to decide what to do about it.

"Or maybe she went home or to Shivweigh's, you know? Doctors can't tell you things like that. She's probably all better and back in her villa or whatever," Stuart offered.

No one replied, though, as the director began to speak in a screechy language at great length. Eventually, the twig folk split into two groups. The decidedly larger group hosted the Twig Queen, and they set off, taking boats to the forest's edge and entering the copse. The other group marched back to the remains of their castle as Professor Kepler rose and crossed over to the flying honey badger island.

"Odd," Fern mused.

"Did they get kicked out?" Stuart asked.

Chezzy watched Professor Kepler as he paused to pet D.O.G. before continuing on to their island. "Enjoying your break?" he asked, greeting them.

"It's pretty alright. Not shabby at all," Stuart replied. "Not that we wouldn't rather be in classes." Fern rolled her eyes with a scoff.

"How's the cleanup?" Fair asked.

"I daresay the staff have gathered most of the remaining cauldrons. Classes should be resuming shortly."

"Oh, good," she added.

"What'd the Twig Queen say?" Fern threw in, nodding her head to the woods as she took another bite of the setters fruit.

"Oh," Professor Kepler flashed her an interested look. "She said the Acid King promised her they could have what remained of the old castle. Seems they were helping to place the cauldrons around and all. But never you mind. You should enjoy your break. It'll be over soon, and then there's so much to do and so much going on."

"What's going on?" Chezzy's voice rose uncomfortably.

"Well, we're going to have some guests at the school pretty soon, I guess you could say. Anyway, you and I will be talking about it before too long, Chezzy." Professor Kepler gave an assuring nod then turned and walked back toward the old castle, staring at his feet as he went.

"He seemed in a mood, didn't he?" Stuart nudged Chezzy with his spiky elbow, but Chezzy paid it little mind. "Anyway, I want to hear more about this Minerocket. You think you're going to try out, Fern?"

"Oh, Sciofalls rarely get put on a team during Alpha year. But maybe come Beta year I could give it a shot. You know, if I wanted to waste my time like that."

"Whatever. I bet an Oxenbor could get put on a team during Alpha year," Stuart boasted.

When classes resumed, Veronica Fayette was still nowhere to be seen. Rumors had been spreading over the entire school about her and Chezzy. Chezzy was frequently met with hushed whispers everywhere he went. Not the normal sort of whispers that had followed him since he had arrived in Boletare, but new and wild speculations. "They're all morons," Fern sighed at breakfast.

"At least the evestry figured out that Nik Daedle was Trick Daedle's son," Fair added.

"So? What? We figured that out forever ago. Did Bag say anything about Trick's witsacking?" Fern asked.

Fair looked back down over the Bag Hoolihow article and shook her head. "No. Nothing about that."

Fern's face scrunched up. "Something's not right. You're sure it was a witsacking?"

Fair shrugged. "That's what my mom said."

Fern shook her head. "The witsacking, Nik Daedle disappearing from school here…" She was twisting her long hair as she thought. "And he wanted to destroy the school. But why?"

"Fern, it's fine." Fair patted Fern's arm in the calming sort of way that she often did with Stuart.

"But," Stuart, who was on his third plate, added, "at least they fixed the dining lab right away," then he speared another gas fried vegetable from a dish that was sliding past him before the plate disappeared through the small, nearby portal.

"Yeah, well, not all of it," blurted Fern while pointing at the wall where the etched message still remained. "We should talk to Professor Kepler."

Chezzy felt himself tense involuntarily. He still wasn't sure what to make of the video, but if Professor Kepler had witsacked Trick Daedle for asking questions, he didn't want to put the others at risk until he knew more. "Have you heard the rumor that I'm the Acid King?" Chezzy asked, hoping to shift the conversation. "I've heard them saying it. They think I'm the Acid King, and that will be my title when I take over Boletare."

"Well, that's ridiculous," mumbled Fern as she stared at her plate.

"Maybe," added Chezzy, "but I've heard of worse titles than that." Then he mouthed, "Prince Watermane," to the others, and they broke into laughter. Chezzy breathed a little easier as he watched Fern's mood shift a little. It helped that Stuart spat out some half chewed vegetables, which sprayed across a Beta year sitting a few seats down.

"Sorry, sorry," Stuart had said between giggles as he struggled to get what food was still covering his lips back into his mouth. "That's great. When did you start calling the Acid King Prince Watermane?"

"What?" Raven barked through Chezzy's versolock as Fern dropped her exasperated head to the table. An embarrassed look overtook Stuart, and he knew he was missing something. A renewed argument between Midnight and Raven had started in a muffle under Chezzy's hand.

"Is Professor Kepler going to show up for your Practicum today?" Fair asked over the row.

"He said he was," Chezzy replied, sobering as he ignored the gripes of Raven. "Speaking of, I'm going to be late. I have to get up to the lab. And I should…" Chezzy nodded to his versolock, "get her out of here." He snatched another biscuit, which let Raven's full volume back out, and many other students glared at him as he hurried out of the dining lab. The eyes followed him from all around, and it wasn't just because of Raven.

He was feeling happy to get away from the other students but considerably less happy about having to face Professor Kepler on his own. Still, he climbed up to the third level of the everling tower, where he stumbled upon Arbiter Bakehour accosting the director. "I don't see why you're so worried," Professor Kepler attempted to calm the man.

"Why I'm so worried?" Arbiter Bakehour nearly spat. "You've had a maniac living at Balefire for years. They're saying he was a moler. And you're asking me why I'm so worried? How did you, of all people, not even know that he was here? Isn't that why you were positioned here in the first place?"

"I wouldn't say it was as simple as that. Which you should fully know about," Aris Kepler replied with a sly sort of look.

Arbiter Kid Bakehour hesitated, then his anger redoubled. "That… has no bearing… Do you even know what Bag Hoolihow has been saying? I'm getting calls night and day." The temples of Arbiter Bakehour were throbbing, and he seemed to be searching for a place to put his hands while it was quite clear he was wanting to put them around Professor Kepler's throat.

"You need to compose yourself," Professor Kepler added. There was a note of threat in the tone.

"Compose? Compose?" Arbiter Bakehour was spurting, but then he caught sight of Chezzy and clamped his mouth shut. "What he did… to Nik," he added in a mumbled mess before shaking his head and storming away.

Professor Kepler sighed heavily and nodded to Chezzy. He knew that many parents and evestry officials had been visiting Balefire daily to harass the director, yet the man gave little indication of concern, which vexed Chezzy all the more. He eyed the director for signs of remorse, but the man was unreadable. "I hear Professor Tampago Brown has been loading you up with all sorts of homework for Gene Production."

"Yes," Chezzy answered.

"Are you keeping up with it well enough?"

"I think so."

"I see." Professor Kepler pondered this a moment, the silence stretching between them.

"I killed him," Chezzy blurted of a sudden.

Kepler regarded Chezzy intently. "Yes."

"Doesn't that... shouldn't that..." Chezzy shrugged, hopelessly.

Professor Kepler gave Chezzy a grim smile. "There's still a lot to talk about... but that won't be today... I'll say this, you saved Veronica Fayette. And I've just seen her, and I know you've been trying to visit her. Still want to?"

Chezzy nodded with a tremble. "Yeah."

"Good, well, the doctor isn't allowing visitors so you might try tonight. When she's not around. And... we'll talk soon." He portaled away, leaving Chezzy alone by the statue of Sannyrion.

That evening, the everling made his way over to the medilab, finding it rather empty and silent. Doctor Tiz'n was nowhere in sight. However, Veronica's chamber was open, and Chezzy approached her cautiously. There she lay, heavily bandaged all across her body with white cloth blending her into the bed.

She peered up at Chezzy with her one unbandaged eye then closed it as if refusing to cry. "Hey, Veronica," Chezzy offered. "How are you doing?"

Without opening her eye, she gritted her teeth and spoke. "Thank you for what you did." Chezzy watched her and wanted to say something more, but her trembling seemed to grow, and he thought better of it. He turned and walked back out, leaving her.

As soon as fall rolled around, the Keris was thrown into the full spectacle of Heuvalween, which was, according to Professor

The Everling and the Acid King

Maxwell, Professor Kepler's favorite holiday. The SIs had all been repaired by Tech McGeehee, and they were reissued with Heuvalween themed skins. Suddenly, there were werewolves and ghouls and zombies and every single kind of haunted creature popping out of walls and from dark corners to scare students. Bogdanov had been made up like a giant spider, and he lurked on a web in the top corner by the entrance to the Chiropa dormitory. He still grumbled at Chezzy every chance he got, which, evidently, was not one of the repairs that Tech McGeehee had made.

That weekend was the first time they were allowed to go back to Sidelight, and all of the students had been buzzing with excitement. There were rumors that the Heuvalween festivities in Sidelight had morphed the whole town into a haunted village for everyone to explore. To top it all off, a massive game had been declared. They were saying that a special token had been hidden in the village that would net the finder a free power borrower that the Burroughs Brothers had recently created specifically for the competition. Fern was near to bursting, since they were saying you'd get to become the monster in the later part of the game. She desperately wanted to be the one to find the token.

"What do you think I'd get to be? What kind of monster?" she asked, her face flushed and anxious.

"I don't know," said Stuart, "maybe you'll look like me," and then he grinned at the others.

"Oh, you're not a monster," said Fair.

Stuart didn't respond, but he smiled with embarrassment as the hovercarts came floating up. They had been made up to look like wrecked ships or alien crafts or flying spaghetti creatures. The four of them piled into a cart that resembled a large, reddish blob that reached out to grab the other students as they passed. Marsle Chin came bounding over and asked if he could ride with them.

"Sure, Marsle," said Chezzy. "Hey, I have a question for you," he added with a sudden thought.

Marsle blushed but looked rather eagerly at Chezzy. "Yeah?"

"If we cover our ears, and you made your sound, would it really not affect us?" Chezzy asked with a mischievous glint in his mismatched eyes.

Marsle gave an embarrassed, though slightly conspiratorial, grin. "You'd probably be alright if you covered your ears really, really well."

"That's good to know, Marsle. That's very good to know," replied Chezzy as he met Marsle's grin with one of his own.

They watched Sidelight grow, and when they departed their cart, they found the town a maze of horrors. If you wanted to pop into one of the shops, you had to battle your way past people, SIs, and bots that sprang out like monsters. Students ran wild, searching for the token, and there were whispers of pacts being made. The five of them agreed to stick together and use a randomizer to decide who would get it if any of them found the token. By midafternoon, none had yet claimed the prize.

The group ran through the maize maze with a giant rat in pursuit. It was larger than all of them combined, and it kicked up dirt furiously as it chased. Together, they stumbled out of the field and collapsed in a little clearing near a fountain. They coughed out dirt and laughed while the rat backed away. Chezzy looked around and spied Professor Kepler sat alone on a bench by the fountain. The man was staring off down a path ahead with a wracked expression as the statues spat fake red blood into the stone pond next to him. Chezzy regarded the man. He had continued to avoid Professor Kepler whenever possible, but seeing the director's somber disposition emboldened him.

"Hold on guys. I'll be right back," Chezzy said to the others before taking a deep breath and approaching the director. Chezzy stopped near him and screwed up his failing courage, but the right words didn't come. "Are you playing, Professor?"

Professor Kepler seemed lost in thought, but he turned to Chezzy. "Playing?" He gave Chezzy a sort of sad smile.

"Yeah. Looking for the token and all," Chezzy explained, his nerves afire.

"Oh, yes. I suppose I am." He had turned his eyes downward as he toyed with something in his hand.

Chezzy took another breath and looked over the director. Maybe everything was finally hitting the man. Or perhaps he had been hiding this all along. "Are you alright, Professor?"

Professor Kepler looked back to Chezzy with another sad smile. "Yes. I'm alright. I've just… I've seen a glimpse of something more, is all."

"Is it bad?" Chezzy's stomach turned. He thought of Nik Daedle, and he thought of his friends. "Are we safe? Are… are they safe?" Chezzy gestured back to the others and wondered if the implications of the question were apparent to Professor Kepler.

"It's not so bad. Don't worry now. You should be playing with your friends, you know. It's a thing many take for granted."

"Well, yeah, I know but," Chezzy hesitated, "will you need help with something?"

"No. Not yet."

Chezzy twisted his foot in the dirt as he attempted to still himself and say what he wanted to say. "I saw the video of you and Nik Daedle." Chezzy cleared his throat. "And Greyire."

"Yes," Professor Kepler replied calmly.

Chezzy waited, as if for an explanation, though none came. "But you had reasons, right?" Chezzy could feel his legs shaking beneath him.

"Yes," the man added, looking at Chezzy.

Chezzy felt uncomfortable under his gaze. "Okay."

"You should go join the others." Professor Kepler motioned to the group.

Chezzy glanced back to them for a moment. "Yeah. We have to find that token."

Professor Kepler gave what was almost a real smile as he held up his hand. "I already found the token. Just thought the students should have a little more adventure before it gets turned in."

The token glinted in the afternoon light as it sat in his hand. "You've had it all along?" Chezzy asked.

Professor Kepler gave a wry look. "Well, it wasn't too difficult to find." He glanced back to the others who were in debate about the various clues they had found around. "You on another date?" He gave a laugh, but it was hardly happy. "It's alright. Why don't you take this over there? Tell them you found it and give it to her?" He offered the token to Chezzy.

"Are you sure?" Chezzy eyed the coin and the director uncertainly.

"Very," said Professor Kepler. "I can turn into all sorts of monsters, and I don't need a token to do it."

Chezzy took the coin and stared back at Professor Kepler. For a moment, he couldn't find the words, and when he did, they came at an almost fearful whisper. "Thanks, Professor Kepler."

Professor Kepler gave a nod before turning his eyes back down the path. Chezzy retreated and returned to the others. They looked at him quizzically, and he held up the token. "What?" Fern screamed. She and Fair rushed forward and swept Chezzy up in a hug. Chezzy looked back to Professor Kepler, but he was gone. Chezzy tried to spy down the path, but he couldn't see the man there either. His friends held him and cheered, but Chezzy's eyes didn't leave the empty alley. Something inside of him was stirring as he wondered what the director had seen.

The End.

Reviews help authors.

Please submit your feedback on Amazon, Goodreads, or your favorite review platform.

If you would like to stay up to date on **The Everling Series**, please visit **wastrelbooks.com** and sign up for our newsletter.

www.ingramcontent.com/pod-product-compliance
Lightning Source LLC
Jackson TN
JSHW081643040126
96281JS00001B/3